Marlowe reached 1 climbing into the cackling dementedly as their flames consumed them. The g___, turned day-bright. The only remaining shadows gathered behind Marlowe's back, taking refuge there from the lights that assailed them.

"Barcas rises again, not as a man, no, not as a man but as the glorious Phoenix!" And now the playwright waved his arms like wings, and the shadows responded, forming a bird beneath him, etched against the light. "And love is triumphant, magnificent, and immortal!"

Marlowe stayed that way for a moment, arms held high, the light blazing. But then the torches guttered and went out, spent, leaving the darkness to reclaim the theatre once more.

"Now if only I could write the damned thing," he muttered, pushing himself up and resting on his elbows. He sighed. "And if only wishes had wings, they might fly."

To my Transatlantic Twin, with thanks for getting this ball rolling

For Jenifer, Adara, and Arthur, who always boost my creativity

Crazy 8 Press is an imprint of Clockworks

TIME
OF
THE PHOENIX

AARON ROSENBERG

BOOK ONE WITH STEVEN SAVILE

CRAZY 8 PRESS

OTHER NOVELS
BY AARON ROSENBERG

The Adventures of DuckBob Spinowitz
No Small Bills
Too Small For Tall
Three Small Coinkydinks
Not for Small Minds

The Relicant Chronicles
Bones of Empire
Trails of Bone
Crossed Bones
Bones at Rest

Tales of the Scattered Earth
The Birth of the Dread Remora
Honor of the Dread Remora

O.C.L.T.
Incursion
Digging Deep
Focal Point

The Daemon Gates trilogy
Day of the Daemon
Night of the Daemon
Hour of the Daemon

Star Trek Corps of Engineers
Creative Couplings
Collective Hindsight
The Riddled Post

Shadowrun: Shadow Dance
Height of the Storm
World of WarCraft: Tides of Darkness
Worlds of WarCraft: Beyond the Dark Portal
StarCraft: Queen of Blades
Exalted: The Carnelian Flame
Exalted: False Images
Eureka: Substitution Method (as Cris Ramsay)
Eureka: The Road Less Traveled (as Cris Ramsay)
Gone to Ground
Stargate: Atlantis: Hunt and Run
Indefinite Renewal

CONTENTS

FOREWORD

It's strange writing with someone you've never actually seen.

Steve Savile and I first met on a writer's forum for tie-in writers. We quickly discovered we had a lot in common, right down to our birthdays—we were born only one day apart. We also proved very good at bouncing ideas off each other and quickly developed a half dozen or more story ideas and novel projects.

One of those started as an notion Steve had about a historic figure, the brilliant playwright Christopher Marlowe, who was secretly a supernatural creature, the legendary Phoenix. Oddly enough, I'd created a tabletop roleplaying game called *Chosen* just a year or two earlier that was all about mythic Beasts who appeared throughout history, choosing avatars to represent them and champion creativity and imagination—and the Phoenix was one of those. We put the two pieces together and eventually wrote a novella we titled "For This Is Hell," which we released in 2011 with the intent of making it the first book in a series.

Several years passed, but finally I decided we needed to get back to the Phoenix's story. Steve was bogged down with other projects at the time, but graciously agreed to let me continue the series on my own. So in 2019 I put out the second installment, "One Haunted Summer," which takes place at the Villa Diodati in the summer of 1816—a rather famous moment in literary history and in some ways the birth of a genre.

The next year I released Book Three, "Death in Silents," which is set in Hollywood in the mid-1920s and centers on the most famous silent film star in the world.

And this year I finished the story with "Cross the Road,"

the concluding book, occurring in the Mississippi Delta during the 1930s and focused on perhaps the greatest Blues musician of all time.

The story evolved as it went, as most good tales do. I hadn't realized when we started that I would focus on a different type of creative endeavor in each book, but once I did make that connection several of the pieces fell neatly into place. I rebuilt the original covers to match those sensibilities as well. Steve and I had originally planned a very different end to the story, but given world events since then I felt that was no longer going to work, so I came up with a new direction and something that, for me, was a much more satisfying conclusion anyway.

This volume collects all four books, together and in print for the first time.

I hope you enjoy the Time of the Phoenix.

Aaron Rosenberg
September 20, 2021

Book One
For This Is Hell

SCENE ONE

Wherein our hero, confounded without a muse,
travels to the Shining City and the Court of Elissa, daughter of Dido

"I stand before you naked, not of body but of soul. Here am I, a man stripped bare of those charming words I would use as sword and shield. I'd as well be a peasant, tongue-tied by such a simple thing as beauty, my purpose undone by a single look. A mute peasant! Oh yes, my mouth moves, my tongue licks and tastes the air, but those damned words refuse to make pretty and so, instead, I blather like a fool in all his motley. You have reduced me to this, my beautiful queen. With just one look my brain is addled, but then that is the same as it ever was when walking in the presence of beauty." *Where is the love?* he thought from the shadows as the leading man stumbled his way to the end of the soliloquy. *Where is the passion? Where is the music?* It was wretched. Mercifully, the actor's delivery was so weak his voice barely made it beyond the groundlings pit. No one would hear in the heavens.

He covered his eyes, but that did not stop *him* hearing.

"But I am not your queen, am I? So what other falsehoods coil in your mouth? Doth mine lips call to mind a rose in full bloom? Doth the full ripe redness of them recall the velvet petals of the flower? Would you part them with your whispered promises, as above so below? Are those the words you so struggle to call to mind? Seductions? Whence I smile do you see the harlot behind the kiss or the sweet innocent maiden you dream me to be? Might I be both? Or must it always be one or t'other? So again, I am not your queen, that much is true, but wouldst thou then fashion me your whore?" She fluttered her long, lush eyelashes at her suitor, but whether in amusement or interest there was no way of knowing from the words alone.

As she laid a hand on his, he froze, trapped like a fly in her honeyed words. He could not look away from her, but he could smile. Barely. The expression was utterly pained and bore the stiff rigor of a look rarely used and much forced.

"The whole of the world lives and laughs and loves, dear lady, that is the nature of life, if we are but lucky enough to understand it as it unfolds around us. Time might choose to brand thee the whore queen of Carthage who doth bathe in asses' milk and call lovers to her chambers by the hundreds, or to remember you more kindly. I suspect it will depend upon others, men humbled and humiliated, to decide how it will be—not, alas, for me nor you to decide. A man's vanity does not love strong women. A man's ego less so. You belittle your foes, best to leave them dead in the dust, that is the way of this ugly world, but even so their words might live on if they are spiteful enough shades. Yet," he paused, offering what by rights ought to have been an immodest smile, "if such a wondrous gift were mine to bestow, I trust I would remember thee fairly and beautifully, as a woman unlike any other."

"I see you have found a few pretty words at last, Iarbas."

"I never doubted they would come, Elissa. Now, perhaps, if thine lips were to press up against mine so that I might taste thee in my mouth, more would come alive as I attain my desire?"

Now, by the laughter lines that crinkled in the corners of her eyes, he could read her expression. The playful quirk of her lips confirmed it. She was teasing him. It really ought to have been more obvious than that.

"And were that so, sir, surely thou wouldst not begrudge me a little—"

"Enough! Enough! Enough enough enough!" The two potential lovers pulled apart, startled by the sudden outburst, as a dark figure burst upon them like some shadowy flame. "Hell's balls! I cannot take another word of this malignant butchery of the Queen's Tongue! Would that I had a dagger to pierce my sodding eardrums and silence the lot of you!"

"What's wrong this time, Kit?" the young "lady" asked, stumbling back a step to make room for the newcomer as he pushed his way between the actors to the center of the stage. "Did I mangle the lines again? 'Surely thou wouldst not begrudge me a little—'"

"I said enough!"

Then a second thought hit the "lady." "Oh, hell and damnation, you'd think I'd never done this before. Mother, maiden, whore. That's it, isn't it? She's the maiden and I'm serving up the whore. I'm sorry, Kit." Out of the scene, the actor's voice was considerably lower and rough, its natural timbre lacking anything approaching the dulcet tones of a beautiful warrior queen. Indeed, out of character, it was decidedly manly.

"That's not what's wrong with the damned thing. Trust me, you were fine, Sam," the shadowy man interrupted, resting a hand on the youth's shoulder. "Your Elissa is as fine as anyone could ask for. Dido wouldn't know you from her own daughter."

The fair maiden's erstwhile suitor snorted. "Easy enough to say, certes," he said, dropping into the vulgate and offering a wink, "given she's been pushing up daisies for centuries now. Your performance ought to be a damned sight fresher."

"Yes, quite, thanks for that, Ned." Kit snapped, his patience frayed thin by the catastrophe he had witnessed unfurling around him. "Always helpful when you decide to share your tuppence with us." The playwright turned on his heel, and seemed, for just a moment, as though he were about to wrench a fistful of hair from his forelock. "I shall endeavor to use your insight as a spur for my creativity, if, in turn, you promise to harness the same and find new ability when I ask you to bloody well act. Do we have a deal?"

Ned Alleyn bristled. "You've lost all sense of humor, Kit. It was a jest, nothing more. Time was, yours was the first voice to crack wise."

"Time was, I wasn't a talentless hack and could actually make the damned language sing, and penning a scene where a few well-practiced words could have a woman part her legs was no challenge at all. Now I can barely raise a smile, never mind anything more ardent, and what's worse, I can hear bloody Will's echo in there. Will, of all people. Talent's a feckless bitch, my friend. Forgive me, Ned. You're quite right." Marlowe rubbed the bridge of his nose, and clapped the tall performer on the arm. "The scene is bunk, the sentiment phony. The whole thing mocks me, through no fault of yours or Sam's, but by Christ on the Cross it has me vexed."

"I cannot argue with you there," Ned agreed, risking the playwright's wrath simply by agreeing with him. "There's no flow to the words, and try as we might they come across as unwieldy and insincere. They are like boys playing at soldier with sticks too long for their grip, off-balance and out of true."

Kit granted his friend a weary smile. "When your own words are finer than any I can put into your mouth, then indeed the world has turned upside down and inside out, and madness runs among us. I melt in your shadow, my friend."

"Ha!" Now it was Ned's turn to slap him on the back, and as comradely as the gesture was, the slap came within an inch of bowling the slender playwright from his feet. "Glad to see you've not completely lost your sense of humor. Just needs a bit of prodding to get it out."

"More like lubricating," Sam suggested, a considerably more natural smile on his beardless lips now. "What say we repair to the alehouse and see whether a flagon or two might stir that genius of yours to greater heights, shall we?"

"I'll see you boys there anon," Kit assured him. "But I would grapple with this beast of mine awhile longer, and where better than here, upon the place of its birth? Or stillbirth, as it is proving to be! But mark my words, lads, I *will* best it. I will prove upon its body once and for all that I am its lord and master. I will stomp and pound upon its flesh until it bends to my will like the supple willow beneath the stern north wind. I am the word and the word is everything. The word is God." He teased a pair of tarnished coins from his belt pouch and palmed them into the young man's hand. "Here, mine's the first round to make up for my foul humor, good strong ale all around, and I trust that mine will not be empty when I arrive to claim it."

Sam laughed. "I will guard it with my life," he assured Kit, "and the bottom shall still be damp, at the least, though how deep, only time will tell." He touched his forehead, as though making a prediction. "The longer the time, the shallower the ale," he said. He and Ned leaped down from the stage and strode across the Playhouse's empty pit, heading toward the front doors. The remaining players glanced about, uncertain as to whether they should stay or go. Kit urged them all out with shooing motions of his hands.

"Go. Begone. Away. Out of here! Follow your leads," he told the rest of the Admiral's Men. "Drink is good, and free drink better. So, to the alehouse with the lot of you, and warm its benches for my arse, so that when I join you I might delight in the warmth of both company and posterior!"

That drew several laughs, and more than a few sighs of relief at this turn in their playwright's humor, and the other men followed Ned and Sam out, calling back over their shoulders and promising that they would reserve a choice spot for his rear's eventual appearance.

It was only once they were gone, the doors slammed firmly shut behind them, leaving the gallery desolate, that the dark man sank to his knees upon the stage. His head fell heavily into his hands.

"Where hast thou gone?" he demanded of his palms, and then reared back to repeat the cry, beseeching the uncaring rafters painted as sky and clouds high above. "Where hast thou gone? Why hast thou forsaken me?"

No answer came even long after his plea had finished echoing through the heavens. He allowed himself to sink still further, until he was sprawled full-length across the stage, arms and legs akimbo, head turned now toward the real sky.

But still, for Christopher "Kit" Marlowe, the world chose not to reply.

After several dull and decidedly uneventful moments had ticked past—broken only by the sound of his own breath rattling in his chest—Marlowe hauled himself to his feet once more. Clearly throwing himself upon the mercy of the cosmos was not the answer. Melodrama would not stir his misfiring Muse.

But what, then, would?

Martin, who had been minding the script and calling out prompts as needed, had let the broadsheets fall in his haste to drink of Marlowe's generosity. Marlowe hopped down from the stage and gathered the scattered pages, ordering them once

more. He glanced through them, his own scrawled words looking so lifeless and flat on the page. His scowl deepened with
each line he read until at last he could bear it no longer, and
flung them once more to the rushes strewn over the hard-
packed dirt of the pit floor.

"Pure unadulterated rubbish!" he snarled at the pages
where they fluttered away from him. "Words? Are these all that
remain? Pah! These so-called words shame the very pages upon
which they are scratched! They defile the very ink with which
they stain, and the very quill that scratched them! These are not
words, they are an abomination!"

He clutched at his temples, driving dirt-smeared fingernails
into his flesh. "You are a disgrace to this mind, to this imagination! You are a pox upon my name and my reputation, a diseased canker that, should it burst, would surely coat my former
glory with filth that would burn away all that I ever achieved
and turn away even the most wretched wreck of humanity!"

He lashed out at the nearest page with his foot, and sent it
fluttering briefly into the air. It came down ink-side to the dirt.
"Begone, thou hideous reminder, thou foul demonstration of
mine failings! Begone, and trouble me no more!"

The page offered no reply, nor had he expected it to. But
there were responses a-plenty already within his own head.

Crouching, he retrieved the battered broadsheet and
straightened its crumpled face. If only it were as easy to smooth
out the words therein. He began anew the task of gathering its
fellows and restoring them to some semblance of order. He was
being difficult, he knew. Difficult and demanding and childish.
Precious and petulant. This tantrum was but the latest in an
ever-lengthening string of tirades, and it had only been through
force of will that he had sent the players away before unleashing it. They had seen enough of his anger already, and were as
close to out of patience as made no difference. He acted the
tortured artist, the misunderstood genius. He demanded the
very best of them but could only offer these words, the worst
of him. Marlowe scarcely deserved their forbearance. By rights
they should have run, and run far far away at that, leaving him
to bluster and blaspheme alone on the gilded stage.

The players were as blameless as these pages he held. They were his instruments—if he lacked the skill to wield them how could that ever be their fault?

No, the fault truly was his and his alone.

This new play was too dear to his heart. *Dido, Queen of Carthage* had been the first of his plays to be performed, and it had sounded across the London theatre scene like a shot across the bow of a ship at sea, a clarion call alerting all that a bright new talent had arrived to take their world by storm. Christopher Marlowe was his name, and his talent shone true and clear, dazzling all that beheld it.

It seemed only fitting, then, that he would now return to that same setting for this latest play. Young Dido was no more, dead by her own hand upon the funeral byre, a testament to her love for the departed Aeneas. But she had left behind a daughter, Elissa, to rule in her stead. And now it was Elissa, grown into the full bloom of womanhood, who must face the travails of love as her mother once had.

But this play was far more than that. It was not merely a tale of love and betrayal, noble though such stories could be. It was a tale of creation, the birth of a wondrous creature, a figure of pure myth, a shining symbol of life and passion and the endless cycle of all things—

The Phoenix.

That majestic flamebird rose from the ashes of its own demise, restored to full vigor by the flames that warmed its golden plumage, to cast its glow upon the world and illumine by its flight.

And the Phoenix, at least according to one set of ancient tales, first beat its majestic wings in Phoenicia and then Persia.

Phoenicia, from whence the Carthaginians came.

Marlowe was determined that his new work would bring the legend of the Phoenix to London, allowing its light to shine forth against the Thames and the Tower and the stern brick houses and the narrow, cobbled streets.

For the legend was at the very core of his being. It glimmered within him, demanding to be set free upon the world once more.

And he aimed to do it justice.

If only these thrice-damned words would bend to his will.

His fists clenched, instinctively trying to wring the pages like the neck of a hen. He barely checked himself. Parchment was pricey enough that it wasn't worth venting his frustration upon. He would just have to find other outlets for it.

He had the plot fully formed in his head—which, in many ways, made it all the more frustrating that he could not translate it into words. It was as clear as day in his mind's eye. Elissa as Queen of Carthage, young and beautiful. The wizard Iarbas, wealthy and powerful, who seeks her hand in marriage. The counsel of elders who advise her, and who approve of the match, for it would strengthen Carthage and the throne both at once. And Barcas, the handsome young guard who has pledged his own heart to his queen, though he knows that she could never notice, much less return, the affections of one such as he.

Marlowe paced the stage, the story unfolding before him as clearly as if Ned and Sam were returned to act it out for him. "Iarbas arrives and woos the young queen," his words rang out across the empty Rose Theatre, where his only audience was comprised of parchment and wood and painted cloth. "Elissa is flattered by the wizard's attentions, and recognizes the value of such a match, yet her heart is not in it. And why should it be? Her heart belongs elsewhere, though she does not know this yet, as is ever the curse of youthful love."

He stood in the dead center of the stage and folded crossed arms against his chest, tapping out a staccato rhythm with his foot to count off the beats. "Pragmatic counselors urge her to accept, of course they do, citing Iarbas's vast wealth and estates—he is a powerful man, and clearly her first duty is to her people." Marlowe rushed across the stage to the balcony as though about to deliver an impassioned plea to some beauty up in her ivory tower. "Elissa wanders her gardens, seeking answers, and in her daze nearly stumbles from the balcony to her death, but lo, a young guard leaps forward to save her. Of course it is Barcas. Their eyes meet, and Elissa sees the love in his gaze—pure and selfless and fiery, while Iarbas's looks are cold and calculating. Never was there a better measure of a man than through the windows into his soul. She finds herself drawn to the handsome guard, whose love burns still hotter from this return to his affections. She resolves to refuse Iarbas's suit, and to take Barcas as her husband instead, though it fly in the face of all tradition. Let them come at her with their swords of scorn!" He skipped across the stage, animated now, the power of the narrative flooding through him as he twirled about, pretending at being a giggling girl, anticipating the joy the two lovers would demonstrate. The torches that still burned along the walls brightened, their flames swaying to follow his movements.

Then he stopped dead in his tracks and glowered at an imagined foe. "But Iarbas sees the lovesick sidelong glances the young queen receives her guardsman, and worse for him by far, like daggers to his own heart, he sees the return of those ardent looks. He begs the counselors to intercede on his behalf, hoping they might sway Elissa to his favor—but it is not love that motivates him now, now it is about power and shame. He warns of dire consequences if he does not win her. Frightened, the counselors forbid Elissa to wed Barcas and demand that she marry the wizard instead." Marlowe turned and turned about before stepping back half a pace. He shook his head at the patch of ground he had just vacated. "But Elissa's love has made her strong in ways none could have anticipated, and she finds it in her to defy the council, rising to true rulership at last and reminding them that they exist to serve at her pleasure, not she at theirs. It is true love. She and Barcas pledge their mutual devotion, and plan to wed." Another skipping, giggling turn about the stage. This was his world.

"When Iarbas learns of this, he is not merely vexed, he is *furious*. His anger knows no bounds," Marlowe muttered, ceasing his cantering and capering in favor of a fearsome pose. The torches guttered, drawn to flicker toward him as he crossed his arms once more and glowered at his imaginary foe. The firelight gleamed within his dark eyes. "He vows that if he cannot have the queen, no one shall, and so blackened is his soul he resorts to the darkest of arts. He steals Elissa from the safety of her palace and spirits her away to his lair, there to take her life forever. But all is not lost! Barcas gives chase, mind set on saving his love with all haste, and bursts in upon them as Iarbas prepares to feed Elissa to the flames he has conjured for this black purpose!"

The flames danced higher around the gallery, as if excited by this mention of their brethren—their glow cast long shadows across the full length of the stage, but Marlowe's face was lit as though from within. On the planks at his feet, the shadows swept outward, much like the wings of a majestic bird.

"Barcas leaps forward, love lending speed to his limbs. He pushes Elissa to safety, and hurls himself at the wizard. But Iarbas is too strong for him!" Marlowe mimed the conflict, swaying back and forth as though he too fought an overpowering foe. "Barcas knows he cannot hold his rival for long, and most certainly cannot win. And yet he cannot allow Iarbas to emerge victorious, for it will mean the death of Elissa! What is he to do? How can he save his love? In desperation, the young guard hurls himself backward into the very flames intended to consume the queen—and drags the wizard with him!"

Marlowe hurled himself backward, echoing his words, and landed hard on his back, sprawled across the stage floor. The shadows scattered around him, skittering to the corners and leaving him a pool of reflected light from the torches, which now burned merrily, sensing their moment was at hand.

"Iarbas dies screaming! His pain within the heat of the fire is all-consuming! Barcas burns as well, but there is salvation in the flames. His noble sacrifice is not the end for the young guard. Instead he is reborn!" Marlowe reached for the sky, mimicking the rising firebird climbing into the air. The torches burst apart, snapping and cackling dementedly as their flames consumed them. The gallery turned day-bright. The only remaining shadows gathered behind Marlowe's back, taking refuge there from the lights that assailed them.

"Barcas rises again, not as a man, no, not as a man but as the glorious Phoenix!" And now the playwright waved his arms like wings, and the shadows responded, forming a bird beneath him, etched against the light. "And love is triumphant, magnificent, and immortal!"

Marlowe stayed that way for a moment, arms held high, the

light blazing. But then the torches guttered and went out, spent, leaving the darkness to reclaim the theatre once more.

"Now if only I could write the damned thing," he muttered, pushing himself up and resting on his elbows. He sighed. "And if only wishes had wings, they might fly."

Damn it all to hell. The story was there, just waiting to be told. It was eager, even. He could feel it bursting up inside him like the firebird itself. So why, then, why why why were the words so resistant? It was as though something were holding them back, a block within him, and try as he might he could not force them to come, nor could he coax them, or beg or bully. They simply refused to emerge.

"But I will persevere," he vowed, clambering back to his feet. "I will master those ill-tempered words. For I am Marlowe, and my words will shine forth like the light of the Phoenix!"

With that, the playwright strode from the stage, the words lingering behind him in the gloom, their promise hanging in the air even as the shadows consumed the space utterly.

SCENE TWO

As our hero is forced to defend himself
against three fat men who would silence him forever

"Come on, come on!" Marlowe struck his forehead with the side of his fist again and again as though trying to drive the point home. "Think, damn you! Think! Use that benighted brain of yours to make magic! Spew words! Let them spill forth in a froth of wit and wisdom! Let them entertain, draw laughter and gasps of shock, let them make grown men shiver and grown women too, men in fear and women in anticipation! Work your magic, Marlowe! Give me a glimpse of the language and imagery that makes you so bloody famous!"

He held the quill poised, its tip hovering a scant whisper above the parchment. The ink pooled at its knife-sharpened point, waiting the opportunity to transform the page from blank sheet to finished scene.

Yet nothing came.

There was no inspiration. His muse had deserted him.

Marlowe hurled the quill from him. It flew across the room and struck point-first the heavy curtains hanging round his bed, the tip embedding itself, quivering, in the velvet. He came near to tossing the parchment after it, or consigning it to the fire, but thought the better of it. Instead he kicked back the stool upon which he had supported his backside and stalked around the room, gesticulating like a man possessed as if he hoped to beat the air into submission and wring forth from its vapors the bloody words he lacked.

"This cannot be," he muttered, chewing his lips as he paced. "I am Marlowe! Expert at every turn of phrase, every cadence, every jest. Rich imagery is mine to conjure forth. Poignant cries are mine to elicit from gawpers. Words are my sword, and it is mine to make grown men weep with the thrust of my sharp blade! And yet, and yet—and yet I cannot write two bloody lines together that do not sound as though wrought by the feeble-mind of a moron. What is this damned fever dream I cannot awake from? Where are the sweats to accompany my delirium?"

Anguished, he ground his fists into his eyes, pushing hard enough for light to explode behind his lids and fill the world with a sunburst of color that momentarily drove away the dismal reality of London. Alas, when he opened his eyes again, the mundane world and the blank broadsheet returned to haunt him.

"Is this it? Is this what I have become? Am I reduced to this? A man with no redeeming features and no gift? Damned and double damned." Marlowe stared down at his hands as though he might see something either etched into the skin, or absent, that would explain the loss of his talent. The well, it seemed, was not bottomless. And, now he was dry.

"No!" he roared, slamming both hands down upon the table. It shivered and creaked beneath the impact, but did not crack. "No," he said again, less certainly this time. Surely some talent yet remained to him? Yes. Of course it did. If he closed his eyes he could feel it tingling throughout his body. He could feel it prickling at his fingertips, and on the tip of his tongue. It was in his eyes and in his ears. It filled his head. The stories were there to be written down. There was still talent a-plenty. And why not? "I am Marlowe," he reminded the otherwise empty room, but there was no force behind his words this time. And then the thought struck him and he breathed, "I am the Phoenix, fiery and free, guiding all toward a path of rebirth, imagination, and delight."

Yet for all his assertions the words still refused to come, and no spell nor incantation of self-belief could summon them.

"Bah!" Marlowe snorted, pushing the parchment to one side. He leaned back against the table and sighed. He had been locked in this silent losing battle for hours. He had retired to his rooms from the Rose, convinced that now, this time, his sure, sharp visions of the play would be captured if he just sat himself at the table before they could fade. But, though he could still see portions of the play within his mind's eye, there were no words this time, and a play without dialogue was no play at all. His inner ear had turned deaf just when he most required it. And without it, he was lost.

"Enough of this," he told himself. "Recriminations are for the courts, they are useless out here and serve only to sour already bitter dispositions." He capped the inkpot, set aside the quill, and rolled the parchment, returning it to a stack which he then slid into its leather case. "If the muse refuses to visit me here and now, why then I will go forth—I will not sit here and plead for her return when there is good ale going sour. Tis far better to carouse with a band of brothers than to sit and mope alone."

Snatching up his hat, Marlowe made for the door. Enough worrying. He would find his friends, see whether Sam had in fact set aside a flagon for him, and drain it dry in a single swallow, then order two more for good measure. Maybe the muse would return if he drank enough to lose whatever self-consciousness held her back? It was possible, if not probable.

With one last glance around the room, Marlowe pulled open the door and stepped through. The candle set upon his desk winked out obligingly as he tugged the door shut behind him and set forth in search of the Admiral's Men.

He was nearly to the street when a voice called out behind him. "Ho! Marlowe!"

Marlowe found himself facing three men of the most disconcerting demeanor. None of them were young, none of them fit or muscular—indeed their clothes all bore a similar cut and style that bespoke some money and a love of good food and, more worryingly, some authority. He looked them up and down openly, taking the measure of them. He knew their kind all too well. They were servants of the Queen, though what they did for Her Majesty, or at least in Her name, was anybody's guess. But, given their presence at his door, and his name on their lips, he could take a reasonable stab that they wanted something from him.

"You have me at a disadvantage, gentlemen. You turn up at my door knowing my name, where all I know about you is that you are both lickspittles and lackeys of those knaves, the Privy Council," he said, closing the distance between them with purposeful strides. The fattest of them backed off. The other two stood their ground. "So tell me, what would the Council have of me today, gentlemen? Have they, perhaps, chosen to levy a new fine against all men, or merely thespians? Or would they have me partake upon a mission most deadly and dire and go murder some rotten baron? Tell me, is there a story in it? For if there isn't, then I must say I am not interested in the slightest."

The thinnest of the men—and given the company that was not saying much—smiled at him. It was an expression that left a chill into the air around them. "Most droll," he acknowledged in a voice dry as dust. "Yet surely you understand that scorning ourselves and disparaging our employers is unlikely to make us more amenable . . . so then one must conclude that you are merely an ass, Marlowe."

"I am renowned for it, I think you'll find. Tis the curse of a quick mouth and quicker wit. So, pray tell, why should I be remotely interested in your favor?" Marlowe was close enough now to catch the smallest of details, such as the fleck of silver at the tips of the speaker's hair and the matching buttons holding his cloak. These were no mere lackeys, he realized, but his anger at their ambush made him impudent. "And when have your paymasters ever been amenable to this playwright? When have they ever done anything for anyone that did not benefit them more?" He laughed, knowing full well the bitterness it conveyed. He struck the same pose he'd held on the stage while pretending at being Iarbas, jutting his chin out. "Hast thou not caused enough harm to me and mine?" he asked theatrically. "Must there be more of this never-ending barrage of blows and insults and movements that might be one or t'other but cannot stem the tide any more than a twig might dam a raging river?" He was enjoying himself now and could scarcely hide it.

All three men's scowls deepened, but Marlowe did not care one whit. They had sought to hinder his work in one way or another for years, but over the last few months their attempts had shifted from coercion to bully-boy threat, showing new-found boldness and increasing desperation. Something had stirred that damned nest of vipers, but clearly not enough to draw either the Queen's ire or her censure, so still they continued to throw their ample weight about unchecked. They had attempted to shut the Rose Theatre more than once, usually spouting preposterous claims of "unsafe business practices" and "unclean work conditions" and "indecent subject matter." Thus far Marlowe, along with Philip Henslowe, the Rose's owner, had managed to fend off any such accusations and keep the theater open. But it was only a matter of time before threats were followed with action and the Rose burned to the ground or suffered some other ill fate.

Especially in a year such as this. 1592 had seen the return of the Plague. It was no secret that many had died and that disease and sickness were rampant. Months past the new year, 1593 was proving no better. The sickly sweet scent of charred bodies still lingered over great swathes of London town. Many a good establishment had closed or been closed, their staff now too ill to cook or clean or keep shop. Many more had fled to the countryside, gambling on the protective nature of the clean country air, and streets that had once bustled now echoed with each footstep. But against all expectation the Rose remained open. Henslowe had made it abundantly clear how he felt: people needed an outlet in such troubled times. They needed a bright spot against the darkness. They needed to be distracted and entertained. And thus far, the crowds had proved him right.

Those thoughts brought Marlowe's mind back to his present dilemma, and the half-smile he could feel tugging at his lips vanished. "So what insult do you have to heap upon me now? Be done with it and begone," he ordered, turning his back to the men. "I have no patience for the sport, and less inclination to hear you out."

"Be that as it may, Marlowe, best you listen," the middle man urged, speaking for the first time. "Unless a stay within one of our city's finest gaols takes your fancy?"

"Ha, is that old chestnut the best you have, boys? Frankly,

I am disappointed. I laugh in the face of your empty threats."
Marlowe walked to the nearest of the men. "I would have thought
that by now you had realized—gaol and me, we are old friends,
her cells as warm and comforting as any maiden I've bedded."

"Which says plenty about the company you choose to keep,
Marlowe."

"Indeed it does," Marlowe replied, "Your not-so-good selves,
for instance. Worse than any whore I've ever taken to the mattress, for you're a damned sight more expensive and without the
pleasure."

There was truth behind the humor. Marlowe had been
detained on all manner of charges, some trumped up, some oh
so dreadfully true—the most recent mere months ago—and
had found the gaol cells pleasant enough. They offered solitude
if not quiet in which to contemplate the scene taking shape in
his head. His contentment never failed to rattle the guards, who
invariably hauled him out of the clink with warnings to "mend
his evil ways." But he was an inveterate . . . well . . . everything:
gambler, womanizer, and drunkard. It was ingrained into the
very fabric of his being. Might as well teach a three-legged mutt
new tricks.

"This new play—" the middle man began.

"The play indeed. What of it?"

"The Privy Council would see it," he continued, finding his
voice. "They would judge it for what it is—that is, upon its own
merits—and determine whether it is acceptable for general performance, or whether it must be closeted away like some dark
poison."

"Let me consider my answer a moment," Marlowe declared,
appearing to mull it over with all due gravity. Inside he was
seething. He felt the urge to scream rising up through his
craw. He wanted to yell in their pox-scarred faces that there
would be no play for them to see and that their masters could
loosen their girdles because the damned thing would never be
finished, much less performed. But he did not. Better to make
them sweat on it a while. Instead he donned his cheekiest grin.

"There is little time, Marlowe. They should see it with all
due haste."

"Then let them buy tickets," he told the three fat men, forcing a laugh to follow the statement despite his foul humor. "They can then watch to their heart's content and make my coffers bulge at the same time. That, mine friends, is what is known as a winning situation all the way round." He bowed low, sweeping his arm before him in a grandiose gesture, then turned on his heel and walked away.

"Marlowe, you whoreson!" one of the men yelled at his back, "come back here! You do *not* walk away from us!" But Marlowe didn't give him the satisfaction of turning or looking back. Let them spit and curse him. They were too fat and comfortable in their equally fat lives to actually give chase. He was well beyond the reach of their sticks and stones, and soon enough he would be clear of their words, too.

The Privy Council! A gathering of evils, both lesser and greater, more like. And to say that they had never liked him was to use the poet's gift for understatement. It was more than that—they actively disliked him, though as to why Marlowe was at a loss to say. There were other young playwrights in this not so fair city, and some even feigned at rebelliousness, though none, he liked to think, had quite his flair for pissing in the face of authority, and every now and then, whence the moon was blue, one of them would be called before the council to face an accusation that his writing did not meet the council's expectations. But rather than the curse of the blue moon, this sort of meddling was Marlowe's everyday. And now the bastards weren't content to wait for the plays to be staged before trying to close them down. Damn them, they weren't even content to wait for the ink to dry before throwing their weight around, and fat bastards they were, to a man, either of belly or head. Mayhap he should decry them for witchcraft and see the Church burn them, for surely this most recent turn for the absurd spoke of some mad gift of prescience? Had they seen into the future and observed the play? If they had, then for once he was actually jealous of them—it was a gift he would have killed for right now, plagued as he was. How much easier then would it be to finish the play as it should be finished, knowing already what words were spoken because he had seen them performed, perfect?

It mattered not, he was not about to wait upon their plea-sure, and nor would he cater to their whims. He would rather burn. They would not distract him from his work.

Not now.

Not ever.

His works was all he had left.

SCENE THREE

In which, whilst slaking his thirst, our hero finds his inspiration

"Ah, the man of the hour! Here he is at last!" Tommy Towne spotted Marlowe pushing open the tap room doors and leapt to his feet, waving the playwright over to the table around which the Admiral's Men clustered, deep in their cups. "We had begun to think you had deserted us, Master Playwright."

"Aye, and left us to pay for our own ale," Sam chuckled.

"And, of course, it is better I desert you than my coin does," Marlowe agreed, "or, heaven forefend, that my genius deserts us all!" As was so often the case, he found it easy to slip into jocularity around these players. They were more than actors. They were *his* actors. They were his friends. And that warmed him enough to offset the growing chill beyond the tavern's doors. "Either would be far more a disaster, I fear."

"Oh hells, yes indeed," Ned answered, smacking his lips after a hearty slug of ale. "Well, come and sit, drink what your purse has already paid for. We've even set aside the choicest throne at the head of the table, and dear old Sam has guarded your flagon with his life."

"Which means," Sam added, "I may have drunk it down into my belly where it would be safest."

Marlowe laughed and slid into the proffered seat, which was hard up against the chimney breast. He could feel the warmth through the bricks on his back, making it a fine spot, indeed. In a few moments he was content, warm and with a view of the alehouse spread before him. If there was a better place in the world he would have been hard pressed to find it. Marlowe reached for the leather jack Sam slid across the table, and as he raised it he felt as a king surveying his subjects.

"To the Admiral's Men," he toasted those around the table, hoisting the flagon high. "Long may your antics upon the stage win the hearts and minds of those fortunate enough to witness your genius, my friends!"

"Hear, hear!" Other jacks were raised, then all drank deep.

"So, Kit, was your solitude rewarding? Did you break the back of the scene?" one of the players, Tim who often played a priest, asked from the far end. Every head turned to Marlowe to hear his answer.

"We playwrights are a fickle lot, moody, cantankerous, insecure, and selfish—it is all part of our charm, as well you know. And at times we must have privacy, else our imaginations cannot roam and you boys would have no words to say." He gave them his most confident smile. "Now I have had my romp, my imaginings unfettered, and all is right with the world."

"Had your romp, have you?" This was a new voice, low and sultry, spoken close enough to Marlowe's ear that it prickled his skin and tickled deep into his eardrum, sending shivers through him. "Alas, that I was not there to join thee."

He shifted slightly, inclining his head. There was a barmaid beside him, already refilling his jack though he had not yet lowered it back to the table. Although her hands were steady on the flagon and the pitcher, she only had eyes for him. Warmth that had nothing to do with the hot bricks at his back soared through Marlowe as he took in the full glossy length of her dark hair, her fine porcelain features and slender figure, her ample yet frighteningly pert bosom, and the curve of her hips beneath her apron. Alone any one of those might have taken his breath away. Together they stilled his heart. But still they were nothing beside the laughter in her dark eyes and the smile upon her full lips. With those she owned him.

"I shall bear you in mind for all future romps, my good woman."

"There's nothing good about me, good sir," she retorted.

He offered her a playful grin. "Mayhap I should be the judge of that?"

"You, sir, are a rogue and flatterer."

"And don't pretend you do not relish my words. You would

be the only woman in London who did not want me for what my silver tongue can do."

"Add to that knave and scoundrel," she accused, smiling even as she did. "Pretty words, prettier face, but tell me, how might you know anything about me beyond my looks? How then could you possibly know whether a duet between us would be to your liking? Not all dancers keep the same time, after all."

"Ah, sweet lady, I am a man of the world," he assured her, attraction loosening his tongue and making him bold, "and a playwright besides—I can judge a soul upon an instant, and tell how two might fit together, for well or ill." He deliberately let his gaze travel the hills and valleys of her body once more, then met her eyes and gave her his cheekiest smile. "Truly, thou and I would fit together like a hand in a glove, so close none could tear us apart, so smooth our every movement would be as one."

"And pray tell, who would be the hand, and who the glove?" came her reply, her free hand resting upon her hip, yet for all the challenge in it she could not have looked more inviting. "Or, who would hold dominance, and who surrender all volition?"

"Why, neither, sweet lady," Marlowe answered, the words coming readily. If only Iarbas' flirtation could be half so sweet, or Barcas' half so convincing! "For surely gloves have adorned such lovely fingers before?" And her hands were lovely, he saw—long and slender, not the roughened digits one might expect from a serving girl. "The glove coats the hand, and thus might be considered master, yet it bends as the fingers bend, so in that it allows the flesh to take the lead. The hand controls the movement, and thus could be said to be dominant, yet all sensation must pass first through the glove, so in that way it trails behind. They are paired, you see, a perfect match, neither ascendant o'er the other."

"Beautifully put, wordsmith—each still strives for mastery," she whispered, her sweet voice going throaty as he leaned in, her breath against his ear once more, her bosom pressed up around his arm. He could feel her weight against him, and the frisson where mere cloth separated them. "But in this contest, there are no losers."

"Indeed," he agreed, finding it hard to ply his voice. His

mouth was suddenly dry despite the ale he had just quaffed. "And certes, it is a contest I would happily engage in."

She laughed then, silver jingling within a chest. "Oh, would you, now?" It was her turn to eye him up and down, boldly and without haste. "That is good to know. And who can say, perhaps you will, if you continue to amuse me."

There was no room for him to rise, and certainly not to his full height, though other parts of him might, but Marlowe sketched a passable bow from his seat. "That, madam, sounds like a challenge. I shall make it my quest to amuse you."

"I hope so." Her lips curved in a silent promise. "Very much so indeed." Then, with an exaggerated sashay of hip, she was away to wait upon other thirsty tables.

"Well, well, well. I do believe the playwright has rediscovered his muse," Ned clapped him on the back. "And a fine and buxom one she is. Cleavage like that could drive even me to verse, if I thought she might smother my face in those beauties. Imagine the ecstatic prose that would flow from my mouth!"

"I would really rather not," Marlowe demurred, grinning despite himself.

Other, similarly ribald comments followed as the cups were drunk deeper, and Marlowe joined in, his spirits rising. Ned was right, this was exactly what he had needed. Brooding alone in his rooms was good for nothing. A man should bask in the company of friends and good humor. And, to be frank, in an entirely other form of companionship as well. His eyes followed the barmaid around the room, watching her move from table to table, somehow avoiding those pawing hands. She glanced his way more than once, every bit as interested in Marlowe as he was in her, and laughed to see his so-open admiration.

Already he could feel his creative urges rising.

"Vanquished so soon? I had hoped for more of a fight," the barmaid purred behind him as Marlowe stood to wrestle his way from behind the table. She had somehow slithered up beside him unnoticed, a feat no doubt aided by the quantity of ale he had downed, and he felt a delicious thrill chase down his spine as he turned and all but fell into her dark eyes.

"Nay, merely respite. One must part with those fine ales already sampled," he replied, indicating his now-empty leather jack, "but then the way shall be clear for yet more ambrosia." He leaned in closer to her. "Be that ale or lips, if thou art the deliverer of such delights I know which I would prefer."

That produced one of her tinkling laughs. "You, sir, are incorrigible." She pushed him away, but gently. "Do you think I am just another keg of ale to be tapped, pulled and quaffed as you wish?"

"Hardly. A fine wine. A delicate liquor. Something to be sipped and savored."

"Charm, charm, and more charm. Pretty words," she said, smiling and twisting so that her backside was pressed against him as he slid past. "But perhaps I shall let you have a taste of mine delights, though only a taste."

"Name the place and the hour, and I will be your servant in the sack," he promised, making sure she felt the iron of his conviction hot against her.

"Keep thy senses as sharp as your tongue and perhaps you will be lucky enough to serve me. You never know." She winked at Marlowe, pushing back just long enough to enflame his every nerve, and then she was off again. It was all he could do to stagger to the door and out into the street, where he dropped his breeches at once and relieved himself against a nearby wall in a steady stream of steaming piss. That was the beauty of the many alehouses of London, the privy was wherever one chose to see it—even in the taproom should it so amuse, he thought, fastening up again.

He turned back toward the tavern but didn't manage a single step. For there, gliding toward him, her gait so smooth it might have been the ripple of a gentle wave, came the very object of his ardor.

She pressed her finger to her lip, saying nothing as she slipped past him. Her hips were heavy with promise. She turned slightly, drawing him on with a curl of her finger. Marlowe moved as if bewitched, following in her wake. His steps were rough and cloddish echoes of her grace.

She led him slowly down to the banks of the Thames,

looking again and again over her shoulder with seductive promise. Their path took them less than a stone's throw from the alehouse, and then they skirted a pair of ramshackle huts to take shelter in an old ruined boathouse, though in truth it was little more than the crumbled corner of what had been. The rough-hewn stack of stone still rose above their heads, and where the walls met enough remained to shield them from the eyes of those strolling past. Especially now, with the encroaching dark serving to cast deep shadows in which to hide.

She turned and snaked into his arms, the length of her body pressed up against his. "Surely there are spots of more comfort and privacy?" he mumbled. "My own rooms—"

She silenced him with a fierce kiss.

He could feel her laughter through their conjoined lips.

A heady rush swept through him, beginning with a cool, floating sensation that shivered from his lips into his mouth, through his tongue and down his throat to quench the inner fire even as it stoked his passion.

Then she had slipped through his grasp once more with a shimmy and a twist, a continuous sinuous motion. Her dress gathered in a pool at her feet. She stepped out of it and into the shadows. Their darkness added to that already cupped below her breasts and between her legs. Her face was all but hidden beneath the waterfall of her hair as it spilled across her brow and cheek. Suddenly she was moving again, turning away from him, gliding through his fingers like water, impossible to hold onto, and dashing two, three quick steps. The last became a leap that saw her arch her back and rise into the air, and for a frozen fraction of a moment the thin moonlight caressed her alabaster-smooth skin as she dove, piercing the midnight-black waters of the Thames with barely a splash as the filthy river swallowed her whole.

He stared at the still water, unable to believe she had actually thrown herself into the Thames when people pissed and puked in it, when every effulgent and effluent was emptied into it from bowels to refuse to bilge from the tall ships down the river. Seconds ticked past and still she didn't reemerge. There was not so much as a ripple on the black skin of the water.

Then her head broke the surface.

Again without a word, she beckoned him to her with one long, wet, and glistening arm.

"I—I am not much for swimming, lady, even given the delights on offer," Marlowe admitted, but even so found himself taking a faltering step toward the water's edge. "I'm more for dryness and a warm bed. Perhaps we could adjourn somewhere less polluted?"

"Come," she whispered, opening her arms wide. He stared at the water sheening her nakedness and he was powerless to do anything but comply. Before he could come to his senses and stop himself from such recklessness, Marlowe stripped away his own clothes and launched himself into the water to join his newfound muse.

The cold hit him hard, a furious body blow that drove the very wind out of his lungs and gripped his balls tight, shriveling him. Still she drew him, and so he struck out to swim toward her, sinking beneath the surface. He broke through again an instant later, sputtering and coughing up the foul water and flailing his arms even as the river attempted to drag him under a second time. His entire body rebelled, shivering uncontrollably.

Suddenly she was beside him, wrapped around him, her arms and legs like the damp tendrils of her night-black hair. Her body undulated against his, seeming to touch him everywhere, every inch of his skin thrilling at her touch, and he found himself beginning to respond in a dim portion of his mind. The numbness was still there now that the shock of absolute cold had subsided, though now it had become an almost pleasing fog, cool and calm and comforting as it wrapped him tight. He felt the tantalizing coolness of her water-slick skin and the undeniable heat elsewhere, and let his mind drift free of his body, lost to waves of pleasure as they washed around him.

Somehow she kept them both afloat as they coupled amid the currents, the river rippling about them as if it too were part of their lovemaking. Perhaps it was.

Sated, she drew him back up to the shore and helped him stumble, dazed and confused, onto dry land. It was only then, when the raw night air hit his bare skin, that Marlowe's body began to shiver again, as though his flesh had just remembered it was freezing. She laughed at him, not unkindly, and shook herself lightly before slipping into her clothes once more.

"So," she asked playfully, "how do you like the water now?"

"Well enough," he admitted with a grin, "though let's be plain, it was more the lovely welcoming woman than the wet embrace of the river that pleased me. A lady whom, it strikes me now, I have no name with which to serenade."

She helped him tug his shirt over his head, then kissed him lightly again, her lips still cool and wet from their dip. "Lorelei," she breathed into his parted lips, filling him with her name. "My name is Lorelei."

And then she was gone, a glimmer of pale skin and damp hair bustling back up the slope to the alehouse and work. But before she slipped from sight, the single lingering glance she threw his way intimated this would not be the only time he would feel her come around him.

Marlowe sighed and shivered, content despite the cold as he wrapped his arms about his chest. He considered returning to the tavern. Surely Ned and Sam and the rest still sat at their table, drinking and jesting and laughing? But he felt the overwhelming need for dry clothes, a tisane of hot tea, and something else, something he had feared he would never feel again since his talent had deserted him—he felt the burning need to *write.*

SCENE FOUR

Wherein the villain flirts outrageously with his Queen,
drawing similarity between ale and women

"Forgive me, my beauteous queen," Ned declared, relishing the guise of the sinister Iarbas, "for thine beauty leaves me somewhat unmanned, and disarmed of the guile necessary for fine words I find myself incapable of the delicate speech."

"And art thou vanquished so soon?" Elissa taunted, batting her lashes at the tall, dark suitor. "I would have thought thee made of sturdier stuff."

Ned smiled, and in that smile every last trace of him disappeared. Only Iarbas remained. "Indeed, madam, my stuff if sound enough, 'Tis only mine lips that disobey"—his smile became a leer—"And if thou wert mine, t'would not be mine lips I would wish thee focused upon."

The young queen feigned shock but it was obvious she was more than enjoying the indelicate flirtation. "Naughty wretch!" she scolded. "Dost thou think me but a mere ale to be quaffed in haste and cast aside after thy thirst is quenched?"

"Not so, dear lady, not so. No ale, thou. Rather," he thought on his feet, looking for a suitable metaphor, "A delicate liquor, a fine wine, something to be sipped and savored. Thou art a true treasure worthy of being wooed and won—and kept safe at hand thereafter."

"You men always find such pretty words to raise a lady's skirts," Elissa said, some bitterness rising above the flirtatious banter, "yet surely thou knowest me not at all—you see my face, my shape, and it fires your blood. There is nothing noble there. So pray tell me how, then, can thou be so certain my *vintage* would lay sweet upon the palate?"

Iarbas allowed himself a deep, knowing chuckle. "I have traveled the world, your majesty, supped many a vintage and seen far more, every shape and size of cask and bottle, and sights far beyond the normal ken. I am a man with a discerning palate, I assure you. One must drink the odd tapped cask to know a truly good vintage. Look at me. My eyes. With these eyes I can judge a soul upon an instant. Thee and I would fit together, certes, like a hand in a glove, so close none could tell one from t'other, our every movement as one."

"Would we now? And who then would be the hand, and whom the glove?" Elissa allowed a hint of iron to show in her tone. She was not some simple child to be bedded with a few clever twists of phrase. She was so much more than that. "Which would hold dominion? More telling, Iarbas, which surrender all will?" She arched an eyebrow. "For thou art a noble lord, wealthy and no doubt well-endowed," she let that hang in the air between them a moment, the double entendre slightly labored, "Yet I am Queen of all Carthage!"

"I meant no disrespect, majesty," her suitor insisted, bowing low and long this time, "nor to suggest usurpation of those rights and duties conferred by royal lineage. I spoke carelessly. I meant only matters such as a couple might share, the delicious moments in which there are no rulers, no subjects—they are paired, a perfect match, neither ascendant o'er the other. Equal in all things, bested only by pleasure."

The queen nodded, satisfied by his answer. "Indeed, then to torture your conceit somewhat, the hand doth control all movement, yet the glove is guardian of sensation. Neither masters the other."

"Yet both strive to be the greater benefactor to their partner," Iarbas claimed, "and in that contest, there can be no losers." He dared a lascivious wink. "And even so, with you it is a contest in which I would most happily risk a rare defeat."

"Perhaps, perhaps, if thou dost continue to amuse me thus."

"Then amuse you I *must*, great lady." He bowed once more, before straightening and making his exit in a flurry of cloak and cap and extravagant feathers.

"Better! Much better!" Marlowe clapped from his place on

the balcony. "Nobly aped, good Ned! Gracefully stated, dear Sam! We'll make a play of this yet!"

Ned turned and bowed up at him. "All thanks to you, my good friend!" He called out, his trained voice easily reaching across the distance. "You put the words in our mouths, and with these any dullard could put on a show fit for a barrister." He smiled. "Though I flatter myself to think my recitation fit enough for a duke, at the least."

"Ha! Far beyond such pond scum, Master Alleyn!" Marlowe assured his friend. "The very Queen herself marvels at your histrionics, as you well know, for certes she has summoned you enough to perform before her."

"In all seriousness, these new lines are good, Kit," Sam put in, his voice shifting back toward its natural register as he sloughed off the character of Elissa. It was a subtle transformation as first he resumed his own gait and then his mannerisms. "There is something wonderfully familiar about them—might I infer you found inspiration in your dalliance last night? She was a rather fine looking woman, that barmaid."

"That she was," Jimmy Tunstall agreed. "And I did note how she returned shortly after you departed, soaking wet and smiling, and hummed and sang the rest of the evening, clearly well pleased with herself. Would that be the one?"

"Aye, the very same," Marlowe agreed. He sprung over the balcony rail and dropped down to speak more on level with his friends. "Lorelei, her name is, and believe me when I say she uncorked the fountain within me, gentlemen!"

"Well, that's one way of putting it," Ned whispered to Sam, who giggled like one of the girls he so often portrayed.

"You think I'd deny it? Damn, but she was something else, lads," Marlowe admitted, chuckling along with them. "But so much more important, her words, the cut-and-thrust of her flirtation, acted as the spur my weary brain needed. She goaded me into a gallop in more ways than one, and these pages are the result, scribbled last night after I left your company—and hers." He gestured toward the broadsheets Martin held. "And best of all, I've not run dry yet!"

"Well, I should hope not, for her sake as well as ours, friend

Kit!" Sam quipped, raising another round of laughter among the players. The mood throughout the theatre was far lighter than it had been for days—hell, weeks!—and Marlowe felt his own spirits blaze still brighter from the joy all around him. As he had stumbled back home last night, he had known that the words had come unstuck within his soul. He had crawled from the Thames reborn. He was Kit Marlowe!

And action had proved him right. Upon returning to his rooms, stoking the fire, and pulling on dry clothes, he had begun to write.

Really write.

Like he hadn't written in years, with the fire of the prose burning through his veins. The lines had flickered and flared to brilliance, sparking one another to greater heights, until the whole of the first scene had taken fire and blazed bright as a funeral pyre.

Marlowe had thrown open the shutters on the morning sun and crowed like a cock. His gift had returned! He was alive again! Alive!

They were still laughing when the Playhouse's front door banged open.

A short, stout figure stumbled in. The man looked as though he had been dragged through a hedgerow backwards.

"Where is Master Henslowe?" He demanded, his voice hoarse.

"Ed?" Marlowe squinted against the sudden glare of the daylight beyond. "What the devil is wrong, man?" Ed Juby was a part of their company, most often seen in the role of the clever servant whose job it was to cause endless jests at his master's expense.

"It's bad, Kit," Ed replied, shaking his head as he made his way across the gallery. The front door slammed shut again behind him, allowing the gloom to swallow the gallery once more. "Where's Henslowe?"

"I'm here, Ed," Henslowe called out as he emerged from the office hidden away behind the stage area. "What is it, lad?"

"John Cholmley, sir." Ed paused and gulped for air, or perhaps something stronger—Ned obliged, handing the shorter man a small silver flask. Ed took it and swigged down a mouth-ful of fiery liquid from before continuing. "John Cholmley—is dead."

That was not the news Kit had expected, but it explained poor Ed's fractured nerves.

"Dead?" Henslowe sagged against a pillar. "How?" Ned stepped to his side to comfort the older man. Henslowe was not merely their friend, and their landlord—he was Ned's father by marriage, binding him as tight as a parent to the whole troop.

The others fell silent.

Cholmley had been Henslowe's partner years ago. The pair had bought a stretch of land known as "Little Rose" and built a small playhouse there. Henslowe had only recently renovated that into the spacious gallery and stage where they now stood. He had bought Cholmley's share off him, ending their busi-ness relationship, but the two had remained close. And though no longer one of their landlords, Cholmley had been a good friend to the Admiral's Men, too. He had never missed a single performance.

Ed looked uncomfortable. "Threw himself in front of a horse, sir, or slipped and fell. Either way, it was quick, at least, if that's a mercy—one hoof to the head and his spirit fled."

"This is ill news," Marlowe commented quietly.

Henslowe was clearly shaken.

A pall descended upon the other players.

"Who's to say it wasn't assisted by a push?" Ned asked. Kit turned to look at him. The thought had been in his mind, too, but he'd never have voiced it. Enough people out there wished him ill, it was not impossible to believe one might resort to a shove to get things done. Could the same have been true for the old gentleman? "Suicide? No. I cannot believe John Cholmley would have thrown himself under the hooves of a thundering horse! He was not that sort of man. He was always sensible. Logical. Why then so illogical in his last action?"

Nods rippled across the gallery. "But who would wish to hurt John?" Pyk asked. "He was such a... such a decent man. A *kind* man. I don't think I ever heard a cross word pass his lips." Which was undoubtedly a lie, Marlowe reflected silently, but only in so much as even good men, kind men, lose their tempers and say things they regret. It is not the heat of words that defines them, he thought, but the cool calm rationality of the rest of their lives which far outweighs any fire. Men like him were ruled by heat, passion, fire, but men like Cholmley were water to his flame, placid, still, and running deep.

"Your question is too broad," Ed mused. "Or perhaps too narrow. I very much doubt there is a 'who' involved." He made the sign of the cross over his broad chest. "More like a 'what.'"

"I've got no time for riddles, Ed. Speak plainly or shut the hell up," Henslowe said, pushing away from the column to confront the stout player. "So tell me, what do you mean, 'what'?"

Ed hung his head, forcing Marlowe to strain to catch his hushed reply. "They say—they say he was ranting as he stumbled into the street. Proper shouting and screaming, and lashing out and shuddering back from invisible foes like a man possessed. A man fighting ghosts. His cries were of serpents, said they were writhing about him, biting at his flesh. It's not natural, you ask me. He never even saw the rider 'cause his eyes were fixed on sights unseen by mortal man."

Murmurs sprang up among the players.

"This isn't the first such tale I've heard," Tom Downton observed quietly. They turned to him. "There was an old beggar woman, said she heard hisses at her ear every hour, felt coils about her limbs." He waited, drawing them in with each unspoken word. Sometimes those were the strongest. "They found her drowned in an alley on a dry morning, no traces of water anywhere save for the dribble flowing from her mouth." He shook his head. "They waved it away as she'd gone mad and drank herself into a stupor, then collapsed in a fit. But it was mere water on her lips, making her the first woman drunk on it. It's not natural. But then, so much ain't these days."

"Aye, there was a fisherman pleading for help the other evening," Sam reported. "I was done and ready for home when I saw him. A pitiful wretch on his boat, begging for coin that he might take himself off the river for the night. I'll be honest, I thought it a clever beggar's ploy, but I couldn't resist asking why he would require a room when he stood within a perfectly serviceable boat." The young performer shuddered. "'There's a creature haunting these waters,' the man replied. 'She is clothed as a woman, all curves and peaks, a thing of beauty, but she is no woman, this—more a snake, sibilant and deadly. She calls to me with her siren song, and I grow weaker by the night. I can't resist her forever. Soon, I'll fall. All I ask is a coin, something to buy a night free of her song. Help me and I will repay you a thousand times!'" Sam looked away. "I gave him a coin or two, I'll admit. I'm a soft touch, though it wasn't enough for the price of a bed." He shook his head. "The next morning his boat was there. He was not. I have not seen him since, though I have heard other fishermen whispering about the death of one of their own, drowned and washed up bloated like some diseased carp."

"The plague," Ned stated plainly. "'Tis the plague returned. What other explanation could there be? Fevers and the dreams that burn within them, nothing more." Others nodded, clearly happy to believe him. Marlowe considered it a clear sign of their underlying fear that they would wish the Black Death back rather than seek another explanation.

For himself though, he was less sure. No, that was mere caviling. He knew this was nothing so banal as a symptom of the Black Death. He had seen that particular monster up close and knew it all too well. Neither, though, was he a stranger to such tales as his men were now repeating. They had occurred before, though not here, and perhaps not within the living memory of any other present, but there could be no mistake. The fevers, the whispers, the visions, the waking dreams, the loss of control—

These were the signs of a Beast.

Somewhere in London, a Beast had begun to stir.

But which one, he wondered.

Serpents could be the device of several.

And where?

If these deaths were occurring all across the city, he would be unable to pinpoint their source. It was possible the Beast was already on the move. He would have to find it, Marlowe realized. But there lay the risk, because without knowing which Beast he faced there was no way for him to determine how best to bring it down. Each incarnation was different. Was it set to oppose his own plans? Or was it content to continue its activities and allow him the space for his? That was the question. He needed a fortnight, perhaps less. Then the play would be complete. That was all he asked. It was not so much, was it?

Yet deep inside him, a sinking feeling, a smooth-sided pebble of doubt, reminded him that fond wishes seldom if ever came true.

Before he could add anything to the tales, the front doors opened for the second time to announce a new arrival. They slammed back with a loud clatter. This time the intruders would have been far less welcome, even if their news had been joyous—a trio of grim-faced and forbidding men dressed all in dark uniforms stood beneath the lintel. Marlowe had seen them only yesterday, and if he had never seen them again it would have been too soon.

"If you have come to see us perform, gentlemen," Marlowe called, detaching himself from the rest of the troupe. He strode toward the three to block their advance, meeting them just inside the gallery entrance, "Alas, you are premature by at *least* a week, more like two. You cannot rush genius—at least, I can't. I urge you to return when we have polished our speeches and honed our wit, that you might better appreciate our art. So, as I would banish a demon, I say begone." Marlowe smiled sweetly.

"I believe we have sufficient appreciation for your *art*, Marlowe," the silvered gentleman in the center mocked.

"Why, such venom, good sir! You would think I bedded your donkey or some such." Marlowe staggered back a step as though shocked. He made sure to keep himself directly in their path all the same. "So, what have I done to deserve such a treatment? I am Marlowe, decried as one of the foremost dramatists in all of England!"

"Aye, that you are. And there's a gent in the alleys by the docks who is the finest pederast in all the land," the man to the left retorted, "but you'll not hear him announcing his reputation quite so proudly!"

"Well, no, obviously, a pederast would have shame, would he not? I am sure you intended to be scathing in your jibe,

but perhaps the talking is better left to those more evolved?"
Marlowe masked the anger he felt rising, a heat of rage blazing up from deep inside, but even so the fire in his eyes was
bright enough to give the trio pause for thought. "If you would
insult me, at least get the words right, *sirrah*. A pederast skew-
ers a single boy, and then only with his flesh. I am far more
potent. And more dangerous. My genius is such that it trans-
fixes *multitudes* at once. Any fool can stick his cock in places it
shouldn't go. Just ask dear Pater." He swept into a low bow, and
was pleased to see when he straightened that he had stunned
them into silence. Let that show the fools how dangerous it was
to confront him in his own nest!

"What would you here, gentlemen?" Henslowe asked, stepping forward to stand beside Marlowe. Marlowe felt a rush of
warmth at the clear support from his friend. "Or have you come
simply to bandy insults with my playwright? If so, a word to
the wise, you will leave here badly bested. This boy's tongue is
vicious."

"We are here upon the Queen's own business, and it's none
of yours, old man," the man in the middle said flatly. He straightened to his full height, which while imposing fell far short of the
towering Ned, who had moved to stand at Marlowe's other side.
"I carry here a notice," he stated as he produced a broadsheet,
which he thrust at Henslowe, "stating that this Playhouse is to
be shut down at once!"

"What? Why?" Ned demanded. "What possible reason could
you have fabricated, you pathetic weasel?"

The silvered man only smiled at him, his expression growing ever colder. The smile barely twitched his lips and was
lost utterly in his neat goatee. "Concerns of public health," he
answered. "Gathering crowds in close confines such as this is
unsafe given the recent reoccurrences of plague."

"What of the Theatre?" Henslowe asked, referring to one of
their two rival playhouses. "Or the Curtain? I assume they are
to be shut as well?"

The man did not answer. After a moment's pause, the gentleman to his left coughed. He licked his lips. "Each playhouse
will be considered on its own merits," he replied coldly. "And

will be dealt with as deemed necessary."

"And in the language of the common man, you're screwing us," Ned snarled. "Despite the size of our *gallery*"—somehow he made that sound decidedly sexual—"which allows more space for the audience than either of the others. Plague fears, my arse. If you were truly worried about close quarters, you'd shut them first. There's a reason they call 'em the stinkies. It's a rancid pit. You're crammed in so tight you can barely breathe."

"Indeed," Henslowe agreed, inclining his head towards his son-in-law. "Ned has the right of it. When the Queen determines that *all* playhouses are unsafe for gatherings, we will comply with Her royal command. Until then, mark my words, gentlemen—this is an abuse of your authority, I assume for some personal vendetta against Marlowe, and I'm having none of it." He raised the broadsheet in both hands and tore it asunder, throwing the two halves back in the trio's startled faces. "Take your lies and stick them up your rectal passage, lad. Any more nonsense and I will take your villainy to the good Queen Herself!"

"Would you, now? You would do well to remember that the Privy Council serves at Her Majesty's pleasure, not yours," the central man informed them all coldly. "We act on Her behalf in everything we do, and you ignore Her decrees at your own peril." He turned on his heel. "We shall return to enforce this proclamation, with force if necessary." As agents of the Queen, the Privy Council had the authority to command soldiers, or at least the local guard. It was not, perhaps, the wisest fight Henslowe had ever picked, but Marlowe loved him for it.

"Bring whatever blades you wish," Ned rasped. "We have steel of our own, and fine knowledge of its use—come at us, and you will see how players defend themselves!"

"In a dress, I assume," the third man sneered, his eyes flicking toward Sam.

"We will shut this playhouse," the silvered man warned them all, "and that play will never reach its audience. You have our solemn oath on that, Marlowe. I would urge you to rein your fools in. It will only hurt you if we are forced to resort to other methods to bring the curtain down." He turned on his heel, as did his companions, and together the three of them departed.

"Miserable creatures. I'm surprised you have spine enough to walk like men," Ned called after them. "Slither back to your nest!"

"Enough, Ned—they've gone," Henslowe urged. Even so, it took Ned a moment to calm down. "Though they will return. And it won't end well, boys."

"Aye, and the fault lies with me," Marlowe admitted. "They are frightened of this play, though I cannot for the life of me think why. It is just a play, a performance, no great truth, yet they seem desperate to prevent it. I dread to think how far they'll go to see we never set foot on the stage."

"Well, frankly, bollocks, my friend. They can try and they can try," Henslowe replied, with a grin, "But the show *will* go on. We will combat them with every tool at our disposal, the sharpest being your words."

That drew a smile from Marlowe. "Yes, of course." He turned back toward Ned and the rest of the Admiral's Men. "So, once more through the scene then?" They nodded and scurried back toward the stage and their places. But even though he followed them and gave them his best attention, Marlowe found it impossible to work when he was so troubled. Both by the actions of the Privy Council—and the ominous warning they had left behind—and by the stories his friends had recounted. Curious events were occurring, for sure, but what did it all mean?

SCENE FIVE
*During which our hero ponders the nature of love's fires
and tests the mettle of pen over sword*

"Thou dost seem troubled, my love." Lorelei slid forward, the water rippling around her, offering tantalizing glimpses of pale flesh. She rested a cool, damp palm along his cheek. "Do I not please you? Have you grown bored so soon?" She batted her eyelashes at him, a flutter of motion behind the waterfall of her hair.

"Nay, rest assured you are still more than enough to drive a man from his right mind," Marlowe promised, tilting his head to kiss her hand. A tingle arose from his lips at their touch. They were lounging in the large brass tub that stood in the corner of his rooms. The tub was filled with cool water and scented soaps and the two of them, entwined. "Forgive me, my sweet. Truly the fault lies not with you—thou art as near perfection as mortal flesh could bear, I swear. Other matters nag at me."

"This new play of yours?" She slithered closer, her breasts rubbing across his legs, belly, and chest as she stretched herself across him. She stopped with her face a hair from his, her lips so close he could breathe her in. "I had thought my role as muse was successful?"

"Beyond all compare," he assured her, leaning forward to kiss her lips. The cool sensation swept down through him, leaving Marlowe both aroused and becalmed, like a panicked ship in a dead sea. "The problem lies not with the writing, for the words flow marvelously—my pen has scarce been able to keep pace with my fevered imagination." He held up his writing hand to show her the calluses and blisters and ink stains there, mute evidence of his claim, and she kissed each finger in turn, leaving them free of aches at last. "The difficulty presents itself in the staging, or at least the performance, of all things, for there are people intent on seeing this tale die unspoken."

"So speak it to me now, then," Lorelei urged, a grin touching her full lips. "Make *me* your rapt audience of one, and delight me with your genius." One of her hands snaked between them and grasped his manhood in a grip slippery yet firm. "And I will delight thee in return."

"How could I resist?" He coughed, and the sound became a groan as her fingers proved too dexterous for him. "Very well. What would you hear?"

"You have shared the conceit already," she reminded him, "and told me some of the opening. So, something else. Entertain me with some other scene. Is there a moment where the lovers speak their true feelings to one another? I would like to hear that."

"My pleasure." He kissed her again, and then leaned his head back, shut his eyes, and let the scene spring to life behind his eyelids. "Elissa is walking the gardens," he explained, painting the picture for her with words. "She seeks solitude and wisdom, for though Iarbas presents a wise match there is no warmth there. Her foot catches on a root and she stumbles by the balcony's edge. One step behind her, Barcas catches her before she can fall, and at his touch the young queen feels a rush of heat. She meets his gaze and falls deep into his eyes, into the passion she sees boiling there. And there, she burns…

"'Never shall I let thee fall,' he tells her, 'for mine own heart is tied to thy fate, and werest thou to plummet I needs must follow—those strings of love bind me so tight I could never be far from thee, even though we must both meet our doom on the courtyard below.'

"'And wouldst thou die in such a fashion?' she asks, "Shattered against cold stone, thy queen lifeless beside thee? I had thought all young warriors sought death in battle, glorious and blood-drenched?'

"'To die beside thee would be glorious beyond measure, believe me, my queen,' Barcas answers, 'and to be so close, even in death, is all I might wish and more.' He glances away then, realizing he has said too much, but he cannot help himself. 'For indeed I know my place, and it is in the ranks, guarding over thee, and never closer, though my heart might yearn for it.'

"'Tell me something, Barcas.'

"'Anything.'

"'Am I not thy queen?' Elissa demands.

"'Body and soul,' he answers without hesitation. "Thou dost reign over me.'

"'Then surely thy place is where I will it?' she contends, 'and at whatever distance I determine, no?' She steps closer, so close his breath mingles with hers, becoming one, theirs. 'And I would have thee near, dear Barcas, always. For the heat I feel from thee doth warm my lonely soul, and cause my heart to blaze and take flight as if carried upon a skyward flame.'"

"Ah, the flames of lust," Lorelei commented with a throaty chuckle, her hand continuing to caress him. "It burns so bright, and so hot, but for so brief a time. Is it not better to fall into a deep pool of abiding—enduring—affection? Is it not more potent to drown in love than burn up in it?"

"The two are not exclusive or adverse, surely?" Marlowe replied, let his own hands sweep along her curves, tracing her lines above and then beneath the water. "Deep emotion can burn as well as simmer steadily below the surface. I would hate to think our fire would burn out, wouldn't you? So for Barcas and Elissa, though their love is new—this bright burning thing, filled with gouts of flame—it rises from a glow banked deep within, and will remain stoked as long as there are coals to burn and breath in their lungs."

"Ever the poet, yet you cannot deny that fires do gutter and die, it is their nature," came her counter, "but currents flow unabated. The sea never fades or dwindles, and its edges are bounded only by our imagination. A wave hits the shore, it breaks, and yet even as it breaks it begins to form anew out in the deep water, ready to roll in towards the shore once more. Ever was it so, and ever shall it be."

"True, and yet even the greatest ocean is subject to the moon," Marlowe pointed out, "and in that it is subservient, whereas fire knows no limits. It can overcome all obstacles—it may even leap through the empty air, to dance from tree to tree or bridge a river or lake, carried aloft by the wind with no cessation to its heat. So is love, great love—under adversity it may be banked, but as long as a single coal contains an ember, a spark, within, then that fire may rise again, restored to a blaze even beyond its former glory."

"And water may drown fire, just like that!" Lorelei snapped her fingers. "Quenched. Drenched beyond its ability to withstand," she countered, her grasp bordering upon painful now as she tugged him down in the tub. Marlowe's head slipped below the surface. He opened his mouth, gasping, bubbles rising. His vision swam, and as she pushed him down he could barely make her out beyond a haze of swirled shadows and light, a twisting, writhing mass of hair and limbs that tangled all about him.

He pulled himself away from her just long enough to surface, and gulped down a deep breath. Water sprayed all about as he shook his head. "But fire can transform water to steam," he replied, grinning, "and boil it away until the pot turns dry." The bathwater, previously gone cold, began to warm once more, until tendrils of that same steam rose all about them and Marlowe felt his cold-paled skin turning rosy.

Lorelei shrieked and swatted at his hands, her hair rising in the steam to coil about her head and shoulders. "What have you done, you rogue! Are you trying to broil me like some trout? What next? Would you fillet my meat at your leisure?"

"Ha! Hardly, woman, though I would gladly spear you," he replied with a grin, leaning forward in the tub and scooping her up onto his lap. "Come, let's play fisherman, shall we? I rather like the idea of you dancing at the end of my pole."

"Fie, I am not about to be caught so easy." She pushed him away and swam to the far side of the tub. "I come when I will, *sirrah*, and not when you demand."

"Indeed, then it is obviously my good fortune that you would come so often." His grin widened. "Surely you are the most obliging fish I've ever encountered. Will you not take the bait once more?"

"Hmph!" She slapped the water, sending a splash across his

chest and face. "Perhaps this fish should withhold its affections for a time? Might be you would come to appreciate them more if you were forced to do without?"

"Madam, believe me, no one could appreciate you more than I," he protested, laughing as he shook the droplets off. "Willingness in no way lessens delight." She smirked at that. It wasn't a smile, though. And the look changed further, to surprise and then dismay as he began to lever himself up out of the tub. "Alas, now, I fear, you must excuse me. There can be no rest for the wicked. And I think we have confirmed that at the very best I am truly wicked."

"What?" She leaned across the tub's lip, her breasts pressing temptingly against the cool metal. It would have been so easy to succumb, to climb back into the water and lose himself in her anew. "Are you casting me aside so casually?"

"Never, my sweet," he assured her, leaning in for a kiss. He pulled back as her arms attempted to snake about his neck and draw him back down into her watery embrace. "You only have yourself to blame, sweet Lorelei—you have enflamed me once more, and new lines spring to mind, burning their words within me. I need to write—they must hit the page before they turn to ash and blow away like smoke on a blustery shore." He bowed, naked and soaked but still wrapped in dignity. "However, I would dearly like to resume our . . . engagement at some later time, after my words stain the pages... assuming you are willing?"

"You are a bad, bad man, Kit Marlowe. I should hate you, turning your back on me like this, but how can I resent being your muse? What girl wouldn't wish to inspire a man to great art?" She snorted as she rose from the tub herself, very deliberately allowing him to see exactly what he was giving up to go and write. "I will wait, wet, for you."

"And I for thee—well, not wet, obviously, I'd catch my death," Marlowe said, extending a hand to help her step down and offering her a towel that had been warmed by the fire. She accepted the first but waved away the second. "Believe me, it is only the play that draws me away, and only for so long as it takes to find the right words."

"She is a jealous mistress, this bitch, demanding all your attention," Lorelei commented. "Suddenly we are rivals for both your heart and your time, this thing I created." She reached out and gave his manhood a not-so gentle reminder. "But remember this, writer man—it lacks the power to please you in the same ways I can." She looked at him knowingly, her gaze dropping below his waist, where her hands had just lingered. "That will bring you back to my bed soon enough."

"You won't hear me arguing," he agreed, though he was tempted to point out that, in fact, they had not once been in her bed, or even to her lodgings for that matter. He knew better than to wade in such waters, though—her humor was already at dangerously low ebb.

"Go then, Marlowe. Go. Write." She playfully mocked him as she tugged her clothing on once more. The fabric clung to her still-damp skin. "But it's a risk, is it not? You might well have to sink to your knees and beg me to return once you've finished your masterpiece." And with that and a parting kiss she swept from his rooms.

Marlowe stared after her even past the point where the door swung shut and she was long gone.

"And who said women were a mystery?" the playwright muttered to himself as he toweled the damp from his body. He let the flames warm his flesh, enjoying the feeling of sensation returning. Finally he pulled on a loose shirt and pants. He caught his reflection in the window. "And this one... all fire on the surface, but ice-cold water beneath, alluring and numbing." He shook his head to clear it. Now was not the time to dwell upon the mystery that was Lorelei. Not when the words wanted out of his head.

"But she knows you well enough, my jealous little mistress," he said softly as he sat at his desk, smoothing out a clean broadsheet before him. "Demanding as you are. Still, with you I always know precisely where I stand. There's something to be said for that." And right now she was warm and willing, and he dove into her heat body and soul, dipping his quill and scribbling away, the words dancing into his mind and out again so quickly he scrambled to write them down before they swept away from him.

He had finished the balcony scene and was just painting the scene around Iarbas's final understanding, that moment when it becomes all too easy for him to see Elissa's affection for Barcas, when he paused. Beside him, the candle's flame flickered. A cool breeze tickled the back of Marlowe's neck. That gave him a second pause. Surely he had left the window pulled shut? The nights were cold and he was hardly one to invite the freezing weather within his home.

He leaned back, shifting to glimpse the window in question—and a knotted cord brushed his cheek as his head moved. He caught the reflection of man in the glass, and twisted violently as the cord snapped tight, quick as a striking snake.

Marlowe shouted incoherently, simply for the sake of making noise and hoping to draw attention, and kicked up from his stool. He wrapped his hand in the cord and dragged it aside before it could bite into his throat. With the other hand he reached for the candle. "You'll have to do better than this, *assassin!*" Marlowe rasped. The cord, still in his hand, smoldered and caught fire. The masked man dropped it with a muffled curse. But even before the burning rope had hit the floorboards, a blade appeared in his hand.

He lunged at Marlowe.

"Damn, but you are persistent! Who are you, then? Let's see about unmasking you, shall we?" Marlowe demanded, knocking the dagger hand aside with his forearm. He allowed a smile to touch his lips. The heat from the contact, brief as it was, suffused the blade and made the stranger gasp. "Have you been sent by one of the many brokenhearted left behind? Or perhaps you are a cuckolded husband? I'm sorry, of course, but I never stick it where it isn't wanted. And if you've come to collect on some debt, then surely poking me full of holes would rather preclude any sort of repayment." Marlowe danced back a step, keeping just out of reach of the dagger. "So, then, have I perhaps insulted some lord, either titled or criminal in nature, without my knowing?"

Still the man said nothing.

Instead he lunged forward, trying with the dagger a second time.

Marlowe dealt with that easily enough, all the while assessing. His attacker was of average height, slender but strong. He handled the blade well enough, so was certainly trained. He wore dark clothes, a jacket and trousers paired with soft black boots and matching gloves, with a black scarf wound about his head to disguise his features. Only the eyes gleamed forth, dark and cold.

"Come sir, you're making it very difficult to like you. Why don't we sit down and talk this out like gentlemen?" Marlow insisted. "How about a gesture of good will? Show me your face. It's so much easier to discuss terms face-to-face rather than face-to-scarf."

The stranger stabbed at him again. The fact that he insisted on stabbing over slashing, which would have caused more lasting damage, gave Marlowe hope. It also made him predictable. He waited for the fourth thrust, knowing it must come, and as it did Marlowe caught the man's wrist, drawing him in close. His attacker struggled but could not pull free, and Marlowe smiled dangerously as the man gasped at the heat of his grip. He felt the man's skin blister.

"Well, I've had my fun, so enough of this," Marlowe said. "I'd rather not kill you. So, please, unless you want me to rain the fires of holy hell down upon your corpse, don't force my hand." Once upon a time, in another life, the fire would always have been his first resort, but he had moved past that. Christopher Marlowe was a man of words, not of steel. "Let us speak, please, and part ways with both still able to draw breath."

The man snarled wordlessly and twisted, yanking his arm free of Marlowe's grasp.

"Well, that rather answers that, doesn't it?" Marlowe sighed.

His attacker stepped in again, driving the dagger up hard toward Marlowe's midriff.

Marlowe sidestepped the blow, barely. He felt the blade's edge slice through shirt and skin alike, parting both with alarming ease. A sudden intense surge of heat nearly undid him. He gritted his teeth, ignoring the raging pain, and replied with a lunge of his own.

His candle, still alight, roared then, blazing wildly into a veritable blade of fire. He stabbed at the stranger's eyes, the tongue of flame searing sight from his enemy forever. The man screamed. It was a sickening sound, hopeless and desperate. "I tried," Marlowe whispered. "I begged you, but you did this."

The man flailed about wildly, dropping the dagger. He stumbled back a step—

—and plummeted from the open window, falling three stories to hit the ground with a sickening thud.

Dead.

Which, all things considered, was a most unfortunate turn of events for both of them.

"Damn it all to the seven hells!" Marlowe spat, covering the distance to the window in three steps. He pulled it shut, closing it as gently as he could. Anyone could have been watching, and a man trying to fly out of his chamber window was not easily explained. Marlowe suspected he already knew what the assassin would have said, had he but talked: he had jilted no lovers of late, nor accrued any great debts to be called in, or even bothered to insult anyone of importance—at least, not since the incident with the placards, and that was hardly the sort to engender such a brutal response. No, there was only one group who would silence him and his work, and they'd promised as much: The Privy Council.

They had threatened violence, and clearly felt the need to follow through. With Marlowe dead his play would remain unfinished and unseen forever.

But the move surprised him. It was one thing to waylay him in an alleyway and make it look like a drunken accident, but to send someone to kill him in his own home? That spoke of a desperation nearing blind panic. What was it about this play that had them so concerned? It was a love story—admittedly one that did not end entirely happily, but a love story all the same. Yes, there was a queen involved, but she was no reflection upon Elizabeth, and comparison would not have been unfavorable even if she were, as Elissa was strong and clever and in control of her own life and of her court. Was it the ending? Barcas's impossible transformation into the Phoenix, a herald of beauty and creativity? Surely not? Where was the harm in reminding all and sundry that they could rise above their fates and cast light upon the world with their creations?

It made no sense to him. Not one whit.

He had no proof that they had been the assassin's employers, of course. The man hadn't exactly been caught redhanded with a writ from the Council, seal and all, declaring Marlowe must die. Indeed, he had left behind only his dagger, which was a simple weapon, finely crafted and well cared for, but without any distinguishing marks to identify it. If Marlowe were to accuse the Privy Council it would come down to his word against theirs, and for all his fame he was just a playwright, whilst they were Her Majesty's appointed agents.

There was nothing he could do about it, Marlowe decided with a sigh.

He set the dagger upon his desk, a reminder of the danger he faced, and then returned the candle to the writing surface. His fingers found the cut in his shirt and slid within to probe the tender flesh there, but already the sting had retreated, his flesh knitting. By morning it would be little more than sore.

Well, now they knew he was no easy victim—not, at least, within the confines of his own home where his fury could blaze unabated. But for now he could only watch and wait. They would try and stop him again, he was sure of it.

In the meantime, he had several more scenes to write before he could lose himself in the heat of coupling with his muse. Marlowe lifted his quill from where it had rolled when he had dropped it, re-sharpened the tip, dipped it in the inkwell, and began again.

SCENE SIX

Whence our hero is thwarted in art and love

Marlowe was whistling to himself as he walked. He had a sheaf of fresh pages tucked securely under his arm, and a spring in his step. He was in high spirits, and why not? He had finished all but the last act of the play. True, he was bone tired, wrung dry, and felt as though he were viewing the world through a haze, but none of that mattered. The play was nearly finished, and it was his masterpiece.

His good humor vanished as he came within sight of the Playhouse and saw the boards nailed savagely across its front doors.

"No!" He broke into a run.

A parchment had been affixed where the boards crossed. As he closed the distance he recognized the royal seal.

"Closed by order of Her flaming Majesty," Marlowe read aloud, his anger getting the better of him. He slammed his shoulder into the door, then backed up a pace and did it again, but the door didn't budge. " 'Concerns of the public health,' my hairy backside! Open the damned door!" He slammed a palm against the door in frustration.

"This is a joke, a bad, bloody joke," he muttered, turning away. He stalked around the building to the actors' entrance in the rear. That, mercifully, remained unsealed. He threw the door open so hard it hit the limits of hinge and frame and rebounded against him. "Henslowe!"

"I'm here, Kit," their landlord answered from within. "We all are. Come in, lad, come in."

Marlowe stepped inside and shut the door behind him. He had not gone ten paces, blinking and squinting as his eyes struggled to adjust to the dimmer light, when a figure appeared out of the shadows. A tall, tall figure. Marlowe's hand moved instinctively for his belt and the weapon sheathed there, memories of the assassin still fresh. But before he could skewer Ned the big man stepped out of the shadows and laid a hand on Marlowe's arm. He followed his friend through the maze of back rooms to the stage. The Admiral's Men were gathered there. The mood was sour.

"We thought it must be you trying to beat the door down with your bare fists," Tom Downton said with a sad laugh. "It's not like we ever have an audience quite so eager to get in."

"What happened?" Marlowe asked, then supplied an answer of his own. "Those cursed bastards of the Privy Council back with their lies and accusations?"

Henslowe shook his head. "In part, I'm sure, but not solely them. Worse, though—Kit, this is no mere vendetta against us. They've shut the Curtain and the Theatre as well. We are all closed down." He looked tired. "And it's not like the stage is alone in its suffering."

"All over London, businesses are shut," Sam agreed. "Some by choice, others by force. And still others by Death himself." The young player shuddered, and several made signs against ill omen.

Marlowe glanced about, trying to take it all in. He found it impossible to believe that the plague had returned so virulently. He had just walked down these streets and seen no sign of fever or suffering—he remembered the bells and the carts and everything else quite clearly. The atmosphere in his city was different now, true, but it was not thick with sickness and desperation. "So, the plague? No lie?" He rubbed at his eyes.

"Not whole neighborhoods," Ned admitted, "but near enough as to have the whole city in panic. There were more deaths discovered this morn: a young man, barely grown into whiskers, dangling from a bridge; a lady, older and most regal, tangled in a fisherman's nets, bloated and gone fish-belly pale; a man, escaped from Bedlam, impaled upon the spar of a clipper newly anchored."

"More madness, as well," Ed added. "A woman running

unclothed through the streets bearing a knife and a spoon, shrieking and striking at all within reach. A man dancing upon a cart, shouting that only by living within the music's thrum could he evade the serpents at his feet. Children tearing at one another, screaming that they must slay the monsters if they are to survive." He shivered, his usually merry face gone sallow and grim. "The world has truly gone to Hell, Kit."

"Aye, it has," Marlowe agreed, frowning as he attempted to sort through their reports. If all were true, and frankly he no reason to doubt they were, matters had grown worse, and rapidly so. He felt the heat rise within him. It was one thing to know your own nature, but something else entirely to know the nature of your enemy. His had many names, but they were all the same beast. Just as he had woken, so, too, had one of his counterparts. Marlowe was a man with enemies. But his enemies were unlike most. Their enmity, for one thing, went back centuries and lives. They hunted each other across the world, vying for ascendancy. In this time and this place he had thought himself safe, at least for a while, and had given in to his urge to create and inspire. And in his vanity, this Beast had woken without him knowing. Who knew what guise it was wearing this time? As to what it wanted? Chaos. It was always thus.

And it wasn't like there was only one of them. Each of the elements had their own incarnations, or Beasts: Earth, Air, Water, and his own, Fire.

Each of the deaths seemed to share the same motif: water. That limited the incarnations he might be facing. The Hydra, perhaps? The Kraken? The Dragon was not adverse to submersion, but he thought he would recognize his brother's hand in things. Hydra and Kraken, those two were most likely, and both had an affinity for madness. He suppressed a shudder of his own. If he were facing the Hydra or the Kraken he would need to be more than wary; both were fearsome opponents, wily and powerful.

"Like it or not, there is sod all we can do," Henslowe was saying as Marlowe turned his thoughts and senses once more to the world around him. Slipping like that was dangerous, and given the likelihood that the Beast was abroad, could prove fatal.

He needed to remain focused on the here and now. "It's not as though we can ignore the proclamation. It's the Queen, we'd end up in the Tower. So we've got no choice but to wait until the danger has past and hope that the order was rescinded. We'll be ready to reopen the second it is, let's just hope there's an audience left to watch."

"Well, perhaps it is something of an anticlimax now, all things considered," Marlowe stated, pulling the broadsheets from beneath his arm, "but I present to you Acts Two, Three, and Four." He grinned. "All that remains to be penned is the final act, and that, dear friends, will be remedied soon."

The players stared at Marlowe, only half-believing. "You finished *all* that since last we rehearsed?" Martin asked. "What's got into you, man? Some demon of the Word, no doubt. Hell's Teeth, I can barely think and even then only half as fast as you write."

"Or did you simply stay awake all night? Burning the wick at both ends, so to speak, and scribbling your quill to a nub?" Ned chimed in.

Marlowe blew out a breath and grinned, shrugging. "I don't know how I fastened my breeches this morning, put it that way. But at least I can write now—it's been a long time coming."

"Knowing you, you had that fine woman fasten them for you!" John shouted, drawing both laughs and whistles, and Marlowe gave a slight bow in reply but said nothing more. The men took that as acknowledgement, and spent several more minutes suggesting ways in which the fair Lorelei might have aided Marlowe in his attempts to clothe himself—though most of the suggestions seemed to require the exact opposite.

Marlowe joined in as best he was able, despite the fact that his thoughts kept drifting to the Beasts, water, and the mythical incarnations tied to them. He kept thinking of the last time he had faced the Kraken and failed, losing a life he had rather enjoyed at the time—but then, he'd been reborn into this one eventually and he was rather fond of it, too. And it felt good to laugh with the company even if only for a little while. The Playhouse was closed, yes, but so were their competitors, so at least they were not losing fans to their rivals. This twist of fate would grant him time to finish the play, and for them to rehearse it. When the scare had passed and the ban was lifted they would reopen and perform *Birth of the Phoenix* at last, before a rapt audience. It *would* be a triumph.

The players took their places and started to run through the new lines.

Marlowe's mood had begun to sour again before the day was out. By the time he walked from the darkened theatre to the alehouse, it was black as pitch, and near as foul.

The day's rehearsals had gone well—very well, in fact, with everyone agreeing that the new scenes were some of the finest he had written. Everyone did their best to speak of the closure, and the chaos and death that had caused it, as only a temporary obstacle. An adversity. The plague would pass soon, and then they would perform again.

But upon leaving the theatre that evening, Marlowe had seen the reality. The plague was growing worse.

People wandered past him, dazed. Those that weren't trapped in confusion were enraged, shouting and swearing, or terrified, blubbering like children and scarcely able to stumble along for fear. For the first time he noticed that many buildings showed signs of damage; there were great rents in wood and cloth and even stone as if some creature had walked the boulevard, scraping scimitar-sharp nails against them.

That image was not so far from truth, Marlowe knew, though the Beast in question had almost certainly effected its destruction through human agents, not demonic ones. It was a taint that worked its way into the minds of all those within reach. He could smell its presence now that he was aware it had awoken, and knew that it was the source of both the rage and the fear. It was intent on driving all of London mad.

"And so it falls to me, again, to put an end to this," Marlowe muttered to himself as he walked, sidestepping a prone man who gibbered and howled as he scratched at the mud beneath his hands. But how? Without knowing the true nature of the Beast or where it lurked, how could he possibly stand against it? London was vast, riddled with alleys and back alleys and so many nooks and crannies the Beast could hide here forever, unseen. He himself had, he was all too aware of that. He needed to think. In part it didn't matter—whichever Beast it was, the creature was clever. And it had certainly sensed him as well; they were bound like that, in torment. So it would have taken steps to remain hidden until such time as it desired a confrontation. He would not suddenly stumble upon it, taking the Beast unawares. That did not happen.

He reached for the latch of the alehouse door, but a slender hand emerged from the twilight and grasped his wrist.

"Come to me, sweet writer man," a husky voice whispered, and he smiled even as he felt the cool, calming touch of her hand send a shiver racing up his arm.

Marlowe grinned as Lorelei dragged him into the shadows beside the door. Her mouth found his, preventing words—not that he was particularly interested in conversation at that moment. Her body pressed against him insistently.

As always her kisses were like a cool rain shower, refreshing him and washing away his cares, leaving him muddled and adrift in a tide of emotion and stray thought. When her hands slid into his breeches and grasped the rising heat of his hard phallus he gasped but did not pull away. His hands crept up beneath her loose blouse to cup her breasts. Her skin was almost icy to the touch.

"Here?" he managed as he pulled back to catch his breath. Her only response was to leap upon him, her long legs wrapping about his waist, her arms coiled around his neck, drawing his head towards her so that she could kiss him again, fiercely. His hands moved lower, gripping her thighs to keep her aloft, then he stumbled a step, driving her up against the wall even as she guided him into her. Some distant part of his brain wondered that no plumes of steam arose as his heat found her dampness and the two sizzled and seared together amid their frenzied coupling. It was not tender. There was no love. It was brutal. Animalistic. Harsh. He existed in a fog of sensation, acting without thought or restraint, high on a haze of pleasure.

It was a miracle the Watch didn't come running with cries of murder, so loud was she.

Afterward she still clung to him, her hair a tangled mess of sweat-soaked tendrils that stuck to him every bit as possessively as her limbs. He kissed her neck, his lips almost numb from the sudden chill in the air, and twisted so that his back met the alehouse wall. Her skirts had slid back down behind, making them appear almost respectable.

She stroked his cheek. "Still so serious, my love?" Lorelei whispered in his ear before biting it with sharp teeth. She stopped just short of breaking the skin. "What more can I do to make you forget your troubles?"

"You drown my sorrows," Marlowe answered, leaning in to kiss her and getting only her cheek as she nipped at his neck once more. "I am in a haze of bliss, unable to think beyond your body."

"And that is how it should be," she agreed. "Let me sate you, body and soul, and fill you with delight. What else, sweet playwright, exists of value in this world, beyond ecstasy?"

For an instant, Marlowe had no answer. Then the thought came, a single point of light piercing the mental fog, and his mind came alive once more.

"The play," he replied, grinning. "That has value. Words and deeds and emotion, wrapped together upon the stage to create and display and transfix, to enlighten and enliven. To amaze and educate and entertain. To share what is inside here," he tapped his temple with a fingertip. "These things have value. They exist long after any physical delight is gone, lost to memory, and they carry our heritage to the peoples of the world, not just those here to see it today and tomorrow but those who will come after and after and after. Imagine that they may read my words in five hundred years. Imagine, because I barely can."

"Five hundred years and beyond, Christopher Marlowe. The world will remember you, and worship your name as a master of the arts," Lorelei assured him. "But it is late, and dark, and grown cold. What say we leave history to itself for another night and enjoy the warmth of your bed, and fill our hearts with joy and your head with dreams? There will be time enough to write tomorrow, and you will be the greater for it, inspired by your muse."

It was a struggle—despite the fact he had just found release, she did something to him he couldn't begin to explain—but Marlowe shook his head. "No, I must go," he said. He wrestled to free himself from her grasp, but Lorelei wasn't about to let him go quite so easily. She clung to him all the tighter, arms and legs and hair all woven around him, but slowly Marlowe extricated himself here and there, easing to the side with each inch of freedom gained, until her feet were on the ground once more and she was leaning on the wall beside him.

She sighed theatrically. "Does your *other* mistress call, then?" Lorelei asked, affecting a pout even as her eyes drank him in and promised much in return. "She has allures of her own, but can she promise to leave you breathless and limp, awash in sensation, all but out of your body from sheer over-whelming rapture?" She winked at him.

Marlowe almost succumbed. What was one more night, in the scheme of things? He might have, had another patron not stumbled past and unlatched the alehouse door. A blast of heat and light and sound washed over Marlowe, warming him against the chill and clearing his head of her spell. He straight-ened, pushing away from wall and woman both.

"True," he conceded, "she cannot offer such *physical* delights, but she promises a joy more subtle and sublime when finished." He laughed ruefully. "But until that moment she is a demand-ing fiend and as such cannot be denied for long, so I must go to her once more."

"I might not be here when you return, Marlowe," Lorelei warned, a bite to her words though she smiled around them. "I am a jealous lover and there are many who would offer me their every waking moment with an eager heart and a firm . . . resolve." The look she gave him was sharp as a serpent's tooth. "Think upon it, playwright. I would hate to have to find a new partner for my passions. And I should like to think that you regret your decision and, who knows, perhaps even miss me?"

Marlowe smiled and touched her cheek. "I already do," he assured her, bowing again and blowing her a kiss even as he backed away. "My heart, my soul, and my flesh, they are yours . . . and when the play is done, my mind shall be as well."

"I will wait, but not forever," she called after him as he turned on his heel. "If the tide runs out . . ." she shrugged as though to say she had no idea what might happen then.

"Then I shall fly into your arms, fear not," he answered, raising his voice as the distance betwixt them grew.

"Go, then, and write if you must. I will wait as long as my humor abides!" She laughed, the sound carrying through the night, and then affected the voice of Elissa from his pages and shouted, "For enamored I am of thee, and wouldst fain lie in thy arms for all eternity!"

Marlowe did not reply. Instead he waved at her and then the alehouse was gone from view, swallowed up in the night. He turned once more to the road before him. His head still felt full of fog and shadow. He picked up the pace, letting the cool night air revive him.

What was it about Lorelei, he wondered, that stole his wits from him? One touch was enough to leave him breathless and thoughtless, numb and cold, as if dunked in a rain bucket on a winter morning. One touch. It was as though she worked some sort of magic on his soul, and it wasn't as though he'd not loved before. It was unlike him to fall so hard, so far and so fast, and to feel so different, so bewitched and becalmed.

That thought gave him pause. It was such a contradiction to his normal state of fire and heat and furious energy that it felt . . . unnatural.

And perhaps, he though for the first time, it was.

And for once he started to *think*.

Marlowe exercised that great mind of his to ask questions: *What if Lorelei's allure were somehow wrapped within all the other curiosities that had surrounded them of late? What if the very madness that had ensnared so many others had seeped into his brain as well, only his fire had kept it partially at bay? What if whatever had driven others mad had merely sapped him of his will and made him susceptible to Lorelei's considerable charms? Or what if it was worse?*

He thought upon that as he walked, the steady sound of his footsteps on the ground a reassuring beat that brought him back to his senses with every pace.

Think.

Lorelei had first claimed she would serve as his Muse, he remembered, and aid him in unlocking the play that had smoldered inside him so intensely, there but refusing to blaze forth. She had offered him what his heart most desired, and now she viewed that same play as a rival for his affections, and begrudged him every moment spent writing. Surely, if she were his Muse, she would delight in the furthering of his art, knowing she was at the root of its forward motion?

Had she truly been his Muse? It seemed doubtful to him now.

So then, was it merely a ploy to gain his attentions? To get close to him?

If you can't find an answer looking at a problem from one end, turn it around and look again: what if she had, in fact, been opposed to the play from the first knowledge of its existence? He let that thought simmer within him, and scoured his memories for moments to test the possibility. He dried desperately to think. He wanted to scream. When—even once—had she truly encouraged his art? She had *claimed* to be aiding him, but had tried to draw him from his writing at every single turn. Indeed, given the sheer distraction of her touch, she had become the chief obstacle to his finishing the play, far beyond anything his own stubborn mind had thrown up to stop him in the past.

She had no desire to see the play's completion.

Rather, she had deliberately muddled his mind and his senses to keep him lulled and docile, a pet for her own play, though hers had no words.

Which could only mean she knew full well the effect her touch had on him, and had used it deliberately and without mercy to bind him to her and keep him unaware.

Marlowe stopped in his tracks, unwilling to believe he had been so wholly and easily deceived.

Lorelei was not caught up in the madness—she *was* the madness!

He'd been so preoccupied with the notion of another Beast lurking out there he hadn't even considered that it had been writhing about him, circling his flesh and coiled in his bed all along. At least he knew now which creature he faced. Given her affinity for water, her sinuous nature, the serpents many had sighted, and the madness billowing out from her, there was only one possible answer: Lorelei, sweet, sensuous, seductive Lorelei, was the monstrous, maddening sea Beast known as the Kraken.

At the very least she bore one of its Aspects; that was how the Beasts worked, they sought out those of like thought and disposition and bonded with them, granting them Aspects of the Beast's own nature. With most Beasts, those chosen fell into competition then, one against the other, defeating each other in some fashion before one rose the victor and bore the Beast's full visage unopposed.

Lorelei would have begun as the Nix, the water nymph.

He remembered with a shudder their midnight swim in the filthy Thames.

Nix were seductive. Water was her element. So at least he knew why he had fallen so quickly under her spell.

And those deaths . . . he realized now that many of them, if not all, must have been her rivals! Not those who had succumbed to madness, like poor John Cholmley, but the others found dead by violence, either in or beside the water. Lorelei had been besting her competition, edging ever closer to oneness with the Beast. After Nix came the Vodyanoi, more powerful and implacable, and beyond that the tentacle-wrapped Uam Boaz. Each was stronger than the last, and so with each new stage Lorelei's hold upon not only him but London in general had tightened, and her madness had spread and taken root. Now she was powerful, so powerful, that if not the Kraken awakened she was barely one step removed. When she achieved that final goal, he realized sickly, all London would fall to her fever dreams and writhing maladies of the mind.

The city entire would crumble into chaos...

And it was his fault. Marlowe knew that with a cold certainty that nonetheless fanned the flames of rage rising within him. His presence here had served as a beacon, alerting the Kraken to this place and time. And his plays, his performances, even his thoughts, the plans to write about the Phoenix, all of the minor rebellions had fanned that fire, stirring the people just as he had hoped but also drawing more attention from the other Beasts until, finally, one could no longer resist its lure.

Now the Kraken was here, and preparing to wrest the city from his grasp and devour it whole.

He would not let it happen.

Marlowe pounded his fist against a nearby wall, the fire flaring inside him. He felt it blister up against his skin and wrestled with it, trying to calm himself. He could not—would not—burn outright. "No," he whispered, the syllable rising into the night. "You shall not have my city," he promised.

The play would have to wait, so in that regard she would win, but it could not be helped. The coming of the Kraken placed all of London in danger, and he was the only one capable of stopping her. She might think that water drowned fire, but he knew better. Fire steamed water away to nothing.

He turned and strode toward home, plans already forming in his head.

Behind him, the imprint of knuckles and fingers remained, seared into the solid stone as though the sturdy building were a slab of mud ripe for the molding. The impression left by his fist steamed in the cold shadows, its heat slowly swallowed by the long, damp night.

SCENE SEVEN

In which passion burns deep and true, conquering all

"Good day, fair lady. I trust the morning finds you well?" Lorelei studied him, hands planted upon her hips, head cocked to one side, eyes narrow, lips playing with a smile. Her long, dark hair showed more bounce than he recalled, more vitality as it curled about her head and shoulders. Marlowe suppressed a shudder as he pictured the strands as snakes and tentacles instead. Fortunately, being the man to put words in actors' mouths had taught him something of their art, and he kept his face cheerful and his voice enthusiastic.

"I received your message," she replied after a moment's pause. "Most thoughtful of you to leave it with my employer."

"Considering you have yet to share where you make your home, it was the next best thing." Marlowe had dropped the note off at the alehouse the previous night, once he had most of his plans in place, and had trusted that she would receive it in time. Whether she would accept his invitation to meet her outside his rooms at first light was another matter, but he had judged her curiosity—and her covetousness for him—strong enough to lure her out in daylight.

"And here I am," she said, stepping forward to close the gap between them. She wrapped her arms possessively around his neck. "Will you not invite me in? It is warm inside, and my body is inviting…" She kissed him, and Marlowe felt the tingling sensation spread from his lips, down his throat towards his heart, and into his blood. But now he knew her game, and was prepared. This time the cold didn't work its magic. This time, aware of what he faced, he had kept his fires banked deep, where her chill could not dowse them, ready to rise at a moment's notice.

He knew what she expected from him, though, and allowed himself to shudder slightly, as though lost in the kiss, and let his face slacken, pretending that the contact had dulled his senses and sapped his will once more.

"I would," he whispered in her ear after a moment, breathless and eager, "but we have already enjoyed such dalliances, and no doubt will again. The day is fair, my sweet, and I thought to take advantage of it." And that, at least, was true. It was a fine day, warm and clear, and much to his advantage. He could see by the way she squinted against the sunlight that Lorelei did not share his pleasure in the morning sun. It was the most potent form of his own element, after all.

He had chosen his moment well.

Seeing him determined, she put a cheerful face upon the matter. "And what had you in mind?" She kissed his lips once more, then his cheek, and then his ear, ending with a sharp bite to the lobe as well. "Given that I would happily let you take advantage of *me* as well as the day."

"A change of venue, first. But that does not mean I don't fully intend to drink deep of your charms as the day wears on," Marlowe assured her. "We are lovers, and lovers deserve an idyllic locale for their passions." He put two fingers to his mouth and whistled sharply, and the carriage driver waiting down the way cracked his whip, urging his horses forward. The carriage came to a halt directly before them, and Marlowe opened the door with the finest bow he could muster. "Allow me to whisk you away, madam, for a day of leisure and delight."

Lorelei giggled and curtsied. "Leisure *and* delight? How excellent." She let herself be guided into the carriage and settled across one of the seats.

"My very thoughts and hopes." Marlowe slid in beside her, pulling the door shut behind him. He rapped twice on the roof near the front.

They fell against each other as the carriage lurched forward, and Marlowe forced himself to put all thoughts of Beasts and deaths and madness aside, determined to see his companion as nothing more than a lovely lady eager for his affection. Otherwise, if he let thoughts of her true nature fill his head, it was almost certain he wouldn't be master of his own flesh, and more than anything that would give him away. No, better to savor her and be damned.

Besides, if he was being honest with himself, as much as she was the enemy, it was the best way imaginable to pass the journey.

They were still lounging against one another, enjoying the languid afterglow, when the carriage slowed to a halt. Glancing out the curtained window, Marlowe saw a handful of buildings about them and straightened up. He adjusted his breeches and shirt as best he could, making himself decent.

"We have arrived," he informed Lorelei.

"More's the pity," she replied, her words nearly slurred from pleasure.

He opened the carriage door and clambered out, then turned to offer her a hand. For a moment, the silence between heartbeats, deep in the dark of the carriage she appeared not as the lovely young woman he had just bedded but as a monstrous creature, all tentacles and serpents and scales, but then she stepped into the doorway and the light and the apparition was gone. It was no specter of his imagination, however—there in the shadows he had seen her true form, confirming what he had already guessed.

The glimpse buoyed his spirits rather than dampened them. Marlowe knew beyond doubt that his plans were not only necessary but just. It was easy to feign cheer as he helped Lorelei to the ground. He shut the carriage door behind her, then reached up to accept the covered basket the driver handed down.

"Welcome to Deptford." He gestured toward the houses and shops and taverns.

She took in her surroundings. "I don't think I've ever been this far from London."

"Really? We are but a few hours' ride from the wall—even my prowess is not that distracting, surely?" He won a sly smile from her. "This is a charming little village, and beyond is the most inviting valley, with meadows filled of clover and trees of apple and pear—and a sweet little brook, cool and clear. It is paradise."

Her face brightened at the mention of a stream, as he had known it would. Water was her strength—and her weakness. "A brook? Oh, that sounds lovely indeed—may we take a dip?"

"I am sure we will. We have food fit for lovers, grapes and bread and cheese, cold roast duck and stuffed figs, and wine with which to cleanse our palates, and a dining room fit for the gods themselves. We will make a morning of it, walking and talking and then eating and laughing, and dipping our feet in the water."

"Heaven," she agreed. "The water will wash away the grime from walking, and the sweat from coupling." She rubbed across his chest and legs and groin, and he felt himself stir again.

"Something to look forward to then," he agreed. She was now in high spirits as she offered him her arm. Marlowe drew her close and led her down the road, out of the village, and toward the valley beyond. The carriage driver would wait for them to return—Marlowe had already engaged him for the full day. But he fully intended to return alone. He would deal with any questions that caused if and when the time came.

"It really is lovely," Lorelei commented, spinning around a beech tree so her hair streamed out behind her. She sighed, content. "And the shade... perfect. This is a wonderful, wonderful spot, Marlowe... but, I see no sign of the brook you promised? I am near parched and would slake my thirst on cool mountain water."

"Patience, my love," Marlowe replied, catching her in a quick embrace as she swung past him in one of her circles, then feigning a sigh as she laughed and pulled free of him once more. "It is just over the rise, then down a ways to the valley floor. But if you hunger, why don't we just have our meal here? As you say, the shade is perfect."

She smiled sweetly. "It is, but I would so *love* to dip my feet in the water before eating—and everything else that will follow, my love," came her answer. Lorelei released the trunk of the beech to swivel about and begin racing up the hill, her pale skin flashing as she passed through patches of sunlight. Marlowe was in no hurry to catch her. He followed at a more leisurely pace, reaching her just as she crested the hill and gazed out upon the valley below.

It was a breathtaking sight, sweeping and wide, a sea of waving green speckled with gold and tan. This was nature at her finest and most stunning. Silver birches formed a cordon about the valley, dark and silvery trunks creating a dappled border beneath dark leaves. The sun blazed high overhead, approaching its zenith, and Marlowe felt it warming him. He inhaled slowly, allowing it to feed him, the touch of it granting him strength.

The air smelled of fresh grass and early flowers and pine.

There was one obvious thing missing from the panorama.

Lorelei turned on him.

"So, he of honeyed words, where is this fabled brook of yours?" Lorelei was obviously unsure, not angry yet, but far from at ease. She had her hands upon her hips, and a storm gathering behind her eyes. "I fail to see it. Tell me Marlowe, is it a creature of your imagination?"

"Oh, there is a brook, a fabulous one, but not here," Marlowe replied setting the basket at his feet. "It is a full league and more back on the other side of town. There isn't a drop of water nearer." He looked at her then, studying her beautiful face. "I felt it wise to put as much distance between us and water as possible. But, talking of creatures, surely you are one yourself— a true Beast, if you would—and all London shudders in your wake."

He had not been sure how Lorelei would react to the confrontation. Anger? Fear? Denial? Mockery?

She threw back her head, hair streaming out behind her, and laughed long and loud and low. It was a deep rumble that sent shivers through him.

"And *finally* the playwright with his great mind tumbles to the truth," Lorelei declared, shaking her head. "I'd truly begun to despair that after all these years you'd forgotten me. It took you long enough. I had begun to think I was going to have to guide you by your very manhood to the sea and drown you in truth before you actually caught on."

"Oh, I know you, Beast," Marlowe responded. "Kraken, I name thee, and in the power of naming order you gone. London is *my* city. She lies beneath my wings. I take umbrage at all who enter her fine streets uninvited and aching for blood."

"You think you're so clever, don't you, *Phoenix*? Oh, yes, I know you. Do I really need to tell you that you have no authority over me? I will, however, point out that London is not yours. You have made it your home, but you have never claimed it. Now I have. My visage lies behind every nightmare, every fever dream, every waking vision. I am throughout this city of yours, little firebird, in every damp corner, and all there tremble in my grasp. It is more mine that it ever was yours."

"Leave now, and I will not follow. You have my word. Stay, and I must destroy you."

Her laughter this time was shorter and sharper, a harsh sound not meant to allure but to humiliate. "You think a great deal of yourself, little flametongue. Do I really need to point out how thoroughly you succumbed to my charms, or how willingly, since our first meeting? What makes thee think this time any different?" She began to stalk toward him slowly, arms raised as her body swayed, and despite himself Marlowe could feel something inside him stir. She was like a serpent charmer… his flesh ached to respond.

But the warm sunlight overhead softened the impact of her seduction.

"Once, twice, a dozen times, yes, but that was always in your element," Marlowe pointed out, and Lorelei froze in her tracks. He enjoyed seeing her surprise. "And of course I was out of mine." He spun, spreading his arms wide. 'Behold, Lorelei! Deptfordshire. No water for leagues in any direction, a blazing sun overhead. You have become, my dear, a fish out of water. Don't make me kill you."

She edged closer, at a crouch now, resembling nothing so much as a snake in the grass, slithering carefully toward its prey. "The grass here is lush and strong, and wet with the morning dew. There is water everywhere. Water is life. Nothing will burn here, little matchstick."

"Would you bet your life on that?" Marlowe stooped and thrust one hand into the basket by his feet, all the while keeping Lorelei in his gaze. When he stood once more, the bottle of wine was in his grasp. "Let's be civilized about this, shall we? My lady, I promised nectar to slake our thirsts and toast our love. Shall we?" The wine warmed in his grasp until the cork popped loose, and he swung the bottle in a slashing motion across his chest. The ruby liquid sprayed from it in a wide arc, splashing liberally across Lorelei's face, arms, and bosom. She stared at him, livid, shocked at the insult.

"Does it taste of fruit and love and promises?" Marlowe asked her. "Or bitterness and ash? Let it be our farewell cup. Depart now, Lorelei, go and never trouble these shores again, or your life is forfeit." He doused her a second time in the wine. "Either way, it ends here, now. I shall not ask again. What is it to be?"

"You are truly a fool, aren't you, Phoenix?" She snarled in reply, "You coat me in liquid and then threaten me? Water is my *lifeblood*, and what is wine but water mingled with spirits to frenzy the soul?" She advanced once more, hands held low, fingers writhing as if each were a serpent preparing to strike. Her shadow lengthened before her as she moved, stretching to sweep around him and gather him into its dark folds. It was monstrous, a massive figure ringed round with flailing tentacles and crowned with a circlet of snakes. He could feel their presence against his mind, hissing and swaying, seeking entry that they might tear his very self asunder and inject their foul poisons deep within his brain to rot away his identity from within.

"What *else* is it?" Marlowe reminded softly. "*Think*, Lorelei. Or shall I spoil the surprise and tell you?" He sighed. Then he gathered himself and focused, raking the coals deep within so their flames burst forth, filling the air around him with light and color and heat. The shadows fled at once, driven away by his radiance, and the sun shone down upon him, adding its strength to his own. "It is water that *burns*, Kraken. And now it is your death, Lorelei. I wish you had just left." And with that he swept both arms toward her, the fire lancing along his skin like great wings of flame until their tips just barely brushed Lorelei's wine-soaked flesh.

That was all it needed.

The flames leapt eagerly across, dancing with glee about her glorious body, and she shrieked. There was nothing glorious about her cries. She raised both arms, beating at her body, trying to bat the flames away. But the blaze could not be shaken off, and grew stronger as the wine fed it. In moments she was a living torch, shrouded in fire and smoke, shuddering and shaking and swaying and moaning in a desperate attempt to break free. But the flames were implacable.

And so was Marlowe.

He stood there, watching. He didn't move to help her. He didn't move to end her suffering. He simply stood there, ensuring that Lorelei could not escape. The flames ate into her. He emptied the last of the wine over her face and hair, drawing the fire up on its searing quest to purge her. She fell to her knees, and then crumpled to the ground and lay there writhing and twitching until at last she was still. The flames continued to lick at her as would hungry dogs, until finally even they could find no more to consume and snuffed out, leaving only a charred figure behind.

"Farewell, sweet Lorelei," Marlowe whispered, kneeling beside her and resting his palm upon her forehead. "It seems we have our answer to which would win in love, fire or water. And, perhaps, despite it all, you truly were my muse. A portion of my soul resisted you, and that resistance forced me awake once more, giving light and life to a new bout of creativity. For that, I thank you. For the rest, though—for the deaths and the madness—I damn you."

He rose and brushed the dirt from his knees, then turned and began to make his way back down the hill. He left the basket.

Behind him, Lorelei's remains crumbled to ash. Then they scattered upon the wind. They would feed the plants below, but nevermore would they find their way to water.

The Kraken would trouble London no longer.

SCENE EIGHT

Wherein harsh words lead to foul and fatal deeds

"Civilization at last," Marlowe muttered to himself as he saw the first of the buildings that marked the edges of Deptford. He increased his pace. The walk back had taken less time than the journey there because he'd walked it alone and had no desire to dawdle or admire the beauty all around him, but still it had seemed a long trek. The sun had vanished behind a slurry of clouds, leaving the day cool and gray.

At times he'd thought he could still hear Lorelei's laughter upon the breeze.

Yet he knew that was not so.

Life had fled her, he was certain of it, and the Kraken had been banished. Not destroyed, for the Beasts were immortal, woven into the very fabric of creation itself. The Kraken would return in time, but it would require an age to recover from this defeat, and then would have to begin the process of choosing new Avatars to vie for its mark. Many Beasts slumbered for decades, even centuries, between excursions into the mortal world. Perhaps the Kraken would do the same. Regardless, it would certainly steer clear of London for years to come, giving him some peace to work. That was all he wanted.

Back in the heart of the city, Marlowe had no doubt the madness had vanished, brushed aside by a cool breeze and warm sunshine. Those who had survived its touch would emerge, blinking and confused, disturbed in their slumbers for a while yet but still whole. And those who died at its behest, or whose minds had been bent beyond repair—well, they would be counted among the fallen still, unfortunate victims of this skirmish, though none would ever know the true nature of the conflict that had claimed them, or its combatants.

He was tired.

Tired but elated.

The Kraken had been strong, even though not fully trans-
formed, and its looming shadows and tendrils of wispy madness had pressed hard upon his defenses. But he had prevailed.
That was all that mattered. The danger was past. And in his
head there rested a new treasure, born in part from this battle
and its outcome.

He knew the last act of his play.

He would return and commit it to ink and parchment at
once, before a single precious word could slip loose.

But glancing about, he saw neither the carriage nor its driver.

Where had the man gone?

Marlowe sighed. No doubt the driver had not expected
him to return from an apparent dalliance so quickly—and why
would he? In his place, surely the man would have spent hours
upon the hill and inside the woman. Marlowe could scour the
town for him, but it would be far easier to simply find an alehouse to sit, drink and waste the hours, and then look for the
man later.

Glancing about, Marlowe spotted a tall, stately house of red
brick.

He had been this way in the past. More than once, touring
had brought the players out to Deptford. It took him a moment
to recall her name, but it came to him. It was the home of the
widow, Eleanor Bull. She maintained herself and her house by
renting rooms, and by serving food and drink in the common
room downstairs. He was hungry. He was tired. Where better to wait for his missing carriage? And perhaps they might
even have pen and parchment for him to scribble upon while
he waited.

Knocking quickly on the front door, Marlowe was granted
entrance by a maid, who showed him into the common room
and accepted his order of a meat pie and an ale, though she was
sad to say they could not fulfill his other request. She curtsied
and departed quickly, leaving him to lean back and relax while
he waited. He was running through the dialogue of the fifth act

in his mind when she returned with a pewter flagon and set it before him.

"Many thanks, miss." Marlowe saluted her with the full cup, handing her a coin in exchange. She blushed and was gone once more, no doubt to wait upon other guests—there were a handful of men scattered at the other tables about the room. The lighting was dim and he could not discern faces, but he was fairly certain his absent driver was not among them. Well, he would eat now and worry about it later.

Marlowe had swallowed only a single mouthful of ale when he felt someone brush up behind him. The next thing he knew, chairs were being pulled out at his table and heavy figures were dropping into them. Two men sat to one side of him, between Marlowe and the door, while a third lounged in the chair behind. Even in the poorly lit space he recognized them at once.

They were the agents of the Privy Council.

"Have you followed me out here to finish what your shadow-assassin could not?" Marlowe rasped in a low voice. He leaned in toward the silvered man, who sat closest beside him. "Or is this more gamesmanship designed to provoke me into something ill-conceived? I can act without thinking, believe me, my temper grows shorter and more explosive with each of these encounters of ours."

"Cease work upon the play at once, and turn over the pages you have written," the man advised in equally quiet tones, ignoring Marlowe's questions or his threat. "Or else I am afraid it will end badly for you, Marlowe."

"You have no hold over me," Marlowe declared, aware how similar those words were to Lorelei's only a few hours before, "nor any say in my work. I write as I will, and this play *will* be finished before I return to London. On that you have my word."

"I urge you again to reconsider. You are following an unwise course of action," his unwanted companion warned. "Orders have been given, and must be met. This play shall not reach its conclusion, and anything you do to defy me will only make your own more swift."

"Do not threaten me," Marlowe replied, causing the candle

upon his table to flare to life. The other man reared back, squinting against the sudden blaze. He made the sign of the cross over his chest. "People who come against me burn at my touch, and blacken in my grasp. Do I make myself understood?"

He stood to depart, wanting to be rid of these men and their odious presence. All he wanted to do was eat, rest, and write. Why was the world conspiring against him still? They stood as well, moving to surround him.

Before he could push past, the silvered man spoke again, but now he pitched his voice louder, that all around might hear it.

"The bill must be paid," he announced, grasping Marlowe by the shoulder. "And it is your turn, miser. Cough up your coin!"

"I don't know what game you are playing at," Marlowe retorted, pulling free of the man's hand, "But I assure you *my* bill is settled in full, and I won't be held accountable for yours. Now leave me be. You have cost me far more than your company could ever be worth."

"I say again, *friend*, the bill must be paid," the other man insisted. "Now dip into your purse and pay our hostess," he shoved Marlowe then, a hard push across the chest, and sent him staggering back into the man behind him.

"What is with you, man? You pick a fight over such pettiness as our evening's fare?" that man roared, slamming Marlowe forward before he could properly find his balance, so that he stumbled into the silvered man.

"Stand away, stand away!" Marlowe shouted, waving his arms to make space, but the men crowded him nonetheless. Then his eye caught the flash of steel, and he spun, grappling the man for his dagger before the blade could be plunged into his back.

"Ah, so it is *murder* then?" Marlowe yelled, but his words were swallowed in the general hubbub as all three men rushed close and pressed in upon him.

He forced the dagger away, hearing it clatter on the floor as he broke the man's grip, but a reflected sliver of light betrayed the fact that a second weapon had been drawn, and too close for him to deflect as easily. He turned nonetheless, determined to bring the full weight of his burning gaze upon the damned fool, let him burn and be done with it and all of them and their bickering and their games—

—and fell back, a curse springing to his lips but slipping away unvoiced as that same blade plunged full force into the flesh above his eye, sending a great gout of pain surging through his skull and then his body.

He was barely aware that he was falling before he hit the hard planks of the floor. He couldn't feel a thing. It was much as when Lorelei had held him in her poisonous coils, numb and cold, and a part of him wondered if she had survived her immolation and returned to take him unawares. But there were the three Privy Council men standing above him, peering down as if at the mouth of a well, and he knew that this was no Beast's doing. The lucky blow of a mortal fool had struck him down.

Then the pain swept all thought clear, and darkness claimed Marlowe.

EPILOGUE
In which our hero's life is revisited

St. Mary's church, Deptford, in the dead of the night. A small plot out back served as the final resting place of the unfortunate, those who had died without name or kin to claim them. Among the flattened earth a single plot stood higher, its mound not yet tamped down, its soil still damp and worm-ridden from being recently turned.

And then that selfsame earth began to shift and shudder, stirring from within.

At last a hand burst forth, black soil clinging to cracked nails as it clawed its way free.

A second hand soon followed, and then a head, the golden-brown hair now matted and dirt-clumped.

Marlowe spat the dirt from his lips and mouth as he pulled himself free and fell gasping upon his back, there beside his own unmarked grave.

He knew what had happened. Though powerless to stop it, he had retained enough awareness to take note as they had pronounced him dead "of a tavern brawl" and sewed him into rough burlap, then dumped him here in the ground and shoveled it down atop him. It had seemed wisest to lay still and assume the deathly pose they had already pronounced, rather than attempt to explain how he had survived such a blow.

He blinked and tested his eye and brow gingerly with one finger. Yes, still tender, but already healed enough to grant him sight and reason once more.

And that was not something to be believed, not even when spoken by a wordsmith such as himself.

He sat up and sighed, tousling the soil from his hair and

brushing it clean of his face. There was no hope for it, he knew. By now word of his demise would have spread to London, and to the Playhouse. The dramatic world would know that Marlowe was no more. He could not return without questions, too many of them and most whose answers were too fantastical even for those who played regularly at ghosts and ghouls and unquiet spirits to swallow.

No, that life was dead to him now.

The late, lamented Christopher Marlowe.

He used a nearby cross to lever himself to his feet. Even if he penned that final act it would never see the light of day. To the world *The Birth of the Phoenix* would go unfinished forevermore, none but the Admiral's Men even familiar with a single line, and as with any incomplete work it would fast fade from all memory. Within the space of a dozen years none would know of what should have been his masterwork.

He sighed again.

So it went. There was little for it now. Marlowe was dead and gone, as Malguin of Toulouse and Altan Kahn had been before him.

Yet the Phoenix lived on.

Who would he become now?

Sifting through his belt pouch, the man who had been Marlowe discovered coins still tucked within the fabric. Most likely those who had handled his body had thought it unwise to rob so ill-omened a corpse. God love a superstitious murderer, he thought. He possessed enough to see him clear of London and environs, and perhaps to flee England altogether. He could away to Scotland, or to Ireland, or even to distant lands as yet untroubled. A new name, a new life, a chance to create and inspire and embolden anew. He would rise from the ashes, aflame as always.

With a smile, he stepped away from the grave that had been his, then turned and pushed the soil back into place once more. No need for any to realize Marlowe resided there in name alone. Not yet, at least.

"Marlowe, the scourge of the Beast must die," he said, misquoting the final moment of what would now forever be his greatest work. *Tamburlaine.* "*Meet heaven and earth, and here let all things end! For earth hath spent pride of all her fruit, and heaven consumed his choicest living fire. Let earth and heaven timeless death deplore, for both their worths will equal him no more.*"

Then, with a last bow to the life he had left behind, the Phoenix turned and walked off into the last dregs of sunlight. Soon all that was left of him was a hazy image among the twilight, and a memory that would burn ever brighter as his words continued to enflame the hearts and minds of any who heard them.

Exeunt

𝕭𝖔𝖔𝖐 𝕿𝖜𝖔

ONE HAUNTED SUMMER

VILLA DIODATI
1816

CHAPTER ONE
In which our players meet and grow to be acquainted,
even as they acquire a change in scenery

"Bit of a pile, I'd say," the dashing young lord declared, leaning upon his walking stick even as he gazed up at the large, porticoed house before him. "Wouldn't you agree, Polly Dolly?"

"It's certainly a damn sight more than we require," his companion agreed, ignoring the nickname as always while studying the impressive salmon-colored building. "Only a handful of us, really." He frowned, the expression settling easily upon his narrow features as if it were an old friend returning home. "Not counting your menagerie, that is." His rather pointed gaze settled upon the dog, monkey, and peacock being handled by various attendants behind them.

"Now, is that any way to speak of our guests?" the first man asked, laughing at his own joke—with his dark good looks and regal bearing he was the very picture of saturnine humor.

Beside him, another man chuckled, his own slighter build and softer features making him seem almost a child beside the handsome nobleman. The woman to his left shook her head, her delicate features displaying some displeasure, but the taller, more robust woman to his right laughed and dared lay a familiar hand upon the first man's arm.

"Oh, I think it's lovely, Georgie," she insisted, pressing up against him and causing his grin to shift to an irritated scowl. "Just think of all the fun we'll have here!"

"Yes, well, it is a handsome place, to be sure," the third man offered a little diffidently, "and we shall visit as often as you like, seeing as how we're a mere stone's throw away." His thoughtful gray eyes drifted to the woman still at his side, concern writ large upon his features. "Shan't we, Mary?"

"Yes, of course," she agreed, though there was little pleasure evident in her tone. "But we won't want to be a bother." Her voice made it clear she intended to be scarce enough to never run that risk.

"Nonsense," the narrow gentleman, whose proper name was in fact John, insisted. "You must come over every day and help us entertain ourselves—otherwise we're sure to go out of our minds, rattling around this place all alone."

"Yes," George agreed easily, turning to face the others now, his smile returning even as he subtly shifted his arm free of the hand still questing for it. "You absolutely must. Please, say you will. I won't hear anything else."

His earnestness was endearing, charming, and impossible to resist. "Yes, yes, all right," Mary agreed, laughing despite herself. "We will come over every day."

"Capital!" George announced, clapping his hands together. "Let us go in and admire this little villa of ours, then, shall we? This Villa Diodati."

"I believe it is in fact the Villa Belle Rive," John corrected, his tone reminiscent of a tutor reprimanding a bright but willful student.

And, indeed, his friend waved the statement away. "Nonsense, Polly Dolly dear," he insisted airily. "It is owned by the noble Signore Diodati, is it not? Distant relative of Charles Diodati, whose good friend was none other than John Milton? Is that not the owner's name there, upon the post?" And, indeed, it was carved into the stone that framed the wrought-iron front gate. "Therefore, the Villa Diodati it must be. I have spoken, and it is so." He said that with full confidence that his every word must be obeyed, as it so often was. For George Gordon, Lord Byron, was accustomed to having his way—with words, with people, and with life in general.

John William Polidori, his friend, companion, and personal physician, sighed but saw little point in arguing further. Debating with Byron rarely got anyone anywhere besides exhausted, and it was a minor enough point, besides. Instead, shaking his head, he followed the young nobleman across the courtyard and into the manor house proper.

"It is certainly a damn sight better than that ghastly hotel," Byron stated as he studied the impressive front hall, with its gran, sweeping staircase to the upper floors. "Not least of which because it lacks all those horrid tourists."

"And perhaps because its proprietor is not so concerned about your reputation and possible activities," John murmured behind him, though not so loudly as to be overheard, perhaps. It was true that the Hotel d'Angleterre had grown rapidly less welcoming over the few days they had spent there, as its proprietor realized what an infamous collection had gathered under his roof, and what sort of scandals might soon follow. Though never saying so directly, and always maintaining a polite and professional air, he had dropped enough hints to make it clear that they were no longer welcome there, and had best seek other lodgings. Fortunately this manor had been for rent, and Byron had been quick to claim it for himself and John, while the other three had opted for the more modest chalet Montalègre nearby. For they lacked the same sort of funds as their newfound friend, and had not the acquaintance nor the presumption to borrow money from him so soon.

"It's grand," the taller woman stated breathily, trailing close behind Byron and gazing as much upon him as upon the room. "I like it very much indeed." Claire Clairmont was given to emphatic statements and equally decisive actions.

"Yes, it is nice," her sister agreed, having followed the rest of them in. "Very light and airy, isn't it, Percy?"

"Very well-aspected indeed, my love," Percy Shelley, poet and philosopher, agreed, giving his lovely young fiancée a smile and a quick hug. "Just the sort of place for the like-minded to gather and discuss all manner of things."

"Quite right," John called out from a room off that grand hall, "and I believe this is the precise space for such lively conversation." He stood in a handsomely appointed sitting room, large and airy with tall windows looking out over the hill and toward Lake Geneva itself, for the manor sat near the edge of the town of Cologny, affording it both privacy and a view. A large fireplace stood centered on the wall between the windows, and couches and chairs were arrayed before it like an audience before a stage, tables beside them holding candelabras and books and small objects d'art. It was a fine room, and all of them agreed at once that it would make a perfect spot in which to gather. Indeed, it felt warmer than the rest of the manor somehow, and more inviting, though John put that down to the liveliness of its occupants.

"We must see to our own residence, I'm afraid," Percy stated, clearly hesitant to leave such finery behind, yet cognizant of their role as guests and also of the fatigue visible in Mary's eyes and drawn expression. "But we shall return as soon as you like."

"Oh, come back for dinner, do," Byron insisted, pacing out the room like a caged tiger, only the slightest hint of his limp evident, hands clasped behind his back. "We'll make a lively night of it, old chap. Living it up in the same space as Milton himself once did." He clapped the younger man on the shoulder for all the world as if they had been close companions since childhood, though in fact they had known each other only a few days. But such was Byron's way, and also proof of the connection he and Percy had formed immediately upon being introduced by Claire.

All in all, it was exactly as John had hoped. For Byron, for all the scandals that brewed about him like storms upon the ocean, was considered one of the finest poets in the world, his fame already assured by such works as "Childe Harold's Pilgrimage" and "The Bride of Abydos." And Shelley had already won attention and acclaim for such poems as "Queen Mab" and such essays as "A Refutation of Deism." The two men were among the most creative minds of their age—and John had managed events to bring them together, in the hopes that this would engender even more inspiration for them both.

This was his lot in life, after all. He had learned his lesson, back in the Plague Years, after all. His was not to create for himself, but to nurture that divine spark in others, to help them reach even higher heights, their minds and souls aflame with delight and energy and imagination.

For was he not the Phoenix, the very essence of such creative force that it shone from his very being, granting him eternal life and youth? What was the point to such a gift if he could not use it to help others fuel their own inner fires?

He had attached himself to Byron, and had been pleased to see the young lord's talents blossom even further during their acquaintance. When tales of his most recent sordid affairs—including the one with his own sister—surfaced, John had had little difficulty convincing his new friend to leave London and England altogether and make for warmer, sunnier shores.

The message from Claire Clairmont had come as a surprise as they traveled—Byron had already dallied with her back in England and had shown no real desire to repeat the experience, but it seemed the young lady had a far happier recollection of their time together and was still enthusiastic for more. Byron might have simply ignored her, but John had seen the note as well, which had explained that she was traveling with her sister Mary Godwin and Mary's fiancé, one Percy Bysshe Shelley. That had changed matters considerably! John had taken it upon himself to write back, letting her know that they would be in Lake Geneva shortly, and the address of the hotel where they would be staying. When they had finally arrived, it was to find the trio already waiting.

Neither John nor Byron had ever met Shelley before, but even at first glance he had been all that a young poet should be, slender and winsome, with large, fine dark eyes and a high brow above which sprang curls as soft as the curve of his cheek. Though Byron was all flame and passion and energy, looking into the younger man's eyes as they met, John could see a fire burning there as well, more thoughtful but no less bright.

And then there had been his lady. Mary was a bit of a surprise and a revelation, for John had expected no more than a smaller, slightly older version of Claire, silly and soft and eager to please. Instead he found himself greeting a lovely young woman with fine features and glorious auburn hair, but it was the intelligence gleaming from her eyes and the wit evident in her quiet, calm face that impressed him most. Here was not one but two more who already carried the spark of genius within them, two whose brilliance he could fan to greater heights! John was nearly beside himself at the very thought. It had taken all his will to keep himself back so that Byron might take the lead, as befitted the master of their little expedition.

Fortunately, Byron was only too happy to comply. He and Shelley had taken to one another at once, recognizing like minds geared toward not only beauty but truth and similar interests in words and their uses. Too, Shelley had an open, friendly, easy-going nature which complemented Byron's more forceful personality, allowing them to get along without a battle for dominance. Even their gifts were compatible, Byron being more given to epic poetry and Shelley more to both short odes and thoughtful treatises. There would be no scrabbling for the same expression or form between these two! They had quickly begun to have long, deep, wide-ranging conversations, covering art, music, beauty, history, landscapes, politics, religion, and even science. Perhaps it had been those topics, and the heat and abandon with which the pair had spoken on them, that had frightened their host as much as anything. But that had proven all to the best, for now they were rid of that cramped hotel and here at a villa, where they could continue to discuss until late into the night without fear of disturbing anyone.

John had the feeling this was going to be a most magical summer.

CHAPTER TWO
In which our players' revels begin

"Ah, there you are!" Byron declared as Shelley led Mary and Claire, one lady on each arm, across the final steps from the path to the villa's back patio.

"And right on time!" Indeed, the sun was even now beginning to set, sending great streaks of color across the sky like the mad dashes of a frantic painter hoping to capture the light before it slipped away.

"Come on, then, dinner is waiting and I am famished!" And with that he spun on his heel—his bad one, which though less agile than the other was at least useful for performing as a post—and practically danced back inside, waving for the others to follow.

John waited instead for the trio to reach him. "And how do you find your lodgings, Ms. Godwin?" he asked politely, offering his arm to Mary, who took it with a polite nod and, he noted, no check of her fiancé for his reaction or approval. That was hardly surprising, however, considering her pedigree—her mother, Mary Wollstonecraft, had been a great proponent of women's rights, and would no doubt have raised her daughters to think for themselves, rather than letting any man claim such a privilege on their behalf.

"It is quite lovely, thank you, doctor," she replied, her voice soft but clear. "And has an excellent view of the lake. Little William seems quite taken with it, and is already sound asleep, thanks no doubt to the crisp breeze and the scent of the water." William was her baby by Shelley, who John had only seen once or twice in the care of the nurse, though it was clear Mary doted on the child nonetheless.

"Yes, it's all very nice," Claire agreed behind them, walking with Shelley, "but I still don't see why we couldn't just stay here, all of us together. You certainly have enough room!"

They did indeed, for upon touring the place after they had departed John had counted no fewer than eleven bedrooms. Still, it was not his place to make such an offer, as Shelley's pained expression showed the poet knew and understood full well. Convincing the young and flighty Claire, however, was clearly another matter.

The doors slammed shut behind them, agitated by a sudden breeze, and all of them jumped, then laughed at themselves for doing so. At least, with those entries sealing out the night's chill, the house became even more cozy.

"Come in and sit down," Byron called. He was standing at the head of the table in the large dining room, his back to the fireplace where a blaze raged, for the air was surprisingly cool for summer. Servants were setting out a tureen of soup, baskets of bread, and carafes of wine and water. "Shelley, come sit beside me," the lord insisted, indicating the seat to his right. "Polly Dolly, you take the left. The ladies can sit next to you both." Which neatly prevented Claire from getting too close to him again, John noted silently. Well played, that.

They all took their appointed chairs—Claire not without a pout and a loud sigh—and the first course was served. But the food, though it was excellent, quickly took a back seat to the lively conversation that flowed as readily as the oft-replenished wine. Mostly it was Byron and Shelley, good-naturedly bickering back and forth about nature and science and religion and art. John offered a comment from time to time but was content to sit back and let the two poets handle the bulk of the conversation, for such talk could only exercise their brains and their creativity. Mary made comment now and again, but her natural reticence and her slight physical remove made it difficult for her to interrupt the flow long enough to be heard. Claire showed little interest in anything more than gazing longingly at Byron, drinking heavily, nibbling at her food, and occasionally making a random outburst when some word or phrase struck her as amusing.

After dinner they retired to the salon, lounging upon the couches there and taking more wine, brandy, and, for the men, cigars. The two poets were a fascinating study in counterpoints, John thought, watching them both—Byron stalking hither and yon, gesturing wildly to make each point, while Shelley sat and considered, those slender, elegant hands interlaced, before offering compelling statements in that quiet, clear voice and soft but unbowed manner. And the women were well matched to the men they admired, Claire being outspoken and impulsive while Mary was quiet and thoughtful. It was a fine night, and all too soon the dawn was breaking over them, its light creeping in through the windows as the five of them rubbed their eyes and covered yawns with the back of their hands.

"We'd best be getting back," Mary pointed out, rising to her feet, and Shelley was quick to follow. "William will be waking soon, and I'll want to see to him."

"Of course." Shelley nodded at John before turning back to their host. "Thank you for a most excellent evening."

"My pleasure, old man," Byron replied, clasping his hand. "No question. Come back over once you've had a little rest and we'll start the whole thing up again." He laughed, as did the others, and John saw the couple to the door, pausing only when he realized that Claire had not yet moved to follow.

"I will be along shortly," the young woman claimed, but her eyes went to Byron and her hand to her bosom, and when the lord grinned John knew he would be the only one in the villa to be getting any rest in the next few hours. Still, creativity fed on passion, and at times such passion required expression of its own. Well he remembered the joys of the flesh, and though he no longer felt such a need for himself he understood and encouraged such behavior in those around him, if only to keep them better attuned to sensation and emotion. Therefore he politely turned away, not looking as Byron reached out and took Claire's hand to lead her toward his rooms, and instead saw Shelley and Mary out, though they had to struggle a bit to exit, the wind having picked up again.

It had been a fine evening indeed.

The next day proved more of the same, for Shelley and Mary did indeed return as sunset neared, like creatures of the night stirring to prowl and hunt and feast once the shadows grew long enough to shield them from the fiery light of day. Claire had remained, and was lounging on the patio when they arrived, looking flushed and self-satisfied. Byron had taken to the bath, and emerged a short while later, his dark hair still dripping water down his collar, all relaxation and good humor.

Dinner that night was much like the first had been, filled with food, wine, and good conversation. Byron utterly ignored Claire throughout the meal, lavishing all his attention on Shelley, and so John did his best to assuage the young lady's hurt by playing at host himself, keeping her and Mary entertained with witticisms and light banter. He succeeded well enough that Claire was only slightly put out by the time the meal ended, and brightened considerably when he suggested they all adjourn to the billiard room and play in teams.

The activity allowed for both movement and talk, and both women found themselves more able to partake in the conversation now that they no longer had a length of trays and bowls and platters separating them, so it was a more casual and free-flowing chatter that took place, with a good deal more frivolity and flirting. Shelley focused most of his attention on Mary, but did not ignore Claire, who teased him back but still gave the bulk of her own regard to Byron. Their host was only too willing to play that game, as flirting was a natural mode of communication for him, almost as native as poetry or scandal, and John kept himself back but chimed in with a compliment or a verbal riposte whenever a pause threatened to occur. And thus the night whiled away a second time, the morning taking them unawares yet again and sending Shelley and his paramour scurrying away through the chill once more like thieves escaping with the good silver, as Claire once again took to Byron's bed.

John was pleased, for he had already heard both men muttering scraps of poetry throughout the evening, and from time to time pausing to scribble a note to themselves. Their brains were indeed in high gear, and their constant verbal sparring was spurring them both on, forcing them to think faster and grander than ever before.

He could feel the flames within them rising higher with each passing day. Soon, they would have no choice but to burst into fits of creation, as their imaginations spilled forth beyond their power to contain.

And that was exactly as it should be.

CHAPTER THREE
In which the weather takes a sharp and unexpected turn

"Oh, what beastly luck this is!" Byron groused, leaning against the door frame and staring out at the cold gray tumult beyond. Posed like that, his shirt open at the collar and the sleeves, cane carelessly held at this side, hair in mild disarray, he was the very picture of "a handsome young noble whose plans have been thwarted by forces beyond his control."

Try as he might, John could not feel the same way.

"Into every life a little rain must fall," Shelley murmured, and laughed when his friend turned enough to glare at him where he sat upon one of the couches, Mary nestled at his side. "Calm yourself, it is only a brief shower. I'm sure it will pass, and then we can resume."

What they intended to resume was a walk through the vineyards that adjoined the villa, circling around through them and toward the lakeshore, where they would find an opportune spot to enjoy the picnic lunch that sat packed away in its basket at Mary's feet. When they had made the plan the day before the weather had been a trifle cool but clear, the sky a cloudless blue, the sun beating down in a vain attempt to offset the unseasonal chill. But this morning the sun had been nowhere to be seen, its fiery presence hidden behind a solid sheet of gray broken only by darker shadows chasing themselves across the horizon, and Shelley, Mary, and Claire had barely made it to the patio before the sky had opened up, getting very nearly soaked in just the few seconds it took them to dash inside.

Now they had dried off and were enjoying the warmth of the fire as it fought to best the surprisingly cool air all around them, but Byron continued to glower at the world outside as if the rain had occurred solely to ruin his plans and his mood.

"Oh, do come and sit down, George," John suggested from his comfortable armchair. "There's nothing to be done for it, so let's make the best of our situation."

"I fail to see how to make the most of being trapped in one's own house," Byron snapped, turning his back on the storm to scowl at John instead.

"Well, to begin with, we are all here together," Mary offered, bravely taking some of the brunt of the young lord's displeasure so that John would not have to face it alone. He smiled his thanks at her, and she colored slightly but returned the expression.

"Oh, yes!" Claire agreed, clapping her hands together. "And we have comfy seats by the fire, and plenty of good food and better wine." She patted the spot beside her on the couch to emphasize that first point, but Byron ignored that, as he often did. John always felt a twinge at how badly his friend treated the young lady, spurning her affections except to slake his lust with them, but every private remonstrance he had made on that matter had been shrugged off. "What could I do?" Byron had replied, showing little concern and no remorse. "She is a foolish girl, who, in spite of all I could say or do – would come after me. I never loved her nor pretended to love her but a man is a man and if a girl of eighteen comes prancing to you at all hours of the night, there is but one way."

"You are a beast to behave so," John had answered, but in truth he found it hard to argue the point, for Claire was clearly more than willing—indeed, she was decidedly the aggressor here. And had he himself not often said that passion in love, or at least lust, went hand in hand with passion in the creative arts? If he hoped to drive Byron to such heights in the one, how could he castigate him for becoming enflamed with the other? Still, he had begged his friend to be kinder toward Claire, if possible. "You may not love her," he had pointed out, "but she loves you, and your casual indifference wounds as much as any other's vicious attack might do." Byron had promised to try his best, but right now, in his pique, his usual callousness was winning out.

Still, he had turned from the window, which was a start,

and slowly moved over to lean against the fireplace instead, facing the rest of them, which was a sight better. "Very well," he breathed at last, though the sulk was still full upon his face and in his voice. "Since it is clear we shall not be venturing forth any time soon, what shall we do instead?" The chill in the room seemed to fade as he spoke, as if his brightening mood were affecting the atmosphere itself.

"Talk, of course," Shelley answered with a laugh. "And why not? We would have done much the same if our plans had held, and in the same company. The only difference shall be our setting."

Byron considered that and finally inclined his head, allowing himself to be swayed by his friend's logic. "In that case," he declared, "what was it you were saying last night, Polly Dolly? About how science must surely win out over art when the two stood at odds? You are wrong, you know—utterly wrong. And here is why—"

As their host began his diatribe against cold rationality, John leaned back in his chair and smiled. He had posed the question precisely because he knew it likely to rile both of the other men, and was happy to see that he had succeeded. Let them paint him the villain in their debates. He was only too happy to provide such a spur for their minds and souls.

Byron became more and more animated as he spoke, pacing before the fire, gesturing with hands and cane. Shelley chimed in from time to time, his softer voice a counterpoint to his friend's dramatic statements. Mary and Claire listened intently, the former occasionally offering a comment of her own, the latter mostly just clapping her hands at particularly clever turns of phrase.

And all the while, the rain continued to pour down outside.

"But surely it must let up soon?" Mary asked for the third or fourth time. Though the sun had never deigned to pierce its heavy veil, the change in light would have told them that evening was approaching even if their pocket watches had not already warned of impending dusk. The rain, however, had continued without pause for the entire day. Only now, instead of a soothing backdrop and an excuse to stay cozily indoors, it had become a barrier, preventing the young mother from returning to her infant son.

"It is showing no sign of that," her betrothed replied, though gently, his arm around her shoulders and squeezing her to him. "But I am sure William is fine, dearest. Nurse will be taking good care of him."

"I must go to him," Mary insisted, her eyes slightly wide and wild, her face growing flushed. "What if he takes ill? What if something happens and I am not there?" She made as if to break for the door, but Shelley held her fast.

The door itself suddenly sprang open, as if answering her desire, but what blew in was a sudden blast of cold, wet air, and enough spray to spatter the pair. They jumped back quickly to keep from becoming drenched, and servants hurried to secure the door again.

"You will do no one any good if you take a chill yourself, pet," Shelley reminded his lady softly, mopping the moisture from her face with a pocket square. "And you are only recently recovered from your last bout." They had told Byron and John, back when they'd met at the hotel, how Mary had been sick for much of their journey through the Swiss Alps, and indeed she was still pale even now, after days in the sun. "If it lets up, we will head for the chalet at once, I promise you, but going now would only get us all sick, and then how would you help William? Trust me, Nurse has things well in hand there, and I am sure they are just as tucked in and warm as we are here."

Mary stared out into the storm, as if she could pierce the curtains of rain with the force of her desire, but finally she sighed and let herself be led back to the couches. "I suppose you are right," she agreed slowly. "I certainly cannot risk getting sick and then infecting him with it. You think he is all right, though?"

"He is fine," Shelley assured her again. "I am certain of it. Now come, sit. I will fetch you a sherry."

"It is strange," Byron mused to John as they watched this little scene play out from off to one side, providing their friends with at least the semblance of privacy. "This storm seemed to appear from nowhere, and to stay so steadily and for so long? I've never seen such a thing."

"No, nor I," John agreed, though in fact he had once or twice through the long years. Such weather was rare, however, and certainly out of place here, especially in the middle of summer. "But this entire summer the world has been behaving oddly. Perhaps this is just the pinnacle of the odd weather, and from here everything will begin returning to normal."

"I hope so," his friend agreed. "I had planned many long walks and leisurely boat rides, not staying caged within one house, however large it might be." Then, as if forcibly banishing such thoughts from his mind, he briskly rubbed his hands together and rejoined the others, the loud gesture signaling his return much like ringing the bell, so that they had time to compose themselves before he was upon them.

"Since it seems we are all trapped here together for the moment," Byron announced cheerfully, "I hope you will consent to dine with John and I, for I am famished, and such good company can only make the meal that much more pleasant." He bowed and offered his arm to Mary, who could not help giggling as she accepted the gallant gesture. Then, to avoid any suggestion of rudeness, their host extended a matching offer to Claire, who eagerly accepted. The three of them proceeded toward the dining room, and John clapped Shelley on the shoulder as the two of them laughed and hurried after.

The dinner that followed was a lively one, with scintillating conversation and a great deal of laughter, no doubt aided by the copious amounts of wine they all consumed. The rain continued throughout, its steady susurration creating an intimacy around the table, as if the five of them were cut off from the rest of the world, with only their words remaining to offset that steady patter. And the noise was just enough to force them all to raise their voices to be heard, which then encouraged them to be more forceful in their statements as well as their enunciation. What before had been delicate and nuanced conversation became broader, sometimes coarser, but also more exuberant, and they were all still laughing as they made their way to the salon afterward.

"I fear this storm means to outlast us," Byron stated, for though they could no longer see the rain now that night had fallen the sound assured them that it still fell with the same force as before. "That being the case, I will have beds made up for you. We have ample room, and you know you are most welcome." He smiled. "Indeed, I will consider this a happy accident, for now we may converse until we are all so tired we can barely hold our eyes open, without concern for leaving off when you are still alert enough to make your way back to your chalet."

Mary had, if not accepted, at least resigned herself to the fact that she would not see her baby that night, and nodded. "Thank you for your gracious offer," she told him. "We regret imposing, but appreciate your hospitality."

"It is no imposition, dear lady," John assured her. "None at all."

Secretly, he continued to be well pleased. To have all of them here under the same roof was more than he had dared hope when they had quit the hotel, but now this storm had accomplished what Byron's entreaties could not. For being around like-minded people often served as kindling to a fire, proximity lending more fuel to the blaze, and even after they all ceased speaking their mere presence would keep their thoughts and emotions racing at top speed. He had seen it before, when a group of playwrights or poets came together and then all slept in the same inn or house—he could almost see the energy linking their minds through the night, feeding upon one another subconsciously even as they slept, so that in the morning they all awoke refreshed but also still inspired, still energized, and eager to resume previous discussions and projects. And though small, this group possessed minds such as he had rarely seen before, and spirits brighter than the sun itself.

Which was why, though he knew it was selfish of him, John hoped the storm would continue, keeping them trapped here together another day. And perhaps more beyond that. But he was already happy with recent events, and resolved not to get greedy, but merely to accept and be grateful for whatever he received.

He was still trying to convince himself of that many hours

later, when he was forced to help a barely conscious Shelley guide an equally tired Mary to the room that had been set aside for them, before staggering to his own chamber and collapsing upon his bed.

His dreams, when they came, were of science and art and beauty, of rain and wind, and of women screaming and laughing and dancing around and around.

CHAPTER FOUR

*As our players enjoy a brief respite from the weather,
and take full advantage of it*

When they rose the next morning the rain had ceased, and Mary and Shelley departed immediately after breakfast for the chalet and their beloved baby. Claire showed little inclination to leave Byron's side, trailing after him like an obedient pup, but her sister prevailed upon her at last to accompany them, and the trio soon absented themselves. "I cannot tell," Byron stated, watching them go, "whether I am happy they are leaving or eager for them to return. Perhaps both."

"I would not worry much on that score," John assured him. "They will be back, and within the day, lest I mistake."

Nor was he wrong, though when they returned it was not to dine nor to spend the evening. Rather, the three young people came skipping back in high spirits and full of plans. "It is clear out today," Mary pointed out happily, gesturing at the cloudless blue sky above. "Let us go out on the water while we can."

Byron readily agreed, for like Shelley he had a great fondness for boating. John was less enamored of the water—fire was his element, and he had unpleasant memories of being nearly drowned in the Thames—but agreed rather than further dividing the small party. So the five of them traipsed down the hill, armed only with a picnic basket and their intellect, plus Byron's walking stick.

It was a pleasant enough walk, through the vineyards which were lush and green after so much rain. They paused at the chalet so that Mary could show off her son, and John and Byron, neither of them much inclined toward small children, made polite noises over how big and handsome he was. Then they were off once more.

A small dock stood just below the chalet, and at its end was moored a pair of rowboats. Shelley helped Mary into one, and Byron leaped into the other before gallantly taking Claire's hand to guide her to a seat. John was left to fend for himself getting in, and nearly tipped into the water in the process.

"Good lord, man, you call yourself an Englishman!" Byron teased, and John felt himself blush to be called out so.

"I am not comfortable on the water," he returned stiffly, taking a seat in the gunwale and clinging to the tiny boat's hull with both hands. "You know this." For, indeed, his friend had teased him about his awkwardness every time they had put out to sea.

"Yes, yes, there's not comfortable and then there's behaving like an ox," Byron retorted, unshipping the oars. Slipping them into their locks he took his place on the rowing bench and quickly, skillfully guided the rowboat away from the dock and out onto the lake. Shelley was right behind him, and soon the little boats were well out upon the water.

It was truly a beautiful day, the lake as blue as sapphire and the water so clear they could see small fish darting along below them. The sun shone overhead, as if apologizing for its absence the day before, and John let himself relax a little, lulled by the boat's motion and the soft breeze and the warmth upon his face.

There was very little conversation, but it proved unnecessary, for each of them were lost in their appreciation of the world around them. Once or twice Shelley muttered a few lines of poetry, and once Claire surprised them all by bursting into song, her voice sweet and lovely as it carried up into the warm summer air. Mary soon joined her, then Shelley, and finally even Byron, the four of them doing a creditable quartet. "Bravo!" John declared when they had done, clapping enthusiastically—and then having to grasp at the boat again when his motion caused it to rock and him to slide about in an alarming fashion. That made the others laugh, but it was good-natured enough that he soon joined them.

After an hour or so Byron shipped his oars, Shelley doing the same, and the two boats sat side by side in peaceful, companionable silence, their inhabitants enjoying the lovely weather and the sight of the great lake all around them.

"This seems an ideal picnic spot," Mary declared, and opened the basket to begin handing out pieces of roast chicken, crisp rolls, slices of cheese, clusters of grapes, and more. They ate there upon the water, the gentle rocking of the boats mild enough not to interfere with such actions, even when Mary produced a bottle of wine and Shelley poured glasses for everyone without spilling a drop. They were all in a fine mood when they finally headed back to shore, even John, who decided that this was perhaps the finest way to enjoy boating. Especially since Byron did not even consider asking him to take a turn at the oars.

"Well, I'm famished," Byron declared as they strolled back off the docks and onto dry land once more. "Exercise and water always give me an appetite. Shall we return to the villa together?"

Shelley started to agree, but Mary's gentle hand on his arm stopped him. "I think we will dine at the chalet tonight," she answered for them, "though of course we appreciate the offer, and will no doubt take you up on it if the invitation were to be repeated at a later date. It's only that, after being kept away from him for a full day and night, we feel we should spend a little time with our Wilmouse. I'm sure you understand."

Byron did not, that much was clear from his countenance, but he was too much a gentleman to say so. "Of course," he stated instead. "The needs of your family must come first. Perhaps tomorrow night, then?"

"That would be lovely, thank you," Mary affirmed with a warm smile. Watching her, John was again reminded how he had initially assumed she would be mild and meek and retiring. What a pleasure it was to see how wrong he had been on that score! If anything, she was the leader of the pair, and Shelley only too happy to follow her directives, amiable as they often were. Claire pouted, of course, but since the invitation had been extended to her sister and future brother-in-law and her only by extension she had little choice but to follow their lead and remain behind at the chalet with them as John and Byron walked on.

"What shall we two do tonight, then, Polly Dolly?" Byron asked as they continued to retrace their steps toward the villa. "For the house is sure to feel empty with no one else around."

No one except the many servants, John thought, and of course your pets—the animal variety. But he did not say that, for he knew his friend well enough to know that such a statement would only confuse him. "A quiet evening of contemplation, I think," he answered instead. "A little light reading, a stroll about the grounds, and a decent night's sleep."

"Ah, you'll turn me into an old maid," the young lord replied, shuddering for effect.

"Consider it doctor's orders," John suggested. After all, ostensibly he had been brought along on this trip as Byron's personal physician, even though the young lord was as healthy as him—and often moreso—and really had only wanted an excuse to bring him along after John had wrangled an introduction and impressed the poet with his own knowledge. Still, the title existed, and every so often John found it useful to drag forth, such as now.

"Ah, that's how it is, is it?" Byron asked, laughing. "What a strange sort of doctor you must be!"

"Would you prefer leeches and bloodletting?" John asked. That produced a genuine shudder, for his friend detested such things, popular though they might be.

"Very well," he stated at last. "A quiet night it shall be. But just this once."

John hid a smile at that. He knew Byron was too animated to like such silence and stillness for long—indeed, it always amazed him that his friend could sit still in a boat, but then his full attention was upon the wonders around him. Still, a quiet night would serve as an excellent pause between bouts of creativity and conversation, and would only leave them more eager to resume such activities after. He was sure Shelley felt the same, and even Mary, now that she had satisfied her maternal urges for the nonce. It would be a lively party upon the morrow, he was sure.

CHAPTER FIVE
In which our players are treated to strange visions

As he had predicted, Shelley, Mary, and Claire returned the following day, and, the weather being chilly and gray but dry for the nonce, the quintet opted to stroll the villa's grounds rather than venturing farther afield. This proved wise, as the darkness thickened overhead and finally unleashed its torrent upon them, forcing them to duck under the portico and then from there indoors for respite. Though not as fierce as the storm the night before, this downpour was still steady enough and punishing enough that none of them wished to endure it, and so they enjoyed a light lunch and then took themselves to the billiard room, seeking to spend the hours with at least some form of exercise and motion.

"I swear, I have never seen a summer quite like this," Shelley stated as he lined up his shot, his gray gaze intent upon the cue and the ball before it. "Thoughtfulness in repose," John dubbed the image, imagining it as a painting or a statue, the young poet's curls and intelligent features captured forever in oils or bronze. "It is more like England in fall than Switzerland in summer, I'd say."

He was not wrong, of course. Traveling from Waterloo and then staying at the hotel in Cologne, John and Byron had heard others remarking on the unseasonable weather as well. Colder than it should be, and far more damp and gray. It was as if the whole world had fallen into a massive sulk, casting dreariness as far as the eye could see.

"The sun will return," Mary assured her fiancé, looking up from the book she had pulled from the room's shelves. "And when it does we will all look back upon these cool, gray days and think, 'ah, if only it were not so beastly hot, as it was then!'"

"Perhaps so," Byron agreed, taking the cue as it was now his turn. "For often our reminiscences are softened by distance. When we are old we will curse the heat and long for these cooler nights, but right now they are vile and burdensome." He took his shot, neatly pocketing the ball, then glanced at Mary. "What have you found there?"

"Oh, it's a collection of stories," she answered, holding the leather-bound volume up for them all to see. It was a hefty little tome, and its title was stamped in gold upon the cover, but was clearly not in English. "*Fantasmagoriana*," she read out. "It's in French, but I don't believe it started so, not the way these sentences are formed—I'd wager it was translated from some other language first."

"May I?" John held out his hand, and Mary placed the book there. "Yes, it's originally German," he stated after flipping through a few pages. "Ah, it states so here, in the indicia." He returned it to her. "Good eye."

"And what sort of tales are they?" Claire asked. "Romances? Adventures? Mysteries?"

"Ghost stories, I think," her stepsister replied. "And other scares." She sounded intrigued, but then John was not surprised. A mind as quick as hers was apt to enjoy such tales of the unknowable.

"Read us one, then," Byron instructed, already bent over the table again. "That will make for an excellent backdrop to our game."

Obligingly, Mary turned to a page, read silently for a moment, and then began. She had a calm, clear reading voice, with excellent diction, and she proved to be a skilled storyteller, injecting emotion into the dialogue and a certain foreboding into the narrative. The rest of them listened, so rapt Shelley and Byron forgot all about their game, and when she had reached the rather horrific conclusion she was treated to four sets of hands joining in applause.

"Oh, well done, Mary!" Claire told her. "That was truly eerie! Do another!"

"Yes, quite," Byron agreed, and Shelley and John were quick

to add their voices to the request. Mary smiled, ducking her head a little, but began the next tale in the collection.

After that one she begged off, citing a certain dryness in her throat. Shelley brought her a sherry at once, and Claire offered to take up the book next. She proved a more breathless narrator but a skilled one, and more inclined to give each character a distinctive voice.

She read two, then passed the book to John. He allowed himself to get lost in the tales, hearkening back to an earlier age when such stories would pour forth from his own fingertips, and after finishing the first glanced up to find his friends staring at him, their eyes wide and their mouths open.

"Ye gods, man!" Byron exclaimed, finally breaking the silence, "you are wasted on medicine! You should be on the stage!"

"He's right," Mary said, her eyes bright. "You read that beautifully, as if it were a play and you the principal actor."

"No, no," John demurred, though he could feel his own cheeks warming at the praise. "Thank you for the kind words, but I would never be able to perform before an audience. I would trip over my own tongue, and then over my feet, and then both at once."

"Well, perhaps," his friend allowed, smiling. "Still, that was brilliant. Read another."

He did, eager to set aside this particular conversation, and did his best not to perform quite so well on this second tale. All the while, he was chiding himself inside. How careless of him to forget who he was in this time and place! He was not that man any longer, and had not been for longer than any of his friends had been alive. Here he was only John William Polidori, poor Polly Dolly, brilliant young doctor and friend to poets and philosophers. The center stage was no longer his to brighten—his role now was strictly in the wings, or as a supporting role.

When it came to Shelley to read, John sat back, eager to hear the young poet's rendition of the stories and also to forget his own. Listening, letting the story wash over him, he began to get the strangest sense that they were not alone, that there was another in the room listening to these tales with them. Carefully, he glanced about. The rain continued, but dusk was also upon them, its shadows creeping steadily into the room, and for an instant, it seemed that one dark corner might have more substance to it than not, as if someone stood there within the gloom. But when he peered more intently, he could not make anyone out. Perhaps it was only the tone of the tales that was causing this sense of unease and subtle dread?

Shelley was an excellent reader, his voice soft but throbbing with emotion, and he skillfully kept all of them on the edges of their seat as each story neared its climax. When he had done his pair, they all sank into their chairs, exhausted, and none moreso than the narrator himself, who looked as if he had just run a mile, his face red from effort and his curls plastered to his forehead from sweat.

"Perhaps a pause from these is in order," Mary suggested, fanning herself. "They are well-written and properly terrifying, but a little of that can go a long way."

"Yes, I'd like something a bit lighter, please," Claire agreed. "At least for now."

"I do not know if this is exactly lighter," Byron offered, removing a slim pamphlet from his jacket and opening it, "but it is at least in our native tongue, so surely that will help." And then, clearing his throat, he began in his deep, strong voice:

"'Tis the middle of night by the castle clock,
And the owls have awakened the crowing cock;
Tu-whit! Tu-whoo!
And hark, again! The crowing cock,
How drowsily it crew."

"What have you there?" Shelley asked. "I do not recognize it, nor its cadence."

"It's a new work by Coleridge," their host replied. "A narrative ballad titled 'Christabel.'"

Shelley snorted. "Coleridge!" He stated derisively. "What does that old fool have to say that's worth hearing anymore?"

"Shelley!" That from Mary, with a far sharper tone than John had yet heard her employ. "Be nice! Mister Coleridge is a dear, sweet man, and a wonderful poet. Just because he and his friends are not to your taste does mean you should belittle them!"

It was the first time John had really seen the couple argue, and he was surprised when the young man did not back down but instead glared right back at his fiancée and declared, "I know that he is an old friend of your family, and thus you are excused for your blind partiality, but he and his group refuse to leave the past behind and accept that there are other ways to write, other forms worth exploring. They would have everyone follow only their example, stifling any attempts at originality, and I stand opposed to that, and to them."

"Yes, fine, you do not like him," Byron cut in, seeming exasperated at being interrupted during his recitation. "But let us hear what he has to say in this new piece and then decide upon it, rather than the other way 'round, hm?" And, with a stern look at his young friend, he continued.

The poem was striking, John had to agree. It told of the beautiful young Christabel, who had gone into the woods to pray and there encountered a stranger named Geraldine. The woman claimed to have been abducted, but there was an air of seductive menace about her that suggested she was not the innocent victim she claimed. Still, Christabel was moved to pity and invited Geraldine into her home, where her own father becomes enamored of the mysterious young woman.

As Byron read, the shadows seemed to grow closer, denser, and the air became thick and heavy. The sounds of rain outside blended into almost a hum, a curtain that surrounded them and left the billiard room silent save their breathing and the words of the poem. Almost John could picture the story coming to life before him, figures forming from the darkness to represent Christabel, her father, and the strange and alluring Geraldine.

The first two faded quickly, as figments of the imagination often did, but the third remained. Indeed, as Byron continued she grew more and more distinct, until John could see her clearly. She was tall and striking, with broad shoulders and handsome curves beneath a white silken robe, gems woven into her long, dark hair. But where her face should have been, beautiful and cold, he saw only a skull, its empty sockets glaring back at him.

All at once Shelley leaped to his feet. "No!" the young poet screamed, and fled the room as if demons were at his heels.

"Percy!" Mary cried out, starting to rise as well, but John had already risen.

"We will see to him," he assured her, beckoning Byron to accompany him. "Do not trouble yourself. No doubt he was just overcome by the poem."

They hurried from the room and did not have far to go, for they found Shelley in the hall, leaning against the mantle there. "Are you well, sir?" Byron asked, resting a hand on his friend's arm, and Shelley jumped at the contact. He turned to face them, and John saw that the young man's face was dripping with sweat, his eyes wide and wide, his lips trembling.

"What ails you?" he asked, resting the back of his hand against Shelley's forehead. He was not warm but cold and clammy, which at least meant no fever had taken him. Only a terror of some sort, it seemed.

"I—" Shelley began, but shook his head, unable to continue. John turned away and, with a few quick steps, reached a small table nearby, and more importantly the decanter it held. Pouring brandy into one of the cups there, he offered it to the poet, who gulped the liquor down straightaway. That brought color back to his cheeks, at least! "Thank you," he managed after a moment. "I will be fine, I believe. I was just overtaken by a vision."

"Oh?" Now that the danger had passed, Byron quirked an eyebrow, his lips forming into a smirk. "So perhaps old Coleridge has a thing or two to teach about poetry after all, hm?"

Shelley did not deny that, which was unusual in and of itself. He merely shuddered and shook, though those tremors were beginning to fade as the brandy did its work.

"What did you see?" John asked softly.

"I saw Geraldine," the poet answered slowly, as if struggling to stop the words from emerging. "Only it was Mary, my own sweet Mary. But she was garbed as the lady of the poem, all in white, stern and cold. But that garment was undone, just as in the poem, and the 'sight to dream of, not to tell,' the strange mark she bore—" He paused, then continued in a rush, "upon her breasts were eyes, eyes where nipples would be! It was horrible!"

Byron frowned, digesting this, but John had an additional question for their young friend. "Did you see her face clearly?" he asked. "Are you sure it was Mary?"

"What? Of course it was," Shelley replied. He faltered a second. "Though—there was something strange about her features. They were . . . pale. No, not that, more . . . translucent. As if they were merely painted upon a thin pane, with light shining on them to show them as a mere veil for what lay behind."

And what would have been behind, John thought, but a skull? He felt certain he and Shelley had somehow just had the same vision, or at least visions of the same subject, only from different angles and with attention to different details.

But how was that possible? And what did it mean?

CHAPTER SIX

*Our hero ponders recent events
and arrives at certain unpleasant conclusions.*

"Are you all right?" Mary asked, all her attention focused on her betrothed as he returned to the billiard room, Byron and John at either elbow to lend support if needed.

"I am fine, fine," Shelley insisted, and indeed though still pale he was able to cross the room unaided and with only a faint trembling still to his limbs. He and Mary embraced and then he carefully reclaimed his seat upon the couch. "I was merely overcome for a moment, that is all." His lips quirked in amusement. "It appears I may owe your friend Coleridge an apology after all."

Mary brushed that aside. "I am sure he would be happy to hear that," she answered, "but right now that is the least of my concerns. We should get you home—a good night's sleep will set you right, I am sure of it."

"Yes, perhaps so," he agreed amiably, levering himself back to his feet. "It does appear that the rain has let up, at least enough for us to assay the journey. Gentlemen," he said, turning to Byron and then John, "Thank you for a most stimulating evening. Claire, are you joining us?"

She started to answer but was interrupted by a tremendous boom as thunder clapped almost directly over their heads. They all jumped from the sudden noise, and the very house appeared to tremble from it. The sound was still echoing through the room when a brilliant flash of light split the night, visible through the windows. It was followed by a pounding as the rain increased tenfold, pouring down where an instant before it had been barely a drizzle.

"Oh!" Mary exclaimed, her hand going to her mouth. "Where did that come from?"

They all made their way to the nearest window and stared out. The night was black as pitch, illuminated by brief flashes concurrent with tremendous thunderclaps. They could see the lake clearly, and even the tops of the trees up on Mount Jura beyond, then a second later all would be darkness once more.

"It is lovely," Mary stated, staring out at the scene. "But I'd rather it had waited until we were in our own rooms before starting this again."

"I'd say you are staying here again tonight, instead," Byron agreed. "You are most welcome, of course. And there's no thought of you venturing forth in all this."

There certainly was not, especially with Shelley still looking a bit peaked and Mary still nervous about getting sick around little William. Byron rang for one of the servants and ordered the same guest room as before made up, and the couple soon bade the rest good night and retreated to that chamber to seek the restorative powers of a night's slumber.

That left Byron, John, and Claire. But not for long—John had been unsurprised to see the young lady sidle up to their host as soon as her sister and soon-to-be brother-in-law were gone, whispering something to him even as her hands slid down his arm and chest. Byron's reply was a mere rumble but it made her laugh, and a moment later they were kissing.

"I'll bid you both a good night, then," John said, and exited without waiting upon a reply. He was not prudish, but felt there was little reason to remain and watch their amorous adventures.

Besides, he had other matters to consider.

"Something strange is happening here," he told himself as he paced the long hall, heading not up to his own rooms but rather toward the back of the house where he could find both privacy and a view of the lake. "The question is, what?"

It was not natural, whatever it might be. Of that he was now certain. He had begun to have suspicions over the last few days, what with the unseasonable weather, but after Shelley's vision he was certain. The young poet was unusually sensitive to the emotions of those around him and to the underlying feel of his very surroundings, and in this case those had manifested as that strange image of the woman with eyes upon her naked bosom. That was the very heart of this mystery, he was sure of it. He just had to figure out what that meant.

Could it be another Beast, like the last time? This felt different, however. Whenever he was around one of his brethren, he could feel their presence, but unless they were facing off it was more diffuse, more ethereal, as they pursued their plans and he furthered his own—if there was an intersection it was usually by chance rather than design. This felt closer, more immediate, more personal. The only way that could be the case if is one of his companions was a fellow Beast, and that much he was certain was not true. After Lorelei he had been very careful to scrutinize those around him against such a possibility.

What, then, was occurring here? He was in the dining room now, staring out the glass doors there as the lightning occasionally lit the sky. The rain was still pelting down, and he frowned, considering that. It was not only that the weather was unusually cool for the season, but this rain, so persistent and so powerful, was entirely out of keeping with their locale. And the way it had ramped back up again just when Mary and Shelley had spoken of leaving—could that be more than mere coincidence?

Curious, he crossed the room and took the small door leading into the kitchen. This was the servants' area, where normally he would not go, but right now he had need of certain equipment he suspected they might possess. Sure enough, at the back of the kitchen, by the rear door, there were several sets of heavy oilcloth raincoats hanging from hooks, with broad-brimmed hats above and tall galoshes below. A few moments of searching secured a set that fit him well enough, and another brief period had him fully garbed and ready for the storm outside.

Then, thus attired, John flung open the door and stepped out into the rain.

Instantly he was hammered by a fierce wind that almost drove him back through the door by main force. It was only by planting his feet that he was able to stagger first one step, then another, and slam the door shut behind him. The rain was hitting him hard as well, each droplet slamming against him with the impact of a rock fired from a sling, but the oilcloth kept him from getting soaked. Marshalling his strength, he forced his way a few steps farther from the house, the storm seeming to double its own efforts with each pace he won. This was no mere storm, brought by chance. It had intent, and power, and a will.

But so did he.

"You will not win," he swore through gritted teeth as he battled to increase the distance from the house. "I am John William Polidori. I am the Phoenix!" Rain hissed as it struck him, turning to steam upon contact, and the darkness around him parted, driven back by the light he knew he was emanating. No matter what drove this storm, it could not best him, for he was one of the Great Beasts, an eternal force of creativity and imagination. He could not be vanquished by a meteorological phenomena, no matter how intense!

And it seemed the storm recognized that, for all at once he passed through it, the wind dropping away, the rain vanishing, as if he had pushed through a curtain. Behind him the storm still raged, but ahead of him he saw the lake, and the clear night sky above, the stars visible as tiny twinkling lights scattered across the velvet firmament.

"There," he stated, straightening and tugging off his hat. "As I said. You cannot win against me."

The storm did not appear to have heard. Now that he was beyond it, it spared him no further thought. But still it battered against the villa, as if trying to break in.

No, John realized. Not trying to break in at all, for it was heaviest just past the doors and windows. It was not interested in getting in. It was there to keep those inside from getting out.

For although it had finally conceded and allowed him to pass, it was more than a match for his friends, mortal as they were. It might not have him anymore, but it still had Byron, Shelley, Mary, and Claire. And he had no doubt it intended to keep them.

But why? What did the storm stand to gain from that?

Ah, but perhaps it was not the storm acting here, but merely something else acting through it. Something that did benefit from having them all trapped within the villa.

Something—like the villa itself.

It came to him in a flash of inspiration. Of course! This house had been host to such creative minds before! It had once been home to John Milton himself, that great poet of old. And now it had Byron and Shelley, and yes Mary as well. It somehow thrived on their creativity, almost as John himself did, except that he fed and nurtured their sparks, whereas he suspected the villa wished to feed upon them instead. That was the woman he had seen, the same Shelley had. She was the spirit of the house.

Had she always been part of the villa, he wondered. Or had she been bound to it in some way? Regardless, their presence had awakened her, and their continued acts of creativity had given her strength. That was why the storm had appeared—she had summoned it to keep them within, so that she could grow even more powerful.

And what would happen when she had enough power? Would she somehow break free of those four walls? What would she do, if let loose upon the world, with her appetite for others' imagination?

John had no desire to find out. Indeed, his very *raison d'etre* put him in direct opposition to such an entity—she sought to drain others' creativity, while he existed to protect it.

Though he had not done so intentionally, he had just found himself at war with the very place he inhabited.

Nor was it a battle he could walk away from. Even if they had not been his friends, those minds within the villa were some of the finest of this generation. He could not allow them to be depleted for the sake of some entity's monstrous appetite.

Which meant he would have to find a way to defeat it, and free them all.

He did not yet know how he would do such a thing, but one thing was certain—he could not accomplish anything from out here.

"Very well," he stated, facing the sheet of rain separating him from his friends. "You desired to keep me within? I accept your proposal." And, with a deep breath, he jammed the hat back upon his head and charged directly into the storm again.

Wind lashed out at him, trying to knock him off his feet, or turn him around, or simply hold him in place. Rain came side-ways, spattering his face, blinding him as he blinked the water from his eyes, forcing him to spit it from his mouth to breathe. He had no doubt he would be chilled to the bone already, but his temper was still high and steam was still rising from his flesh, insulating him against the cold. Armed with that heat, he forced his way back to the villa, though it felt like hours just to cross that lawn. Finally, his hand closed upon the latch to the kitchen door and, with some blind fumbling, he forced it open and stumbled inside.

It was as if a switch had been flipped. The rain stopped exactly at the door, as if afraid to cross the threshold. The cold remained with it, the kitchen proving comfortably warm even though the ovens had been shut for hours. Shedding his bor-rowed rain gear, John sighed with relief.

Still, he knew that he had only solved the first piece of this riddle. He knew who and what his foe was, now, and had an inkling as to its goal. What he did not yet know was how to defeat it, particularly while protecting the others. He could not simply burn the spirit out, not without damaging the villa and putting his friends at risk.

Which meant he would have to find another way. And quickly, because if it was growing stronger with each passing night, as he suspected, he probably did not have much time left.

CHAPTER SEVEN

Our hero hits upon a method to remedy matters,
utilizing the particular skills of those present.

"Goodness, what a night!" Claire stated, yawning dramatically and making a point of stretching widely. "What with the rain and all, we barely slept a wink!" She followed that statement with the aforementioned wink directed at Byron, whose terse nod was his only acknowledgement to her blatant declaration of their previous activities. It was odd that, for a man who delighted in flaunting his affairs to the world, he could be curiously reticent sometimes. Though John knew that was also part of his studied attempt to dissuade Claire from thinking theirs was anything more than a casual, carnal affair. Thus far, his efforts appeared to be wholly unsuccessful, but that was their concern, and John felt he had meddled in it more than enough already. They were both adults, after all, though Claire only just. Besides which, he had far larger concerns.

"Yes, the storm certainly picked up, didn't it?" Mary agreed, smothering a more delicate yawn herself. "And it shows no sign of abating yet!" She seemed surprisingly sanguine with this, however, perhaps because after the last time they had been trapped here she had found William safe and warm and happy, just as Shelley had promised. If their entrapment lasted more than a few days, however, John suspected the young mother would again grow anxious to be reunited with her son, which was more than reasonable.

"It certainly does not," Shelley stated, sitting himself beside her at the breakfast table and snatching a roll from the pile plated up before them. He had evidently recovered from his shock the previous night, and looked fully himself again, all charm and kindness and thoughtfulness. "We will simply have to amuse ourselves again. Fortunately, I find myself in altogether amusing company." His eyes twinkled at that last one, and the other laughed with him. For a party trapped by a strange and unwelcome storm, they were all in high spirits.

That word of course brought John back to his current dilemma, and the question of how to handle it. He considered telling the others what he had discovered last night, but immediately rejected the notion. Even if they were to believe him—and it was a rather incredible tale, straight out of that book they had been taking turns reading—what would be the benefit? Surely they would all become alarmed at the thought that the house itself had a consciousness and that this presiding spirit was intent upon keeping them here and feeding off them in some way? How would sending everyone into a panic help anything? No, far better to keep them in the dark as to what was really occurring—let them blame the freak weather upon some far-flung natural disaster or a rare conjunction of the stars or whatever else they could accept.

What made that all the trickier was that John suspected he might need their help in freeing them all from this trap. He could win himself free, after all—he had done so last night, and could again. But that was himself alone, and such a brute-force response would not work for his friends. Still, something would have to be done, and quickly.

Could he destroy the spirit somehow? Certainly reducing the villa itself to ash would accomplish that, but he already knew that was out of the question as long as they were all still within its confines. Without that level of damage, however, he was not sure how to extract the spirit from the building so that he could get at it directly. An exorcism? Such a thing might work, but he did not possess the necessary mindframe for that particular task. Nor did the others—not in this group of free-thinking radicals! None of them had any real faith to speak of, and it would take something of that nature to separate spirit from structure.

That was out of the question, then. Indeed, he suspected destruction was entirely off the table. If he could not destroy the spirit, though, what were the alternatives? It did not seem inclined to treat with him, or to negotiate—and why should it, when at the moment it held most of the cards? All it had to do was wait them out, maintaining the storm overhead and holding them here until it had what it needed to break free.

Break free—perhaps there was something there. Idly, John accepted a roll and a tub of jam from Mary, slathering the one upon the other and stuffing it into his mouth, barely noticing the laughter that ensued from his ungentlemanly display. His thoughts were focused upon that last notion, which he sensed might be the key to all this.

The spirit was trapped here. It was trying to break free. They had not heard any tales of the place being haunted, so it seemed likely the spirit had been quiescent all this time, from whenever it first was bound to this location until now, when they had arrived and reawakened it.

Which, he realized with a pang, was most likely his own fault. His was the power to invigorate, to stimulate, to excite. He had directed those impulses toward his friends, particularly Byron and Shelley, but no doubt some energy had leaked out around the edges. Mary had certainly benefited from it as well, and even Claire. What was to say it had stopped there? What if his very presence, and the power emanating from him, was responsible for awakening the spirit herein? The timing was too convenient to think otherwise. If he had stayed away, the spirit here would still be dormant, perhaps forevermore.

What was done was done, however, and not worth thinking upon, not when there was so much to be done. If his power had awakened the spirit, though, it stood to reason that he could also return it to its slumber. The question was how? That was not within his purview—others among the Beasts were skilled at somnambulance, at dreams and fogs, but not him. He burned too brightly to ever encourage a limiting of the senses.

No, he would have to work some other way. Encourage it to sleep, channel his power to that end, but through some other medium. To bind it tightly once more, so tightly it would never again be able to even test its bonds, much less break them.

He would need something that could imprison a spirit that

drew its strength from creativity, he thought, sipping water to wash down the roll, and all at once an image flashed into his head, from ancient myth. Ouroboros. The ancient world serpent, like the great Midgard Serpent Jormungandir, that swallowed its own tail. A binding that drew from the spirit's own strength to keep it imprisoned.

Creativity. That was the key. He would use his friends' creativity, the very spark the spirit hungered for, to trap it more securely, and force it to sleep forever.

He became aware of the conversation around him once more, which centered on the question of how to amuse themselves while stuck in the villa for another day. Mary was advocating reading more stories from *Fantasmagoriana*. Claire was shuddering and begging them not to, saying that the previous tales had left her with nightmares. Byron, for all that he hated agreeing with his current paramour, also seemed disinclined to return to that book, though John thought his friend's reasons were less about being frightened and more about the innate passivity of listening to stories someone else had written. Shelley seemed torn. He had enjoyed those stories, and was clearly interested in hearing more of them. At the same time, he no doubt worried about a repeat of last night's rather extreme reaction, and was more than willing to consider some other activity that might allow him to retain more control over himself.

"I have an idea on what we might do," John stated, the inspiration bursting into his mind fully formed. "Let us not read those old tales again but, rather, take them for our inspiration and each of us create a ghost story of our own. We can then read our efforts to one another. It will be a novel experience, and an interesting experiment to see how different minds react to the same stimuli, for here we all are, in the exact same place, under the exact same circumstances, yet I daresay it is safe to assume each of our tales will be unique."

Byron clapped his hands. "A capital idea, Polly Dolly! Would that I had tumbled to it myself, but I wholeheartedly endorse it! Yes, we've got a first-rate crew of poets and authors here, surely we can come up with better than that musty old book? And we'll have a few laughs at our results, at any rate!" John had known such a scheme would appeal to their host, of course—it was an excuse to be creative but in an unusually sociable fashion, and those were two of Byron's greatest strengths.

"Hm." Shelley stroked his chin, considering the notion—as ever, he was thoughtfulness to Byron's impulsiveness. "Yes," he said after a moment, "I like it as well. It will be an interesting experience, you are right, and a shared one between the five of us, for no matter who reads these tales afterward, no one but us will have the same connection to them, all of us having been here together at their mutual birth." Leave it to the young poet to state his agreement so gracefully and with such dramatic flair!

They all turned to the two women, then. "Oh, I'm not much of a writer," Claire stated, hand pressed to her chest, "but I'm happy to give it a go, and to cheer on the rest of you!"

That left only Mary. Many an individual, faced with the eagerness of a Byron and a Shelley, would simply have capitulated. She did not, however, impressing John yet again—here was a woman who knew her own mind, and had no intention of letting anyone else make it up for her! "I suppose," she said slowly, still thinking things through, "that it would not hurt, and it would be all in fun—just so long as it is not taken as competition, for you know I dislike such things! Friends should not pit themselves against one another!"

"Well said, dearest!" Shelley agreed at once, placing an arm over her shoulders. "And I quite agree. We are not competing, but rather collaborating, encouraging each other to do our best, each in our own fashion!"

She smiled and nodded, and Byron practically crowed with delight. "It is agreed, then!" he stated. "We will each attempt our own tales, and then share them together when we are done. What an excellent way to spend a rainy day!" He then turned to John. "And as this was your plan, Polly Dolly, are there any rules you would like to impose upon us?"

John smiled at that, for he could not have planned this part better. "Only the one," he stated. "It must be a story of the terrifying and macabre. Specifically, it must feature an element of the unnatural impinging upon the mortal realm, and mundane heroes struggling to defeat those outside forces."

Take that, spirit, he thought triumphantly as they all hurried to finish their breakfast and rise to find writing materials and adequate space to think and compose. Five tales, at least two of them by master wordsmiths, each backed by the power of the Phoenix, and all about people such as these battling to defeat beings such as yourself. Stories of the supernatural being bound, and those stories themselves used as a binding for a supernatural.

It was the perfect solution—provided it worked.

CHAPTER EIGHT
Our players set themselves to the task,
though not without complications

The day passed largely in silence, each of them engrossed in their task. It was not the type that could be wrought in unison, even though they were all embarked upon the same journey—rather, each of them must reach the same destination alone, by their own route. Some might have benefited from discussing their plans with others, but that was for them to say. John had resolved not to force himself upon any of his friends, but to make himself available should they wish to confer or vent.

The first to find him was Claire, of course. "I am bored," she declared, flopping down on the couch, for he was currently in one of the sitting rooms, working at the writing desk there. Already several pages were covered in his scrawling hand, and it was with a touch of reluctance that he set his pen aside to face his guest, for it had been a very long time since he had felt the touch of such inspiration himself. He had forgotten the heady rush that came with crafting a story and fixing it into words, and was nearly giddy as he twisted to study the young lady scowling so dramatically across the room.

"What seems to be the problem, Claire?" he asked her, putting on his best bedside manner. "Trouble with your story?"

He could have predicted her answer nearly word for word. "There is no story!" she complained, pouting. "I am not a writer like the rest of you! Even dear Mary far surpasses me! I like reading well enough, and drawing, and painting, but that is enough for me!"

"I thought you had wanted to become a writer as well?" John asked. "Was that not how you made Byron's acquaintance in the first place?" His understanding had been that she had written the young lord, stating that she hoped to be a dramatist, and had asked for his advice. A correspondence had sprung up from that connection, which had led to her ultimately visiting him in London, at which point they had become lovers.

"Yes, I had such aspirations," Claire agreed now, waving them aside like so much dust in the air, "but I've long since realized that is not for me. I'd much rather attend a play than write one!" She stretched, and winced a little as she did. "I'm just so restless! And I've not been sleeping well, and I've felt ill when I've woken up, and I just don't know what to do with myself!"

Restless, ill, and not sleeping? John turned his attention toward her more closely, and specifically toward the life force he could feel brimming within her. A life force, he now saw, that seemed so full in part because it had in fact doubled. Ah. That would explain a great deal—no doubt it had occurred back in London, but was only now making itself felt. He considered telling her, but decided that now was not the right moment, when they were trapped in this house and needed everyone else to remain focused if they hoped to escape. He would inform her of her condition as soon as that was resolved. There was yet time.

Instead he said, "I'm sorry you feel that way, Claire. Hm. Perhaps you could check with the servants and make sure lunch will be served soon? I know that Byron has a tendency to forget meals when he is in the grips of creation, and I suspect Shelley and Mary could be the same. It would be a great kindness if someone were to remind them when they needed to eat."

The thought of being useful brightened Claire's face at once. "Oh, yes, of course!" she answered, springing to her feet. "I'll see to that at once! Thank you, Polly Dolly!" And she bounded from the room, happy to have a task, especially one that might earn her a kind word from her distracted lover.

Satisfied that was at least handled, John returned his own attention to his writing. But he paused only a few words later, for now he was curious as to how the others fared. The more he wondered about that—for so much rested on their success!—the less he was able to focus on his story, until finally with a sigh he set the pen down again and rose to his feet. He had best check on them.

He found Byron in the salon, only a door away. The young lord had dragged a stool over to one of the sets of French doors, which he had flung open so that the sound of the rain filled the room, as did the thick mugginess. As John entered Byron rose to his feet and paced the length of the room and back again, pausing on the return to lean against the mantle, chin upon his hand. He was the very picture of "A Poet in Thought." But after a only a few seconds he regained motion and resumed his path, reclaiming the stool and then quickly jotting something down upon the paper he'd held furled in one hand.

John was not surprised. He had seen Byron write while in the carriage, while sitting at lunch, while climbing a hill. He had even observed the other man jotting down lines on the back of a cannon when they had been at Waterloo! The man could write anywhere, it seemed, as long as he was inspired, and right now it was clear that his creative well was overflowing. Claire might find it difficult to drag him to the dining table, but eventually the young lord would acquiesce, only he would bring his paper and pen with him, and continue to work as he ate. Still, that would satisfy both hunger and creation, so John considered it well enough.

Next he went searching for Shelley. The younger man was up in the bedroom he had been sharing with Mary, and John hesitated before knocking, fearful of disturbing the poet's process. Instead he leaned his head against the door and expanded his senses, seeing into the room despite the heavy paneled door barring his actual sight.

Shelley was also pacing, but his steps were more frantic, his face more anguished. There was paper and pen sitting upon the small writing desk under one window, but each time he approached them he hesitated, then turned away. Shifting his attention to those implements, John saw that the paper was very nearly blank, with only a few lines inscribed there and two of those crossed out.

As he watched, Shelley returned to the paper, wrote something, scratched it out, and then, with a soft cry, hurled the offending sheet from him before crumpling to the floor himself. He curled up there, head in his hands, weeping piteously and muttering something to himself. It took John a few seconds to make out the words: "I am worthless, worthless, worthless . . ." The young poet was repeating them over and over again.

This was disastrous. John reached for the door knob, intending to enter and comfort his young friend, but paused. What would he say, beyond assuring Shelley of his skill and value, things the poet surely knew already? John had wrestled with despair enough times himself—and lost the battle more than once—to know that such intellectual awareness mattered naught when you were overwhelmed by those feelings, nor did reassurance from a friend who must surely be biased in your favor help defeat those beliefs. Only time could conquer such a depression, though the kindness of a loved one could help ease it slightly, as could public approbation. Since the latter was barred them while they were imprisoned here, he went to seek Mary instead.

John found the final member of their quintet sitting in one of the drawing rooms. The lights were all out save a single lamp beside her couch, and in the shadows he nearly missed her, for she sat motionless, head clasped in her hands. Upon her lap sat a small lap desk, and atop it a single blank page, the pen resting across it almost accusingly. She glanced up as he approached, for he was careful to scuff his feet on the floor so as not to startle her. "Oh!" she said.

"Sorry to bother you, Mary," he told her gently, reaching the couch and resting a hand there. "How goes it for you, then?"

"Not well, I'm afraid," she answered truthfully, shaking her head and tapping the page as proof. "I just cannot think of anything that seems appropriately . . . spooky. Nothing worth turning into a tale, at any rate." She managed a wan smile. "And you? The others?"

"Oh, mine is coming alone," John told her modestly. "Thank you. Byron seems caught up in his as well. Claire has already conceded the race, so I asked her to see to lunch being served." Mary smiled at that, but not meanly—rather, her expression seemed gratitude for his finding her stepsister something to occupy herself. "But I'm concerned about Shelley," he added, and she stilled, the smile dropping away. "I went upstairs and, well, I think I may have heard something from your bedroom. It sounded like"—he hesitated, not sure how to put this delicately—"well, it sounded like he might be in some distress."

Mary rose at once, setting the lap desk aside. "Thank you, John. I will check on him. He wrestles with dark thoughts at times, and I know the rain has been dampening his mood as well as the air." She bustled out, and a moment later John heard quick footsteps upon the stairs. Good. He regretted disturbing her but perhaps this would actually benefit both—Shelley by having her comfort him and draw him from his darkness, and Mary by giving her something to focus on rather than the story that would not come. He knew from bitter experience that sometimes that was the only way to start, by letting yourself get distracted so that your own anxieties could not constrict the flow of ideas so tightly none could get through.

When Claire called them all to lunch a few minutes later, John was happy to see Mary leading Shelley to join them, even as Claire dragged Byron to the table. A little food, some wine, and some light conversation might do everyone good, he felt.

To that end, rather than ask how anyone else's tale was progressing, or talking about his own, John instead stated, "You know, I forgot to mention the other day but I was reading the most interesting article about galvanism . . ." He proceeded to discuss the article, which had detailed the recent strides that had been made with such an application of electricity, and had offered several ideas as to where that might lead in future. "Imagine," he concluded, "if the author is correct, and they can indeed discover a way to revitalize dead tissue! Why, someone with a damaged limb might be able to regain the use of it!"

"Ha," Byron scoffed, "that hardly seems likely, does it? No, once the animating force has departed, neither heaven nor hell shall see it functioning again."

"But what of science?" Shelley asked, the first words he had uttered that meal beyond a few mumbled politenesses. He seemed only too eager to fasten on some topic that did not pertain to himself and his own perceived flaws. "Surely that is manmade and therefore neither celestial nor demonic, and thus exempt from your proscription!"

Beside him, Mary shuddered. "Is it?" she asked, fiddling with her napkin. "I would think that, while science itself might be a tool of man, its usage could qualify it as either heavenly or hellish in its scope. And reaching beyond death, reversing that natural process, that does not strike me as anything sanctioned by the Almighty."

"Well said, Mary!" Byron agreed, thumping the table for emphasis. "Yes, the impulses must come from above or below, regardless of the tools used! And neither would wish to see their own domains so arrogantly trespassed upon by mere mortals!"

The argument raged back and forth, John contributing here and there but mainly letting Byron and Mary debate Shelley about both the plausibility and, more importantly, the morality of attempting such scientific marvels. By the time the meal had ended Shelley was fired up from the conversation, and though he announced that he was returning to the bedroom John felt confident the young poet would not be giving way to such dark impulses again. Byron took to the billiard room with Claire, carrying his papers with him and no doubt intending to continue his own writing in between shots. Mary headed back toward the drawing room, hopefully now inspired as well, though by her expression John feared she might still be unable to push her insecurities aside long enough to breathe an idea to life. For himself, he went back to his desk, and the story waiting there, and wrote furiously until dinner. It had been so long, he had forgotten what an incredible rush it was to feel the tale racing through his veins like this, burning in its eagerness to burst forth, and it was all he could do to keep up with it as the words leaped into his mind and demanded to be set down upon the page.

CHAPTER NINE

In which our players relate the tales they have created—
with unexpected effect

The next morning dawned bright and clear—or would have, if not for the shroud of rain and fog cast all about them, dampening their view and their mood.

All except Mary, who looked, if not rested, at least bright-eyed, alert, and even eager, her cheeks flushed. "It came to me last night," she explained hurriedly as they sat to breakfast, not waiting for anyone else to speak first, which was unusual for her in and of itself. "I've been having difficulties sleeping, you know, what with all this horrid rain constantly beating down upon us like Judgement Day itself. And I was nowhere with my story, positively nowhere. Until last night. I finally fell asleep, at I know not what hour, and then I had a vision." She paused to take a sip of water before continuing. "I saw the pale student of unhallowed arts kneeling beside the thing he had put together," she said, her eyes unfocusing as she looked beyond them, beyond the rain, to another plane altogether, a plane of pure imagination. "I saw the hideous phantasm of a man stretched out, and then, on the working of some powerful engine, show signs of life, and stir with an uneasy, half vital motion." Glancing about, she realized that the others were all staring at her, hanging upon her every word, and laughed, blushing as she lowered her head. "So I wrote it all down," she ended, unable to keep from looking up again and displaying her triumphant smile. "I was up the rest of the night, but I don't mind. Because I have my story!"

"Oh, good for you, Mary!" Claire told her, clapping. "I can't wait to hear it! To hear all of them!"

"Yes, well . . ." Shelley stirred beside his betrothed, scrubbing at his face with one slightly shaky and reaching for his wine-glass with the other. "I will read what I have, if you so desire, but I warn you that it is not much, nor is it complete." He looked shamefaced, like a little boy who has failed to do a lesson for his favorite teacher. "I fear I have not succeeded at this task we all agreed upon, and have thus failed you all."

"Nonsense," Byron told him, lounging at the head of the table as always. "First of all, it was merely a diversion, wasn't it, Polly Dolly? A way to pass the time. You owe us nothing more than the pleasure of your company, which I assure you is great indeed. Besides which," their host continued, politely overlooking how his young guest flushed at the compliment, "I am sure that even a few random scribblings of yours will be worth ten times the finished, polished prose of most of our so-called celebrated authors." He yawned, stretched, and leaned his head back to rest it against the chairback. "For myself, I have completed mine, though I warn you it is short. Still, I am pleased enough with it, and trust it will find a sympathetic audience here."

The others all nodded, and John cleared his throat. "Perhaps, then, we should adjourn to the salon," he suggested, "and there we can read what we have wrought, so that we might be further entertained on this dark and rainy day."

Everyone seemed agreeable to this idea and, after nibbling a little at the food there—for none of them were overly hungry, it seemed, or at least not for mere food and drink—they did as he'd suggested and returned to the salon where they had already spent so much of their time.

"I shall go last, if that is acceptable to everyone," John stated as they returned to the couches and armchairs they had each adopted as their own. How quickly such a thing becomes habit, he thought. "But I will leave it up to the group of us who should go first."

"I will," Shelley stated, rising to his feet and drawing several folded pages from his shirt. "Might as well start with the meanest of the lot, eh?" No one objected, though Byron made a rude noise at the self-inflicted insult, and so Shelley cleared his throat and began to read.

His voice was as soft and smooth and clear as ever, his words precise and filled with emotion and meaning. Though the story was, in truth, little more than the fragment he had claimed, still it was powerful and evocative. It told the tale of a young boy who found himself dreaming of a strange, unearthly woman each night, and who reached the point where he was too terrified to sleep. His parents despaired, for the boy grew weaker each day, but nothing they did was any help. Nor could the doctor, when he was called. Or the priest. "In the end, it was only the boy who could save himself," Shelley asserted. "Which he did by the simple yet difficult trick of reminding himself that the woman was not real, that she existed only in his own mind, and that therefore he must have dominion over her, should he only choose to exert it." That proved to be the end, for he coughed, folded the papers back up, and abruptly took his seat.

There was a second of silence, as if they were all waiting in case he was tricking them and was about to continue. Then Byron rose to his feet, clapping loudly. "Oh, well done!" he stated. "Short, yes, and perhaps only a sketch, but what a sketch! I swear I could all but see the boy here among us, and feel his anguish!"

The others all chimed in, agreeing with Byron's assessment, for it had been powerful. Moreso, because John had quietly lent the roughhewn tale some assistance. As Shelley had read he had concentrated upon the poet's words, his voice, and most importantly the tale he was presenting. He had channeled his own energy into that story, giving it a life beyond what most narratives could ever hope, making it not only a channel for his power, and a vessel, but also a conduit and a casing. He put the creative power of the Phoenix into Shelley's words, and built of them a chain wrapped tightly around the spirit residing her with them, pinning it back to the building it inhabited and restricting its ability to reach them.

Outside, the storm slackened a little, patches of light starting to show through the clouds. Then it darkened again, a new crop of thunderheads rolling in, and the rain trebled in force and speed, sounding like a thousand arrows dashing themselves to pieces against the roof and walls.

The spirit had realized what John was about. And it was fighting back.

"I'll go next, shall I?" Byron offered. His papers were resting on the table beside him, and he raised them and started in, stating, "It happened that in the midst of the dissipations attendant upon a London winter, there appeared at the various parties of the leaders of the ton a nobleman, more remarkable for his singularities, than his rank." Though he had been lounging the young lord now rose to his feet and began to pace as he read, telling them the story of young Aubrey, "an orphan left with an only sister in the possession of great wealth," and how he met the aforementioned gentleman, one Lord Ruthven. The two became acquainted and, when Ruthven departed London for Rome, Aubrey accompanied him. They separated, however, after the noble seduced a friend's daughter—disgusted, Aubrey traveled on to Greece alone, and there fell in love with the beautiful Ianthe, an innkeeper's daughter. It was she who told him the legends of the vampire, "who had passed years amidst his friends, and dearest ties, forced every year, by feeding upon the life of a lovely female to prolong his existence for the ensuing months." Aubrey does not believe his beloved until one night she is found dead, "upon her throat were the marks of teeth having opened the vein." Aubrey then falls ill, and Ruthven arrives as if summoned by the young man's ravings and cares for him during his illness. Afterward, the pair roam the countryside together. They are set upon by bandits and Ruthven is mortally wounded. He makes Aubrey swear an oath not to reveal "your knowledge of my crimes or death to any living being in any way" for a year and a day, and then the strange, intense, predatory nobleman sinks back into his pillow and dies.

Beyond the villa's windows, the wind shrieked and howled and battered against the building, but could do little more than stir the heavy drapes and send a few loose papers scattering to the floor.

John hid a smile, lest his friends mistake that for his reaction to the grim and horrific tale Byron had just recited. Yet he was inwardly well pleased, for this was exactly as he had hoped. Byron's tale was perfect—the story of a being that fed off others to survive, and then died itself? Clearly the young lord had also picked up on the struggle they were trapped in, at least at an unconscious level. And, with the Phoenix lending the very magic of the universe to that story, "The Vampyre" became more than just a short horror story—it became a prophecy, carrying within its words the dark fate that awaited the spirit they battled here.

They all applauded, and indeed it had been masterfully done, each line vivid and precise, the characters lifelike in only a few brief descriptions. Byron seemed well pleased with their response, and executed a quick, graceful bow before resuming his seat. "And now," he stated grandly, gesturing toward Mary, "I believe it is the lady's turn to dazzle us with her creation."

"I don't know about dazzling," she replied, reaching for a notebook by her side and then standing with it opened before her like a prayer book. "But I hope to at least intrigue and engage. Beyond that, we shall see."

She cleared her throat as John marshalled his own resources. "Frankenstein," she began, in her clear voice, "or The Modern Prometheus." And then, pausing and taking a deep breath, she continued, "To Mrs Saville, England. St. Petersburgh, Dec. 11th, 17-. You will rejoice to hear that no disaster has accompanied the commencement of an enterprise which you have regarded with such evil forebodings. I arrived here yesterday, and my first task is to assure my dear sister of my welfare and increasing confidence in the success of my undertaking."

As she read the sky outside grew dark as night, and John quickly lit the candelabras that stood at hand, placing them around the room and setting one right beside Mary on the table so that she could see to read. She nodded her thanks before continuing, quickly enthralling them with the tale of poor Victor Frankenstein and his passion for science, for "It was the secrets of heaven and earth that I desired to learn; and whether it was the outward substance of things or the inner spirit of nature and the mysterious soul of man that occupied me, still my inquiries were directed to the metaphysical, or in it highest sense, the physical secrets of the world." To that end he became a student at the university of Ingolstadt, and it was there that he learned enough about nature and human physiology and electricity to begin his mad experiment, to usurp God's own role and "infuse a spark of being into the lifeless thing that lay at my feet."

When Mary told about the experiment's success, the storm surrounding the villa increased, the spirit clearly liking this example of life brought out of nothingness, of the inanimate made animate. But her tale did not stop there, and she told how Victor turned away from his own creation, horrified by what he had wrought.

Lightning flashed overhead and thunder boomed, but Mary continued, and the rest of them sat, enthralled, as she wove her tale, speaking of the monster's desire for revenge. The lightning became more intense, the thunder rolling together into one long crackle like laughter, as she related how the creature killed Victor's beloved Elizabeth on their wedding night and then led his creator on a chase across Europe and Russia and finally up to the Arctic Circle, where the story began.

The thunder at last ceased, the lightning stopping, the clouds rolling back enough for some light to once more reach into the room, as if the storm was now eager to hear the end of this tale. But oh! Mary proved to be a consummate storyteller, turning the tables on her audience yet again, for in the final act Victor perished and the monster, returning to study the corpse of its creator, declared, "Fear not that I shall be the instrument of future mischief. My work is nearly complete. Neither yours nor any man's death is needed to consummate the series of my being and accomplish that which must be done, but it requires my own." The creature continued, explaining that, "I shall collect my funeral pile and consume to ashes this miserable frame, that its remains may afford no light to any curious and unhallowed wretch who would create such another as I have been."

John wanted to cheer, and had to restrain himself from doing so. Oh, how perfect! Not only the monster dying at its own hand, but by fire, his own element! "I shall ascend my funeral pile triumphantly," Mary read out, the air itself hushed with anticipation and dread, "and exult in the agony of the torturing flames. The light of that conflagration will fade away;

my ashes will be swept into the sea by the winds. My spirit will sleep in peace, or if it thinks, it will not surely think thus. Farewell."

When she finished and lowered her notebook, allowing it to close, there was naught but silence surrounding them, the calm before the storm, the perfect stillness at the eye of the torrent. Then the others all leapt to their feet, clapping as if to wake the dead, and Mary blushed, bowing her head and dropping into an elegant curtsy.

"Magnificent!" Byron proclaimed. "Truly incredible! What a tale! Why, I confirm I have been bested, and that in truth it is no contest! That was fantastic!"

"Yes, utterly wonderful," Shelley agreed. He hugged his fiancé and kissed her enthusiastically on the cheek, not at all upset to have been so clearly upstaged. "Fantastic, Mary, simply fantastic. In fact, you should expand upon it, turn it into a full novel."

Though the storm still blocked the sun outside, it might as well have been transparent as glass, for Mary shone so brightly in her joy that it nearly hurt their eyes to look upon her. Not was the entirely a metaphor, for John's power had lit her from within even as it sparked to life with her words, and the salon was truly illuminated, though all of them were so transfixed by the tale they had just heard that they barely seemed to notice.

Outside, the clouds began to thin again, and the rain to drop off. The storm was beginning to crumble away, now that the spirit guiding and controlling it was being bound back into its former prison and thus was losing its ability to influence aught beyond the creak of floors and the squeak of doors.

One final touch remained, one last nail to seal the coffin shut. John allowed Mary her moment of glory, for she more than deserved it, but at last, as the compliments began to slow, he rose to his feet, the fruits of his labor in hand as ink upon paper. "As promised," he stated, "the last piece of our little experiment. I call it 'Haunted.'"

His story was shorter than Mary's, though not so short as Byron's, and it was a complete tale, albeit a simple one. It told of a band of friends who came upon a house and chose to stay there, only to discover that they were not alone. For the house was possessed of a spirit itself, a malignant force that sought to feed upon them and use their lives as the prybar with which it freed itself from the walls and doors that shaped it. But the friends, when they realized the nature of their foe, did not despair or succumb. Instead they closed ranks, rallying one another with good cheer and warm affection, keeping each other's spirits high—and thus preventing that low spirit from draining them away. Instead it spent itself in its efforts, all in vain, and grew steadily weaker and weaker, until finally, after one last attempt that was easily rebuffed, it faded away to nothingness, leaving the house nothing more than a collection of wood and brick and mortar and plaster and the friends free to leave, alive and unharmed.

As he read, John allowed more and more of his own nature to uncloak and shine through, the light bursting into being around him. It stretched out its limbs, like great wings of flame, and did not scorch the people sitting there, nor the furniture, nor the walls. Instead it passed out through the windows and walls, and where it touched the storm beyond that collection of moisture and shadow was burned away, leaving great swathes of open, empty air behind. His wings rose higher, reaching up past the roof, and tore holes in the clouds above, letting the sun stream down, its light golden and warm and enticing. The smell of the lake reached them, passing through the dampness of the rain, and a light breeze brought with it the scent of flowers and of grapes on the vine. When he reached the end of his tale there was a thunderous clap, but not like that of the storm before— this was more the sound of a pair of hands slamming together, creating a shockwave that tore the thunderclouds apart and scattered them to the four corners, leaving nothing but a clear blue sky overhead. With the storm went the sense of heaviness and foreboding that had been weighing down upon them all these past few days, and it was with a sigh of relief and joy that they all collapsed back into their seats, and fell into a deep and restful sleep.

CHAPTER TEN

Being the aftermath of those tales, including certain unpleasant choices that must be made for the greater good.

"**B**loody hell!"

The mumbled shout woke John, who had been dozing in his armchair. He sat up quickly, glancing about, but it was only Byron, stretching and rubbing at the back of his neck from his own seat.

"What the devil was I thinking, falling asleep sitting up like that?" the young lord demanded of no one but himself, rising jerkily to his feet and stretching this way and that. "I'm stiff as a post!"

"Indeed," Shelley agreed, yawning and shifting a bit where he and Mary had passed out on the sofa. "It does seem that we all succumbed to fatigue at once, does it not?"

"Well, it was a frightful storm," Mary offered beside him, adjusting her posture and discreetly tugging at her dress to make sure it was still more or less situated. "Plus all the stories we told—we were all wrung out, by the end. It's little wonder we all fell asleep down here!"

Claire bounded to her feet and raced to the nearest set of windows, throwing the curtains wide. "It's stopped!" she shouted, tossing them a beaming smile over her shoulder that was nearly as bright as the sun shining down on them from outside. "The sun is out!"

John frowned at that—not at the change in weather, which he welcomed, but at the note of surprise in her voice. Did they not remember when the storm had broken? But it soon became evident that they did not. Nor was that the only element of last night's activities that his friends had forgotten.

"I must say again, Mary," Byron offered now that he had finished his calisthenics, "that story of yours was truly excellent." He leaned over and clapped John on the shoulder. "Shame about yours, old chap, but don't tear yourself up over it—Shelley couldn't come up with a complete one either."

Judging by the way the others added their condolences, John realized that none of them remembered his story. That made sense, in a way—it had been so intrinsically tied to the spirit binding them here, and with the spirit now forced back into the depths of the house and into stillness and slumber, evidently all traces of his story had gone with it. Well, if that was the price, so be it. He had wrought the tale for that sole purpose, and was content for it to remain unknown, provided it continued to serve as the chains holding that spirit down, and as the lock that fixed them in place. So he merely smiled, dipped his head, and accepted his friends' comments, doing his best to look mildly disappointed in himself when in fact he was delighted with his previous night's success.

"Don't know about the rest of you," Byron remarked joining Claire at the window, "but I think I've been in this house long enough. I'm of a mind to be out on the water, under the sun and the open sky. Perhaps for several days or more. Shelley, what say you? Care to join me?"

Shelley brightened at the thought of sailing. "This is where Julie was set," he stated, speaking of Rousseau's epistolary love story. "Even the Château de Chillon is not far from here. It would take a few days by boat, but perhaps we might see that?"

"Absolutely," his friend replied. "Let's make a week of it, shall we? I'll have the servants gather some victuals, and we'll set out at once." Belatedly he glanced at the ladies and at John. "All of you are welcome to join us, of course."

But Mary shook her head. "I think I'll repair to the chalet," she answered, "both for some proper rest and for some time with William. I would not want him to feel neglected! But thank you for the invitation. And do be careful," she warned with a special look for Shelley, who had confided the other day that he did not know how to swim.

Claire looked torn, but finally shook her head. "I don't think

I can stand to be night and day on the water," she explained. "And I'm not feeling all the well, besides. Mary, I'll come back with you instead."

That left John, but he also kindly refused the offer. "I think I'll retire to my room and get some sleep as well," he claimed, but he knew that he would be doing no such thing. Instead he planned to patrol the villa and the grounds, checking for any signs that the spirit might still be active. He would have to be vigilant for the rest of their stay here.

In under an hour Byron and Shelley had set out for the dock and their boat tour, and Mary and Claire had gone with them as far as the chalet. That left John in the house all alone, save for the servants. He did not mind—a little quiet right now would do him good, for he had exhausted himself with his actions of the previous eve. Still, the trick had worked. Even extending his senses to their fullest, he could find no trace of the spirit. It had either been destroyed or forced back down so deep it would most likely never find its way back to the waking world ever again.

Byron and Shelley were gone a full week, and returned sun-burned and happy. They had even been inspired by the trip, for Byron had stayed up late writing a poem he called *"The Prisoner of Chillon"*, and Shelley worked on a philosophical tract he titled Hymn to Intellectual Beauty. Mary was able to rest, to tend to her son, and to make some notes on her story—it seemed she was taking her fiancée's suggestion seriously, and considering enlarging the original into a fuller tale. Claire did not sleep well that week, and was often sick in the mornings, to the point that it became impossible to conceal her condition any longer. She confronted Byron about it, asserting that the child was clearly his, and though displeased with the notion he agreed to help support it once it was born. He did not, however, want anything further to do with Claire herself, feeling that she had trapped him, and after only a few more weeks she and Shelley and Mary departed, heading back to England.

John was sorry to see the trio go, but could hardly fault them. He also felt some relief at their departure, because he had continued to worry that repeated bouts of creativity might awaken the spirit yet again. Now, with only himself and Byron left, that became less likely.

Byron withdrew into himself a bit afterward, and John let him. He had begun to realize that staying so close to the young lord could also serve as a lightning rod for the spirit or any others drawn to energy and passion and creativity and chaos. Thus when Byron declared at the end of September that he was thinking of quitting the villa as well and traveling on to Italy, John stated that he would not be traveling with him.

"What?" Byron looked genuinely shocked at this news. "But, Polly Dolly, why ever not?"

There was no way John could tell him the truth. Instead he claimed, "I'm sorry, this has been a lovely, idyllic interlude, but I fear I must return to reality now. My family has requested my return to London, and it is high time I put into practice the medicine I studied so hard to master."

Though his friend had never worked a day in his life, at least that call of duty was something he could understand and accept. They parted ways amicably, and Byron headed toward Italy—with John secretly trailing behind him. That continued for another week or more, until John was sure his friend was no longer under the spirit's influence in any way. Then he truly did go back to London and open up a private medical practice while he decided what to do with his life next.

It was almost a year before John heard from Byron again, and when he did receive a letter he was surprised and more than a little dismayed by its contents. "I have been dreaming about that story I wrote in Switzerland," the young lord wrote. "There was more to the tale, it seems, and so I have written that part now as well. I enclose it here for your perusal, since you were not only present at its inception but can claim some role in its birth."

With mounting horror John read the pages attached to that note. The story of "The Vampyre" did indeed continue. In them, Aubrey returned to London, reunited with his sister, and then watched as Ruthven appeared, seemingly risen from the dead, seduced the young lady, and obtained her hand in marriage.

Aubrey tried in vain to prevent the match but failed and, over-come, died—and that very night Ruthven killed his sister and drank her blood to prolong his own life, then disappeared.

"No!" John cried, hurling the papers from him. This would undo everything he had wrought! The spirit must have made one final gambit and somehow wormed its way into Byron's mind, then lain dormant, waiting until it felt the danger had passed. Now it had pressed its suit and won his attentions, lur-ing him into changing his story with this new addition. Since the tale still contained traces of the Phoenix's creative force, such an alteration would also receive that might, and could be enough to shatter the spirit's bonds once more. He could not allow that to happen.

Writing quickly back, John begged Byron to reconsider. "Your tale does not require such an end," he wrote, "and in fact that only diminishes its power. It would be far better to pre-serve it in its original form."

Byron refused, however. "That was incomplete," he wrote back. "This is not. And this is far more terrifying, which was the goal you set for us."

"Yes, but to then overcome that terror," John's next letter replied. "Which your original tale did. In this version, the ter-ror is the victor, and leaves none alive who did dare oppose it!"

They continued to write back and forth, but Byron still would not change his mind. John finally accepted that he would have to resort to more desperate measures if he were to once more block the spirit's path to freedom.

Visiting the offices of Byron's publisher, who he had been in contact with before their fateful trip, John presented "The Vampyre"—but as his own creation. Using his gifts he con-vinced the man to publish the story under his name. Doing so bound the tale to the might of the Phoenix, placing it entirely under his control, and thus cut off any access the spirit might have gained to the power therein.

Byron was furious, of course. He threatened to come after John once he heard, but John pointed out that he knew far more damaging things about Byron he could release to the public if pressed. Besides, the story was not up to the young lord's usual standards, and did he really want his name associated with it? In the end, he was able to convince Byron to see things his way, and the nobleman even openly disavowed the piece.

Still, John knew their friendship was now over. What was more, the longer he remained in this guise the more likely the spirit might find some way to overcome the restraints he had placed upon it. In order to seal them once and for all, John William Polidori had to die.

Two years later, on August 24, 1821, he did exactly that. Faking a death by ingestion of prussic acid and bribing the coroner to confirm his end, the man who had been John Polidori slipped away at dusk—once more only the Phoenix, and once more alone. As he drifted away into the London night, he could not help but feel that he had become nothing more than a restless spirit himself, untethered and unseen, wandering this way and that in a desperate attempt to influence the uncaring world around him.

The End

HOLLYWOODLAND
BOOK THREE
DEATH
IN SILENTS

CHAPTER ONE
FADE IN:
INT. HALLWAY – NIGHT
A shadowed door in a shabby but respectable apartment building. It is deepest night, and only a single light in the hall offers any illumination. Two people stand in the partially open doorway, one on either side, facing one another.

"Thank you for a lovely evening," the young lady said, leaning against the door to peer around it, yet keep it between them, almost as a physical manifestation of some guardian to any remaining chastity. "It was wonderful."

"The pleasure was all mine, I assure you," the gentleman replied, hat still held in his hands, head bowed slightly as if in supplication. Then he lifted his gaze to her, and his eyes gleamed mischievously even in the dim light. "Or dare I hope not all?"

She colored prettily and allowed herself a momentary smirk before swatting him on the arm. Her bare hand only just brushed the fine linen of his suit, for he was fully attired, if hastily, casually so, his tie only loosely knotted, his collar button still undone, his hair falling free of its usual slick perfection. As was she, in fact, even to the extent of still having on the light makeup she had applied earlier that day and the simple locket on a chain that was her own jewelry. Only her gloves and shoes and cap were missing, having been set aside upon returning home.

"Oh, behave!" she told him, but softened the reprimand with a smile that bore more than a little sauce. "At least, for now." A noise somewhere in the hall or lobby made her start slightly, and she glanced about, then sighed. "You'd best go, though."

"Are you certain?" he asked, with a slightly predatory gaze upon her lips and what little he could see of her figure. "I could stay, if you liked." Despite the shadows he seemed almost wreathed with light, a beautiful beacon in the dark.

She only laughed at that. "And have Mrs. Bischoff catch you here?" she asked. "Trust me, you'll thank me for keeping you out of her grasp! She'd lay you out flat with a rolling pin, then call the police and have them cart you off! Not exactly the sort of headline you'd want." She smiled fondly at the image, and the thought behind it. "She's very protective of us girls."

"As she should be." He executed a flawless bow, full of liquid grace, and set the hat atop his head, automatically sharpening the brim. "In that case, I depart knowing that you are in good hands. But I hope to see you again. Dare I ask for it to be as soon as tomorrow?"

Her blush was visible despite the gloom. "That would be lovely." Leaning forward, she gave him a brief kiss, just the flutter of her lips on his, before pulling back behind the safety of the door. "Good night."

"Good night." With a smile and a touch of his hand to his lips he turned and strolled down the hall and from thence down the stairs. She watched until he was out of sight, then shut the door and leaned against it with another, deeper sigh.

Such a man! She still could hardly believe it. The whole night had been, well, in a word—magical.

Stepping away from the door, she executed a quick twirl across the room, singing softly to herself, before collapsing giddily backward onto her still neatly made bed, giggling like the girl she very nearly still was. A large stuffed animal, an elephant with comically large ears, perched nearby and she grabbed it up, hugging it to her chest and burying her face in its soft gray fur.

Oh, she was so happy she could die!

She felt a sharp pang then, in her stomach, and paused in her delighted giggles, frowning. That's right, she had only picked at her dinner, convinced that men did not like to see a young lady with a healthy appetite. How foolish! She'd best find something now, or she'd hardly be able to sleep. And she had to get some rest—she had a big day tomorrow!

Rising to her feet, still clutching the elephant to her chest, she glanced toward the small icebox in the corner. She'd brought home the remains of her dinner, of course—one didn't waste good food, especially in this day and age! She could nibble a bit of that and still have enough left for at least tomorrow's lunch. Yes, that made sense.

She'd only managed a few steps before the pain returned. It was stronger now, more emphatic, enough to make her double over. This was no mere hunger pang! Had there been something wrong with the food? But if so, why hadn't it bothered her earlier? Why now, hours later? Regardless, it hurt so much she could barely think straight, but still she staggered toward the corner. Now her objective was not the icebox, however, but the sink beside it. Reaching that, she turned the tap and splashed cold water on her face, then cupped some in her hand and sipped at it. Ah! That felt good going down!

For an instant, she felt some relief. Then the pain returned. With a cry she crumpled to the ground, the elephant falling from her grip to roll several paces away. The pain was intense, worse than anything she'd ever known. And it was no longer just in her stomach, either. The agony had spread, traveling up through her chest. Each breath felt like shards of glass stabbing into her, and her gasps rattled and wavered like that of an old man. What was wrong with her?

She needed help! The phone sat on a small table nearby, beside her one good chair. The room was small, barely ten feet to a side, and the table no more than two feet from her now, yet it felt like miles as she reached out, stretching one arm in an attempt to reach it. Her grasping fingers fell short, however, and the pain intensified, causing her to reflexively curl up, wrapping both arms around her middle in an attempt to make it stop. Please, make it stop!

But it did not stop. Instead it intensified, until she could barely see, her vision clouded and constricted to a narrow cone, her breath wheezing and irregular, sweat breaking out all over her body. Her chest felt hot, then cold, waves of what felt like fever washing over her, and her limbs began to jerk, her back spasming as the agony grew still worse. She tried to call out but her throat had locked up, only a strangled gasp emerging. She could feel the panicked beat of her heart, thumping madly inside her as it struggled to continue against this strange and sudden onslaught.

Then, with one final pounding, it gave up the fight, and ceased its motion.

Her eyes bulged and she tried to scream, clawing at her chest as if she could force her heart back to beating. No sound emerged, and her weakening fingers only slid off her own flesh. She could feel the strength leaving her, and could only watch, horrified, as her hands shriveled before her weakening eyes, her limbs twisting and narrowing, her very skin drying and spotting.

Then that cone of dim light narrowed into a pinprick before disappearing completely, her eyes rolled back, her mouth fell open to allow a single rattling noise to escape between rotting teeth, and she collapsed in a heap, the shadows converging eagerly to devour her as the spark of life fled her defeated flesh.

The stuffed elephant lay nearby, its button eyes turned toward its former owner, and its expression appeared woeful, as if sorry it had been forced to witness such a sad end.

CHAPTER TWO
EXT. FILM SET – DAY
A busy set on the studio lot, midday. People moving
with great purpose, the air filled with chatter and good cheer.

"Hey, Buster!" someone called, and one of the men sitting among the crowd of cast and crew glanced up. "Give me a hand?"

"Sure thing." He jumped up at once, ceding the overturned crate he'd been using as a stool to someone else as he hurried over, for Buster Gallagher was nothing if not helpful. And why not? His own role as "second stunt double" wasn't exactly demanding—he was basically here in case George wasn't up to handling a particular stunt for some reason, or if the director decided to try it with each of them and see which looked better on film. That was fine, though. He was happy just to be on set, drinking it all in.

It was wonderful! Even after several years he still marveled at the magic of the movie industry. Such an amazing thing, being able to capture not only your likeness but your very motion, your expressions and actions, on screen! And then to be able to play that back, not just once but as many times as desired, and to duplicate it so that it could be played in many places all at once! Why, it was like the theater all over again, only now you could perform for thousands of people all around the country, and continue to do so over and over again! Truly amazing!

Of course, in the theater you'd had a voice—indeed, it could be said that the voice had been the most important part of a play. They had not yet reached that stage here, sadly. Attaching sound to a film was proving difficult, something to do with recording both and then connecting them together correctly so when you spoke your words matched your lips? He was not entirely sure. They would figure it out some day, he was sure of that. Humanity was nothing if not inventive.

But in the meantime, oh, the cleverness! The film itself might be silent but the viewing experience was anything but! There was an orchestra to play music, setting the mood by swelling dramatically or trilling happily or pounding dreadfully. There were sound effects. And then there were the title cards! Dialogue or explanation, displayed on the screen for all to see, no danger of being misheard or garbled or overlooked, not even an interruption to the story but part and parcel of it, built into the very narrative flow! It was astounding!

His fingers itched to take up the pen again, as he had when he was Marlowe, and again briefly when he was Polidori. But he still did not fully understand the wax and wane of this bur-geoning new medium. Its process was still more intuition than sense, at least to him, and he had not yet grasped its pulse and taken that rhythm and flow into himself. Until he did, he would not attempt to write for it.

Instead he immersed himself in the craft itself, learning all he could about how movies were made. That was why he had cast himself—in more ways than one!—as "Buster Gallagher," crew member, stunt double, and even aspiring actor. It meant that he could be here on the set, taking everything in, being right in the thick of things, feeling the excitement of the movie process washing over him. Last year he had managed to get on film himself for the first time, doing stunts on a movie called *Ben-Hur: A Tale of the Christ*, and he had loved it so much he had jumped at the chance to be in this production when it started. It was so exhilarating! He had not felt this alive in over a century!

So for now the immortal Phoenix, avatar of humanity's cre-ativity, was content to haul furniture and fetch water and hold lights. Whatever was required.

By the time he got back to the side where the others were still sitting and talking, something had changed. He noticed it at once—there was a sudden electricity among the group, far more than from just the thrill of making a movie. This new energy was darker, more savage. Something had happened—something bad.

It did not take him long to find out what. "Did you hear?" One of the girls, Maud, asked, turning to him as he sat and placing a hand on his arm. Maud was like that—she was a dancer, employed mainly in background scenes, and very given to physical contact. Which, given her lithe form and pretty face, was not at all unwelcome. Now, however, her touch seemed more a demand for comfort and reassurance than a flirtation, and her eyes were awash with tears. "Oh, it's just awful!"

He wrapped an arm around her, pulling her close for support, and peering over her dark curls at the others. "What's wrong? What happened?"

"It's Lucy," one of the other men, Tom, managed to say through a throat roughened with grief. "She's dead."

"What?" Lucy Wyman was another member of the cast, a sweet girl desperate to shed her Iowa farmgirl roots and appear worldly and sophisticated, despite her wholesome good looks and friendly nature being two of her best features. She had not shown up for work this morning and they had all been surprised and a little worried, because in addition to being ambitious Lucy was conscientious and never missed a call time. Now they knew why. "What happened?"

Tom shook his head, unable to go on, but Carl picked up the narrative. "Nobody knows, exactly," his fellow stuntman—Carl was actually getting billed as "riding double," a pretty sweet credit, to be sure---explained, his face taut with sorrow and suspicion. "All the cops are saying is she was found dead in her room, and it looked like she'd wasted away from some kind of illness."

"Which makes no sense!" Another dancer, Nina, burst out. "We just saw her yesterday! She was the picture of health!"

"Yeah," Maud nodded against his chest. "She was practically glowing, she was so happy!"

"Happy?" Buster hadn't seen Lucy much yesterday himself—he'd actually been called to do some shooting, a rare but welcome event, and had spent the day filming a scene where he'd had to leap over something and duck a blow from someone. "Happy about what?"

Most of the others glanced away, unwilling to divulge secrets. It was a funny little community, he'd found—eager for gossip about those around them but highly protective of their own, always quick to defend a friend and surprisingly reticent to tear down a rival from within the group but vicious at ripping into anyone outside their circle.

Still, this was still within the confines of their peculiar brand of keeping confidences, and Lucy was not around to complain about the breach, so eventually Nina mumbled, "she had a date."

"A date?" That shouldn't have been a surprise—Lucy had been lovely and sweet and most of the men on set had shown interest in her far beyond the professional. But she'd always been very careful not to accept any advances, determined to improve her career through talent alone and to focus on work and friendships rather than romance. "I'll look for love after I'm a star," she would say whenever anyone asked her out, which was often. "Until then, it'll have to wait."

Which meant she had broken her own rule last night. But why? And with whom?

"Who was this date with?" he asked, and Nina started to reply—then glanced up, startled, as a shadow fell across them all, and her mouth clamped shut faster than an eye blink.

Buster turned to see who had caused such a protective hush to fall over their circle and found himself frowning up at a trim man in a fine suit. The face was well familiar, of course, and not just because its handsome, slightly dark features had graced movie posters for the past several years. No, he knew the man well because it was the very actor he had been hired to double for on occasions like yesterday.

After all, Rudolph Valentino could hardly be expected to risk his own life and limb—and face—ducking punches!

"Is everyone well here?" Valentino asked, his words as always tinged with the accent from his native Italy. He was sharply dressed and impeccably coiffed, as always, but there was something about the cast of his eyes and the set of his mouth that made Buster think the famed movie star was unsettled about something.

"Did you hear about Lucy?" Tom replied in what sounded suspiciously like an accusation. "She's dead!"

The leading actor hung his head. "Yes, I did hear," he replied heavily, shaking his head. "Such a tragedy. She was a lovely young woman, and had such promise."

"The police are looking into it," Nina declared, glaring at Valentino—which was odd, because every woman Buster had ever seen gazed longingly at the handsome actor instead. "They say she was ravaged by disease. Did you seem okay to you, last time you saw her?"

The leading man started a little at that, though it was hard to tell if that was from the question itself or from the naked hostility around it. "Yes, of course, she seemed fine," he stammered. "The very picture of health." He frowned. "If you will excuse me." And, with a slight bow, he turned on his heel and walked away, moving more quickly than was his usual wont.

Buster followed the man's retreat with his eyes, then cut back to his friends. They were all glowering in Valentino's direction, and their glares confirmed what their words had already suggested to him.

It had been none other than Valentino himself that Lucy had gone out with last night.

In a way, that made sense. The man was a renowned womanizer, using his looks and charms to woo many an eligible young lady—and more than a few who would not normally have been available, if the rumors were true. She would have had a hard time resisting him, even with her determination not to let dalliances distract her.

Of course, rumor was that Valentino was seeing Pola Negri, herself a star of the silent film. Some even said they were engaged. Still, he hardly seemed the type of man to let a little something like impending wedding vows stop him from courting other women—supposedly he'd continued to see and sleep with other women all throughout both of his two previous marriages. Which might be the very reason they failed!

Plus, Valentino was the star of the picture they were all

working on, *Son of the Sheik*—itself a sequel to one of his previous successes. If he had taken an interest in Lucy, he had the influence to advance her career by leaps and bounds.

Provided she was willing to make him happy enough to want to help her.

But had she? Lucy had been strong-willed and determined. Would she really have set aside her resolutions, even for a man such as that?

Perhaps—or perhaps she had not been willing to go as far as the famous Latin Lover had wanted, and he had somehow forced the issue.

With lethal results.

Buster knew that he would not be able to rest until he had determined exactly what had happened to Lucy—and who was responsible. And then, well, the Phoenix was not above finding a little justice for a fallen friend.

CHAPTER THREE
EXT. STUDIO ENTRANCE – NIGHT

That night, when a handsome figure in a well-tailored suit emerged from the studio lot, he had a shadow behind him that was not his own.

Buster watched as Valentino crossed the street. The famous actor looked nonchalant, relaxed, completely unaffected by the recent death of one of his fellow cast members. Could the man truly be so cold as to not feel anything for poor Lucy? That only hardened Buster's suspicions about the leading man. And made him more curious about where he might be going now.

But as he watched, the subject of his scrutiny slipped into a sleek convertible that was parked on the other side of the street. Damn and blast—of course the man had his own automobile! He was known for liking fast cars almost as much as fast women! Buster, meanwhile, had never managed to retain much money despite his many centuries of life—somehow there were always more important things to consider than wealth and belongings—and so he did not own any sort of vehicle himself, usually being content to walk or take the bus. Now, however, he stood in impotent frustration as Valentino peeled away from the curb, narrowly missing another car in the lane, and then accelerated away.

He did not see, behind him, how the very shadows writhed and fled, expelled from the region by a momentary flare to the light, as if someone had lit a small bonfire there at studio front. But Buster had had many years to practice self-control, and that brilliance quickly diminished, leaving any who had seen it to wonder if they had simply imagined the effect.

Still, he would have to take steps to make sure he was not so easily lost a second time.

A few nights later, when work was called to a stop for the day, Buster was quick to make his goodbyes. His friends were all surprised, for normally the stuntman was good for a cheap meal and a few rounds of drinks with them, and typically seemed to have nor want nothing better than to sit and talk and laugh together. He had been different since Lucy's death, though— more withdrawn, more somber—and they all chalked his strange behavior up to that, as they were indeed all still feeling that same pall of grief over their friend.

Buster said his farewells, promising to spend more time with everyone next evening, and hurried away. He rushed across the street, heading straight for the shiny new vehicle that was Valentino's—but then swerved to the right and moved several cars down, finally stopping at a battered old pickup truck. It was dingy and rusted in places, held together by tape and baling wire in others, but it was the only vehicle he had been able to afford. The important thing was that it did in fact run. He had to yank hard to wrench the door open but finally managed it and slid inside, ignoring the lumps in the seat cushion as he inserted the key and started the engine. It took a few tries for the old machine to catch, but eventually it coughed to life and he sat, hands taut on the wheel, staring straight ahead. Waiting.

Only a handful more minutes passed, his truck belching out dark, greasy smoke, before Buster caught movement from the corner of his eye. There! Valentino was sauntering out again, looking like he had not a care in the world. He crossed the street almost without looking at the cars whizzing by, trusting them to stop for him instead of the other way around. His laid-back demeanor was at complete odds with the way he raced the engine once he was in his car, or how he pulled out quickly in order to speed away.

But this time Buster was ready for him. He had started easing out into traffic when the star had still been opening the door, and as a result wound up right behind the convertible as it edged into the road. Got you, he thought exultantly, and had to tamp down his enthusiasm when the steering wheel started to smoke slightly in his grip.

CUT TO:
EXT. STREET – NIGHT
A quiet residential street

Following Valentino proved to still be difficult, even with an automobile of his own. First, the famous actor was a daredevil behind the wheel, speeding recklessly, taking turns sharply and at the last minute, fearlessly threading through the other cars on the road. Second, although the Phoenix had lived many lifetimes and was a being of nearly incomparable power, this was only the third or fourth time he had actually attempted to drive, and the first time it had involved more than a leisurely jaunt down a country lane or, the other day, the tense navigating of streets from the lot where he'd bought this ailing beast to a space he could park near the boarding house where he had a room.

Everything was so different when you did not have solid ground beneath your own two feet, when you were separated from the world by a steel box! He felt like a caged bird, his wings pinned, his fire banked, and it was all he could do not to burst into flame and ignite the entire damnable contraption! Only through sheer force of will, driven by the need to discover the truth behind and then avenge poor Lucy's death, did he manage to restrain himself and keep driving.

But what a drive! He had not felt such terror, such personal fear, since the Black Death had haunted the streets of London! All his reflexes and daring were being tested here to keep the Latin Lover in sight, and if not for the fact that Valentino's car was easily spotted he would have lost the man several times.

It was with a heavy sigh of relief that Buster finally saw the other car slow and then pull to a stop. They were on a quiet little side street filled with old, stately residences, most of which looked as if they'd been converted into boarding houses of one sort or another. Valentino parked and hopped out while his

engine was still cooling down, straightening his suit and resetting his hat before strolling down the avenue toward a particular building.

There were no other parking spots nearby, and Buster was
forced to drive past. He did so slowly—fortunately there was no
other traffic along this street!—and kept glancing at his mirror
as he did. He was able to ascertain that the actor did indeed go
to the door of that house, and rang the bell. Then he'd reached
the end of the block and was forced to circle around it.

By the time he'd returned to the scene, Buster saw that
Valentino was back at his car. The handsome actor was no longer alone, however. He had a young lady on his arm, and after
a moment Buster knew her, though she was not on *Son of the
Sheik*. But he recognized those curls, and the smile she bestowed
upon her companion—it was Winona Wilkes! He had seen her
a year or two before in that Western film, *Sell 'em Cowboy!* She
had been striking enough to make an impression, and he'd been
surprised not to see her in anything since, but had heard she
had moved behind the camera and was writing now instead.

That struck him as interesting, and he pondered what that
might mean here, if anything, while he slowed to a crawl, giving
the Latin Lover time to hand his current partner into her seat
and then step swiftly around to take his own before gunning
the car and leaping out into the street, nearly colliding with
Buster's truck. Fortunately Valentino did not even spare him a
glance before pulling out ahead—Winona did, twisting about
with a shocked look, but relaxed once she saw that vehicle and
driver were unharmed. She was laughing as they sped away.

Buster followed as the pair wended their way out of the
residential neighborhood and down to a busier section of Los
Angeles, one filled with all manner of shops and restaurants.
He was not terribly surprised when they pulled up in front of
Musso & Frank's, though he would have thought Valentino to
be more of a Café Montmartre sort, where you went to see and
be seen. Musso & Frank's was still a fine establishment—heck,
he couldn't afford to eat there except maybe once a month!—
but it was a good deal quieter and frequented more by successful businessmen than by movie stars.

Still, just the type of place you might take a date if you did not wish to be seen or recognized.

Since he could hardly afford to order there, and didn't know how long they might be, Buster found a parking space within sight of the restaurant and just sat in his truck, watching and waiting. He wondered again, though, at how Valentino could be so relaxed, so cavalier, so charming with Winona, when Lucy was barely cold in the grave. Before this, he would have described the leading man as surprisingly down to earth, almost humble, and always friendly to everyone, from the water boy to his leading lady. The man had always taken the time to stop and check in with the rest of the cast and crew, and would chat with them as if he were no different from anyone, talking about weather and cars and sports and food and whatever else came to mind. Buster had always admired that about him, and had thought the man a good sort, likeable and talented without being arrogant about it.

Now, however, he was beginning to revise his initial assessment. Had it all been an act? Especially if the rumors were true and Valentino really had taken Lucy out, howe could he not be broken up over her death?

Unless he was the one who had killed her.

It would not be the first time the Phoenix had seen someone who presented one face while secretly possessing another. He thought of the lovely Lorelei and shuddered. No, he knew only too well how fair could mask foul from view.

He was still musing this and other past encounters when he saw the couple in question emerge. It seemed several hours had passed during his reverie, judging by the night sky now in full evidence above, and he was forced to squint in order to see Valentino help her into the car once it was brought round by the valet. Time to go, then. It was a relief to switch on the headlights—or headlight, as the truck's right front light barely flickered and was too weak to shed any real light on his surroundings—and steer back into traffic after the convertible once again leaped away.

The return journey did not seem nearly as long, though that might have just been guessing the intended destination, and

Buster found a spot right on the corner from which he could watch Valentino escorting Winona back to her room. Now came the question, however. Did he abandon the truck and try to get closer? Did he trust the Latin Lover alone with the lovely young lady, especially after recent events? Or did he stay here for when the star returned to his car, in order to follow him to wherever he went next?

The internal debate became even more urgent when the Latin Lover re-emerged only a short time later. Odd, that. From everything he had heard, Buster would have expected the couple to be . . . occupied for hours, at the least! Had Winona managed somehow to stand firm against the star's charms? Certainly Valentino did not look as pleased, from this vantage point, as he had when he had parked the car, and he kept glancing back toward the residence, a frown visible on his face even from a distance. So he was not completely irresistible, then! Good for Winona!

That brought Lucy back to mind, however. Surely she had also held to her virtue? Was that why she had died? If Valentino had killed her, was it because of that? If that was the case, had Winona now become a victim as well?

Buster watched, face furrowed into almost a grimace, as the movie star hopped into his car and started the convertible up again. What to do? If he went to check on Winona he would lose Valentino, without question. But what if he allowed himself to be led away and it later turned out she had needed his help? He was torn.

The convertible roared out onto the street and Buster was forced to make a decision. He pulled out after it, glad he had never shut off the truck's engine for fear it might not start again when needed. He would follow Valentino for now. Then, once he knew the star was settled for the night, he could come back and check on Winona. This way, if the man were still out in search of a victim, he could be on hand to put a stop to that right away.

They drove for some time, Valentino continuing to weave in and out of traffic and Buster following from a distance, content merely to have the convertible in his sights. They were leaving the more heavily populated areas, heading slowly toward the city's outskirts, where palatial mansions dominated, and Buster began to suspect where they were going. His guess solidified as they made their way around Benedict Canyon, and confirmed when the convertible pulled into a long, winding private drive. That confirmed the star's destination even before they reached the top of the hill, where a set of tall iron gates barred further entry. Buster, who had paused back down the drive a ways to remain out of sight, pounded a hand against his steering wheel. So Valentino was returning home after all, to Falcon Lair, the sprawling estate he had purchased last year and named after his ill-fated film *The Hooded Falcon*. Well, at least now he knew for certain!

As soon as the gates had shut again behind the convertible, sealing the actor in for the night, Buster turned his truck around and started to retrace his steps. Now that he knew Valentino was in for the night, he could check on Winona and make sure she was all right.

Of course, how to go about that was still a question. They had only met once, in passing, at a party. He doubted she would remember him. So how to explain suddenly showing up on her doorstep, especially the same night she had gone out with the man whose film he was currently in?

Buster was still testing out possible scenarios as he pulled up in front of her boarding house. It was then that he realized there was a second problem: it was most likely after hours, and if this was anything like most residences, the matron would have locked the doors and would not be allowing anyone else in, especially not unattached young men! So how was he going to make sure Winona was okay?

With a sigh and a shake of his head, he stepped out of the truck and trudged toward the house, stopping under a tree just out of sight of the front door. After all these years, he still sometimes forgot that he did not have the same limits as the men he pretended to be!

There was an ornamental fence separating the property from the sidewalk, stone below and wrought iron above, with bushes planted just beyond. Gathering himself, the Phoenix flowed from the tree's shadows and across the walk, then up and over fence and bush both, in a single liquid motion, like fire seeking the path of least resistance. He turned his senses toward the large, stately brick building now before him, seeking the aura that had been visible around Winona when he had seen her earlier, young and lively and full of energy and creativity. He found it after a moment, there on the fourth floor—but something was wrong! It was flickering like his broken headlight, fluttering like a caged moth, and weakening by the second!

With a silent roar, he leaped forward and then pushed off from the ground, letting his anger and concern propel him upward. The ground fell away, the wind ruffling his hair and tugging at his collar as he soared across the remaining distance, pushing back just before he reached the building so that his collision with the wall outside Winona's room produced only a muffled thump. There was a window just to his right, and he shifted position, fingers clinging to the ornamental stonework above the floor and shoe tips perched on a similar lip just below, so that he could peer in.

What he saw nearly froze even his fiery blood.

Winona Wilkes, actress and now writer, was sprawled on the floor. Her mouth was open and her eyes wide, her face drawn in a look of shock and sheer horror, every line drawn in agony.

And there were many lines.

Though he had only seen her earlier tonight from a distance, Buster had seen the same lovely young woman he had noticed on screen and then at a party. Before him now, however, was a wizened old crone, a woman who had led a long, hard life which had wrung every ounce of vitality from her withered flesh and twisted limbs.

She was dead, without a question. And there had been nothing natural about it.

With a sigh that was more like a rumble of thunder, the Phoenix allowed himself to fall backward, letting the air carry him back away from the house and return him to the ground just beneath the tree where he had started. There was little sense in bursting into the room or even trying to gain entry, as nothing could be done for poor Winona now.

Nothing except to add her name beside Lucy's in his head, as someone who had been torn from life far too soon.

Someone whose untimely and unnatural death required vengeance.

Making his way back to his truck, Buster vowed that both girls would have it.

CHAPTER FOUR

EXT. FILM SET – DAY

The next morning, on the set of Son of the Sheik

It was a somber group among the crates and stools the next morning.

"Poor Winona!" Nina exclaimed, clinging to Tom for support, a gesture he willingly if somewhat absently returned. "She was a real sweetheart!"

Several of the others nodded. Even though the lady in question had not been on this picture with them, the industry was still small enough that many people knew each other. Buster had always heard, and seen from the outside, how that was true of those at the top of the profession—how Greta Garbo might wind up chatting with Harry Houdini or Charlie Chaplin, despite their being on different pictures at different lots for different studios. He hadn't known, however, until he was one himself just how much the less illustrious members of cast and crew mingled, but it was certainly so—wander over to one of the nearby diners and you could wind up sharing stories with actors from RKO, dancers from Columbia, set designers from Warner.

And there was no rivalry about it, either. At their level, there didn't need to be. There was plenty of work to go around, so much so that people often started a conversation with, "Hey, how's life treating you, need some work?"

Nor was it a competition to get your name up in lights or get top billing. These were people who showed up in the credits in a group, as "Dancers" or "Harem Girls" or "Cowboys" or "Mobsters," if they made it onto the screen at all. It was more important to make sure the picture had everyone it needed to be a success than it was to try and one-up someone else for a slightly higher spot in the credits of a buck more in your pocket.

Besides which, people often switched studios, or worked for several at once—the big-name stars were usually signed to exclusive contracts but for bit parts and background characters or for crew you didn't get paid enough to agree to such conditions, so you picked up work wherever you could, which also meant you tried to stay friends with everyone you could, in case they knew of a job you could fill.

Thus, everyone there knew Winona, at least well enough to have picked her out of a crowd and to have had coffee with her.

Besides which, her death, coming so soon after Lucy's, was hitting doubly hard.

"What does it mean?" Carl asked, pounding his fist against the crate he perched on. "First Lucy, now Winona? Neither of 'em a day over twenty-five! Is it some kind of bug or something?"

Footsteps clattered on the pavement just behind them, and Buster straightened. "Yeah, I'd say it was a bug, all right," he growled, twisting about to glare at the man who had stepped up to the circle but still stood outside it, his pristine suit at odds with their more worn-in attire. "What do you think, Mister Valentino?" He practically hurled the words at their leading man.

Valentino's high, clear brow creased. "What do I think about what?" he asked. His hat remained perched on his head, which was fair since they were outdoors and the mid-morning sun was beating down on them, but still rankled Buster, as if the man were showing bad manners by not baring himself. This despite the fact that all the other men there still wore their hats, and several of the women as well.

"About Winona's death." Buster turned still further, so he could glare at the movie star. "Awfully peculiar, isn't it? Her being so young and all."

The other man did not bother to hide his wince. "Yes, it is indeed," he agreed slowly. "And horribly sad, as well. She was a bright light, snuffed out far too soon." Now he did remove his hat, holding it to his chest for a second, head bowed as if in prayer, before resettling it.

But Buster wasn't fooled. Nor was he willing to let the matter go. "None of us had seen her in some time," he continued. "Had you?"

That brought the Latin Lover's head up in a hurry, and his sharp, dark gaze fixed upon Buster. "Why do you ask?" he inquired, but his words were as pointed as his stare.

"Wondering who saw her last," Buster replied. "I'm sure the police will want to speak to whoever that was."

"I heard she died of some sort of illness," Valentino snapped. "That can hardly be a matter for the police."

"Appearances can be deceiving, though, can't they?" Buster rose to his feet, turning to face the actor squarely. They were of a height, part of the reason he'd been cast as his stunt double, and had a similar, wiry build, but of course Valentino was dark, almost swarthy, while Buster could feel himself practically glowing as his rage built up, stoking the fires within. "You'd know all about that, right?" he demanded, letting the accusation hang a moment before adding, "what with being a famous actor and all."

"Yes, I suppose that's true," the leading man retorted, stepping in closer until their faces were mere inches apart, his skin flushing slightly, though whether from anger, embarrassment, or just proximity to the Phoenix's flame, Buster could not say. "Things are certainly not always what they seem—for better or for worse." He glanced away, his shoulders slumping a little, and a small, sad smile touched his lips. "In this case, however, I believe it to be true. Miss Wilkes died before her time, certainly, but at no one's hand. Not even her own." That last was set with some asperity, and not without reason, for suicide was all too common among the Hollywood set, though rarely for one so young. Still, his sorrow over her death and his concern for her reputation seemed almost genuine, and the Phoenix felt a prick of doubt. Could he have been wrong about the man?

Yet there was no doubt as to what he had seen last night. Valentino had been out to dinner with her, had walked her home, had escorted her to her room, and had then left—and Winona had been dead a short while later, inside that room, after hours, when no one else but another boarder or the matron could have been to see her.

He also did not miss the fact that the actor had evaded his original question. "So you're saying you hadn't seen her recently?" he asked again, more pointedly, and the others all stiffened, glancing at their star with the first glimmers of suspicion in their eyes.

Caught out like that, Valentino could no longer dissemble. "I did see her recently, in fact," he answered at last, each word emerging from his lips as if dragged out. "She had retired from the screen, you know—which I felt was a great loss—and had turned to writing, and wanted me to consider a script she was working on. We met to discuss it, and it held some promise—I told her to let me know when it was done." He shook his head. "That was the last time I saw her, though. I suppose we will never see that film now."

"What was it called?" Buster demanded, not willing to let the actor off the hook so easily. The question burst forth with such vehemence that Valentino started back slightly.

"It was—it was called *The Boarder*," he said after a moment. "It was about a young man who takes a room with an older couple and falls for their daughter. But she can't leave her ailing parents, she's the one taking care of them, and won't consider her own happiness as long as they need her." It was a plausible story. It was also one that had been told a hundred times before, in various ways and often with an added element, such as the boarder being suspected of a recent spate of killings or the couple hiding some dark secret.

Still—"Hardly your usual fare," Buster noted. "No action at all? No racing horses across the dunes or leaping from balconies or swinging swords? A quiet man in a quiet house? Are you turning to dramas now? And only one young lady to woo— people will think you're losing your touch."

Valentino bristled at his tone, which was only fair, for it had been said with a sneer. "I am losing nothing!" he replied hotly. "I am the great Rudolph Valentino! The Latin Lover, adored by women everywhere, envied by men! I am the great romancer, the dashing hero, the suave villain! Not some mild milquetoast in a cardigan, sitting on the front stoop!"

"So, not really the role for you, then?" Buster asked. "Funny she would have thought it was, or that you'd agree to even consider it."

"Ah." That rebuke brought the actor back to himself, and back to the context of their conversation. "Yes. Well. I met her as a favor, you understand. One actor to another. And I said I would look at it when it was done—I never said I would agree to be in it."

The trap was sprung, and the Phoenix pounced, going for the throat. "Then I guess it turned out well for you, eh, that she won't be around to finish it!" Nina and Maud and some of the others gasped at his effrontery, his audacity—to accuse the great Valentino of such a thing, even obliquely! But Buster ignored them. His eyes were fixed on the man before him, trying to discern the actor's reaction to his words, to his implied condemnation.

There! Valentino's gaze darkened, brow lowering, lips flattening into a thin line. He was angry! Furious, in fact. But there was more to it than that. The tautness of his cheeks, the quiver of his jaw, the fire in his eyes—was that fear? Fear at being caught out in the lie, or perhaps in something far worse?

"I do not need to stand here and be insulted like this!" the movie star declared. With one final glower, Valentino turned on his heel and marched away. Buster thought at first he would simply go back to the small bungalow that had been set aside for him whenever he was not on set, but the man stormed right past that, past actors and set dressers and dancers—right past the director, who turned and called after him to no effect. In a moment the great actor had disappeared from view, and Buster suddenly realized he had gone too far. He had driven Valentino clean off the set!

Grabbing his jacket from where it still sat atop the crate, he raced after the other man, dodging people and furniture and equipment. That had been stupid of him, he cursed himself as he hurried, trying to still look casual if at all possible. He'd been angry, yes, and had wanted to see how Valentino would react upon finding out someone knew. But now he was leaving the set, leaving the lot, and if he made it to his car before Buster could reach his truck he could disappear, go who knows where. What if he went after yet another young woman? There'd be no one to know, no one to see, no one to stop him. And it would be Buster's fault!

He was nearly at the front gates now. But Valentino was already beyond them, already crossing the street—and his convertible was once again parked almost directly across from the studio entrance, for quick and easy access. Abandoning any attempt at stealth or subtlety, Buster burst into a full-out run. His truck was a bit farther down but he nearly flew across the street, key already in hand, and yanked the door open so hard he almost took it off its hinges. He was in the seat and turning the engine over a second later, stomping on the gas—

—and the truck stuttered, gasped, wheezed, coughed—and died.

No! Buster pounded on the steering wheel and then leaned back, forcing himself to calm down. Flooding the engine wouldn't help him any. Right now he needed to be careful, gentle, even slow. He turned the key again, praying for a miracle—

—and this time the engine caught and held. Yes!

With the truck finally rumbling to life, he looked up again—and, through the grimy, scratched windshield, caught a glimpse of a dark, sleek shape disappearing around the corner. Valentino's convertible.

He was too late. The man was gone. And he had absolutely no idea how to even start looking for him, in this city of thousands and more.

Buster slammed his hand against the wheel again, then slumped forward, resting his forehead upon it instead.

Once again, he had let his temper get the best of him—and with potentially disastrous results.

CHAPTER FIVE
EXT. FILM SET – DAY
Early morning, on the studio lot

Buster arrived the next morning to find more bad news waiting for him. This time, it came in the form of Nina, who was weeping unconsolably in Tom's arms. For once, Buster's fellow actor did not look pleased at the little dancer's attentions, but patted her back awkwardly, like a lifelong bachelor who had just been handed a screaming baby and was afraid to so much as move.

"What's happened?" Buster demanded as he stepped into the circle, and his friends all turned to glance his way—all except Nina, whose face was still buried in Tom's shoulder. None of them seemed willing to answer at first, with Maud shaking her head and looking almost as distraught as her friend, but at last Carl spoke up.

"Another girl dead," he stated gruffly, like being callous about it would make it hurt less. "Maria Rittali this time."

"Maria Rittali?" Buster wracked his brain, trying to put a face to a name. He had only vague impressions: long, straight blonde hair, fine as corn-silk; bright blue eyes; a quick smile, and even quicker feet. "The dancer?"

That brought a fresh bout of weeping from Nina, and Maud had to turn away, her own shoulders heaving. Yes, the dancer, he remembered now; and, she had worked with both Nina and Maud before. Not on this film, though—she had been off doing background on another piece, a romance, he thought, when the directors had been casting for *Son of the Sheik*. Otherwise he had no doubt she would have been sitting here alongside the rest of them, laughing and telling jokes and stories to pass the time.

Until last night, evidently. "What happened?" he asked again, though his question had more specificity to it this time.

Carl continued in his self-appointed role as conveyor of information, though he had precious little to offer. "Don't know," came the reply. "Just that she turned up dead this morning. Landlady found her. Sick, they think. Though she was fine last week—we ran into her at the cafeteria." United Artists had a cafeteria on the lot, as did most of the major studios—it was easier to provide food to the cast and crew than to wait on their finding food for themselves. Anyone working on a UA picture could wander in there during meal times and get a decent meal for a decent price, less than it would typically cost elsewhere. It was also a great place to catch up with friends you'd made on one film when you wound up working on different ones for the same studio later.

Buster scowled and had to glance aside when he saw a spark of fear in the other stuntman's eyes. He had to rein in his temper, he knew. It was starting to show again, and normal folk did not fare well with a glimpse of the Phoenix's flames. But he could guess what "sick" meant in Maria's case—drained of life and vitality, just like Winona had been. Just like Lucy probably had been as well. That made three girls in under a week.

The burning question was, had Maria been out to dinner with a certain suave movie star last night?

He intended to find out.

But the day's shooting ended early—because without the film's star there were only a few incidental shots that could be done, and Valentino never showed. Hiding? Buster wondered as he sat off to the side with the others, grumbling and lamenting. Too afraid to show his face? Maybe because of their confrontation the other day—he had to know that Buster was on to him now. But if so, wouldn't the smart thing have been to lay low for a few days, rather than killing again? Or had he done that to sate his unholy appetites for a few days, like a man gorging himself before fasting?

Regardless, since he was too cowardly to show himself,

Buster couldn't confront him. Which meant he'd have to find out the truth about Maria some other way.

"Go home, everyone!" George Fitzmaurice, their director declared. "Get some rest! We'll hope the Sheik deigns to grace us with his presence on the morrow, so be here bright and early, just in case!" And with that the man threw up his hands in disgust and stomped away.

Normally, being released early would have been a cause for celebration, but it was abundantly clear that no one in the group was in the mood to be merry right now. Tom led Nina away, announcing that he would see her safely home, and Carl took charge of Maud, who kept glancing back at Buster as if hoping he would choose to escort her instead. But Buster had other things on his mind. He watched his friends go, sitting and stewing until the rest of the set was completely empty— and then he rose to his feet, his banked fires flaring with purpose.

Right. Time to see what he could find out.

His first stop was only a few dozen paces away, just to the side of their sets—the small cabin used by Valentino himself. The door was locked but that was hardly a problem. Buster applied a little added pressure to the knob as he twisted, and the cheap lock broke with a muffled snap. Ah! Pushing it open and slipping quickly inside, he shut the door again behind him and glanced around, the only light filtering in through the half-drawn curtains but still enough for his eyes to make out details.

It was a small space, a single room with a tiny attached bathroom, just enough for a star to have some privacy, eat without being hounded, read over new lines, touch up makeup, maybe take a quick nap. There was a sofa against one wall and Buster had no doubt it pulled out into a bed. A small table sat opposite, with a pair of chairs, and a small closet stood beside the bathroom, big enough to store a few changes of clothing. That was it.

Valentino had not bothered to add many personal touches, either. There was a cap hanging from a hook on the back of the door, a muffler draped below it. A coffee cup sat empty on the little table, alongside a few pages of the script. In the closet he did find some clothes, a suit and an extra shirt and tie. The bathroom held a toothbrush and toothpaste, and a small bottle of expensive cologne beside a jar of hair oil and a comb. That was all. There was nothing in here to link Valentino to the murders, or to the three women at all—there was nothing in here to indicate a woman had ever even set foot in this space! Buster sighed, kicking the nearer chair aside, but he had not really expected much, in truth. This cabin was only Valentino's for the length of the film, after all. He would hardly keep damning evidence in a place he would be moving out of a few weeks later!

No, to find anything substantial, Buster knew there was only one place to go—Falcon Lair.

With a small growl of frustration he left the tiny cabin, digging in his pocket for his truck key as he went.

CUT TO:
EXT./INT. MANSION – NIGHT – TRACKING
A secluded estate, with a handsome house and extensive grounds

Of course, the problem with Falcon Lair was that Valentino had bought the estate precisely for its privacy, adding a tall concrete wall all around the property to keep his more ardent admirers from disturbing his rest. No doubt there were men guarding the place as well, and the main house was easily visible from anywhere on the grounds, a fact which made it almost impossible to sneak up on its occupants.

Fortunately, the Phoenix was not just some moon-eyed fan.

Parking down the road, he trudged up the hill but turned aside before coming into view if the main house. The star had purchased eight acres in total, most of it given over to untamed land for him to ride his horses, and it was that route that Buster intended to take, coming on the house from the rear where he would be least expected. After glancing around to make sure no one else was about, he drew upon his fire and wreathed himself in its invisible tongues, shaping it into the wings of his birthright. Then the Phoenix took to the air, though only for a moment—just long enough to bound clear over the high wall and land softly, soundlessly, on the grass beyond.

There were indeed several horses about, grazing aimlessly, and a few glanced up at this strange intruder, curiosity clear in their large, gentle eyes. Buster cooed at them, his flames once more banked deep within, and after a second the horses dismissed his presence with a flick of their ears, for he had always had a way with animals. Thus assured that they would not give him away he took off at a swift walk across the grounds, making for the large, handsome two-story Spanish villa perched up ahead.

At one point he heard footsteps somewhere nearby, and ducked behind a nearby tree. The guard wandered past, never seeing Buster there in the shadows, and after a moment he continued on. More trees and bushes ran up to the house from this angle, and so he was able to reach the white stucco walls themselves without being seen. Then it was merely a matter of levering up the nearest window and quickly swinging himself inside, with a grace and agility little Nina might have envied.

Once inside, Buster paused to listen closely. He did not hear anyone, but the house was large enough that it could easily host a dozen people and he might still not know it. Still, he would have to take his chances. He had come this far, he could not back down now. Not without what he came for.

A part of him hoped to encounter Valentino himself, to beard the villain in his own den. At the same time, he still did not have proof that the other man was responsible. Could he really condemn a man on just his suspicions? But could he risk letting him go and possibly dooming another young woman to a grisly death? For that reason, he hoped he did not meet the home's owner—then he would not have to make that difficult decision.

The house itself was a marvel, and despite himself and his focus Buster was impressed. It was large and grand, but more it was the fact that it was filled with veritable treasures—suits of armor, swords of all varieties, paintings and sculptures. Strange trinkets, too, including many he recognized as having some occult significance. And books! So many books! In his long life the Phoenix had visited many of the world's greatest libraries, but still the sight of those tall shelves filled with volume after volume filled him with both delight and awe. And he could tell at a glance that these were no mere window dressing. No, these books looked well-used, loved, even. He had not known that Valentino was much of a reader, and that made him doubt yet again. What else did he not know about the man?

But then he stumbled into a large, airy room that stopped him in his tracks. From the massive table dominating the space and the row of tall-backed, dark wooden chairs surrounding it, this could only be the main dining room. What caught his attention, however, was that the room had evidently been repurposed. For there on the wide expanse of polished wood was not food and drink, plates and glasses, napkins and cutlery, but papers, playbills and script pages and newspaper clippings. Many of them had been drawn upon in pen, and stepping carefully closer Buster saw that there were faces circled as well. Lucy peered up at him from a clipping about the movie she had been in before *Son of the Sheik*. Winona's name was underlined in a script page from *Shoot 'Em Cowboy*. And Maria smiled in the background of a publicity photo from *Cobra*, which had come out last year—and which had featured none other than the Latin Lover himself, smirking in the center of the picture.

That was it, then. Buster straightened, pushing away from the cluttered tabletop. Here he had his proof. Valentino had selected each girl by perusing his vast array of clippings and scripts and photos and other souvenirs from the various films. After he'd chosen a victim he'd stalked them, preyed upon them—and killed them. The "how" was still unclear, but there was enough arcane paraphernalia strewn about the house to show that the movie star was no stranger to the occult. He had clearly found some spell or artifact to do his dirty work, but his was still the will behind it, and thus his was the guilt.

Now all Buster had to do was find the man—and make him pay for his crimes.

Fists clenched, he stalked slowly from the room, not bothering with stealth any longer. If anything, given his current mood he hoped the men hired to guard this den of evil dared to get in his way. Behind him, the pages on the table burst into flame, scorching the lacquered surface as they burned to ash, leaving only charred spaces behind.

CHAPTER SIX

INT. TRUCK – NIGHT – TRAVELING
A truck, cruising down the road. The Phoenix is the sole occupant.
He is driving but distracted and irate.

Two of the men charged with guarding Falcon Lair had indeed confronted Buster as he exited the house via the main door. The men were big and tough—and taken one look at his face, his posture, his hands, and the strange way his shadow writhed behind him, dancing like flame and flaring like a raptor swooping down upon its prey, and quickly backpedaled away. No one else had interfered as he had stalked across the courtyard, past the tinkling Spanish fountain, and pushed upon the wrought iron gates, and he had only barely resisted the impulse to melt those same gates as he passed between them.

The long walk back down the hill gave him time to cool down slightly, and as soon as his thoughts overtook his temper Buster began to curse. Not at Valentino, however. At himself. How could he have been so stupid? Yet again he'd let his temper overwhelm him, and to what end? He'd found those papers, the clippings and photos, and he'd destroyed them. How did that help anyone? Not that the police would have even believed him—especially in this town, where movie stars were like royalty and Valentino was a prince—but still, he could have left everything for them to find!

To make matters worse, when he finally reached his truck he realized he had no idea where to go next. Who was the Latin Lover's next victim? The answer had most likely been in those papers. If he'd taken them, or at least sorted through them, he might have found other names and faces circled. Instead he'd left a pile of ash—and with it, zero chance of stopping the actor from claiming yet another young woman's life.

Furious with himself, Buster hauled open the truck door and threw himself into the seat so forcefully the springs and leather creaked in protest. Where could he go from here? It wasn't like he could check on every pretty young woman in the film industry! There were hundreds of them!

He started the engine and pulled away, heading back toward the center of town just to have a destination. Meanwhile, he thought hard. What did he know for certain? Three women dead, all of them young, all of them pretty, all of them in the movies though not all actresses, and all of them somehow intersecting with Valentino. That still didn't narrow it down much, though—the man had done a dozen or more films, each with a cast of a dozen or so, plus all the rest of the crew. Plus there were always parties and dinners and outings, and he could have picked his victim from any one of those.

He had to be smart about this. Think it through. He was the Phoenix, the embodiment of creativity! Surely he could outsmart some Italian peasant turned dancer turned movie star!

That was something—all three girls had been, if not poor, not well off. Struggling to make ends meet. So heiresses and successful actresses were out.

For that matter, none of the three had been leading ladies, though all could have been some day, if they'd stayed on the path. Talented but young.

And talented in many ways, too. Maria had been a dancer. Winona was a writer. And Lucy—well, she'd had a voice like an angel. She'd started as a backup singer and had then graduated to acting roles.

Of course, that still described a lot of young women. No, he'd still need more to go on.

Was there something in the locations, perhaps? He didn't actually know where Lucy had lived, or Maria, but he had seen Winona's room. Were they all near each other? But so many boarding houses and women's residences were!

The rest of the city came into view around a bend, its lights beginning to shine as darkness fell, and Buster blinked, trying to let his eyes adjust. It always took a second to shift focus and see past the glow in order to make out the details.

He nearly slammed on the brakes in the middle of the street as he straightened and pounded the wheel. That was it!

As the Phoenix, he could make out more than just lights and features. He could see into people's souls, if he chose. He could read their emotions, their feelings, their very lifeforce. It was not a skill he called upon often, for it could leave him drained for a time afterward. Too, he had become more reticient to rely upon power as he had grown older, preferring wit and guile over force. Yet still such tools lay ready and waiting, arrows in his quiver, feathered and ready to fly. He could do so now, looking upon the city below with more than mere eyes.

And one such as Valentino, steeped in hatred and lust and violence, wrapped in whatever magicks he had conjured to do his killing, should stand out like a beacon on a dark plain. All he needed to do was let himself see past the crowd.

Pulling over, Buster hopped out of the truck and then climbed into the back, standing up so he could see over the cab. From here all of Hollywood spread out before him, the dirt and grime hidden by distance and shadow, looking like nothing but a jeweled carpet glittering in the light.

Calling upon his fire, he studied the city. Now he could pick out a different sort of light, the glows of humanity, each bobbing, weaving burst a man or woman or child. Some were dim, some flickered, some were strong and bright.

But one—one strobed with a sickly pulse, throbbing like some diseased heartbeat, its color not healthy, not natural.

Evil.

There was the man he sought.

Fixing the position in his mind, Buster leaped back down to the street, hurled himself inside, put the battered old vehicle back in gear, and took off at a bone-rattling pace, making a beeline for that light.

"I'm coming for you, Valentino," he muttered as he barreled around a corner, the truck tilting onto two wheels before crashing back down onto all four again. "Just you wait. The Phoenix is coming for you."

CUT TO:
EXT. HOUSE – NIGHT
A small home on a quiet street in a pleasant neighborhood

The home he finally pulled up in front of was not a women's residence or a boarding house. It was smaller than those, a simple
two-story house with green shutters and ivy starting to climb
the square pillars supporting the front porch. Buster did not
recognize it, but the mailbox by the front door bore the name
"I. Benton," and that rang a bell.

I. Benton. I, as in "Isadora." Isadora Benton, popularly known
as Dora.

She was not an actress, though. Far from it. Dora's particular talents were actually even more in demand in Hollywood,
however.

She was a seamstress.

And not just any seamstress. Dora could stitch up a costume in the blink of an eye. She could take a man's measure
at a glance, and tailor a suit to him perfectly while he was still
standing there staring. She could turn a pile of rags into a king's
robes, a courtier's fine suit, a lady's evening gown. She was an
absolute wizard with needle and thread, and every studio clam-
ored for her to come work for them. It was considered a major
coup to score Dora to handle the costuming for your film.

Buster was almost certain she had done the costumes on at
least one of Valentino's previous films. And he thought, though
he could not swear to it, that he had seen a picture of her in that
pile on the star's dining room table.

There was no time to waste. Pulling open the screen he
pounded on the front door. And did so again when there was no
answer. He was just contemplating kicking the door in when he
heard someone moving within, and a woman's voice calling out
a moment later, "I'm coming, hold your horses!"

He did not back up at all, so when the door finally creaked
open he was right there, mere inches away. The woman facing
him was nearly as tall as he was and solidly built, with thick
reddish hair and a strong face that was normally very welcoming but right now was scrunched in a frown. She studied him

a second, and he could see that she recognized him but only vaguely. "Yes? What?"

"Dora," he started, pulling off his cap as an afterthought. "Buster Gallagher. We've met a few times." He craned his neck to peer past her into the room, which was only dimly lit despite the lamp he could see casting its light onto a comfortable-looking sofa. Something shifted there in the dark, and then a man stepped forward, emerging from the shadows like a shark rising from waters to strike. Strong features, slicked back hair, and dark eyes that glittered at him over a slight sneer.

Valentino.

Buster shouldered the door open and pushed past Dora, who squawked in protest but lacked the power to stop him from entering and confronting the movie star.

"Surprised to see me?" he asked, for the actor did look it, his eyes having gone wide and the smirk falling away.

"What are you doing here?" Valentino demanded. "Get out! Now!" He was carrying something long and slim, like a cane, but wrapped in a jacket or blanket. Odd.

"Not a chance," Buster replied, stepping closer instead, until they were eye to eye. "You're done here. Not just here—you're done, period."

Now the movie star's eyes narrowed. "You have no idea what you're meddling with," he stated coldly. "You need to leave. Now."

"And leave you alone with Dora? Not a chance." Buster grabbed the man's jacket lapels. "I won't let you hurt anyone else."

"Me?" Valentino stared at him. "Are you insane? I'm trying to save her!"

"What?" That made Buster pause, at least for a second. Then he shook his head—and shook Valentino as well. "No, you're lying. You're just trying to trick me, to get rid of me. But I'm not falling for it!"

The actor reached up and carefully, almost gently detached Buster's hands from his jacket. "I am telling the truth," he stated quietly, calmly. "I swear to you, on my mother's grave, I am not the one perpetrating these heinous crimes. I am trying to stop them, to save these girls." He frowned and glanced away, deflating slightly. "And so far, I have failed miserably." Then he visibly collected himself. "But not tonight!"

Buster reeled back a step, studying the man before him. Could he be telling the truth? Everything thus far had pointed to Valentino being the killer—his guilty behavior, his strange actions, the pictures at his house, his interest in the occult, his being with each girl right before she died. Yet the Phoenix could see no falsehood in him, not right now. Did that mean he'd gotten it all wrong? Or was he simply being fooled by a man who made his living pretending, which was a nicer way to say lying?

Either way, there was a simple solution. "Fine. We'll both go. Then she'll be safe."

He reached out a hand, but Valentino brushed it away. "No! If I leave, she dies! It happened to Lucy, and to Winona, and to Maria! I won't let it happen to Dora!"

"Hang on—let what happen to me?" The woman in question interjected, shoving her way between them. "What exactly is going on here?" She glared at Valentino. "You said you wanted to talk about costumes for your next film! And you—" she scowled over her shoulder at Buster. "I barely even know you!"

"Why don't we all go somewhere?" Valentino suggested, his voice cool and soothing. "We can go get something to eat. My treat." He glanced toward the door, which Dora had shut after Buster's rude entrance. "But we should go now."

But Dora was used to standing firm against actors and their wiles, and she folded her arms across her chest. "I'm not going anywhere. With either of you. Not until somebody explains what's going on." She tapped her foot. "Start talking."

Buster glanced at Valentino, who frowned and gave a faint shrug. "I don't really know myself," Buster told her honestly. "All I do know is, I'm pretty sure you're in danger." He looked past her at the actor and could barely believe it himself as he added, "I think maybe he's got the right idea."

The costumer still didn't look completely convinced, but she didn't argue outright as Buster took her arm on one side and Valentino on the other and they pivoted her toward the door. They'd only managed a few steps, however, before Buster froze, the hairs on the back of his neck rising and his skin pimpling all over as if from sudden cold.

"Something's wrong," he stated, not whispering but speaking clearly. He could see his breath pluming before him. He could feel the shadows suddenly closing in, the lamp fluttering valiantly against it but eventually succumbing, its light winking out and plunging the room into darkness. "Something is here."

"Stay between us, Ms. Benton," Valentino instructed, his voice quavering only slightly. There was a rustle of fabric, presumably from him shifting position to put the lady at his back. "We will keep you safe."

Perhaps, Buster thought. Perhaps. He was now willing to accept that the movie star might not in fact be the killer, that he had been telling the truth, that he was here in attempt to protect her.

But protect her from what?

CHAPTER SEVEN
INT. HOUSE – NIGHT
A living room, cozy and comfortable.
It is only evening but the room is unnaturally dark.

First things first. Time to shed a little light on their situation. "Cover your eyes," Buster warned. Again the sound of cloth in motion, now doubled.

He could feel the cold weighing down on him, its presence almost physical, and concentrated. His inner fire was there, as always, and he stoked it with his will, encouraging it to flare up and out. The lamp was an obvious conduit and, as he focused in the direction he remembered it being, it roared back to life, its bulb suddenly forcing back the darkness with a burst of brilliance that would have been more at home atop a torch than encased in a glass bubble.

And in that sudden light, Buster saw a figure, stripped of its protective shadows, caught for an instant unawares.

It was tall and lean, gaunt, even, shrouded in bits of fluttering cloth that could have been rags as easily as whole garments, dark and dusty like old charcoal or dirty ash. No part of its flesh was visible, nor could Buster see its eyes beyond a faint gleam within the wrappings, and almost he wondered if he might be dealing with a mummy, but since when did such creatures haunt the dark and drench themselves in shadows? Though it would explain the state of its victims.

Whatever its nature, the creature snarled at them, caught out in the light. Valentino gasped, and Buster knew without glancing over that the other man had blinked and looked. That was fine, though. He'd only wanted to avoid blinding him when the lights returned.

"What—?" the actor muttered, but to his credit he did not cower or retreat. Instead, much to Buster's surprise, he unfurled the item he'd been holding, tossing aside the cloth and raising up—a sword. An old one, by the looks of it, long and straight, with a hilt that curved forward like short, blunt claws. There was something vaguely familiar about it, and he was pleased to see that the movie star at least knew how to wield such a weapon, holding it in a comfortable grip. "Begone from here, demon!" he called, his words carrying across the room, and Buster saw Dora start. She at least had kept her hands over her eyes, but now she began to lower them.

"No, don't look," he urged her, tapping her wrist, and perhaps it was the gravity in his voice or the fear and defiance in Valentino's but she complied, keeping her sight safely locked away. If they succeeded in protecting her from whatever this creature was, she would be better for never having looked upon its fearsome visage. And if they failed—well, better not to have it be the last thing she saw.

The creature had overcome its momentary paralysis and was stalking toward them, its shielded gaze still seemingly intent upon the young seamstress. It swept past Valentino, and the movie star swiped at it but clumsily so. His blade missed the creature entirely, and even though its face was covered Buster thought it was grinning in anticipation of its inevitable success.

Well, he was determined to put that outcome in doubt! He might not have a fine sword to hand, but he was the Phoenix, the keeper of mankind's fire, a being of puissance and purpose, made of energy and fire and light! He did not need any other weapon beyond his own will and his flame! Leaping forward to place himself squarely between the interloper and the lady of the house, Buster lashed out, swinging his fist toward where he supposed the creature's jaw to be. Light danced under his flesh and fluttered across his skin as he moved, and when he connected it was with a mighty crash, as of metal against stone. There was a flash as well, like lightning, and the creature stumbled back, its focus now locked on him instead. Well, good! Let it look upon its adversary and despair!

Only, despair did not seem to be the emotion currently filling its narrow frame. Instead he suspected that anger spurred it on as it raised both arms high and wide, wrapped hands outflung, as if willingly making itself a target. Yet its motions seemed confident, even arrogant, and the gesture one of defiance.

No, not a target, Buster quickly realized. A beacon. For the dark responded to the creature's call, every shadow rushing forward and wrapping it tight, cloaking it in a shell that even the lamp's warm glow could not penetrate. It seemed far larger now, more menacing, its cowled head nearly scraping the ceiling, its cloaked figure looming, its long arms seeming to brush the walls as they moved to wrap around the three people caught within its grasp.

Cowled? Where had that come from? Buster frowned, glancing quickly up at the creature again. Yes, that was the only term that truly fit. But that meant . . .

The creature snatched at them and he quickly tabled that thought, blocking the blow with his forearm. Light exploded from the contact and the creature shied away as if burned. Good, it could feel the flame! Buster grinned up at it. "Come on then," he urged softly, his own blood singing from the conflict. "Your darkness versus my light. Let us see who triumphs."

But they were not alone, of course. Valentino leaped forward with a cry, swinging his sword, the blade cutting air with a heavy swoosh. The creature did not seem affected by it, or terribly concerned, but its gaze still shifted between the two men facing it, and Buster could tell it was calculating its odds. It had expected to find a defenseless woman alone. Instead, it found itself dealing with a swordsman and a firebird. And even if the sword was not a serious threat, it was a distraction, and could still be dangerous with a lucky strike.

Buster decided to help it make the right decision. He took a quick step back, pivoted to snatch up the lamp, and then spun and charged forward, wielding it like a spear. Its cord snapped loose from the wall socket but in his hands its light could never die—instead the bulb blazed still brighter, too bright to look upon, becoming a living flame that he sharpened to a point, a fiery lance aimed straight at the center of the creature's chest. Even for one such as that, this blow could spell its doom.

Nor was the creature slow to realize its own risk. It shirked back from that burning weapon, its size diminishing as it contracted defensively, pulling itself in tighter to become more dense, darker, its shadows no longer spread thin but layered for protection. Those began to peel away, however, as Buster moved in closer, burning away the dark one inch at a time. It snarled at him again, its veilings slipping down to reveal a glimpse of naked teeth set in a face as smooth and pale as they were, and it swatted at the spear but pulled back quickly before coming in contact with the incendiary tip. Then, with a final glare, it wrapped both arms around itself, hugging itself in tight—and vanished, tugging the shadows in around it and disappearing within them even as they fled the room, leaving only the regular shade of a deepening dusk and the faint smell of something old and musty.

"Where did it go?" Valentino demanded, still waving the sword about before him as he twisted and turned, studying the room. "Is it gone? Is it over?"

Buster lowered the lamp back to the floor, withdrawing his light from it slowly so as not to shatter the bulb but merely letting it dim and then fade completely. "It's gone, yes," he agreed carefully, extending his own senses to be certain. "And I don't think it will be back soon. Certainly not tonight." He frowned as he recalled what he had seen and thought, and put some of the pieces together. "Something is very, very wrong, though."

"Clearly." The movie star had lowered his weapon at last, and now cast about for its makeshift sheath, grabbing that up and wrapping the sword again. Then he turned to Dora, who still stood like a statue, clearly straining to listen but gamely keeping her hands in place. "You may lower your hands now, Ms. Benton," he assured her, and she did so with a slight flush to her cheeks at the way he said her name.

Still, Dora was hardly one to be easily cowed. "What just happened?" she demanded. "It got really cold and really dark, and it sounded like you were fighting somebody, but I don't see anybody else here. Who was it, and what'd he want with me?" Her eye caught on the object by Buster's side. "And is that my lamp?"

"It is," he agreed, focusing on the easiest answer first. "Sorry for borrowing it without asking." He carried it back to its previous location and plugged it back in, then switched it on. "There, good as new." Now he had a decision to make, and he went with his instinct, crossing the room to take Valentino by the arm, though in a comradely manner rather than that of a captor and prisoner. "I apologize for barging in like this, and for all the confusion. We'll just be going, and leave you to try to regain some peace and quiet."

The Latin Lover, however, was not a man used to being managed. Especially by other men. He shifted his arm, pulling it free of Buster's grasp. "Perhaps I should remain here to make sure Ms. Benton is indeed safe," he suggested archly. "We have only your word that whatever it was is no longer here."

That comment made Buster tilt his head a little as he considered the other man. Only his word for it? Couldn't he see that the shadows and darkness had gone? That the creature was no longer towering above them? But no, perhaps not.

"It is my word, yes," he said finally. "And I can assure you, it is true. She will be perfectly safe. But you and I, we have much to discuss." He flicked his eyes toward the now-wrapped sword clutched beneath Valentino's other arm. "I think it would be better to do so somewhere else, rather than disturbing Dora further."

"Ah." To his credit, the actor was not slow to comprehend the implications to that look, and he nodded, albeit grudgingly. "Yes, very well." Reclaiming his hat from a hook near the door, he doffed it toward his hostess as he swept into a courtly bow. "Ms. Benton, it has been an absolute pleasure, as always. I hope we can discuss costumes and upcoming projects again very soon."

"Oh, well . . ." She smiled, clearly a little flustered, and dipped a quick curtsey. "Thank you." Her eyes found Buster and she frowned but nodded. "And thank you, though I'm still not exactly sure what for."

There was little else to be said after that, and so Buster tipped his own cap and then herded Valentino outside. It was only once the front door had shut solidly behind them and they had traversed the short brick path to the sidewalk that the actor bridled at being treated in such a way.

"All right," he stated, turning to hit Buster with the full force of his displeasure. "Now that we are out of there, perhaps you will explain exactly what you are about? And what that was?"

Buster mulled that over, but only for a second. He had always been one for quick decisions, trusting his gut and his heart, and now was no different. "I will explain," he agreed. "Everything. But let's go somewhere we can talk freely." He shook his head. "Preferably someplace we can get a drink."

I need it, he thought to himself as they made their way toward their two cars.

After all, it wasn't every day he was forced to face down Death itself!

CHAPTER EIGHT
EXT./INT. MANSION – NIGHT – TRACKING
Falcon Lair, a palatial estate high in the hills over Hollywood.

Their destination proved to be the very place from which Buster had so recently emerged: Falcon Lair. "You wished for a place that was quiet, private, secure, and where you could obtain alcohol," the movie star had pointed out as he was sliding into the seat of his convertible. "My home has all these things." And he'd taken off without waiting for reply or agreement, leaving Buster no real choice but to follow.

As he drove, trying to keep the actor's car in sight but not overly concerned since he knew where they were going, Buster mused over this latest turn of events. He could see now, in retrospect, how everything he'd thought had pointed to Valentino being the villain of this piece could also have been him as the failed hero. The guilt over the girls—in many ways, given both the man's public persona and the slightly less guarded side Buster had seen on set, it made far more sense for him to be upset over having tried to protect them and failed than over having killed them. The rush to reach each one—if he'd believed they were in danger, of course he would be in a hurry! Taking each one out to dinner—if he'd thought he could protect them, what better way to keep them close, and in a public place? Even the pictures—he must have somehow used those to divine the identity of each victim.

Which did not explain how Valentino had become involved, how he had known which girl was in danger next, or even what he'd thought he could do about it. But those were answers Buster fully intended to get. At least he no longer believed the man to be a murderer!

The guards at Falcon Lair were understandably bewil-
dered when Buster stepped out of his truck, which he'd parked
behind Valentino's convertible on the circular drive around the
fountain, right in front of the main house. Here was the man
who had emerged from the house just hours before, clearly an
intruder, and had practically dared them to confront him—only
now he was here with the lord of the manor, who was at the
front door and beckoning him to catch up. They did not say
anything, just watched Buster warily, and he wondered if they
would mention it to their employer later or simply chalk it up as
another strangeness of movie folk.

He shouldn't have been surprised himself when Valentino
then led the way to the dining room—and then froze in shock.
"Santa Maria!" the actor muttered, the name spilling from his
lips apparently by reflex as he stared at the ruins on the tabletop, tiny mounds of dark ash all that remained of all those
papers he had gathered. "What has happened here?"

"I'm afraid that was my fault," Buster offered, seeing no
reason to lie about it. He shrugged when Valentino turned a
disbelieving glance his way. "Sorry. I thought you were the one
killing these girls. I was angry."

"Angry?" The movie star stumbled forward and reached out,
sifting the nearest pile of ash through his fingers. "So it would
seem. I am lucky you did not burn the whole house down!" He
turned and studied Buster. "You did something with the lamp
as well, back at Ms. Benton's. You have an affinity for fire and
light."

That was an astute observation, and the Phoenix acknowledged it with a slight nod, though he decided there was no reason to go into his full origins at this time. "I do." He frowned,
considering the actor in turn. "And you see more than just the
surface, don't you?"

Valentino smiled. "I inherited some of the Sight from my
mother and her mother and her mother before her," he acknowledged. "I can at times read a person's emotions, feel their energy,
and even pick up traces of past actions in a place or thing."

So the famous movie star was a sensitive! Buster nodded.
That explained some of recent events—and also perhaps a bit

of why and how Valentino had risen to such fame so quickly. If he could feel the emotions around him he could adapt his performances to them, subconsciously adjusting to produce the desired effect. Actors did that all the time, but he would have had a significant advantage over most.

Which led to another question he'd had since they'd left the seamstress's house. "You couldn't actually see what we were fighting, could you?" he asked.

"No." That confession clearly aggravated the famous man, and he turned away, crossing to the sideboard and pouring two crystal tumblers full of some amber liquid from a matching decanter. Returning, he handed one to Buster and downed a healthy slug from the other. "I knew something was there, and to my eye the room seemed darker, more forbidding, but I could only make out a vague shape, little more."

Which explained why he had missed it with his thrusts, even though he was clearly competent with a sword. Buster took a sip of the proffered drink and nodded appreciatively. It was first-rate Scotch, but from someone of Valentino's refined tastes he'd have expected no less. "Be glad you could not make out more," he assured his host. "Else you might have been driven mad at the sight of it."

"Oh?" Valentino was eyeing him very closely now. "Yet you could see it in full, could you not?" He read the answer in Buster's face. "And you are not mad. Though your language has changed—always I took you for a regular man, friendly enough but nothing odd or untoward. Now there is something different about you. You carry yourself more proudly, speak in what I would consider a far older form of the language—who are you?"

Yes, very astute indeed! Buster smiled and lifted his glass in salute. "You're right, I'm more than just Buster Gallagher, stuntman and would-be actor," he agreed. "And I am older than I look. A lot older. Let's leave the rest for now—we have more important things to worry about." He sighed and took a larger sip of his drink before continuing. "Like the nature of our adversary."

That had the actor's full attention. "You recognized it! Excellent! What are we facing, then? A demon, torn from Hell?

An unquiet spirit? A curse laid upon Hollywood by some disenchanted soul?"

Buster shook his head. There was no way to sugarcoat this. "Death," he replied bluntly. "We are facing Death itself."

He hadn't known at first, of course. Though it seemed a part of him had, deep down—hence his automatically equating the figure's head covering with a cowl. But toward the end, there had been no mistaking that skeletal face, those bottomless eyes. And it all fit together: the shadows, the cold, the sudden and dramatic draining of life. It was the Grim Reaper and no other.

But—"What? Why?" Valentino was demanding. "That makes no sense! Death comes for us all, certainly, but not like this! It may steal in unexpected, like a thief in the night, but this is no quiet burglary but outright assault! When has Death ever taken people in such a fashion, unexpected and without clear cause? And only the young, at that?"

"No, you're right, it is utterly out of character," Buster agreed, swirling his drink and letting his eye get lost in the honey-toned liquid as he thought matters through aloud. "It did not seem utterly itself. At first sight I mistook it for a mummy, for it was more ragged than robed and its hands and face were covered. Almost as if it were trying to disguise itself. And where was its scythe? It is never without that instrument of demise, yet here it had only its hands and its will." He frowned. "And you're correct about its targets, as well. That is not how it operates. No, something is very wrong with Death."

"Perhaps," his host suggested slowly, almost timidly, which was unusual for the man but showed his realization that he was out of his depth here, "it is not acting under its own auspices?" He straightened when Buster's gaze snapped to him, automatically donning an air of feigned confidence as he explained. "If I were such a person as could claim to control natural forces—a sorcerer, wizard, call it what you will—would I not seek mastery over Death itself? There are many such tales, are there not? Typically they are so the individual can avoid dying themselves, but what if it is more than that? What if it is a desire to yoke the power of death, to bend it to your bidding? The first thing you would do, upon chaining such a fearsome force—"

"—is strip away its greatest weapon," Buster finished. "Like muzzling a dog. Or taking a man's gun and promising to return it if he did as instructed." He nodded. "Yes. That makes sense." Yet more proof that the books in this house were not merely for show—Valentino had more of a mind that he'd expected! "So, someone has taken control of Death, and now sends it to do their bidding. But why? Why these women? What did they ever do to draw such a fate to themselves?"

Valentino could not resist a pointed glance at the ash flaking his table. "I had many files," he stated with a hint of reprimand. "I could tell whatever was doing this, it was after young women in film." He shook his head, setting his glass down and placing both hands flat on the table to better survey the damage there. "I gathered everything I had about every woman I knew."

"How did you then figure out who would be next in its sights, though?" Buster asked. That was one of the elements here he had yet to understand.

The smile he received in return had a touch of the bemused as well as a hint of pride. "I cannot rightly say," the famous leading man admitted, dipping his head. "I would look through everything and . . . get a feeling about one of the names or photos. That is all I know." He sighed. "But it worked. It led me to Ms. Wyman, Ms. Wilkes, Ms. Rittali, and tonight to Ms. Benton."

"You were sensing Death's attention on them," Buster guessed. "Normally, that would be a natural thing but this, this is most definitely not, so it's creating a disturbance in the spiritual realm. That's what you're picking up on. And you were using the pictures and scripts and clippings like a crystal ball, sifting through them until you came across the one that resonated." It was a crude method and could only have worked this close to the source of the disturbance, and for someone like Valentino who had interacted with each of the women personally.

"But I failed each time," the Latin Lover confessed, hanging his head in shame. "I would go to them, try to be close enough to protect them—from what, I knew not, only that the danger was imminent—but I could not see a way to explain the situation without seeming mad." He banged his fist on the table, making his glass jump, the remaining whiskey sloshing within the crystal. "They would not even let me stay the night, though I would have done nothing more than watch over them!" The smile that touched his lips now was a bitter one. "My reputation preceded me, and none of them were the type of woman who would have succumbed to seduction if I had attempted it, even with all my charms, but that meant they were also unwilling to allow me in or remain alone with me, despite my assurances that my intentions were strictly honorable."

There was nothing Buster could say to that. It all made sense—as did the fact, he recognized now, that Valentino had continually referred to each woman by her last name rather the more familiar first name—and he found he felt for the man, who had honestly wanted nothing more than to help these women and had been hampered by his own past proclivities. "Even if you had convinced them to let you stay," he offered finally, "it wouldn't have changed anything. Death still would have taken them." He glanced at the wrapped sword, which had been laid atop the sideboard when they'd entered. "You can't hurt Death with a mortal blade."

"Not even this one?" With a quick, brisk motions Valentino crossed to retrieve the weapon, yanked it free of its covering, and raised it high, the light from the chandelier catching along its polished blade and the grooves of its hilt. "For this is no mere sword," he declared, his words ringing out. "This is no less than Colada, the second sword of Rodrigo Díaz de Vivar, El Cid himself!"

It was true that the blade seemed to have an aura about it, one that suggested more than mere steel at work. And the two swords of the legendary Castilian knight and warlord were said to possess mystical properties. He also knew that *The Hooded Falcon*, the unfinished movie for which Valentino had named his estate, had been intended as the story of El Cid. Given the other treasures he'd spied around the place, he could well imagine the movie star seeking to acquire a genuine artifact of the man. And what better weapon to carry when facing an undetermined mystical threat than a magical sword?

"It might be able to hurt Death somewhat," he finally conceded. "Assuming you can land a solid blow."

Valentino nodded, acknowledging that point—which he seemed to accept as speaking, not of his prowess, but of his ability to perceive their unearthly foe—and lowered the weapon, setting it gently across a corner of the table. "I will do my best, an' we meet again," he vowed.

Which brought them back to the question at hand. They knew Death was the killer they sought, and Valentino's theory made sense, that it was under someone's control. But who and why? And how could they track that person down and stop them from unleashing the Grim Reaper on yet another young woman?

CHAPTER NINE
INT. MANSION – NIGHT
A sumptuous dining room in a large and elegant manor house high atop a hill. Two men, their heads bent close together in grave contemplation.

"How do we proceed now?" Valentino asked him then. He gestured at the mess on the table before them. "I cannot consult the images, as I had done previously."

Buster dipped his head briefly, acknowledging the fault, but now was not the time to dwell on past errors. "I don't think anyone else will be targeted tonight," he pointed out. "We stymied it at Dora's, and it will need time to regroup—and for its master, whoever that may be, to choose a new victim. Which means we have a little time." He rubbed at his jaw. "The real question here is, why these four? What do they have in common?"

"They are all women," his host answered at once. "All young. All talented."

"True." He considered that, following those points where they led. "But how would anyone have known that? Lucy was up and coming—I can fully believe that, given a few more years, she could have been a star, but she had only a handful of lines in your movie, and I remember her saying once how thrilled she was, and how it was her largest part yet." He pushed away a pang of grief, for of the three victims thus far, Lucy had been the one he'd known the best, the one he had often sat with and joked with throughout the day's filming. "And Maria? I only met her once—what can you tell me about her?"

"Beautiful," came Valentino's reply. "Fiery. Passionate. A gifted dancer, and a great presence. Yes, she too would have become a star."

"Okay, so somebody jealous of their impending success?

Trying to cut them off now, before they can achieve that fame—maybe to take out the competition?" Buster pondered, but then shook his head. "That doesn't fit our other two, though, does it?" He was asking the air as much as his companion, and answered his own question. "Winona Wilkes wasn't acting anymore—she'd moved on to writing instead. And Dora, she's not an actress at all!"

"True, though both are gifted in their own way," the movie star was quick to point out. "What I'd seen of Winona's writing was first-rate—another year, two at most, and she would have been writing entire scripts herself. And Dora, she is a genius with needle and thread, and not just for fixing and tailoring—she creates whole costumes, designs them herself, and they are fantastic."

"So it's about young talent," Buster summarized, pacing around the table as he spoke. "Particularly young women with talent. Doesn't sound like a jealous rival, then, unless there's a woman out there who's an actress, singer, dancer, writer, and seamstress. Maybe just someone who hates seeing women get ahead at all?" The film industry was unusually forward-thinking, he'd found—women were not only in front of the camera but behind it, including directing and producing. In part that seemed to be because films were still considered by many to be more of a hobby than a serious business, and so a reasonable place for wealthy women or idle wives and widows to focus their attention. But it was also still a young industry itself, and so had not yet had time to form as many rules and restrictions as the older, more hidebound fields where women were still not welcome.

Valentino was chuckling, though the sound had little real mirth behind it. "If that is all we have to go on, the list will be very long indeed," he warned. "There are many who do not think a woman's place is anywhere but in the bed or the kitchen or on a man's arm as an ornament." The way he stated that, with a clear air of disgust, made it obvious he did not agree, and the Phoenix found his estimation of the man rising another notch. Not only gallant and compassionate but open-minded? A rare breed indeed!

He was right, however, about them needing a better lead than this. Which led Buster back to a question he'd already asked. "Whoever is doing this," he reminded his companion and host, is not simply pulling their names from a hat. He has a list of suitable victims. And if he's basing it on young women with talent who have not yet made a name for themselves but certainly will, that means he's seen their talent for himself."

The Latin Lover smiled for real this time, though it was a slightly predatory look that matched well the name of his home. "He has worked with all four of them, or they have worked for him," he agreed. "We must merely connect the dots, see where their careers have intersected, and we will have our man."

"Or at least a place to start," Buster amended. After his nearly fatal misjudgment of Valentino, he knew he would not be so hasty in assigning blame again.

Glancing about, he spied a sheet of paper that had blown off the table onto the floor at some point previous to his earlier visit and so had escaped the tabletop conflagration he'd caused. Scooping that up, he collected a pen from where he'd seen several on the buffet and, taking a seat, poised the one over the other. "Do you remember any other pictures Lucy worked on?" he started, writing her name neatly near the top left of the page.

The other man frowned—he was now the one pacing about the room, hands clasped behind his back as he thought. "Only one," he admitted finally. "She had a small role in *The Songbird's Promise*, as I recall." He smiled, just for a second. "I know because she told me that and I teased that she should have been the songbird, with her lovely voice."

Buster nodded, squelching the renewed burst of rage that threatened to scorch the table further at the reminder that such a lovely voice and lovely lady had been snuffed out all too soon. "What about Maria?" he asked. "I know she was in *Cobra* with you, correct?"

"Correct. And she had been in a film, *Dreaming of a Dream*, shortly before that. I think she had another role already lined up for right after—yes, something about murder, *The Murderer's Touch*!"

"Good." Buster added those to his list, beneath Maria's name.

"And Winona? I know she was in *Shoot 'Em Cowboy*."

"She had background roles before that," Valentino replied. "Nothing large enough to earn her a credit, but she was in several. I do not recall the names—I only know because she mentioned it when I dined with her, as another motivation to move behind the camera." He looked as frustrated as Buster felt.

Studying the meager list, Buster despaired a little. Five films so far, and none of them overlapping. "And Dora?"

"Ah." The sound was full to the brim with defeat. "For her, I suspect the list will be a great deal longer—too long, in fact. She has had a hand in many productions, often at the last minute to help save the costume department from certain disaster. For a time, I believe she was even—"

Suddenly Valentino abandoned his stately pacing and dashed forward, causing Buster to draw back reflexively as the other man rushed him. But he was not the star's target, not exactly—instead Valentino snatched the list from his hand, stared at it a moment, and then held it aloft like a hard-won prize.

"Yes!" he exulted before slamming it back down on the table. "Here!" He stabbed a finger at the one film by Lucy's name. "*The Songbird's Promise*! And here!" This time he jabbed at *The Murderer's Touch*. "Both of these were for the same studio—the very studio that had employed Ms. Benton on retainer last year in order to avail themselves of her services on each and every film they produced! The same one Winona mentioned working for and leaving quickly because she hated the way they had treated her! Stellar Pictures!"

"Stellar Pictures?" He'd heard the name, but the Phoenix felt that might be the extent of his knowledge about the studio. Though most of Hollywood was dominated by the four major houses—Warner Bros, Famous Players, Metro-Goldwyn, and Fox—there were several mid-sized studios like Universal and United Artists and any number of tinier ones that popped up, produced a film or two, and then either fell apart or got bought out by one of their competitors.

"They are in Poverty Row," Valentino clarified, which explained a good deal. That section of Hollywood, centered on the intersection of Sunset Boulevard and Gower Street, was home to most of the smaller—and shadier—studios. Any house that started out there moved away to a larger and more reputable location as soon as they were able. "The owner is a man named Lawrence Ray. I met him at a party once, and have done my best to avoid him ever since." He sniffed. "Distasteful man. Very oily, like a salesman, all over you. I have never heard good things about his productions, though certainly some good people have come out of them—and moved on to better places without a backward glance." He nodded decisively. "Yes, he would be a prime candidate for the man behind these deaths, for he has about him that venal quality, like a man who hates to lose and hates to let anyone go."

"Right, then." Setting the list aside, Buster pushed back from the table and rose to his feet. "What say we pay Mr. Ray a visit?"

"Indeed." Valentino stepped to the sideboard and retrieved Colada before giving Buster a wintery smile. "Come, we will take my car. It would be a shame for you to perish before even having a chance to confront this villain." And he led the way out before the Phoenix could muster an adequate reply.

CHAPTER TEN
EXT./INT. STUDIO – NIGHT
Poverty Row, a rundown business area devoted to film.
It is late at night as a sleek convertible pulls up to the curb.

Stellar Pictures was a narrow lot squeezed in between two others and fronted by a slightly rundown building—if not for the name emblazoned across the front, Buster might have thought they were facing an old and possibly derelict warehouse instead of a functioning film studio. This was not the first studio he'd seen in such a state, however—more and more people were beginning to realize there was money in film and attempting to get in now before it became big business and closed ranks to outsiders and entrepreneurs, which meant many studios were little more than a shack, a handful of staff, and a pair of secondhand cameras. Those that survived added to their ranks and purchased new and better equipment. Those that did not left behind only a reel or two, some pages, and a discarded costume rack—most of the failed ones never even had enough capital to purchase an ad in the papers.

"You think he's here at this hour?" Valentino asked as he parked right in front of the studio's door—at least there were spaces at this hour of night!—and shut off the engine.

"Let's hope so," Buster replied with a touch of gallows humor, unpeeling his fingers from where they had gripped the dash and the door. "Otherwise, I've just risked my life for nothing."

That brought a laugh from his companion, who had already unbuckled and hopped out of the car. "You show no fear at confronting Death itself, yet you tremble like a child from my driving? For shame!" But his teasing was good-natured, and

Buster smiled as he also pried himself from the vehicle.

"Death I can predict," he retorted. "Your driving is chaos itself." Which should have meant he was in his element, for he was a Beast, a paragon of Chaos. Yet he had been white-knuckled the entire ride. Perhaps it had to do with being in someone else's control, rather than his own. Certainly. Valentino had not been nervous—he had kept up a running commentary as he sped around other vehicles, zipping across lanes with no warning, and taking corners so sharply and so quickly the car had often been up on two wheels. The man was fearless, it seemed, and while the Phoenix admired that trait, he had rarely put his own life in such a person's hands.

Still, he could think of worse people to entrust with his safety as, together, they faced the building. All seemed dark, yet Buster thought he could sense the warmth of life somewhere deep within. "He's here," he stated confidently. "Where else would he go to plot such villainy? His home? No, he selects the girls from his roster of past employees, which he would keep in his office. That's where we'll find him."

Valentino shrugged and collected Colada from the space behind his seat, the sword loosely shrouded once again. "Then let us beard the monster in his den!" And he led the way to the studio's front door.

It was locked, of course, but that was hardly an obstacle and Buster had no patience left for niceties. Grasping the doorknob, he let his heat flow forth and grinned as he felt the locking mechanism within melt away. With a twist and a shove the portal flew back and they entered.

"Guards?" Valentino whispered, but Buster shook his head. Now that they were within the walls he had a better sense of its occupants, and there was only the one besides themselves. Which made sense, if Stellar Pictures was as financially strapped as it appeared—why have guards for an empty, locked building with little of value inside? The cameras would be the only items of any real worth, and those would be in an equipment room with a far sturdier lock.

"I'm guessing Ray will be upstairs, corner office," Buster suggested, not bothering to lower his voice. Either the man had heard the door opening and was already aware he was not alone or he was oblivious and would not hear them speaking, either. He led the way down the hall, past rooms labeled "Costumes" and "Makeup" and "Props" until they had reached the back, where an old but still sturdy stairwell led to the upper floors. Quickly they climbed, grateful the building was only three stories. Even so, they both paused by unspoken agreement on the top floor to catch their breath.

"We need to be careful with Ray," Buster reminded his friend—for at some point tonight he had indeed begun to think of Valentino as such. "We have no idea what he is capable of, but we do know he has somehow leashed Death, and that makes him dangerous."

The movie star nodded. In the dim light filtering in from the stairwell windows—for the lights were off, and they had not bothered to find or turn any on—he looked pale but determined as he followed Buster down the hall. This floor was all offices, it seemed, some with lofty titles like "Head of Creative Development" and "Head of Talent Acquisition," and Buster smiled grimly as he recognized the tactic. If you could not pay in money, pay in ego instead.

The final door, all the way at the front, said only "Studio Head." He didn't bother to knock, but tried the knob and, upon finding it unlocked, swung the door open.

Ray's office took up the entire front of the floor. Whereas the hall and stairwell were shabby, with peeling paint and old, worn wood and concrete, this space was pristine, luxurious, with gleaming hardwood and rich paneling and an expensive Oriental rug that boasted an intricate pattern in rich reds and deep blues. Paintings adorned the walls and a massive wooden desk took up one end, while a set of comfortable couches and chairs surrounded a low coffee table at the other. The room's sole occupant had been behind the desk and rose smoothly to his feet as they entered.

"Come in, come in!" Lawrence Ray was not a big man, nor a handsome one. As Valentino had said, he exuded an air of oiliness, a smarmy sheen cast over hunger and greed and lust, and with his slicked-back hair and his suit that might have been expensive but had not been tailored to him and his second-rate cigar he did indeed present the image of a salesman, and not a good one. The smile he offered them as he closed the distance was also smarmy, and Buster recognized in the man's taut grin and too-wide eyes that he had been surprised by their arrival and was concerned, even afraid, of what it portended, but was doing his best to conceal that behind a veneer of brittle confidence and false welcome.

Ray was holding an ebon swagger stick, the dark length tucked beneath that arm and his fingers loosely looped around what appeared to be a bone top, but he extended the other hand to Valentino. "Mister Valentino, always a pleasure!" he exclaimed too heartily, turning the proffered handshake into a pat on the upper arm when the movie star did not return the gesture. He glanced at Buster, sized him up, but clearly could not match a name to the face and was not impressed with what he saw, so settled only for, "Sir," and a curt nod before returning his attention to the Latin Lover. "To what do I owe this unexpected honor?"

Valentino, however, was having none of it. "This is no social call," he snarled, stepping forward to stare the studio head down from mere inches away. "We know what you have done. The murders stop now!" Buster had to admit, he was impressed. This was the smoldering intensity the actor projected onscreen, dark and dangerous, and it was enough to cow most men.

The head of Stellar Pictures proved no exception, cowering back a pace from that glare. "I don't know what you're talking about!" he claimed, but his voice broke over the words and sweat was already sheening his forehead. "I swear!" He took another step back and seemed to regain some of his courage. "Don't come any closer!" And the swagger stick swung forward to block Valentino's path.

But the movie star only sneered at the black stick before him. "So, you wish for trial by combat?" he declared, his voice low and steely. He shook the covering from Colada and raised the ancient blade, its shining length clanging against the swagger stick, its tip aimed right at Ray's left eye. "So be it!"

Ray had only long enough to gulp in fear before Valentino

had knocked the stick aside and extended his reach, the sword now a hairsbreadth from piercing that same eye. "Ahhh!" he shrieked, throwing himself backward, and raised his weapon again, but this time upright before him in both hands as if it were a cross to fend off evil spirits. "Defend me!" he cried out, angling his call upward and out, toward the night sky. "I command you!"

The room had been comfortably, even warmly lit by both overhead lights and several lamps at the corners, but now that dimmed as darkness flowed in from the windows and beyond, filling the space. "Back!" Buster told his friend, resting a hand on his shoulder. His eyes were following the motion of that darkness, which was gathering before them, swirling and condensing into a tall, gaunt figure placed squarely between themselves and Ray.

"It's here, isn't it?" Valentino whispered in return. "I can feel it, but I can't see anything, just a dark patch in the air." He swung his sword loosely in that direction. "But point me toward it and I will see if Colada can indeed harm a spirit."

"No." Buster shifted, sliding forward to put himself in front of the actor. "Let me handle Death. You deal with Ray." His mind returned to and fastened upon the studio head's odd accessory. "The swagger stick, that's the key. Get it from him."

"Consider it done," the movie star promised. Then Buster's attention returned to the creature in front of him, as its form finally emerged from the shadows and its features became visible.

It had abandoned its earlier attempts at subterfuge, he saw at once. No more was it wrapped in layers of darkness. Now its pale skull gleamed forth, its eyes mere pinpricks of light within hollow sockets, and it reached out with its long, skeletal fingers, the tips sharp as claws and intent upon ripping the life clean from his body. Its jaw widened, the bare teeth parting, and it hissed like an angered snake ready to strike as the darkness coiled about it in anticipation.

But the Phoenix had long experience battling snakes, and he was not afraid of this serpent, despite its long history. Indeed, of all the Beasts—of all creatures in the cosmos—he was perhaps the only one who did not fear Death. For what was Death to him?

"Come, then," he said softly, raising himself to his full height and spreading his arms wide. Light blossomed from his body, filling the room and driving back the shadows, extending like wings to either side, and in Death's hollow gaze he saw those pupils widen as it recognized at last its foe. "For I am the Phoenix! I am the immortal embodiment of all that is creativity and life and light! Death, you hold no power over me!"

That proved provocation enough to overcome any momentary fear, and Death lunged with a snarl. Buster leaped forward to meet it.

Light and dark collided, heat and cold, fire and shadow. The flames batted away skeletal hands, but were in turn driven back by bone and shroud. Neither could get a firm grip on the other, and they parted after a moment, both panting, and began circling one another, crouched low and seeking an opening.

Over Death's shoulder, Buster saw Valentino circling back behind the melee, keeping his own attention resolutely on Ray. The studio head stood frozen with fear, watching as his champion battled this glowing, fiery stranger, and did not even seem to notice the movie star's approach.

Growing impatient with this game, Death hissed and swiped with one claw. The Phoenix blocked the blow and batted at the cloaked figure in return, only to be knocked away as well. They were too evenly matched, both supreme in their own element but both unassailable by the other.

Fortunately, all Buster had to do was stall. There was a yelp as Valentino finally reached Ray and, with a single quick, fluid motion, yanked the swagger stick from the man's sweaty grip.

"NO!" It was a cry of pure desperation, the sound of a man who knew at once that he had just lost everything, and it distracted Death, who turned to glance in that direction.

That was the opening the Phoenix had needed, and he stepped forward—but not to attack. "Toss the stick!" he shouted instead, and although one eyebrow quirked in silent question Valentino did not hesitate to comply. The ebon swagger stick spun through the air as it was flung toward the center of the room—and into Death's waiting hands.

As it flew, the rod lengthened, the bone tip distending, its shape warping. By the time it had settled into that skeletal grip it was taller than its wielder, and the tip was nearly half that length, curving viciously out and down in a wicked arc. The Grim Reaper had its scythe once more.

That dark specter turned to study Buster, seeming to swell until its dark presence filled the entire room. This was Death unleashed, once again restored to its full power. Yet it did not strike.

"We have freed you," the Phoenix pointed out. "You are no longer under Ray's control." Then he deliberately furled his fire around himself, bowed his head, and waited.

It was a gamble, he knew. But it was the only way he could see to end this safely, for the rest of the world if not for him. For what if he and Death had continued to battle, and he had somehow won? What then? What would the world be without death to keep life in balance?

There was a shriek, filled with rage beyond knowing, and a sharp, cold wind brushed across his face. But it was merely the backwash as Death leaped—not for him, but for the petrified movie executive. Valentino had the good sense to throw himself backward, and Death ignored him completely as he fell upon Ray like an owl swooping down upon a mouse. Those long, shadow-cloaked arms shifted, bony hands bringing the scythe down sharply, and the man screamed as the weapon's tip pierced his chest, right over his heart. He stiffened, jerking once, twice, before sliding back off the blade to collapse in a lifeless puddle of limbs upon the floor.

Death straightened and turned, its weapon held upright so that its butt rested against the floor. It met Buster's gaze—and dipped its chin once, a nod of respect to a worthy foe and thanks for a deed well done. Its eyes flicked briefly then to Valentino, who had straightened, and its mouth widened into a grin that was nearly a leer. Then it dragged the shadows tight around it, furling them so its bony countenance was hidden away once more, and vanished, taking the dark and the cold with it.

"Is that it?" Valentino asked, and Buster did not fault him the least for the way his voice quivered and shook. "Has it gone? Is it over?"

"It is over," he agreed. He forced the fire back down, banking it once more lest the sight of his immortal flame should drive his friend mad, and then approached, rounding the desk to study the dead body laying there. Lawrence Ray's eyes were wide open and shot with terror, his lips parted in that last, horrible scream. There was not a mark upon him, but Buster did notice a strange pin upon the man's lapel, and plucked it loose to examine. It was a circle, enameled and bright with golds and reds and yellows and blues, and the quartered image seemed vaguely familiar to him, though he could not say from where. Around its edges were letters picked out in gold, and he read them to himself: "Honi soit qui mal y pense." Yes, he knew that from somewhere? But where?

He could not recall, but pocketed the pin to consider again later. In the meantime, he stood and smiled, clapping Valentino on the shoulder. "It's over," he said again. "Now let's depart before we find ourselves answering some difficult questions."

"Oh, indeed." Valentino grinned back as they exited the room, pausing to collect his sword's covering along the way. "I feel the need for strong coffee and rich pie. And I know just the place. Come—I'll drive."

Buster groaned at that, but nonetheless followed his friend out, shutting the door behind him. Death still waited in that room, but now only the ordinary kind. The natural order had been restored.

CHAPTER ELEVEN
EXT. FILM SET – DAY
The film lot for Son of the Sheik. Morning.
Actors and crew, going about their business.

When Buster arrived on the set a few days later, he found Valentino waiting for him.

"No new deaths in several days," the film star stated, smiling widely. He slapped Buster on the back. "It is truly done with!"

"It is," Buster agreed. He'd felt nothing unusual since their encounter with Death and Lawrence Ray, no imbalances in the ether, no waves or ripples in the spiritual realm. All seemed to have returned to normal.

His friend's smile morphed briefly into a frown. "My greatest adventure," the man groused, looking around to make sure no one else was paying attention to them and pitching his voice low, "a true-life battle between good and evil, and I can tell no one! For who would ever believe me?" Then his smile returned. "But perhaps if I make it into a movie instead? The Star and the Sunbird! Together against Death!" He gestured with his hands as he spoke, painting the imaginary title and tagline across the bright blue sky.

Buster laughed. "Fine, but leave me out of it," he warned. "I'm happy being just a bit player."

"I do not understand that either," Valentino confessed. "You are . . . not human, are you? Not truly? You are, as you said that night, the Phoenix? Creativity itself come to life? Yet you labor as"—he glanced around them again—"a stunt double, an extra. Why?"

It felt strange to speak of this to anyone, but he felt the movie star had certainly earned the truth, not to mention his honesty.

"I am human," he answered. "I'm just . . . something else, too. I was human, once. Completely. A long time ago. The Phoenix is bigger than that, bigger than any body or mind could contain. I'm just its embodiment, its avatar, its chosen representative." He shrugged. "As far as the rest—I've been a star before. But I think I'm better supporting others' talents than just advancing my own." He put a hand on his friend's shoulder. "Like yours. You shine on the screen brighter than I ever could."

Valentino accepted the compliment with good grace. "Well, if you ever change your mind, you have but to let me know," he promised. "Then you and I will light the screen together!"

"Fair enough." But Buster knew he never would. He'd grown past that now. And he felt it was for the best.

"There is still something that concerns me in all this," the actor added, still keeping his words soft enough that the other actors and crew milling about preparing for the next scene would not overhear. "How did a man like Ray capture Death? Surely, if he held such knowledge, such power, Stellar Pictures would not have been the small, sad excuse it was?" He used the past tense, for already, with its founder's death, Stellar had been closed, and was in the process of having all its pieces sold off to other studios.

Buster nodded, for he'd wondered that as well. "It could be that he stumbled onto the knowledge," he pointed out. "And had yet to realize what he could truly do with it. In which case, we stopped him just in time. Or"—and this was the thought that chilled him at night—"he was somebody's patsy, handed the power to control Death to see what he did with it, see if it worked, test the process for someone else."

"That is what I think, too," Valentino agreed. "It is how I would do it—why put myself at risk until I have seen that it can be successful? And this way, if it fails, I am not caught up in it." He smacked his hands together. "But if that is the case, the person truly behind this is still at large!"

"Maybe so." Buster's thoughts returned to that lapel pin he'd taken off Ray's body. The words emblazoned around it still haunted him, but he still could not remember where he had seen them before. "But if that is the case, best not to go looking.

You don't know what else that person might be able to do. We stopped this plot, freed Death, and I doubt it will let itself get trapped the same way a second time."

The director called for places, and Buster moved to the side, getting out of the way, but Valentino remained where he was. "It is not enough," he insisted, his face grim and his stance determined. "Whoever did this, they are also to blame for the ladies' deaths, and they must answer for their crimes."

"Leave it alone," Buster warned, but he had a feeling his friend hadn't heard him. They did not get a chance to speak again the rest of the day, and Buster left the set that night with a bad feeling in his gut, as if something terrible were going to happen.

Two months later, reporting to the lot for work as an extra on a new film, a western, Buster was stopped by Maud, who ran up to him, her eyes wet with tears. "Oh, Buster, have you heard?" the dancer declared, throwing her arms around him. "It's so awful!"

"What's wrong?" he asked, his arms reflexively hugging her tight even as cold blossomed in his belly. "Did we lose someone else?" But he'd been so sure it was over!

"Yes!" she answered, sobbing into his shoulder, but pulled back to look him in the eye and speak more clearly. "Valentino himself!"

"What?" Buster pulled loose from her embrace. "What happened?"

She shook her head but after a second was able to compose herself enough to answer. "They're saying it was an ulcer or something," she said softly. "He took sick and wound up having surgery at some hospital out East." The movie star had gone to New York to begin touring to promote *Son of the Sheik*, which had premiered here in Hollywood a few weeks before. "I guess it didn't go well?" She burst out crying again.

Buster did his best to comfort her, but his own thoughts were whirling. He couldn't help thinking that this could not be a coincidence, to have faced down Death only to succumb to him mere months later. Plus, he'd worried that his friend hadn't given up looking into the matter, and had continued trying to trace who Ray might have been working for. What if he'd found something, and had paid the ultimate price for it? The Phoenix knew all too well what that was like—as Marlowe he'd been murdered by the Privy Council for refusing to give in to their demands and for becoming an obstacle in their path.

That memory brought a sudden realization, and Maud cried out and pushed him away, stating, "You burned me!" as she staggered back and then fled. But Buster barely noticed, so caught up was he in the knowledge his reminiscence had shaken loose. That was where he had seen those words before! Not just them but the entire emblem, with its four quarters featuring lions and harp. It was the royal coat of arms, and that particular version in a circle with the wording around it was the mark of the Privy Council. *"Honi soit qui mal y pense,"* meant "Shame on anyone who thinks evil of it."

But what would a Hollywood film producer in 1926 be doing wearing the mark of Elizabeth I's Privy Council from the late sixteenth century? The men he'd faced back then had been mortal, of that he was certain, but there had always been rumors that the council's power was more than simply temporal, that they dabbled in other forces as well. Could that have continued somehow? And made its way here to the Americas, and now into film?

"I will find out," the Phoenix swore, and for a moment his fire was brighter than the sun beaming down overhead as if blithely unaware of the tragedy that had just occurred. "I promise you, my friend, I will find out—and if they are the ones responsible, I will make them pay!"

But for today all he could do was mourn the loss of one of Hollywood's brightest stars, the great Latin Lover, who—like the women he had tried to protect—had been taken from the world far too soon.

FADE TO BLACK

FULL-RANGE RECORDING

Book Four

MADE IN U.S.A.–NOT LICENSED FOR RADIO BROADCAST

CROSS THE ROAD

TRACK ONE

Babe, I may be right or wrong.
Babe, it's your opinion,
Well, I may be right or wrong.
Watch your close friend, baby,
Then your enemies can't do you no harm.[1]

New York, 1927

Christopher Marlowe, the immortal Phoenix, avatar of humanity's creativity, crept into the deserted hospital room through the window.

This was not his preferred method of entry, of course. But he had been denied access via the normal route, as several burly hospital orderlies had been stationed out front of the Polyclinic Hospital and steadfastly refused to allow anyone not seeking medical attention or visiting admitted patients to enter. More guards had been placed along this floor, at stairwells and elevators, and additional men barred the door to prevent even those who slipped into the building from getting into the room itself.

Fortunately, Marlowe had certain advantages others did not. Thus, after waiting for nightfall, he had simply leaped up to the building's roof. Then, determining which room he needed, he had lowered himself down to the window, which had not been locked. After all, they were six stories up. Now he was grateful for all the guards, as their presence meant that he could stand here in the room where a famous man had died without fear of interruption.

"I am sorry, my friend," Marlowe muttered, crossing to

---

[1] All lyrics from Robert Johnson, 1936-1937

the bed and sinking down into a crouch beside it, studying the still-rumpled bedspread and dented pillow. There were flowers strewn all around the place, most of them now long since dried out, as it had taken him some time to make his way here from Hollywood. He could perhaps have taken an airplane, but Marlowe had never experienced air travel in that fashion and did not yet trust it, though little harm could come to him regardless. Still, he had chosen the slower but more reliable bus and had only just arrived in New York this morning.

The city had fascinated him, of course, with its towering buildings and throngs of fast-moving people—Los Angeles was wider, more open, and people did not seem to move at the same pace as they did here. Still, he had not come to sightsee and had made his way here as quickly as possible.

But to what end? That he still did not know. Valentino was already dead, under mysterious and highly suspicious circumstances—particularly as it had been only months since they had battled Death together, and defeated the man controlling that dread and implacable spirit. And thus only months since the famous actor had sworn to find out who had been behind the Grim Reaper's forced servitude. Clearly, he had stumbled upon something, and it had gotten him killed. But what? And by whom?

Looking around the room, Marlowe saw nothing that might help him find answers. His friend had not left him a note or any other sort of clue. No doubt by the time he had been admitted here, ostensibly for an ulcer, he had not been in any condition or frame of mind to leave such messages. Marlowe cast about him with those senses beyond mortal, yet there was no hint of magic here, no scent of strange forces at work. Only the faint tinge of dried flowers, still sweet upon the air, and the sharper, more acrid smell of cleaning agents.

Rising to his feet once more, Marlowe studied the bed a final time. "I will find them," he promised, as he had upon hearing of Valentino's death. "I will."

But clearly not here. With no reason to remain, Marlowe strode to the window and, with only one glance back, stepped through it. He allowed himself to drop lightly to the ground, landing just beside a rosebush—and startling a group of young women clustered there, no doubt hoping to pay homage at the site where their idol had perished. Tipping his hat to them, Marlowe walked away, heading back to the hotel room he had left earlier. Perhaps reflection would yield a new course of action.

A few hours later, while the sun was still hidden and most sensible folks slept, Marlowe was startled by a sharp rap upon his door. "Who is it?" he asked, rising from the room's lone chair where he had been sitting, lost in contemplation.

No answer came from the hall—but the door suddenly burst inward, with enough force that its knob slammed against the wall, cracking the worn plaster there. Three men stepped inside, the third shutting the now-cracked door again behind him.

"So," the one in front said, his voice sharp and clear. "It is true. You live." He was well-dressed, as were his two companions, all of them wearing fine suits clearly tailored to them, with natty ties and matching pocket squares, and carefully shaped fedoras. But it was to their pins that Marlowe's eyes went, unobtrusive though the small enameled circles might have been to others. Yet Marlowe had half-expected them, and indeed carried a matching accessory in his pocket, with its quartered image of lions and harp and the motto *"Honi soit qui mal y pense"* in gold around the edge. It was the symbol of Elizabeth I's Privy Council, the same one he and Valentino had found upon Lawrence Ray when they'd defeated him several months earlier.

These men were the very ones he had been seeking. And it seemed they knew something about him as well.

"You know me, then," he declared, straightening and facing them head-on. "Yet I do not know you. So, perhaps you'd be so kind?"

That drew a laugh from all three, quiet chuckles followed by a shake of their respective heads. "I think not, Mr. Marlowe," the man in front replied, and though his swagger might have fit the city they stood within, his accent certainly did not, sounding far more cultured and vaguely European to Marlowe's ears. "All you need know is that we are Wizards, and you are not wanted here, or anywhere. Begone, before we are forced to deal with you again, in a more permanent fashion than upon our previous meeting."

That made him bristle, as no doubt they had expected. "Our previous meeting?" he repeated. "You mean when you—or your ancestors, at least—stabbed me in the eye during a deliberately staged bar fight? I think not." He glared at them. "This time I am prepared for you."

The two men on either side began to advance, fists already raised, and Marlowe could see the murder in their eyes. Very well, then. It seemed the time for talking was past.

Drawing upon his inner fire, he let it flare, not fully but enough to brighten the room, casting the men's shadows in dark relief against the walls behind them. Then, as they continued to approach albeit with eyes squinting against the sudden light, Marlowe gathered the edge of that fire and cast it toward them, the flames manifesting as they left his hand and racing forward to engulf his two would-be assailants—

—and he stared, mouth falling open, as those same flames washed over the men and past them, fading away as the pair continued forward, unscathed, their auras if anything cooler than they had been a moment before.

"Yes, and we are prepared for you as well," the third man responded with another laugh. "Which one are you, anyway? Dragon? Hydra? Phoenix? Not that it matters." Reaching into his jacket, he drew forth something long and thin and conical. It glittered in the light, a hint of blue trapped in its clear, rough-surfaced form, and Marlowe realized it was an icicle. The man was carrying an icicle in his pocket! That was not the greatest surprise, however, as the stranger—the Wizard—pointed that icicle at him, spoke a series of words under his breath, and the air itself seemed to crystalize from the object's tip, in a widening beam headed straight for him!

Marlowe twisted to the side, the cold searing his shoulder and cheek from its proximity, and again he gaped as the air beside him assumed solidity and mass, and the temperature dropped in the room. There was now a massive block of ice where he had stood a second before, cold radiating from its translucent sides.

"You're quick," one of the other men said, speaking for the first time, his voice low and rough. "But there're three of us, and you've got nowhere to go." He grinned. "Unless you wanna try for the window again?"

Again. That meant they knew about the hospital. No doubt they'd been watching it, waiting to see if anyone should come looking for answers. And he had. Marlowe bit back a curse. He'd blundered right in, never bothering to check the area for others. Then they'd merely had to follow him back here. Which meant, between that and the man's taunt, that they'd somehow barred the window, preventing him from fleeing that way.

He was still strong, far stronger than someone his size ought to be, and fast. But could he fend off all three at once, with the one freezing the very air and all three immune to his flames?

The floor creaked under his feet as he shifted, and an idea came to him. Yes, they might be shielded, and the window barred, the door beyond reach.

But there were other ways out of this space.

He bared his teeth at them all. "You cannot trap me," he warned. "I am the Phoenix. I am freedom itself." As he spoke, he released his flames once more—but this time through his feet. The floorboards barely had time to sizzle before they blackened and burned to ash. Then, with a thunderous crash, they gave way, the weight of the ice block shattering the thin supports underneath and sending both it and Marlowe plummeting to the floor below.

The room there proved to be occupied as well, and the man there squawked in surprise, leaping from his bed half-clothed as the ice block shattered upon the floor, showering the room in small shards and chips and a fine flurry. Marlowe ascended more gently and shrugged apologetically to his temporary host. "Sorry about the mess," he said.

Then he dove out the window.

As he'd hoped, these Wizards had not thought to bar the rest of the building, only the window to his room. The glass here broke easily enough, his flames melting the shards before any could cut him, and he soared out into the night air, landing quickly before anyone could see.

But a shout from a nearby car told him he had been spotted nonetheless. And when the headlights clicked on and the car shot toward him, Marlowe knew the Wizards had left men outside, waiting.

There was nothing for it. He ran. He had hoped for a hunt when he'd come here, but not like this.

Not with him as the hunted.

TRACK TWO

I got to keep movin', I've got to keep movin'
Blues fallin' down like hail, blues fallin' down like hail
Mm mm mm, blues fallin' down like hail, blues fallin' down like hail
And the days keeps on worryin' me of a hellhound on my trail
Hellhound on my trail, hellhound on my trail

New York, 1930

Marlowe might not have admitted it to anyone else, but he was weary.

As he paced his small hotel room, frustration overwhelmed exhilaration. For he had, at long last, shaken the Wizards off his trail.

They had proven implacable, pursuing him avidly and with seemingly inexhaustible energy and resource. Whenever he managed to lose or defeat one group, another appeared in their stead—always well-dressed, always bearing that same pin upon their lapel, and always warded against his flames and armed with ice or some other method to ensnare him. He had fled, never having time to think, to plan, to even question, merely running on instinct, using his skill and experience to slip their net time and time again.

Yet always they had returned before he could catch his breath, just as determined as before.

It was only an inadvertent discovery that had saved him. They had cornered him in a warehouse in Chicago, and Marlowe had set the entire building afire to escape, knowing that even if they could not be harmed by the flames the Wizards would still be dazzled by it and unable to see him duck out through a crumbled portion of the blazing wall. Soot had clung to him as he'd emerged, temporarily darkening his skin, and he had found himself wishing that could remain somehow, disguising his features.

Then he had stared as, beneath the soot, his skin began to darken, taking on a deep, burnished bronze color. His scalp had begun to tingle as well, and reaching up he'd discovered that his hair, normally fine and a soft brown, had thickened and curled, and, a quick glance in a nearby window confirmed, darkened as well.

He looked like a completely different man. Possibly of African descent, possibly Mexican, but certainly not the pale Londoner once known as Christopher Marlowe.

A fresh crew of Wizards had pulled up across from the inferno that was the warehouse, but Marlowe had strolled past them, having brushed any remaining hints of soot from his clothes, and they had not spared him a second glance. He was free!

Which meant that was the time to turn the tables on them.

Destroying that small cluster would have been simple enough, even with their protections, but it would only have been a minor and temporary victory. He wanted far more than that, to put a stop to the Wizards once and for all, and to do that he needed to find their heart, not their fingertips. Which meant biding his time and letting these lackeys lead him back to their masters.

Accordingly, he'd found a convenient perch atop a nearby rooftop and had watched that new group from a distance as they'd sifted through the rubble after the fires had been put out, seeking any signs of him. From there they had dispersed, presumably to their homes. Marlowe had followed one at random, and the man had indeed headed to a residence—he had seen a woman and children greeting the man inside. Having no other ideas, he'd staked out the house through the night, and had seen the same man emerge the next morning, climb into the car he had parked in front the night before, and drive downtown to an office building.

Which he had then disappeared into, and not emerged from until evening.

Marlowe had kept watch the next few days, and though he recognized others from that last search party, none of them did anything unusual or suspicious, and he caught no hint of magic anywhere. Perhaps, then, these were not even true Wizards at all, but merely hirelings, brought in as local muscle? That would fit with the Privy Council's old methods—he still remembered the assassin they had sent after him, back in London all those years ago. If that were the case, however—and these men certainly seemed utterly mundane, not part of a secret, centuries-old sorcerous brotherhood at all—then his only hope was that the Wizards would require them for another job, and would initiate contact once more.

Sadly, that did not happen. The men went to work each day, doing whatever people with little jobs did in little offices all their little lives, and went home each night. Nothing more.

Eventually he had grown frustrated and returned here to New York instead. For surely any true Wizards hidden in Chicago were merely a satellite, called upon by their superiors as needed. New York was where they had first found him, and it was the larger, more influential city. Presumably that would be their base.

Yet he had already been here several days, and had seen no sign of the Wizards. The air here was quiet—thick with noise and music and voices and vehicles, yes, but devoid of magic.

If the Wizards were here, where were they hiding? He had to find them if he hoped to learn anything about them other than the fact that they wielded arcane forces and were determined to find and destroy him.

He was frustrated, yes. But at least now he had time to think and plan. The problem was, he did not know *what* to think.

One thing seemed certain. These men, these Wizards—they had not only killed Valentino a few years ago but had killed Marlowe himself, or at least done their best to do so, several hundred years earlier.

But that made little sense. The men who had balked him so many times as Marlowe, the queen's Privy Council, had been mortal. He was sure of it. Still, it had been their seal he had seen upon the man he and Valentino had faced in Hollywood.

That man, too, had been mortal—as evidenced by his death before their very eyes—and an unfamiliar face. So it seemed more an organization at work here, a long-reaching one, rather than a group of particular individuals—not the Privy Council members he had foiled back then, merely their descendants or successors. That also fit with those who had pursued him, for each time he had defeated one pack of them, another appeared, and none of them faces from his past. Evidently this was no mundane organization, but one with access to powers beyond mortal, powers that at least approached those of him and his brethren. How had they obtained such magic? And what did they use it for, beyond hunting him?

Uncertain where to go or what to do next, Marlowe had holed up in this small hotel and now brooded, pacing the worn floorboards until they creaked a muted symphony, not seeing the cracked plaster of the walls or the sagging mattress or the tilting table as he walked to and fro, his mind attempting to retrace whatever steps had led these shadowy opponents to their deadly actions.

Who were they, and what did they want? That was the question. All he knew about them from before was that they had wielded immense power in London, speaking and acting with the authority of Elizabeth I herself. They had *been* the authorities, and they had wielded that power with a heavy hand, imposing strict rules upon all, but none moreso than the dramatists, who they had hated and attempted to stifle at every turn.

And none so vehemently as him.

Of course, much of that had been his own fault, he freely admitted. He had delighted in throwing his rebellion in their faces, in defying their orders, in ignoring their strictures. He was the Phoenix, after all! He would not be constrained by a pack of old men whingeing from some dark-paneled chamber! He would be free to create, to entertain, to inspire!

Except that he had not, in the end. For, when they finally accepted that they would never be able to control him—they had slain him instead.

He had survived that, of course. He was the Phoenix, after all. Kill him and he arose from his own ashes. But the death had been too public to hide or explain away. Christopher Marlowe had indeed died that day.

He had moved on, however. Found a new place, crafted a new life. Moved on again and again, each time taking a new name, becoming a new person on the surface but always burning with the same fire beneath.

Not this time. His last persona had been Buster Gallagher, stuntman and actor, friend to Valentino. Buster's travels since would be difficult to explain, but no one had bothered to ask, nor had Marlowe felt the need or had the energy to construct a new identity. He was traveling without a mask now, without a disguise, and yet without his true face as well, the semblance of Marlowe gone, perhaps for good.

Now only the Phoenix remained.

But to what end, if he still had no purpose, no goal, no destination? For these men, though he knew they must exist, remained elusive. The only one he knew for certain had been Lawrence Ray, the struggling movie mogul—and he had died, a victim to the collapse of his own scheme. He could not have been acting alone, yet Marlowe had found no trace of the man's co-conspirators at the time. They had vanished as surely as any ghost, emerging from shadows only long enough to strike down Valentino when he had insisted upon pursuing them. And then to come after Marlowe himself when he had come here seeking answers to the actor's death.

But why attack either of them at all? For that matter, why their strange plot in the first place? They had targeted young women with promise, women with creativity and spark—the exact sort of people the Phoenix chose to encourage. Had it all been to thwart him? Or had that been an incidental benefit, the renewal of their old grudge just an added bonus? Why murder such women? To darken the world? To dim its collective fires?

That fit with the Privy Council's actions, to be certain. They had always quashed any play they felt was too daring, too imaginative, too innovative. They had valued order and stability above all else and had been more than willing to sacrifice originality toward that end, allowing change but only at their pace and within their boundaries.

Thus they were the anti-Phoenix—the anti-Beasts, if it came to that, for all of his strange brethren shared that one driving purpose, to elevate humanity's creativity, though each in their own fashion. These men seemingly sought the opposite, to keep mankind dumb and docile.

Which at leave gave him motive. Unfortunately, it helped not at all in determining identity, or location, or current plans.

Fed up with confinement, Marlowe fled the small room, making his way down to the hotel's tiny, cramped bar instead. At least it was different surroundings, and even though it was still early evening there were already others about. Companionship was good. It helped, somewhat.

"What can I get you?" the barman asked as Marlowe claimed a stool by the bar, and he was pleased to see that the man did not eye him askance. That had been a revelation as well, returning here from Chicago in his new guise, for many had frowned upon seeing his newly darkened visage, and a few places had pointedly ignored him, refusing him service for his coloring alone.

"A beer, if you please," Marlowe replied. The man nodded and turned away, selecting a glass and bringing it to the tap. But Marlowe had stopped paying attention. For the radio behind the bar—still a relatively new device, no more than a decade old, but one that in the past few years had started to become a fixture everywhere, as people listened to broadcast music rather than their own phonographs—was playing, and he suddenly found himself captivated by a strange music he had never heard before.

"Listen to my story now, please listen to my song," a man was singing, to the strumming of a guitar. "Can you imagine how I feel now, have mercy my real milkcow gone."

There was something plaintive about his voice, untrained but powerful, and astonishingly authentic. Marlowe was more used to standard broadcast songs, with their careful orchestration and polished singing, but this, this was raw and real and vibrant and thrilled him to his core.

"She's a full-blood Jersey, I'm going to tell you boys the way I know," the singer continued. "She's a full-blood Jersey, I'm going to tell you boys the way I know."

"Who is that?" he asked, and the barman laughed, setting the beer before him on the stained and scratched counter.

"Surprised you don't know," he replied. "That's Freddie Spruell. 'Milk Cow Blues' is the song." He shrugged. "Not my thing, but folks seem to like it. It's that new Delta Blues, you know? From down south, the Mississippi Delta?"

"The Delta Blues," Marlowe repeated, absently setting a dollar down on the counter and taking a sip of the beer as the barman scooped up the bill. "Thanks." He listened to the rest of the song in a half-daze. Such energy! Such natural rhythm! Such honesty! He absolutely loved it.

And he had a feeling the Wizards would, in turn, completely hate it. It went against everything he now suspected they believed in.

Which meant he suddenly had an idea of exactly how to find them.

Finishing his beer, he hopped up from the stool and headed back up to his room, filled with fresh purpose. Fortunately, he had always traveled light. It would take him little time to pack his few belongings, and then he would be on the road once more.

Only this time, he was heading South.

For, if you could not find the animal you were hunting, you instead sought its natural prey and staked that out instead, trusting the predator to find it soon after, and you waiting.

And that was exactly what he planned to do.

TRACK THREE

I believe, I believe I'll go back home
I believe, I believe I'll go back home
You can mistreat me here babe,
But you can't when I'm back home

Memphis, Tennessee, 1930

A week or so later, Marlowe stepped off the bus, stretching to relieve the aches in his back and neck, took a deep breath of clean evening air, and looked around with interest. He had never visited the American South before. Besides which, aside from brief stops along the way from one coast to the other, he had rarely visited small towns in this country, instead focusing on the major cities. Though he was not entirely sure Memphis could be called a small town, even by such cosmopolitan standards. Still, the lanes were far wider here than he'd encountered before, the traffic more spread out. The sidewalks he'd glimpsed on the way in were the same, wide and straight with ample room for everyone to walk. And the buildings were not as tall as in the major cities, shorter and with more room around them, giving the entire city more of an open feel.

The people seemed different as well, he noted as he hefted his one small suitcase and strolled from the bus, out through the station and into the city proper. Most nodded hello to one another as they passed, and all but a few lacked that breakneck pace he'd seen in New York and in Hollywood. Here, apparently even when people had someplace to be, they still took their time getting there.

It was warm here, too, the late afternoon sun still beating down upon them without buildings to block it, so that he was glad the brim of his hat shaded his eyes. Though Marlowe was unaffected by external heat, he quickly removed his jacket and slung it over his shoulder, loosening his shirt collar and rolling up his sleeves to more closely match the other men he saw around him.

Of course, there were other differences on display as well, and some of them far less pleasant. During his trip back to New York, Marlowe had noticed the change in people's attitude toward him, based purely on the difference in his appearance. Taking the bus from there to here, he had been relegated to the back, in the "colored" section, which was far more cramped and uncomfortable, with far less air or light. Now, out on the street, he saw men sneer at him, women frown and turn away, and children jeer. All this because he was several shades darker than them? He had heard about this horrible inequity, of course, and seen it many times, but never before experienced it firsthand.

Fortunately, his was not the only non-white complexion in evidence. Many of the men and women he saw out and about were considerably darker than him, and from them he received polite, even friendly nods and smiles. Nor was it every lighter face that glared or glowered at him. Just many of them.

Still, he had not come here to make friends. As long as those who disdained him did not interfere in his quest, Marlowe resolved to pay them no mind. Instead, he stopped on a street corner a few blocks from the station, turned his face up to the sky, closed his eyes, and listened.

After a few moments, he began to hear exactly what he'd hoped—the faint strains of music, even those distant echoes filled with longing and frustration but also with strength and pride. Yes. That was what he was here to find.

Giving himself a moment more, he finally opened his eyes, nodded, and stepped off the curb, crossing the street and heading in the direction he'd heard that music. The hunt was finally afoot.

It took nearly an hour, and the sun had already set, leaving the sky a deepening blue and the world around cooling to a more palatable temperature helped by the evening breeze, but eventually Marlowe found himself at the corner of Beale Street. Before him to the right stood an impressive building, tall and handsome with its high roofs, chimneys, and intricate detailing. But it was not that elegant home that had captured his attention.

Instead, his gaze was focused upon a smaller, plainer white building across the street and on the next block. A simple cross upon the door and another affixed to the crest of the roof indicated the building's purpose, and the music he had sought emerged from its open door, along with a warm, welcoming light.

"Greetings, brother!" a man declared as he stepped inside, taking Marlowe's hand and shaking it energetically. "Welcome to the Beale Street Church! Come on in, take a load off! Are you hungry? Help yourself, we got plenty!"

Marlowe saw that much of the building was given over to a single large room with whitewashed walls and dark rafters high above worn wood floors. Rows of polished wooden pews lined it on either side of a wide aisle, leading up to a low stage at the front that was currently occupied not by a preacher but by a quartet of men, each playing a banjo or guitar or harmonica. But in back here there were several long tables, each heavily laden with trays of food.

The smell of fried chicken and collard greens and rice and beans and stew made his stomach grumble, and he happily let himself be drawn into the line there, where a plate was piled high with food and then thrust upon him. A jar at the end was labeled "Donations" and he judiciously dropped a rumpled dollar into it, but he suspected from the pleased response that it truly had been more of a suggestion than a requirement. More benches lined the walls, and people were sitting or standing in small groups, eating and talking—and listening to the music that rose above all those other sounds, blending everything together into a wave of song and emotion.

"Welcome, friend!" another man told him as he found a

seat, clapping him on the shoulder but carefully so as not to unsettle the plate he was attempting to balance upon his knees. "Don't think I know you—new to town?"

"I am, yes," Marlowe admitted. "Just arrived this morning." He took a sizable bite of the chicken, the fry crisp and tangy in his mouth, the meat beneath still juicy and tender and piping hot. His new neighbor laughed and handed him a napkin, and he nodded thanks as he mopped at his chin. "Thank you."

"You're right welcome," his companion replied. "Daniel Austin, glad to meet you." The hand he extended was steady, the fingers thick and solid, calluses visible upon the palm. A workman's hand.

"Carl," Marlowe replied, inventing a name upon the spot. "Carl Monroe. A pleasure." He waved his half-eaten chicken leg around the place. "Y'all do this often?" Already he could feel himself slipping somewhat into the cadence of language here, so different from the clipped tones of New York or the equally rapid but lighter sounds of California.

"Every Saturday night," Daniel answered. "A little food, a little talk, and a whole lot of music and dancing." He grinned wide. "Can't be beat."

"No, it sure can't," Marlowe agreed, finishing the piece of chicken and starting on another, with a pause in between to gulp some lemonade from the tall paper cup he'd been given along with his food. Daniel nodded at that, clearly pleased at his confirmation, but kept silent for a moment or two, content to let him finish his meal in peace. And so Marlowe ate and drank, and after a time he chatted more with Daniel and with others who wandered over to introduce themselves and find out who he was and where he hailed from and how long he was staying. But mostly, he listened.

The music was much as he'd heard in that bar, only even moreso now that it was in person. There was that vibrancy to it, that energy, the same as he'd felt when watching performers up on stage during a play, the same as when he'd seen men like Byron or Shelley recite poetry or fiction—the same as Valentino when he had stepped before the cameras.

This was passion. This was truth. This was life.

This was what he lived for.

He'd found the place he'd been seeking. Now he just needed to wait until the Wizards found it as well.

TRACK FOUR

Well, some people tell me that the worried, blues ain't bad
Worst old feelin' I most ever had
Some people tell me that these old worried old blues ain't bad
It's the worst old feelin', I most ever had

Farrell, Mississippi, 1930

Marlowe spat a handful of watermelon seeds upon the ground at his feet, swallowing the rest of the mouthful of sweet, juicy melon. He lifted his hat to wipe the back of one hand across his forehead, then set it back down atop his sweat-damp curls, the brim tilted down to shade his eyes from the fierce noon sun, and leaned back in his chair so the top of the rattan back rattled against the clapboard wall behind him. Several other men sat there upon the front porch, all of them in that same level of semi-slumber brought on by the heat and humidity, and conversation, when it occurred, was a slow, soft hum that barely disturbed the heavy air.

Shaking his head, Marlowe let it fall back and closed his eyes, the half-eaten watermelon still cradled in his lap. There was little else to do, here in Farrell, Mississippi, beyond sit, sleep, talk, and occasionally sing the blues.

That last was why he had come, of course. He had spent nearly a month in Memphis, and while he'd enjoyed the company and the hospitality there had been no sign of the men he sought, these strange Wizards with their sorcery so like yet unlike his own gifts. After a time, he'd begun to wonder if he hadn't got it wrong. Not about those men and their ilk being interested in the Blues—of that he was certain. But perhaps

Memphis would not be their destination. It was, after all, the very uppermost tip of the Mississippi Delta, or so he'd been told by his new friends. The Blues emerged from there and spread hence to the rest of the world, but it originated lower down.

Then, he'd finally decided, lower down was where he had to go. Packing his one bag, he had taken leave of the family who'd given him a bed during his stay and had boarded the one and only bus headed down into the Delta. A day later, he'd disembarked in Friars Point. Even that town felt like it might be too large, too formalized, for what he had in mind, so he'd set out again, this time on foot, following the thin dirt road away from the bus route and ever south.

The next town along the way had been Farrell.

It was not much of a town, in truth. Perhaps half a hundred souls, most likely less, and half of them too old or too young to work. Not that there was a great deal of work to be had hereabouts. The people seemed to make do with a rough and ready combination of fishing, hunting, and personal farming. Their curious glances as he'd passed among the handful of buildings told him they were unaccustomed to visitors, yet for all that they'd been perfectly friendly, offering him a jug of homemade corn whiskey and a pipe filled with local tobacco and a plate of rice and beans.

And here he had been ever since.

The reason why came rising up, as it so often did, swelling and pushing the moist air aside to fill his mind and spirit as a handful of younger men perched on rough benches in front of the porch began to play their instruments and then burst into song. This, this was the true Delta Blues! Unadulterated, not cleaned up for the church crowd or tamed for the radio, just raw and rich and spontaneous, a playful battle between the men as they tossed lines back and forth, daring each other to complete the verse and keep the rhythm going.

It was the music that kept him here, the music that kept his spirit soaring, even as his heart sank lower and lower with each passing day.

Because he'd yet to see the Wizards here, either. Nor had the town's residents ever heard of or seen such men. And surely it would have been impossible for them to stay hidden in a place this size.

Had his entire trek here been a waste, then? Had he spent this time for nothing?

Although it was not as if he had a shortage of the stuff. Indeed, if anything he had far too much of it.

His thoughts slid down that dark road, spiraling deeper and deeper as the heat bore down, his whole body drenched from it, his eyelids heavy as his breathing, and all of it labored. Yes, labored, the same way he had all these years, all these centuries. And for what? He protected humanity, encouraged them, inspired them, but to what end? How had it made any sort of a difference?

When he had been Marlowe, at least he had created great works himself. Even now, some of those lived on, though others had been lost to the years. He'd seen his plays performed in London, in New York, in Boston and Chicago and Los Angeles. His name and his art lived on, even as he did.

But did that help any? Did it change anything? People emerged from the theaters weeping or laughing or somber, depending upon the piece, but were they more than when they went in? Did their lives improve—did *they* improve—for having heard his words and seen them performed?

And what had he done since? Crossed two continents and an ocean, met countless people, inspired many of them—and to what end? Was he truly making a difference, or simply marking time in this apparently endless life of his?

Though it did not have to be endless. He knew that much. After all, had there not been other Phoenix before him?

Marlowe's thoughts flashed back, back to the very beginning. He had still been a young man at the time, just learning his craft at the feet of other, older playwrights and actors, though already he'd begun to show promise, his work still crude but filled with a passion that captivated the listener, an energy that often crackled through the theater like the air before a storm. After one such performance, a man had lingered, his singular appearance attracting as much attention as Marlowe's verse had done, for there were very few Chinese in the city, and none ever beyond the docks where their ships came to trade exotic goods. Yet, this man had sat there on the bench, ignoring the looks and jeers he'd received from his fellow audience members, and had remained there patiently afterward, his hands folded in his lap and an expression of deep calm upon his long, lined face.

"So," he had said in heavily accented but easily understandable English when Marlowe had finally been sent to shoo him away so they could close up the theater for the evening. "You are the one who will succeed me."

"Prithee, I know not what that means," Marlowe had admitted. "Succeed you at what? Who might you be, an' it come to that?"

"My name," the Chinaman had replied, and up close Marlowe could see how deep those lines were, and how thin and nearly translucent his skin, though his hair was still dark and sleek and his eyes still bright, "is Altan Kahn. I have traveled a long way to find you, young Christopher Marlowe." He had sighed, the sound that of a much older man, and had risen to his feet with the creaks and groans of one as well. "Traditionally, we would battle, as I once fought the warrior named Malguin and he no doubt bested others before that, but I am old and you are not, and I find I am tired, my fire nearly spent. So instead I bequeath it to you willingly, my young friend. The eternal flame. The fire at the heart of all creativity. The immortal Phoenix." He had cupped his hands together before him, and within them grew a bright light, flames sprouting there from nothing, not burning his flesh but floating just above it, a great ball of fire so brilliant Marlowe could barely look upon it.

And then the old Chinaman had stepped forward and, in one quick motion, slammed that burning sphere into Marlowe's chest, directly over his heart.

Pain! Marlowe still remembered it now, the agony, as if he were dying, as if he were burning to ash on the spot. He'd fallen to his knees, only just aware that his attacker had dropped as well, both hands going to his chest where the pain seemed centered, his body breaking out in a sweat, his extremities tingling, his vision swimming. It had felt as if he'd been borne up by an enormous wave, one of fire and pain, and it had swept him along, away from the world he knew, leaving the dirt and grime and wood and smoke behind, carrying him high up into the air, into the clouds, up to the very sun itself.

And from there, as if the sun had just burst through those same clouds on a rainy day, he had seen the whole world laid out below him, in all its glory, shining and bright and beautiful, filled with tiny lights he instinctively knew were people. Wonderful, funny, clever, creative people. Their lights were hypnotic, and he'd felt the flames respond to them, intensifying, and draw them higher in return.

And then those same flames had turned inward, as if sucked into him somehow, and he'd fallen again, plummeting back into his body, coming to there on the dirty rushes of the gallery floor, the old Chinaman dead beside him, and his every sense and every inch alive as never before.

He had become the Phoenix. He knew that, deep within. He was now the avatar of creativity, of individuality, of personal freedom. His task was to inspire, and to protect.

But for how long? How old had Altan Kahn been when he'd found him there? How old had been that man he'd mentioned, Malguin, who had sought him in turn? Surely not several hundred years. Why, then, was Marlowe still here? Why had he not found someone to pass the flame to, so that he could rest?

Because, in truth, he was tired. And frustrated. And uncertain where to go or what to do next. And perhaps because it was harder to find such bright souls now, in this modern era, with so many around and so much activity and confusion masking such sparks of creativity.

For now, he took another bite of watermelon, spitting the seeds out to join the rest there on the floor. Chewed and swallowed and listened to the music, let it soothe away the sharpest edges of his pain and fatigue and despair.

What else could he do?

TRACK FIVE

I went to the crossroad, fell down on my knees
I went to the crossroad, fell down on my knees
Asked the Lord above, "Have mercy, save poor Bob if you please"

Somewhere in the Mississippi Delta, October 1930

It was already well past sundown one night in October when Marlowe felt the inexplicable urge to get up off that porch. He was on his feet and standing on the dirt out front before he quite knew what he'd begun, those few of his recent companions who had not toddled off to bed stirring only slightly as his chair banged against the wall, but by then he was already walking, his strides lengthening as he settled into the rhythm of a steady, ground-devouring pace, his face and feet turned toward the south.

What was it that had called to him so strongly, he wondered as he passed quickly through Farrell and beyond, out onto the road, nothing but trees to either side and no sound but the wind through the leaves to keep him company. There was something out there, he was sure of it, but what that might be he could not say. Only that it had called, and he must answer.

He could not have said how long he walked, or how far he traveled. At one point there were lights and the sound of voices to his right, but he did not slow or swerve to investigate, and those soon fell behind him, swallowed up once more by the deepening night. The road continued on, nothing more than a wide dirt track, and Marlowe followed it, his steps firm and steady along the way. He could not see much, though the moon had risen and was full, its silvery light shining down through the trees, for their canopy was still so thick and heavy he could only barely make out the path he knew he must follow.

Eventually, he came to a clearing. The trees huddled back from it as if frightened to approach, and a second track crossed the first, disappearing into the woods to the east and west just as this one continued on south and stretched back behind him to the north. A dog was howling somewhere nearby, or perhaps it was merely the wind. A downed tree lay near the juncture of the two paths, and Marlowe paused there, setting himself atop its fallen trunk. Leaning back, he closed his eyes and let his senses stretch out this way and that, becoming one with the night, feeling his way through it.

Someone was approaching. He felt them first, then heard them, a solitary pair of footsteps much like his own, and no more hurried. A man, he surmised, and young. Approaching from the south. As the sounds grew, Marlowe opened his eyes, and nodded as he saw the figure emerge from the shadows, a young man, slim of build, in a white shirt and dark slacks, suspenders, and the ever-present hat that was the mark of every man in the South. His skin was darker than Marlowe's own, though in this dim light even his appeared black as pitch, and up against his shoulder the newcomer carried a guitar.

As he approached, Marlowe realized he recognized the man as one of those who played and sang the Blues even more than most. This was one who had dedicated his life to the music, not just singing to pass the time but making that his career. His voice was good, and he was handy with the harmonica, but the guitar was his passion.

Sadly, in that area, the youth's desire far outstripped his skill, for he could only barely play the instrument, and badly at that.

Still, Marlowe sensed in the man a kindred spirit, fueled by a desire to create and inspire, and he admired that. Though what was even such an itinerant performer doing out in these woods at such an hour?

"You're out late, Robert Johnson," he declared, sitting up to make his presence known.

That startled the newcomer, who sank to his knees right there at the center of the crossroads. "Maybe so," he agreed, hanging his head. "Yet here I am, and here you are, too."

Marlowe rose to his feet, slowly, and approached the musician. Yes, there was fire there, he saw, but it was banked low,
barely more than embers. Why was that, when he had heard
Johnson sing? It had to be the trouble with the guitar. The
young man cradled it as if it were his own child, as if hoping his
devotion would somehow coax sound from it that his fingers
alone could not.

Well, perhaps Marlowe could help with that.

"Stand up, Robert Johnson," he urged as he reached the
other man. "You want to throw that guitar over there in that
ditch and go back up to Robinsville or Beulah and play the harp
with Willie Brown and Son because you're just another guitar
player like all the rest? Or do you want to play that guitar like
nobody ever played it before? Make a sound nobody ever heard
before?" He leaned in close, and his own flames began to flare,
sparks from it dancing across to the other man, catching in his
eyes. "You want to be the King of the Delta Blues," he asked,
"and have all the whiskey and women you want?" For he knew
of Robert Johnson's favorite vices, as did anyone who had ever
met him or seen him play.

Johnson smiled. "That's a lot of whiskey and women, Devil-
man," he replied, and Marlowe laughed at the appellation. Did
the musician think him the very Devil? Perhaps, for who else
did one meet out here in the dark, beneath the full moon?

"I know you, Robert Johnson," he told the young man
where he still knelt upon the ground. "But do *you* know you?
Do you know what you truly want? Time for you to make up
your mind."

He spread his fire to either side like great burning wings,
then wrapped them around himself and the man at his feet,
letting the light and the warmth and the energy fill them both.
As it did, Marlowe himself began to feel his spirits rise. Why
had he been so down on himself and on the world? Here before
him was proof that he was still needed, and proof as well that
there was still beauty in the world, and life, and soul. He tilted
his head back and laughed, and the sound rose, swirling about
them, drawing from not only his mind and heart but Johnson's

as well, until it soared and swelled and echoed among the trees. It had become the very sound of the Blues, eerie and touching at the same time, thrilling and comforting, soothing and electrifying.

"That sound can be yours, Robert Johnson," he told the musician at his side. "That's the sound of the Delta Blues."

Johnson raised his head, meeting Marlowe's own gaze, and Marlowe was not entirely surprised to see a light glowing within the young man's eyes. Now those fires were fully awake, and roaring to life! "I got to have that sound, Devilman," he declared, his voice ringing and picking up many of those same tones, throbbing with passion and power. "Where do I sign?"

Marlowe smiled, amused that his chance companion should still be clinging to that same initial misconception. But why not? Wasn't one myth as good as another? "You haven't got a pencil, Robert Johnson," he chided gently. "Your word is good enough. All you have to do is keep on walking, and keep on playing. Let your music come from your heart and your soul, and you will be unstoppable." He paused, and felt he owed it to the other man to add, "But you better be prepared. There are consequences."

Johnson stood, swaying slightly beside him, his eyes still aglow from the fires within. "Prepared for what, Devil-man?" he asked.

"There are those who will wish to stop you," Marlowe warned. "They will wish to dim your light and smother your sound. They will not want to see your song sweep forth, for its power will possess people, will free them, and some in the world do not desire to see that. So you could turn around. You could set that guitar down and go back whence you came and content yourself with performing in small towns still, singing and playing harmonica. But if you take up that instrument and that calling, you will have the Blues like never known to this world. Your soul will pour out in your song, and the whole world will hear it. That is what you need to be ready for."

Robert Johnson looked at him a moment. Then he laughed, and the sound was like thunder, his eyes like lightning, the pair of them shattering the silence and the dark as if it were dawn rather than midnight. "Step back, Devil-man," he declared, squaring his slight shoulders even as he settled the guitar against the right side once more. "I'm going to show the world I am the Blues."

Marlowe nodded, pleased that the musician had not balked at the thought of trouble and, for once, basking in a heat that was not his own. "Go on, Robert Johnson," he agreed. "You are the King of the Delta Blues. Go show the world what you can do."

The young musician nodded back and strolled away, headed north the way Marlowe had come, all fatigue and doubt struck from his being, his every movement filled with power and light and song, even his steps falling to a new beat that seemed to stir the trees until their leaves and branches swished and swayed in rhythm. Marlowe watched until Johnson had disappeared from view, the smile never leaving his face nor that newly restored sense of purpose and contentment fading from his chest. This, this was what he had been born for! This was why he was here! Not to sit on a porch and eat watermelon but to walk the Earth and share his light with others, to inspire them to fiery heights of their own!

A part of him thought to follow Johnson, to see what he would become. But he had already given that young man a gift. There were others who might need such support and encouragement as well.

And there were still the Wizards to locate. They had not come to the South, as he'd expected. They might still, but perhaps they did not move as quickly as he. Or perhaps it was too spread out down here, too sparse, the lights too small for them to notice yet.

In which case, he might need to go somewhere with more flames to be lit. Someplace they could not, would not ignore. There was talk of war brewing overseas, he'd heard men say. Troubles in Europe, discontent left over from the Great War now threatening to erupt again. Well, wars were always a time of great and terrible creativity. Many of his brethren would be drawn to such, why not their apparent opposites as well? Surely, if these Wizards wished to lull mankind into a dull and dreary uniformity, they would be present to stamp out those innovations that always arose from such conflicts?

He would go and see. Marlowe smiled and dusted his hands on his pants, took off his hat and slapped it against his knee before resetting it on his head. Yes. He had stayed here long enough. He'd return, at some point. But for now, whatever had been urging him in this direction was gone.

The Phoenix was needed elsewhere, and so that was where he must go.

He walked away, turning his back on Robert Johnson for now, and the crossroads fell quiet as he left them behind.

TRACK SIX

I got stones in my passway
And my road seem dark as night
I got stones in my passway
And my road seem dark as night
I have pains in my hearts
They have taken my appetite

Berlin, Germany, August, 1936

Marlowe hurried down the long hall, his boot heels clattering on the polished marble floor. Damn it! The vote had not been scheduled to occur for another two hours! He had only just been informed that the meeting had been inexplicably moved up, and he was already late for it. He only hoped his compatriots had been more timely in their arrival, or all their work would have been for naught!

He was still a dozen feet from the grand double doors when they swung open, not with any great force but just enough for a pair of figures in gray suits to slip through. Marlowe slowed to avoid running them down, and the men both glanced up at his approach. His heart sank as he saw their faces, both confirming their identities and gathering the news from their stricken expressions.

"Herr Schacht. Herr Doctor Goerdeler." He came to a stop beside them just as they cleared the massive portal. "What has happened? The vote—"

"There will be no vote," Reichsbank President Hjalmar Schacht replied, with no force but an abundance of bitterness. "The Führer has spoken."

"What? No! There must be!" Marlowe insisted, but his two companions both shook their heads.

"It is over, Herr Vogel," Price Commissioner Dr. Carl Friedrich Goerdeler told him in a leaden voice. "He has already made his decision. There is nothing more to be done."

"I don't believe that," Marlowe declared, glaring at them both, stoking his fire and willing it around them, trying to raise their spirits as well. But it was no use. Their flames had already been snuffed out, all their confidence and passion shattered, nothing but cold ash remaining in the dregs of frustration and defeat that filled them now.

"You should believe it, sir," a new voice intruded, and Marlowe turned back toward the door to see another man emerging, this one a square-jawed individual with short dark hair and piercing eyes. A nasty smile tugged at his thin lips, and in his dark suit he looked every inch the consummate businessman, but Marlowe was not fooled, for he knew the man's identity already, and his pedigree.

"Herr Göring," he said politely nonetheless, nodding hello though his shadow flared behind him. Schacht and Goerdeler, perhaps seeing that or simply feeling the shift in air around them, said quick farewells and walked away as rapidly as was feasible without breaking into a run. He could hardly blame them. Few crossed the self-styled ruler of Germany—or his second in command—and lived long to tell of it. "I take it congratulations are in order," Marlowe continued, keeping his voice in check, if only barely.

"Yes, indeed," the Nazi answered, tipping his head in acknowledgement, that small grin never leaving his lips. "Our Führer has chosen to move forward with the Four-Year Plan—and he has placed me in charge." The grin widened into a full-blown smirk. "I realize this is not the outcome you had hoped for, eh?"

"Not quite, no," Marlowe admitted. He had been working for months with Schacht and Goerdeler to gain support for an alternate plan, one which would decrease military spending and both restore and preserve certain civil liberties among the populace. Göring's Four-Year Plan was the exact opposite, putting emphasis on military might at the expense of personal freedoms.

It was everything Marlowe despised, but he had known that the only possible path to defeating it had been working from within the system rather than using brute force from without, using his two allies' clout to win support from others within the government so that they could then put the matter to a vote. Now it seemed even that had failed.

"Yes, I can only imagine," Göring continued, moving closer, a malicious light shining from his eyes. "Curtailing freedoms, restricting creativity, forcing uniformity and obedience—quite the antithesis to your guiding principles, eh? Herr Phönix."

At the term, Marlowe's head rose sharply and he studied the man before him. Upon one lapel Göring bore the swastika, of course, the ancient holy symbol the Nazis had perverted and made their own. But on his other was a different pin, one Marlowe knew all too well—a quartered circle in red and blue and gold.

"What?" Marlowe stared openly at his apparent rival. "You? You're a—"

"A Wizard, yes," Göring answered. "One of many, far more than you can even imagine." He laughed. "You look so surprised, Herr Phönix. How little you know of us—yet we know everything about you." He tutted. "And your name? Herr Kay Vogel? Mister Fire Bird? Truly? Do you think so little of us that you believed we would not see through your little charade?"

Marlowe was still trying to wrap his head around the notion that this man, this odious man, was one of the very foes he had been seeking these past ten years. "How?" he managed through his confusion. "You have no magic, none at all. I would know otherwise." For certainly his every sense told him that this man was cold and inert, mystically speaking, without even a single spark of power.

"Magic?" The Nazi snorted. "Stuff and nonsense. Many of my colleagues believe in such fairy tales, but I am a man of science, Herr Phönix! I live in reality alone!" He moved in closer, until his face was inches from Marlowe's own. "What need have we of so-called magic, I ask you?" the man whispered, his breath warm on Marlowe's lips. "We do not require such things to change the world, my friend. Only our will."

Marlowe stepped back, struggling with this statement and the strange new revelation it had incited within him. All this time, he had been hunting the Wizards by their magic, catching flickers of it here and there, seeing it around those they sent after him in return. But if Göring was telling the truth—if many of the Wizards were mere mortals, without any power at all? No wonder he had been unable to find them. Those men he had followed back in Chicago, the ones he had dismissed as lackeys, outside agents, they had been Wizards after all. Just ones without magic. He had watched them and watched them, assuming they were only a way to find his true enemies, when they had been the enemy themselves, and he had ignored that in his shortsightedness.

Here he had been seeking them everywhere, despairing at not finding any trace, while they had been hiding in plain sight all this time!

He barely noticed as Göring waved at someone else through the still-open door, and a quartet of large, burly men emerged, all dressed in the uniform of the Waffen-SS, the Nazi's own armed enforcers. "Escort our friend here to quieter quarters," the commander instructed his thugs. "Magic or no, there are many strange riddles surrounding his activities and his history. Now at last we will get to the bottom of those. Yes, we have many questions we will wish to have answered at our leisure." Then, with a cavalier nod and a flippant wave, Göring strolled away, laughing at his own not-so-subtle joke.

Everyone knew that the Nazis did not bother to ask politely.

The men approached, and the two in front grabbed Marlowe by either arm. That snapped him out of his fugue and he snarled, his flames flaring outward and flinging the soldiers from him, hard enough to slam them into the gilded walls on either side with a pair of loud cracks. Göring glanced back and what he saw must have alarmed him, for he shouted, "Help! Men! Kill him at once!" even as he turned and ran for his life.

Heeding that cry, more soldiers poured from the chambers beyond those doors, shouting as they bore down upon the slightly built man in their path, but Marlowe did not mind. In fact, he welcomed them. This was something he understood, after all. Anger and violence and pain—yes, these things he knew. These things he excelled at. Violence, after all, could bring with it a certain level of creativity, too.

The hall was soon ablaze with light, fire licking at the tapestries on each wall, windows shattered from the sudden and intense heat, men screaming in agony as their uniforms and hair and very flesh caught fire. It was over soon enough, the shadows creeping back in, the flames diminishing rapidly as if they had been swallowed back up, the cool August breeze blowing in through newly empty window frames.

Afterward, a single man strode from the hall, his form unharmed, fire dancing in his eye and a grim expression on his face. For despite winning that skirmish, Marlowe knew that he had already lost this battle. The Four-Year Plan would be put into effect. Hitler and his regime would grow in power. And anyone who opposed them, who thought to encourage debate and dissent, would be quickly disabused. The opportunity for mannered opposition was past.

Still, it would be some time before the Führer had the strength or confidence to push beyond his nation's own borders. Marlowe would return and deal with him at a later date. For now, he had unfinished business back in the States and a new perspective to bring to his search.

At last he would find the Wizards—and he would end them.

TRACK SEVEN

When I leave this town, I'm gon' bid you fare, farewell
And when I leave this town, I'm gon' bid you fare, farewell
And when I return again, you'll have a great long story to tell

Chicago, October, 1936

Marlowe found Robert Johnson much as he'd left him—only different.

The first change he noticed was locale. He'd traveled from Germany to London and from there to New York, then made his way across half the country to Chicago, expecting to stop over there only a few days before continuing South. He'd had only a vague notion of how to proceed from there, but intended to start where he'd left off unless some better plan presented itself.

Being back in the States was strange. There was not the same cloud of foreboding as in Europe, where most seemed to know war was coming to them sooner rather than later. Here, an entire ocean separated them from the problems Germany was creating for itself and its neighbors. People in America clearly believed that, even if there was a war, it would never come to them, so why should they worry about it?

Besides which, there was more than enough to worry about right here at home. The Great Depression was still in full effect, and people everywhere were suffering. Most of those Marlowe passed had a lean look to them, the result of food shortages and budget reductions. Clothing was more threadbare, more patched. Cars were older. Buildings were dingier. Yet the homes themselves were often more kept up, the gardens more carefully

tended, the lawns more diligently cut, the awnings and window sashes more frequently repainted, as if those little touches
which were still within people's power could help them fend off
thoughts of larger problems they were powerless to overcome.
Marlowe admired their efforts, and their attitude, even if he
knew that ultimately such obfuscations could be fruitless.

One of the ways people were still keeping their spirits up
was through music. The radio made song available to all, and
everywhere he went Marlowe heard those sets turned up, blast-
ing Big Band, crooners, country—and the Blues.

And one of the people he heard mentioned most often was
Robert Johnson.

Not that Johnson's songs were on the radio. No, these were
mentions of his live performances, but the musician seemed
to be everywhere. Which was why, when Marlowe landed in
Chicago, he found that the man would be playing in that very
city, the very next night. Which was both surprising, to find the
musician so far from his old familiar haunts, and serendipitous,
since Marlowe had planned to seek him out regardless.

Naturally, Marlowe immediately made plans to attend the
performance.

The music hall was packed, the air already warm from so
many even in such a large space and thick with the mingled
smells of sweat, perfume, tobacco, and wood polish. People were
standing in the aisles and all across the back, and he wedged
himself in amongst the latter, twisting until he was able to place
his back firmly against the hall's rear wall. Though he had never
been a towering individual, the floor here slanted down toward
the stage, so he had an excellent view of that platform and of
the slender young man who sat upon a stool there, a guitar resting comfortably across one knee.

Robert Johnson still looked much the same. Smooth-
cheeked and clean-chinned, his suit shiny from long use but
pressed and clean, his tie sharp and bright, his hat tilted jaun-
tily to one side and his eyes bright. He smiled out at the crowd,
seemingly at ease, and then, without a word of notice, bent
forward slightly, curling over his instrument, and began to
play.

Marlowe had heard the man before, of course, and had always been impressed by his voice and by his lyrics. But, previously, Johnson's use of the guitar had severely hampered his performance overall. Not so now. The man's fingers were deft and sure as they strummed and stroked across fret and string, producing a set of wailing notes perfectly clear and yet somehow sliding seamlessly from one to the next. There were low notes mixed with the high, and Marlowe realized after a moment that the musician was using a thumb pick for those. This was not a new technique, but to do so this smoothly while also finger picking the high notes was impressive. There was more to the performance, however, and Marlowe concentrated, drawing upon what he had learned when he'd visited the South those few years before. Ah, of course! The slide! Johnson had one of those as well, and was using that at the same time. Even more of a virtuoso performance! Clearly the young man had been studying and practicing since their last meeting, though Marlowe congratulated himself on helping unlock the performer's massive potential.

The rest of the audience was as rapt as he was, and not a sound was heard from the crowd, barely even a breath, until Johnson finished the song. Then thunderous applause arose, filling the place to the rafters. He merely smiled, dipped his head in thanks, and began to pick out the notes for the next song.

Johnson played and sang for two hours straight, pausing now and then to sip from either a glass of whiskey or a tumbler of water. When he finally rose from the stool and bowed, guitar held high, the crowd erupted in praise, clapping and cheering and whistling.

Marlowe was right there with the rest of them. He had been drawn to the South by the Blues, fascinated and enthralled with its power and its passion. Robert Johnson had just demonstrated the very best of it, raw intensity and emotion coupled with perfect mastery of technique. The man truly had become the King of the Delta Blues.

People were converging on the musician, and despite wishing to renew their acquaintance Marlowe instead stayed back where he'd been throughout, watching as Johnson navigated those well-wishers as confidently as he had his chords. Most received a smile and a nod of thanks, gracious but quick, the response of a friendly performer nonetheless worn out from an exhausting performance. Attractive women received a good deal more time and attention, coupled with a far warmer smile and light touches along the arm and side from those dexterous hands.

Then there were the businessmen. Wearing dark, conservative suits, well-made and far better maintained than most, these men were effusive in their praise, if their smiles and broad gestures and handshakes and backslaps were any indication, but at the same time they were all business. Johnson's posture toward them was far different, much more deferential but not at all subservient, Marlowe was pleased to note—the young man presented an attitude of "yes, I respect you and would be happy to work with you, but at the same time I know what I bring to the table, and that you need me more than I need you." The men did not seem displeased with this confidence, though a few appeared taken aback at not having whatever they'd proposed immediately and enthusiastically accepted. Still, they all departed with smiles and nods, suggesting mutually beneficial arrangements were in the works.

His suspicions aroused, Marlowe paid particular attention to those men as they sidled past, none of them noticing him where he stood in the shadows, his skin and hair once more darkened as they'd been on his last sojourn to the States. Some of the businessmen he discounted, for up close he could see that their suits were as worn as the rest, and he could make out hints of desperation in their eyes and at the corners of their mouths. But the final group to depart, their suits were all sturdy and new, hints of fine whiskey and aged tobacco wafting about them as they walked, and their faces were round and pink and full with prosperity.

No magic surrounded these laughing, strutting men, but Marlowe now knew not to ignore them simply for that reason alone. In every other way—powerful, successful, self-important, out to control others—they fit the mental profile of his foes exactly.

He barely needed the multi-colored, quartered pin winking from one's lapel to tell him he had found his prey at last.

The Wizards were indeed here, and now Marlowe had them in his sights.

TRACK EIGHT

My door knob keeps on turnin', it must be spooks around my bed
My door knob keeps on turnin', must be spooks around my bed
I have a warm, old feelin', and the hair risin' on my head

Marlowe followed these men out, but it was already late and they soon parted ways, each hailing a cab and departing the neighborhood. Choosing one at random, Marlowe pursued, and watched as the man was deposited before and soon entered a large, handsome home. Very well. He would watch and wait, as he had before, but this time with clearer eyes, eyes now open to the larger truth.

The next morning, the same man emerged, wearing a similar but fresh suit. A cab was waiting for him, and wasted no time whisking him away, toward the heart of Chicago's business district. Marlowe followed, careful not to draw attention to himself—even if they did not yet recognize him in his altered guise, he saw no reason to risk exposure before he was ready.

The cab brought the Wizard to the same building Marlowe had staked out before, and he cursed himself anew as he watched the businessman stride in through the glass front doors as if he owned the place. So close, all those years ago! If only he'd known! If only he hadn't made such foolish, narrow-minded assumptions!

At least he knew better now.

Approaching the building, Marlowe read the brass plaque displayed prominently above its front door: "North West Tower." He had paid the structure itself little attention before, but now had to admit that it was a striking piece of architecture, tall and triangular, almost like the prow of a ship had been cast in stone there upon the street. It soared at least a hundred feet overhead, a single tower at the top there where the two sides met, and its lines were clean, almost plain, but made impressive by its sheer scale. To his mind it said, "Look at how imposing I am, I require no embellishment to dominate."

How very like the Wizards.

Stepping inside, Marlowe found himself within a handsome lobby, low-ceilinged and dark despite the bright morning sun outside, with thick columns breaking up the space and low leather chairs and round glass tables in small clusters almost like an obstacle course between him and the front desk at the far side. He barely noticed the furnishings, however, for there had been a faint tingle as he'd entered, almost like a shiver across his skin but warm and electric rather than cold.

Magic. There was magic here.

Exulting at being proven right, he glanced about him, trying to discern if any of the people moving to and from the banks of elevators behind that front desk were the opponents he sought. How many true Wizards were there, after all?

A ding from one of the elevators caught his attention, and he focused on it just as the doors opened and a quartet of large men in dark suits came rushing out. They moved in a close-knit formation, crossing the lobby and glaring about them, studying each and every person in turn. Marlowe had already turned away from them, though, guessing their intent, and singled out one of the groups of people nearby. "Excuse me," he asked, approaching them, "might one of you have the time?"

"Oh, of course," one of the men answered, pulling out a pocket watch. "It's ten to nine."

"Thanks so much," Marlowe replied as the security guards swarmed past, barely looking his way—after all, he did not match any description they might have of him, and he was clearly part of a conversation already, whereas surely they were seeking a man alone? "Sorry to have bothered you. Have a good day."

"You too," the others replied politely, and Marlowe turned to go, the guards having already retreated to the front desk to debate their next move—but he paused mid-motion, his eye captured by a pin on the nearest man's lapel.

The mark of the Wizards.

Nor was that gentleman alone, for he quickly realized that the man with the pocket watch had the same pin. As did the other two they'd been speaking with. All of whom were now studying him curiously.

"Sorry, just thought of something I'd forgot," he told them with a shrug and a self-deprecating laugh, and continued his earlier motion, making his way toward the door and back through it at a carefully casual pace, not looking around or glancing behind but also not rushing.

Once he was through the doors and back on the street, however, he all but flew—and the temptation was strong to do exactly that!—across the street, down the block, and around the corner. Only after he had put that much distance between himself and that building did he pause for breath, or risk looking back.

Wizards. They were all Wizards, every one of them. Possibly everyone in that entire building!

Just how large was this enemy of his?

Deciding to test his deadly new theory, Marlowe allowed his skin and hair to resume its original appearance, the color fading from him as it were being washed away. More security guards— presumably led by the same four, though now he counted nearly a dozen—had spilled out through the same front door he had just exited, and were searching the area, clearly surprised to not see him immediately before them.

Stepping out from behind the corner where he'd been sheltering, Marlowe straightened, put two fingers to his lips, and whistled sharply. When the guards' heads snapped up in his direction, he waved.

And then he ran.

Three hours later, Marlowe emerged from an elevated train station. He was once more burnished and curled, and had been riding the trains for the past half hour to make sure he had at last lost any remaining pursuit.

It had been a near thing, however. Especially since, surrounded by innocents, he had not dared take the violent yet expedient measure of immolating his pursuers.

There had been many of them, too. Not just the initial dozen—they had somehow communicated their whereabouts with others, and every time he thought he'd escaped them another pack would appear and converge upon him. He had only managed to evade them at last by darting inside an office building, charging into the stairwell, leaping up five flights in a single bound and then again, and then sprinting to an unused corner office, throwing open the window, and hurling himself out through it into empty air.

As he'd hoped, neither the Wizards nor anyone else thought to look ten stories up, to see a man clothed in flame soar from the building and sail clear across the street, over two smaller buildings, to alight at the far end of a train platform. Dimming his fires and changing his appearance while still hidden in shadow, Marlowe had slipped onto the train there just before its doors had shut, and had sunk down onto the nearest empty seat to catch his breath and watch anxiously out the window.

None of the Wizards had appeared, however, nor had there been any waiting at the next station, or the one beyond that.

Still, that had been close. Far closer than he liked.

Even so, it had also provided invaluable information. The most important of which was that he had drastically underestimated these people.

With so many men at their disposal—and all of them actual members of their organization, even if it seemed most lacked any magic—that entity was significantly larger than he had ever suspected. And, as Göring had both insinuated and demonstrated, far more influential. Marlowe had never imagined that a group spawned from London's ruling council could have power on a global scale, but clearly they did.

And he was forced to admit that they were far too widespread, far too well entrenched, for him to destroy them utterly, as he had previously hoped. He might be able to burn out one root, perhaps even find their dark heart, but with so many people involved in so many industries and aspects, and in so many cities and nations, the Wizards would continue despite his best efforts.

Still, he was not ready to give up the fight entirely.

No, he might not be able to destroy the Wizards, but he could still hurt them. He could hand them a resounding defeat, take away something they had worked toward. Free one aspect of life from their crushing control.

And what better aspect than the one where he had already begun to focus some of his attention? An area teeming with life and possibility, and filled with creativity and individuality?

Yes, he decided. If he could not stop them entirely, he would block them in this one avenue, at least.

He would erase their influence from and shatter their hopes of control over the Delta Blues.

TRACK NINE

Early this mornin', when you knocked upon my door
Early this mornin', ooh, when you knocked upon my door
And I said, "Hello, Satan, I believe it's time to go"

St. Louis, Missouri, November 1936

Robert Johnson had already departed Chicago, the previous night having been the last of his three days of performance there. Marlowe caught up him with next in St. Louis, where the musician had been booked for three days as well.

"Well well," Johnson stated when he answered the door to his hotel room the following morning, to find Marlowe standing outside it. "Hello, Devil-man. Been a while. You here to collect?" He was laughing as he said it, however, and swung the door wide to let Marlowe enter—revealing that he was not alone, for an attractive woman of middle age hastily covered herself with the blankets and sheets strewn about her on the bed. Johnson grinned at her as he sauntered past to the small side table, where he collected a bottle and two glasses and poured a pair of drinks. The first he handed to Marlowe and the second he kept for himself.

"Looks as if you've been doing well for yourself," Marlowe stated, sipping the whiskey and studying the room. It was several cuts up from the ragged little places he usually stayed, but then he had never cared much for finery or frippery—and had rarely had the means to afford such things even if he had. "I heard you play in Chicago. You've come a long way."

"All thanks to you and your gift, friend," Johnson stated, raising his glass in toast before draining half of its contents in one long swallow. "Well, you and a solid year of practice at Ike's feet."

Ah. Marlowe nodded, another piece of the puzzle falling into place. He'd seen Isaiah "Ike" Zimmerman more than once down in Mississippi, and the man was a skilled guitarist. If Johnson had sought him out, and Zimmerman had agreed to teach him, that man's expertise combined with Johnson's innate talent— yes, it made a great deal of sense.

"And now here you are," Marlowe said, swirling the whiskey in his glass. "Living the high life. Traveling all across the country, performing. Drinking." He cast a side eye toward the woman, who had slid out of bed and was attempting to dress while still modestly holding a sheet before her. "Entertaining. And meeting with businessmen."

"Ah, is that what this is all about?" Johnson laughed. "You figure you already got my soul, can't have me selling it to none of those folks, too? What, that mean I'm poaching your belongings?" He shook his head, entirely at ease—and yet outside, clouds had begun to gather, and thunder to rumble. "Don't see how that's none o' your concern, Devil-man. See, I'm still alive, and while I am, my soul's mine, to sell or give away or barter as I please."

"Not to them, it isn't," Marlowe retorted. "Those men, you have no idea who they are or what they are capable of. They will break you, Robert Johnson. They will strip you of your soul, yes, but more importantly they will whitewash your music. They will pare it down, wipe away any and all traces of you from it, and make it bland and boring and just like everything else. They will peddle it as the Blues, but without a single trace of the Blues in it. This you cannot allow to happen."

Johnson laughed again, though the sound had more of an edge to it now, and thunder crackled behind it like some sinister echo. "Break me? Devil-man, don't you know? I'm the King of the Delta Blues. They couldn't break me if they tried." He grinned, flashing his white teeth. "But, boy, do they seem keen to try."

"What have they promised you?" Marlowe demanded, settling down his drink, which had begun to bubble and froth in his hand, the alcohol turning to vapor as his temper rose. "Tell me!"

"Promised? Oh, nothing much," the musician replied, nodding slightly as the woman slipped behind them and darted for the door, shoes and purse and fur stole still in hand. "Just a recording contract. You hear that? They wanna record me. Me! I'm gonna be on records, Devil-man! Maybe even on the radio! Can you imagine? Robert Johnson gonna be playing out of every house, every bar, every cab in this here country! How's that for a boy from backwoods Mississippi?"

But Marlowe was already shaking his head. "No no no! That's exactly what they want! They're luring you in, tempting you with dreams of wealth and fame! They won't deliver! They'll use you instead, but they'll twist you, twist your music, until you can't even recognize yourself in the mirror! You'll look up one day and see some stranger staring back at you, only hazy shadows left of the talent you once possessed, and you'll wonder how you got here, where you went wrong, and weep over what you gave away and can never now reclaim." In his mind's eye Marlowe saw himself, his true form, and the pages of his plays crumbling to dust between his fingers, the stories of Polidori turning to mist before his eyes, his bit parts in Valentino's movies blurring and fading from the film reels. Where had it all gone wrong, indeed?

Laughter brought him back to the here and now, mocking laughter. "You talking about me, Devil-man?" Johnson asked him shrewdly, that light in his eyes growing brighter and brighter. "Or 'bout yourself? Sounds to me like you got plenty of your own regrets, no need to be seeking out any of mine. 'Cause I know what I'm about. They ain't gonna take me unawares. No, sir."

"You don't understand," Marlowe insisted, grabbing the musician by his jacket and hauling him close, until their faces were inches apart. "You cannot know how powerful they are, how insidious. They will destroy you!" The room had been dark when he had first entered, its curtains drawn, but now it was as bright inside as out—brighter, even, for it had become dark as night out there, but incandescent in here—and the curtains had blown back, the air outside thick and heavy with the scent of impending rain.

"Oh, I understand plenty, Devil-man," Johnson replied, tugging his hands free and shoving them away but not stepping
back, staying instead right there to confront him. And now the
slim musician seemed taller, darker, yet with a sinister glow
about him, as if lit from behind, and there was a crackle to his
voice as he spoke, matched by a light arcing within his eyes
and an answering flash from beyond the window. "You afraid.
I can see that. But not me. Maybe you're afraid *for* me—or
maybe you're afraid *of* me. You granted me the crown, remember? What's that make you? The old, fallen king? The forgotten
ruler? The defeated tyrant?" He grasped Marlowe by the arm,
and Marlowe felt the contact like a jolt of electricity, and his arm
tingled and burned from the touch. "I'm in charge now, Devil-
man," Johnson warned softly. "And you'd best take heed, lest
you incur my wrath."

The rational part of Marlowe's mind knew that this conversation had escalated rapidly, and for no clear reason, and that
he needed to calm things down before they blew entirely out of
control. But another, deeper part of him exulted at the conflict,
at the clash of wills occurring between himself and this spirited
young man. And it was that part which answered, flaring to life
so that the room filled with a blinding light and Johnson jerked
his hand away with a yelp, the palm reddening from contact.

"Do not threaten me, Robert Johnson," Marlowe warned,
and within his voice was all the years he had lived, all the lives
he had worn, all the stories he had spun or helped to breathe
into being. "You may be the king, but I am beyond all that. I am
beyond you, beyond even mortality. You face a force far greater
than any man could hope to conquer—defy me and, for all that I
admire and esteem you, I can and will utterly destroy you." The
curtain burst into flames behind them, filling the room with
acrid smoke that would have brought tears to their eyes if either
had been paying any mind.

Yet Johnson's eyes, far from watering, blazed in response,
burning through the fog of fumes. "I can handle myself, Devil-
man," he promised, and the skies lit in agreement, the thunder
crashing down an instant later. "Don't you worry none about
me. But don't you test me none, neither."

Marlowe started forward, fists clenched, wings of flame rising to either side, ready to crush this upstart, this interloper. But something in him stopped that advance, the part of him that had been a lover and a writer rather than a fighter, the part that had struggled to protect and nurture rather than just destroy. He could still feel that heat at his core, burning to go after Johnson, to battle the young musician and defeat him, and could see a matching desire in the young man's eyes. But he forced it down, drove it back, clamped it down tight and bound it with his will, mastering himself once more with a supreme effort when the Phoenix wanted nothing more than to kill or be killed, to defeat or be defeated.

That thought brought back an old memory, one of his earliest, and suddenly it was as if cold water had been dashed upon him, drenching him in calm and control and understanding. Because now, all at once, everything made perfect sense. He knew what was happening, and why.

And that meant he suddenly saw, clear as the light he had so recently shone about this hotel room, exactly what they must do.

Together.

Now if only he could convince this hotheaded young musician, the King of the Delta Blues, to agree.

TRACK TEN

My enemies have betrayed me
Have overtaken poor Bob at last
My enemies have betrayed me
Have overtaken poor Bob at last
And there's one thing certainly
They have stones all in my pass

Jackson, Mississippi, November 1936

"**D**amn him!" Marlowe railed at the air, his anger and frustration boiling over and creating a wash of heat that erupted outward, battering people to the side as they walked along and causing cars to swerve and honk as their tires threatened to melt. "What was he thinking?"

He and Johnson had both headed back down to Mississippi, but separately so as not to draw attention from the Wizards. Johnson had left first, and by the time Marlowe had reached Rosedale, the young musician was already gone. It hadn't been difficult to find out where to, either—"You ain't heard?" one of the local elders had been only too happy to crow about when asked. "That boy, he gone on up to Jackson! Got hisself a meeting with one a' them there record producers. That boy gonna be a star!"

"Not if they have their way, he won't," Marlowe had muttered, storming off before he lashed out at the old gent. It wasn't his fault, after all. He was rightly proud of one of his neighbors, that was all.

But Johnson. That was a whole other story. They'd talked about this! Though "argued round and round" might be more accurate.

"Listen," he'd insisted that morning in St. Louis. "There's no need for us to fight. We are on the same side. Didn't I give you the gift of the Delta Blues? Didn't I anoint you king? I am not trying to take that away from you, or stand in the way of your success. Far from it—I want to see you achieve all that you possibly can, to become the king you were meant to be. That is all. I am not here to usurp, only to advise and support. Please allow me to do that, and grant that, in my longer life, I may have something to offer in that regard."

Johnson had continued to glare at him, jaw set and brow lowered, but then finally he had laughed and it was like the sun had come out from behind the clouds—not just metaphorically, for outside the sky had suddenly cleared, the strange storm vanishing as quickly as it had appeared. "All right, Devil-man," he'd said. "All right. I hear you, and I admit, you older than me, and maybe wiser—leastways, you've managed to keep yourself going all this time, which has to be worth something. So I'll listen to what you got to say. But don't try telling me not to make no records, 'cause that I simply ain't gonna do."

"Fine, fair enough," Marlowe had agreed. "And you're right. Your music not only deserves to be heard on the phonograph and the radio, it should be. It should be heard by one and all, far and wide, all across this nation and beyond." The younger man's smile had widened at that, his whole demeanor shifting, relaxing, the last traces of that combative posture fading away. "But believe me when I tell you, though they may seem it at first those businessmen are not your friends. They are part of an old organization, one that has for centuries sought to stamp out just such bright voices as yours. They would let you keep your crown, but tarnish it and squash it until it was nothing but a dull cap upon your head, and you no more than a puppet to dance at their beck and call, and to their tune."

"That ain't likely to happen," Johnson had insisted, a little of that gleam returning to his eyes. "They're welcome to try, though."

"Try they will," Marlowe had assured him. "But we can make sure they do not succeed. If we work together."

And so they had devised their plan. A fairly simple one, at

that, but no less effective for its lack of complexity. Provided, of course, that the Wizards did not recognize him. A few of them might have caught a quick glimpse back in Chicago, but it had been brief, and mostly from a distance, and he doubted those men were anywhere near here.

Still, he'd decided it was best to be cautious. Hence traveling separately.

Only now Johnson had gone on ahead without him—which had definitely not been part of the plan! Well, nothing for it now but to go after, and hope he could still salvage something of this mess, and of the young man's life while he was at it.

Rosedale to Jackson was no mean distance—the former up by the Arkansas River, the latter on the far side of the Yazoo and down just past Vicksburg. Perhaps a hundred, hundred and fifty miles. Moving at a steady clip, it might take a man a full day to walk that distance, assuming he did not stop or slow.

Marlowe covered in half that. And arrived just in time to see Johnson emerge from a record store, shaking a man's hand. The young musician's smile was bright and proud, a king enjoying his conquest—but the other man's was thinner, and far more sinister, the smirk of a courtier who had just tricked his liege into handing over valuable titles and privileges without realizing.

Or that of a counselor who had just finished betraying his monarch, and was preparing to end him and steal his throne.

Marlowe waited until the other man had turned away, evidently to lock the door of his store, before waving. He was sure that Johnson had seen him, but the musician gave no immediate sign. A moment later, however, Marlowe heard him say, "Here, why don't you give me a minute—I need to relieve myself."

"That's fine," his companion replied at once, all too eager to please. Something about his words and manner just struck Marlowe as oily. "I'll go get the car and bring it round, how's that?"

"Sure, sure," Johnson replied. "Okay I leave my stuff right here, then?" He'd been lugging both his guitar and his suitcase when he'd stepped out, and now had them leaning up against the locked front door.

"Oh, absolutely," his new friend agreed. "Safe as houses right here—no one'll touch them. Back in a jiffy!" And, with a jaunty wave, he hopped down off the step and headed around the corner.

Johnson stepped down as well, going the opposite direction and ducking into the space between the store and the next building over. Marlowe hurried across the street to join him.

"Well, hello, Devil-man," Johnson said when he slid into the alley, which reeked of ammonia from both animals and men relieving themselves on the hard-packed dirt. "Seems you found me."

"Yes, but you were supposed to wait!" Marlowe reminded him sharply, his eyes lighting up the worn wood of the building opposite and casting Johnson's shadow sharply against that wall. "We were going to approach him together! We agreed!"

"You agreed," Johnson corrected easily. "I listened. But I didn't see no need to wait once I got back home and found out they wanted me up here pronto. So I came. And now here I am, and here you are." He grinned. "All nice and easy."

"Who is he?" Marlowe demanded. "And why is he fetching his car?"

"Him? Why, that's H.C. Speir," the musician answered. "This here shop is his, but he don't just sell records—he makes 'em! Well, he finds folks to bring over to the record company, but I figure that's close enough."

"So he's a talent scout." Marlowe nodded. That's what the men in Chicago had told Johnson, that they could recommend him to a good talent scout, who would then listen to him play and decide if he should be given a chance to make a recording. "I take it he liked what he heard?"

"Like? Like?" The younger man straightened, puffing out his modest chest. "He loved it! Couldn't get enough! Said they needed to get me into a studio right damn now, not a moment to lose!"

What was their hurry, Marlowe wondered. Surely the music world did not normally move at such lightning speed? Why try to whisk Johnson away like this? Did they know about him after all? Had they realized he and Johnson were—at least tentatively—in league?

"And what did you tell him?" Marlowe asked now. "Did you mention me, as we planned?" That had been their idea, to have Marlowe go along as a backup musician. That way he could shield Johnson from their influence and he could play to his fullest without interference.

Johnson nodded, but there was a ruefulness in there, and a shrug, that told Marlowe all was not as intended. "I did, right enough," the musician confirmed. "Told 'em you was the only one I'd play with, couldn't trust no one else. Know what he said, old Speir? He said, 'you don't need nobody else! You're a gem, all on your own! Anybody else, they'd just clutter up your sound!' And he ain't half wrong, neither."

"That's not the point," Marlowe reminded him. "I'm not going along to play; I'm going to protect. It's your sound and yours alone I want heard, believe me."

"Maybe so, but that ain't how it turned out, now is it?" The musician pointed out. "I already agreed. What else was I gonna do? Make out like I couldn't play all on my own, when that's what I been doing all these years anyway?" He shrugged it off with another of his easy smiles. "So I said yeah, that's fine, I can go on my own. And I guess that's exactly what's gonna happen. All the way to Texas, if you can believe it. San Antonio, no less! Speir's gonna drive me there himself!"

There was a honk from the mouth of the alley, as if on cue, and both of them glanced up, seeing a shiny new automobile pulled up just beyond. They could make out Speir in the driver's seat, gesturing for Johnson to come on—and squinting down the alley, trying to make him out in the shadows there, and no doubt wondering if he saw someone else there with the young man.

"I gots to go, Devil-man," Johnson told Marlowe then. "Can't keep fame and fortune waiting." He tipped his hat, clapped Marlowe on the shoulder, and, with a bright laugh, turned and sauntered on out of the alley. Marlowe watched, creeping forward but keeping to the shadows, as the musician disappeared for a moment, presumably collecting his instrument and case. Then he was back, hopping into the front passenger seat and lounging back like he owned the place. Speir honked again, and the car zoomed forward, gone from view in an instant.

Leaving Marlowe to grit his teeth and clench his fists in an effort not to burn the entire street down around him.

Damn that man! His arrogance! Why would he not listen? Marlowe had been battling these Wizards, knowingly or not, for centuries! Why did Johnson so blithely assume he could best them all on his own? Oh, the arrogance of youth!

You were young once, too, Marlowe reminded himself, lest he grow too angry and decide to leave Johnson to fend for himself. No, he would go after, and help the young man still, as best he could.

The King of the Delta Blues would have the Phoenix's fires to uplift him—whether he wanted them or not.

TRACK ELEVEN

Mmmm, standin' at the crossroad, I tried to flag a ride
Standin' at the crossroad, I tried to flag a ride
Didn't nobody seem to know me, everybody pass me by

San Antonio, Texas, November 23, 1936

At least, Marlowe thought with just a touch of spite as he studied the grand building before him, his adversaries were determined to do this in style.

After giving himself a few minutes to cool down, he had taken off for San Antonio, eschewing more conventional transportation methods to travel there under his own power. Fortunately for him, there were only two truly viable routes for driving there from Jackson—Speir would either have to take the highways up toward Shreveport and then angle down through Waco and Austin, or head down to Baton Rouge and then straight across to Houston and beyond.

Meanwhile, the Phoenix had no such limitations. Bound only by his own strength and fueled by desperation and no small amount of rage, Marlowe cut straight across the center of Louisiana, through the forests that filled that region, passing just above Alexandria and then into Texas just below Lufkin, in a straight line for San Antonio. Whenever there was a risk of anyone seeing him, he walked, albeit at a pass far beyond the norm. When he was assured of being alone, he ignored the restrictions of gravity and darted through the air, a massive, fiery bird of prey that all mundane wildlife knew to avoid.

In this way, he was able to reach the city several hours before his quarry. Which created a new problem—how was he expected to find them here when they did arrive? San Antonio was no Rosedale or even Jackson—at least a hundred thousand people called the city their home, and likely more than that. Marlowe found himself liking the place despite himself, with its fascinating mix of old and new, Spanish and German influences woven together to create a strange and unique whole. None of which helped him.

Something did, however. As had occurred back before their first encounter, and again in Chicago and even in St. Louis and Jackson, Marlowe realized that there was a strange nagging feeling in the back of his head, almost like a mental itch, akin to the mind reminding him of something he needed to do, but in this case linked to an external factor: Robert Johnson. Following that itch led Marlowe to the eastern outskirts of town, and squinting against the bands of dusk he could just make out a plume of road dust far out along the highway.

They had come by way of Baton Rouge and Houston, then. Fair enough.

Finding a place to lean against the corner of an old adobe building, Marlowe then simply had to wait until Speir's fancy convertible drove past, and follow them from there. That led him to a handsome eleven-story corner building, a fancy covered walkway adorning the second floor. "The Gunter Hotel" the sign out front proclaimed. He waited until Speir had pulled up, handing the car keys to a valet as he climbed out of the vehicle, and then slipped into the lobby and found an empty seat off to one side before Johnson and his guide could follow. As an afterthought, he'd let himself fade back to his native coloration as he'd entered the building, and as a result no one gave him a second glance, just another white man in a hotel.

His timing proved to be excellent—no sooner had he seated himself then he heard the revolving doors swish again, and a pair of feet clatter on the polished marble floor. "Let me just call up and tell them we're here," he heard Speir say, followed by the tromp of footsteps over to the front desk and then, in oily tones, "Could you ring room 414, please."

"Of course, sir," a young woman replied. "Here you are."

"Don?" Marlowe heard, straining his hearing to its utmost.

"It's Harry. We're down in the lobby. Great. They'll be right down, and then we'll get you all set up. You need anything?" Those last statements were louder, no doubt aimed at the man beside him—Marlowe was able to glance past several decorative plants to see Johnson leaning against the polished front desk.

"Nah, I'm good," the musician replied. "Ready to roll."

A few minutes later there was a ding from the elevators, and then another set of footsteps. "There he is!" someone declared in hearty tones and hauntingly familiar traces of a London accent. "Mr. Johnson, I'm Don Law, from Brunswick Records. It's a real pleasure to finally meet you."

"Good to meetcha, Mr. Law," Johnson replied, and Marlowe was sure they were shaking hands, though he could not see that from his vantage point.

"So we've got the room all set up," Law continued, "and my sound engineer, Vincent Liebler, is ready and waiting. Anything we can get you before we get started?"

"Just some water and maybe some whiskey," the musician answered.

"Of course, of course—we have both of those ready and waiting, and food as well," Law assured him, and there were footsteps again, receding now. Heading toward the elevators, Marlowe guessed. "Come on, let's head on up. Thanks for everything, Harry! Talk to you soon!" That was called over his shoulder, from the sound of it, and after another minute Marlowe heard a single set of feet tromping back toward the front door and disappearing through it. So Speir had just been the delivery boy, and was not invited to the party himself? Interesting.

As soon as the elevator dinged, Marlowe was up from his chair and making a beeline for the front desk. "I'd like a room, please," he told the young woman there. "Room 514, if possible—it's my lucky number." He gave her a friendly smile, which she returned, and a part of him couldn't help thinking that her reaction and his reception might have been very different if he were still wearing his darker guise.

"Of course, sir," she answered. "Let me just check—you're in luck, 514 is available. How long will you be staying with us?"

"I don't know yet," he admitted. "Let's say two nights for

now, and if I need to extend that I'll let you know." He had no idea who long a recording session usually took, or if this one would be abbreviated or lengthened due to the Wizards' influence. Because they were definitely here. He could feel it.

"That's fine," she told him. "It's three dollars a night, so that will be six dollars."

Digging into his pocket, he produced a five and a one and slid them across to her, receiving the check-in book and a room key in return. "Thank you." Then he was making for the elevators himself.

It was a handsome room, large and well-appointed, with comfortable furnishings new enough to look clean and fresh but old enough to have some charm as well. Marlowe barely noticed, though. As soon as the door had shut behind him he had kicked off his shoes and crouched down, hands flat on the hardwood, concentrating on the space directly below. Johnson was there, he could feel him, like the heat from a distant fire. Two others were also present, less vibrant, almost cold to his senses. Colder than was natural, as if their very nature had been frozen somehow.

Wizards.

"All set up now?" he heard Law ask. "Great. Whenever you're ready, we'll get started." Then footsteps, across the room and out of it but not into the hall—no, these were through to the room beside, which if it was like his had an adjoining door, Marlowe noted. So sound equipment in one room, performer in the other. Smart.

"Let's do this, then," Johnson declared, still just as confident and cocky as ever. And, without further ado or warning, he began to play.

Marlowe could feel the energy building in the young man beneath him. It was like a fire about to erupt, a swelling of heat and light and activity churning just below the surface, building and building until it finally burst forth, erupting into the world.

Only, in this case, something was holding it back. There was a sort of skin over top of it all, subtle and soft but strong and cool, chilling that fire and blocking it from escaping.

That was the Wizards' work, Marlowe knew at once. And

this was exactly what they'd planned. They were tamping down Johnson's gifts, taming his music, smoothing it out into a blander, more banal version of itself. This was the version they intended to play over the radio. To most it would still sound fresh and original, but that raw intensity would be missing. It would not set people's thoughts and emotions alight, not heard like this.

Fortunately, Marlowe was not about to let that happen.

Releasing some of his own fire, he brought his wings to life—and, following the path of his arms, they projected down through the floor, into the room below.

Where their fiery tips burst the bubble of the Wizards' containment spell, causing its constraints to wither and fall away, cool remnants puddling on the floor as Johnson's music soared free.

Marlowe could feel the consternation from the room beyond, as the Wizards there—for Law and this Liebler were clearly among that number, and of the variety that actually possessed power, from what he could sense—registered the failure of their spell and scrambled to restore it. But every time they tried to wrap Johnson in that ethereal confinement again, Marlowe shattered it. His fire slowly filled the room below, warming it with life and imagination until the Wizards' spell could not even find a place to start, its cold restraint unable to gain a foothold amidst such overwhelming creativity.

Not that Marlowe had to do it all alone. Johnson's music was a veritable bonfire, a font of inspiration, and Marlowe felt himself revitalized by the waves of sound washing over him, feeding his power even as he fed it in return.

Between them, the Wizards didn't stand a chance.

Johnson spent three days recording in that hotel room, with Marlowe crouching just above him providing support and shelter. He recorded a total of sixteen songs in that time, though he did alternate takes on many of those, adjusting rhythm and tempo and even lyrics as he went. They took a break after that, and the tension was palpable through the floor. Marlowe allowed himself to relax and recover as well, certain the ordeal was not yet over.

Nor was he wrong. A few days later, on the twenty-sixth, a third man entered the scene. "Mr. Johnson, I'm Art Satherley from ARC and Vocalion," Marlowe heard him say as he listened in. "You can call me Uncle Art, though, everybody does. Good to finally meet you—Don's told me wonderful things about your music, so much so that I needed to come out here and hear it for myself." Like Law, this Satherley's speech had hints of a British accent, though heavily faded now.

"Pleasure, Uncle Art," Johnson replied, and from his words and tone Marlowe could picture the younger man, still cool as a cucumber. Did he even know about the protection he was receiving from above, Marlowe wondered. Or did the cocky young musician just assume that he was resisting through his own will alone? Had he even noticed the attempted intrusions? There was no way to tell without speaking to him, and Marlowe did not dare risk that.

"I know it's been a long few days," Satherley was saying now, "but I'm hoping you have it in you to do just a little more recording? We want to make sure we make the best use of your time, and ours."

"Sure, sure," Johnson answered. "Ready when you all are." And he strummed his guitar, producing an ululating wail from the finger slide, for emphasis.

"Excellent. It's late, though—we'll start up again first thing in the morning."

That had given Marlowe a little more time, which he'd welcomed. He could go without food or drink or even sleep for extended periods when needed, but it did thin his endurance somewhat. Fortunately, the sheer outpouring of energy from Johnson's music had helped offset that. Still, he was happy to leave the hotel room for a few hours, walk the city, get some fresh air, and find a quiet restaurant with an out of the way table where he could dine on spicy tamales and rich enchiladas accompanied by pale beer and cool water. After which he'd returned and fallen asleep, dreaming of the lives he'd lived and the many he'd touched along the way.

The sessions below had begun again at dawn the next day, and ran that day and the one after. Marlowe had felt at once the difference in the spell, now that three Wizards were pouring their strength into it. Fortunately, it had still been well below his own potency, and he had again shattered their efforts each time they'd attempted to erect them around the young musician. Each try drained the trio of men, and by the time the sun set on the twenty-eighth, which was a Friday, Marlowe knew he had won. At least for now.

"Outstanding!" he heard Law declare, loud enough that he knew the record producer had entered 414 again rather than skulking next door. "Absolutely fantastic! I think we have everything we need for now, Mr. Johnson. We'll need to take these recordings back to our home studio and process them, get those records printed up and out the door. But don't worry, we'll be in touch."

"Sure, sure," Johnson replied. "Sounds good. Just let me know."

"Of course," Law said. "Meantime, here's the recording fee we promised. And a bus ticket back to Jackson, as well. We've got the room paid up through tomorrow, so feel free to relax tonight and enjoy it. Order some room service, live it up a little. You've earned it."

There was a little more chit-chat, then the door between the rooms shut. A short while later, Marlowe felt the strange chilled aura that surrounded those men fade from his awareness. The Wizards had gone.

He considered going downstairs and speaking with Johnson, reprimanding him for his recklessness and pointing out how he had protected the younger man, but decided against it for several reasons. Yelling at him would not change anything that had already happened, and it would only make any future cooperation even less likely. Plus there was always a chance the Wizards were still watching, or had even left some kind of magical guard in place. Instead he simply relaxed himself, but kept a mystical eye on Johnson the whole time. When the musician vacated the room the next day and hopped a bus back to Mississippi, Marlowe was not far behind.

For the next few months, all was quiet. Johnson went back to the life of an itinerant musician, traveling from town to town and city to city and playing everything from tiny front porches

and cramped churches to packed music halls. Marlowe shadowed him, always staying just out of the younger man's view.
More than once he caught a glimpse of Wizards in the audience,
but none of them approached, and Johnson continued to play
freely.

Then, in March, the first of his records finally went on sale.
It was "Terraplane Blues" on one side, with "Kind Hearted
Woman Blues" on the other. The record was a tremendous hit,
particularly in the South, and sold some ten thousand copies,
but Marlowe was pleased to note that it was unadulterated, with
Johnson's music spilling out of the phonograph in all its raw
power and glory. He was pleased, and knew the young musician
must be as well, but was sure the Wizards were livid.

He was also certain they would not let such a slap in the
face stand. They would try again, and in force this time.

Indeed, he was counting on it.

TRACK TWELVE

Well ah leave this morn' of I have to, woh, ride the blind, ah
I've feel mistreated and I don't mind dyin'
Leavin' this morn' ah, I have to ride a blind
Babe, I been mistreated, baby, and I don't mind dyin'

Dallas, Texas, June 19, 1937

When the Wizards did make their move, it was sudden. One day Johnson was on the road, as usual, this time playing in a small but hopping bar in Baton Rouge. The next he had packed up, canceled the next night's performance, said good-bye to the woman he had shacked up with—the young musician had discovered that he could find women to take him in almost anywhere he went, and thus gained both companionship and free room and board—and hopped a bus to Dallas.

Fortunately, Marlowe had been watching still. He immediately took off for Dallas himself, and arrived in time to settle in and watch as the bus pulled into the station. A man in a suit was waiting for Johnson there, and though he'd only glimpsed the fellow once or twice back in San Antonio, Marlowe recognized the voice at once, with its traces of faded London, as the man greeted the arriving musician. It was Don Law.

Law had a car waiting, and whisked Johnson away the second he'd collected himself and his meager luggage. This time they did not head to a hotel, however. Instead, Marlowe followed them to a handsome Art Deco corner building. "508 Park Avenue" read the letters on the black marble around the door, though much of the building was orange-red brick with white marble accents. More than mere architecture, however, was the sense of power coming off the building in less a wave than a steady, solid hum, creating a static field around its walls. Clearly, this was a Wizard facility, and they had prepared it well. That was no doubt why they'd chosen to bring Johnson here—they wanted him someplace where he would be cut off from any help, where he would be defenseless.

But, like so many, the Wizards had failed to take certain basic ideas into consideration. So blinded were they by their routines and structures, their utter lack of imagination, that they made assumptions based only on their own experiences and capabilities.

In short, the walls did indeed appear impregnable to his fire—in fact, Marlowe could tell that they had been physically hardened against flame as well as mystically. And the entrance was particularly well protected.

But the Wizards had not considered that an assault could also come from above. Being bound by gravity, they assumed any foes would be as well, and so they had not bothered to provide protection to the roof.

Marlowe did not approach right away. The building was large enough, with multiple floors, that he would need to know where they were taking Johnson before he could make any move. Fortunately, even through all that shielding he could still detect the young man's aura, radiating heat like a small, mobile bonfire. As Marlowe watched, that glow rose to the third floor and then bounced merrily along to its very end and around to the back corner.

Which certainly made matters even easier, as there was a single-story building of the same brick nestled up against that side of the stronghold.

Circling around behind, Marlowe was able to leap up to the smaller building's roof without difficulty. Then he paced to its edge, where the Wizards' structure reared up above. The roof here was arched enough that it was midway up the second story, and so it was an easy matter to propel himself straight up into the air and cover the remaining distance, landing lightly on the roof of 508 itself. Then he crouched down and crept back until he was directly above the glow that was Johnson.

It was quiet up here, the day calm and clear, the air warm, a light breeze ruffling his hair, and only the occasional sound of a passing car reminding Marlowe that there was anyone else beyond this building and the people in it. He put that from his mind now, however, as he concentrated, extending his wings once more, sliding them down carefully, quietly, through the roof and into the room below.

The wards here were far stronger than those back in San Antonio. There they had been only temporary, hastily erected with the belief that little more would be required. Here they were permanent fixtures, as woven into the building as its electrical wiring and its pipes. The guards were far stronger, far more settled, but at the same time more rigid, and placed as uniformly as any set of crossbeams or supports. Marlowe simply took his time, feeling his way to the spaces between those magical pillars, finding the spots where their power was at its weakest.

Then, rather than pierce it utterly as he had before, he inserted himself, his heat and light, slowly inundating the cool supports until they glowed from his flame, transforming them from barriers to conduits and allowing his might to enter undetected and fill the room beyond.

Johnson had already begun to play, his own fire raging against the boundaries the space was attempting to impose upon him. Marlowe added his own power to the mix now, softening the barriers until they melted, letting the musician's light blaze forth unabated.

It was glorious—as was the wave of frustration and disbelief emanating from the room next door, where the Wizards once more watched and waited, arrogant in their assumptions that they could not fail.

Johnson played the entire day long, pausing only for brief breaks to use the restroom or stretch his legs or sip some water or nibble a sandwich. The Wizards only grew more and more agitated as the recording session continued, the King of the Delta Blues weaving his magic into each and every song, stamping his particular fire onto each recording. Marlowe chuckled to himself, up there on the roof, as he eavesdropped, hearing the Wizards argue with each other underneath him.

"This can't be right!" One of them—from the lack of a British accent, he was guessing Liebler—insisted. "All the wards are in place but he's still not tamped down! Look at these readings!"

"How is he doing this?" Law demanded. "He's little more than a boy, and he's not one of us, there's no spellcasting involved—how is he breaching those barriers?"

"However he's doing it," a third voice, also English-inflected, cut in. Satherley. "We need to put a stop to it." A heavy sigh followed that. "We need to bring him in."

"Are you sure?" Liebler asked. "You know he hates it when his own work is disturbed."

"I'm well aware!" Satherley snapped. "But he likes it even less when things fall apart on him! Get him!"

Marlowe had perked up as the conversation had progressed. This was exactly what he'd hoped for. Law, Liebler, and Satherley were all potent Wizards in their own right, but he'd known they were not the top of the food chain. And that was who he wanted, the top Wizard, or at least the one in charge of this particular venture. Now it sounded like they were bringing in that very man, hoping his presence and power could fix this problem. Which meant, finally, Marlowe would see who he was up against—and would be able to face him directly.

"He'll be here first thing in the morning," Liebler reported a few minutes later, after a hushed one-sided conversation Marlowe gathered had been via telephone.

"Good. Let's break for the night, then," Law suggested. "I'll take him to his hotel, and we'll keep an eye out for any trouble. Then I'll collect him first thing in the morning and we'll finally finish this."

"You think he'll be able to turn things around?" Liebler asked.

"Oh, he'll fix it, one way or another," Satherley insisted, the very soul of confidence. "Whether our young Mr. Johnson will survive the experience, that's a whole other matter." All three of them chuckled, then broke off their discussion and opened the door to the recording studio itself, calling out to the musician in question that it'd been a great day's work and now it was time to get some rest, "for tomorrow we'll really put you through your paces!"

Marlowe scowled, up on the roof, and had to pull back his fire quickly, lest it rage out of control and immolate the men below. How dare they play with Johnson's life like this! But of course he was nothing to them, just another annoyance to be swatted, another creative to be controlled.

Well, they were going to be in for a surprise, come the morning. For Johnson was not alone, and not without aid. He had the Phoenix on his side, and there was about to be a reckoning.

Marlowe briefly considered warning the young man what was coming, but decided against it. Knowing Johnson, he would insist upon throwing the knowledge in the Wizards' face, and that simply wouldn't do. No, better to leave him unawares, the better to play his part. He was just here to record his music, after all. The coming battle was Marlowe's concern.

A part of him whispered, as he hopped down to the roof below and from there to the ground behind it, that he was treating Johnson just as badly as the Wizards were, using him as bait and not even doing him the courtesy of letting him know that. But Marlowe waved that off. He had briefed the young musician before, after all. And if Johnson was paying attention, he would notice Marlowe's presence nearby, and be comforted by it.

Either way, this would all end tomorrow. Marlowe would make sure of that.

TRACK THIRTEEN

Mmmm, the sun goin' down boy, dark goin' catch me here
Oooo ooee eeee, boy dark goin' catch me here
I haven't got no lovin' sweet woman that love and feel my care

June 20 dawned clear, dry, and warm, the air filled with that crackle that often presaged an electrical storm—or a forest fire. Marlowe could feel the world humming around him as he resumed his perch atop 508 Park Ave. He'd made sure to arrive as the sun did, knowing that Johnson would not wish to be rousted so early, no matter what the Wizards had planned.

As he'd expected, it was another hour or more before the young musician finally arrived, chauffeured over by Law once more and whisked immediately inside. Marlowe had worried that they might decide the location itself was a problem and set Johnson up somewhere else, but the ball of heat that was the young man followed the same path as the day before, eventually settling just beneath him in the corner room on the third floor.

Perfect.

Thus far, Marlowe had not felt any difference in the building's wards, and only three of the strangely chilled auras of the Wizards nearby. Perhaps whoever it was they had summoned had been delayed, or called away elsewhere? If so, that would be a disappointment. All this work for nothing.

But, shortly after Johnson began playing again, Marlowe felt it. A sudden cold front washing in from the street out front, dropping the temperature around him until his breath plumed. The mysterious head Wizard they'd summoned had just arrived!

Sure enough, something that tingled in his senses like a walking ice block entered the building and rose to the third floor. It traced the same route Johnson had, stopping just a few yards short to enter the room where the other Wizards huddled instead.

"Sir!" Marlowe heard Law say, though the words were muffled even more than mere stone and brick and metal could explain, as if the cold were blocking his senses as well. "Sorry to have to call you, but—"

"Yes, yes," a testy voice replied, thick and deep and strong. "I can see why. That young man there, he's playing his heart out! And what are you all doing to stop him, eh?"

"We're doing everything we can, sir!" Satherley protested. "But somehow he's shrugging it all off!"

"Is he? Are you sure?" There came a dry, low chuckle that sent a chill up Marlowe's spine. "Or has he had a little help? A guardian angel, perhaps? Something looking down from above, at any rate!"

The attack was swift and sudden, but Marlowe had already tensed from the menace in the stranger's voice, and had instinctively drawn his flames tight about him, stoking them to ward off the frigidity in the air. Thus, when a lance of severe, biting cold shot up through the ceiling, he was able to hurl himself backward, at the same time slapping his hands together to catch the mystical bolt between his palms. Its cold warred with his heat, but in the end his flames overcame, melting away the ice so that steam curled about him.

Still, it was clear that the time for stealth was over. Very well, then. He wished to find out his assailant's identity, anyway.

Gathering his strength, Marlowe swept a hand across as if he were cuffing aside a bothersome fly. His fiery wing, mimicking the motion, slashed deep into the rooftop, carving a massive furrow straight through to the rooms below. A flick of his other hand and the severed portion of roof peeled back, allowing more than enough space for him to drop through, landing lightly on his feet before three astonished men—and one smug, grinning one.

For an instant, Marlowe could not put a name to the face, though he knew he should. The man was stout of build, with a wide, square face, a thick nose, and heavy brows. Despite the fine suit, complete with gold watch chain and black bowtie, he looked more a bruiser than a Wizard. Still, Marlowe could feel the power coming off him in waves, sharp and stiff and angular. He could almost see the energy, the way it shimmered in the air like glass with heat trapped inside it.

That image connected with another, and Marlowe gasped as he put the pieces together. "You!" he burst out, unable to contain his surprise. "But you died years ago! The entire world heard of it!"

"I did," the man agreed with a smirk. "But then, you're not stranger to faking your own death, are you, Mr. Marlowe? And just as it was for you back in 1593, it was time for me in 1931, and long past. I couldn't very well continue my work if people kept gaping at me, asking how I'd cheated Death for so long! So I ended that life, and have continued in the shadows ever since."

Marlowe shook his head, but it made sense. Not just that the Wizards could bestow some crude, no doubt limited version of his own longevity, but that this man in particular would have earned such treatment. And that he would now be here, in charge of operation.

After all, who know more about music and sound and radio than Thomas Edison?

"I knew the boy couldn't be blocking us on his own," Edison declared, and Johnson stiffened, for in tearing open the roof Marlowe had ripped away much of the intervening wall as well, and the studio where the musician played was now open to this observation room as well. "But why intervene at all? What's in it for you?"

Now it was Marlowe's turn to sneer. "That's all your kind ever think about, isn't it?" he accused. "Personal gain. Profit. I fight for something far greater than that. I battle for creativity itself!"

"Yes, yes, I've heard about your kind," Edison replied, dismissing the declaration with a small wave of his hand. A hand that was visibly fuller and less wrinkled than the last image Marlowe had seen of the old inventor, upon news of his death. Likewise, the Wizard's hair was thicker than those final photos, and not nearly so white, being more iron-gray, while his brows were nearly black. So there was some rejuvenation involved, as well. "The Beasts," the famous inventor was saying. "Champions of creativity. Bah!" He snorted. "You know what I hear? Chaos! That's all! And chaos is bad for society! It causes upheaval! Uncertainty! Nobody wants that! They want a nice house, good clothes, full bellies—they want stability and security. And that's what we give them."

"At the cost of their souls," Marlowe shot back. In the other room, Johnson's playing had faltered as he listened in, and the room chilled further as the music began to fade. "Keep playing, Johnson!" he called out. "Do not stop, no matter what!" The younger man frowned, but something in Marlowe's tone spurred him on, and he bent back over his guitar again with renewed energy, his song once more filling the room—and driving away some of that cold.

"You cannot win," Edison insisted. "You are all alone, and I have many at my side." Again the air seemed almost to crystallize around him, sharp, glittering edges nearly visible like a strange geometric mandala.

"I am never alone," Marlowe replied. "All of humanity is with me. Every creative thought, every work of art, every moment of inspiration fuels me, and I in turn ignite them." And, drawing on the inspiration rising from Johnson's music, he flared to life, his wings spread wide, the entire space turning brighter than midday, until the other men all flinched and turned away.

All except Johnson, who swiveled around so his back was to them but kept playing. And Edison, who stood fast, shielded by his icy facets.

"Fine, then," the inventor stated. "The fires of imagination versus the cold stability of logic. Let's see who wins."

He snapped his fingers and a millions shards shot through the air, straight for Marlowe—but he furled his wings about him, melting those bits of ice as they flew, and retaliated with a spray of fire that set the back wall ablaze. Edison's cold extinguished that before it could do much more than blacken the bricks, but Marlowe took advantage of his distraction to step forward, driving the tip of one wing ahead of him like a burning lance, straight for the famous man's midsection. The gold chain there glittered, however, and his fire was rebuffed, though the links darkened slightly.

Edison laughed. "That the best you got?" he scoffed, and tossed what looked like snowball, only made of ice and shaped like a cube. The object grew as it spun through the air, and somehow slid around Marlowe, trapping him in a mirrored cage. But he raised the temperature again, burning white-hot, and the walls melted away, puddling at the floor here and there before finally evaporating completely.

"I could ask the same, old man," Marlowe retorted, and hurled a sphere of his own, this one made of glowing, writhing fire. But Edison produced a lightbulb from his pocket, and the fire was sucked into the glass shell, glowing brightly but utterly contained.

They were too well matched, Marlowe saw. It would be different were he to get Edison somewhere alone, but here, in the center of his power, with the other Wizards close by to lend him their strength, he was too strong. And the longer they spent trading blows, the more time the Wizard would have to summon even more reinforcements, until he had enough magic to overwhelm Marlowe completely. Then the Phoenix would die, and its eternal fire would brighten humanity and inspire them no more.

Marlowe could not allow that to happen. It was time for more drastic measures.

Hurling himself forward, he leaped at Edison. The inventor reeled back, surprised at such a bold and physical move, but Marlowe was upon him in an instant, wrapping his arms and flames tight around the man. He could feel the ice there, cold and rigid, trying to dampen his fire, to snuff out his inner light, but he pushed back against it, tightening his grip even as he stoked his flame to heights never yet attempted. The room was aglow, too bright to see, and the very bricks began to melt from the heat, yet still Marlowe held on. He could feel Edison struggling against him, trying desperately to break free, no longer thinking of battle but only escape. Yet Marlowe would not relax his grip, or reduce his flame. Instead he drew upon Johnson's song once more, and ignited his very core, blossoming into a true bird of fire, all else seared away, nothing left but magic and power and the sheer, savage joy of creation.

Edison cried out, a smothered sound, as his ice melted away. He shriveled in the Phoenix's grasp, his restored youth burned off, old age once more claiming him, and then even that was gone as the flames took all life and thought and power and turned it to ash.

When Marlowe finally let his fire flicker out, he held naught but empty air and the faint hint of smoke.

The other Wizards had all fled, and Marlowe was alone with Johnson, who still played on, unharmed by the conflagration that had occurred just behind him. Now Marlowe stumbled toward the musician, calling his name.

Johnson turned, and when he saw Marlowe's hand was outstretched, he lifted one hand from the guitar and reached out in return. They both strained to bridge that gap, and as their fingers grazed each other there was a spark between them, like a burst of static or the tiniest flicker of fire. Marlowe smiled, a wave of contentment washing over him—

—and then the room exploded, that spark setting off a massive detonation that rocked the entire building on its foundations and shattered glass for blocks around.

When the Wizards crept back close enough to peek in through the shattered remnants of the door, they saw a blackened outline on the floor where Marlowe had last stood. The Phoenix had burned too hot, exhausted its own flame, and been consumed in its own blaze. Edison was no more, the great master of electricity and sound defeated and destroyed in the battle. Of Johnson there was no sign, but his guitar was gone as well, and a song still hung in the air, the rhythm and words fading slowly with the warm light shining down through the shredded roof.

And in the other room, the tapes they had made both the day before and that morning before everything had come to a head? Those survived, miraculously unscathed. Almost as if something had protected them to the very end.

BONUS TRACK

You may bury my body, down by the highway side
(Baby, I don't care where you bury my body when I'm dead and gone)
You may bury my body, ooh, down by the highway side
So my old evil spirit, can catch a Greyhound bus and ride

Greenwood, Mississippi, August 17, 1938

The cemetery at Little Zion Church was quiet, for it was well after midnight. Beneath an old pecan tree sat a mound of dirt, still fresh from being shoveled in the day before.

Now, however, in the dead of night, with no one around but a curious owl and a few furtive mice, the ground itself began to writhe, rippling and bowing upward like a cresting wave. The mice fled, squeaking, as the mound writhed, the earth churning—until a figure suddenly rose from it, sitting bolt upright.

"Well, damn if that ain't a thing," Robert Johnson declared, brushing dirt from his arms and chest and rising to his feet. He had not been entirely certain that would work, despite what Marlowe had shown him.

Still, it had, and here he was. Dead and buried. Faking his own death had seemed a bit extreme on the face of it, but after giving it serious thought Johnson had realized that Marlowe was right. The Wizards would not rest until they had broken him, especially now when his continued survival and success were a slap in their faces after their recent defeat. There was no way for him to go on as he was, and only one way forward that made any sense.

Robert Johnson, the King of the Delta Blues, had to die.

Taking off his hat and shaking it clean, Johnson resettled it on his head. He hated that his music had to end as well, at least as far as recording any new songs went. But at the same time he consoled himself with the thought that his legend, and the music he had already put down, would live on forever.

Besides, he admitted as he held up one hand and the scene around him lit like he were holding a torch, now he had a brand-new gig. And one that promised to be potentially even more interesting.

Leave it to Marlowe, that crafty old thespian, to be a master of staging and misdirection. He had died, yes, and the Wizards had at least consoled themselves that their ancient enemy was now gone for good.

But what was a Phoenix, after all, but a firebird that rose anew from the ashes of its own demise? Fortunately, they had been too busy watching Marlowe's end to see Johnson's own rebirth, or to realize that, in that final instant, Marlowe had passed to him the Phoenix's flame, along with his memories and of course the Beast's guiding purpose.

Now *he* was the spirit of creativity, the mystic patron of the arts. And, with Edison dead and the Wizards believing him gone as well, he was free to travel the world, encouraging others to create just as he had.

Marlowe's memories had hinted at a war coming in Europe. That seemed like a good place to start—new sights to see, new people to meet, and a time of chaos and energy and ingenuity to inspire.

Besides which, he felt he owed a certain Herr Göring some comeuppance on Marlowe's behalf.

Whistling to himself, Johnson tamped the dirt back down with one foot before turning and striding away. His steps left blackened imprints in the ground, fires flickering along their edges, but those soon faded, and all was dark and quiet there once more.

For the Phoenix had moved on to new vistas, bringing his light to other parts of the world.

End Recording

ABOUT THE AUTHOR

A ARON ROSENBERG is the author of the best-selling DuckBob SF comedy series, the Relicant Chronicles epic fantasy series, the *Dread Remora* space-opera series, and, with David Niall Wilson, the O.C.L.T. occult thriller series. Aaron's tie-in work contains novels for *Star Trek*, *Warhammer*, *World of WarCraft*, *Stargate: Atlantis*, *Shadowrun*, *Eureka*, and more. He has written children's books (including the original series STEM Squad and Pete and Penny's Pizza Puzzles, the award-winning *Bandslam: The Junior Novel*, and the #1 best-selling *42: The Jackie Robinson Story*), educational books on a variety of topics, and over seventy roleplaying games (such as the original games *Asylum*, *Spookshow*, and *Chosen*, work for White Wolf, Wizards of the Coast, Fantasy Flight, Pinnacle, and many others, and both the Origins Award-winning *Gamemastering Secrets* and the Gold ENnie-winning *Lure of the Lich Lord*). He is the co-creator of the ReDeus series, and a founding member of Crazy 8 Press. Aaron lives in New York with his family. You can follow him online at gryphonrose.com, on Facebook at facebook.com/gryphonrose, and on Twitter @gryphonrose.

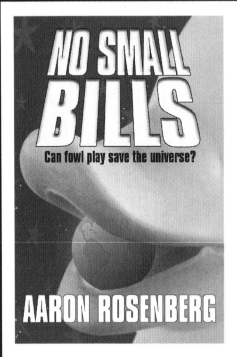

WHEN MAGIC DIES,
ONLY THE DEAD HOLD MAGIC.

Once, the empire of Ritakhou was full of magic. But since the Schism, the realm, renamed Rimbaku, is a pale whisper of its former majesty. Now the only magic is the Relicant Touch, a power allowing talents to be drawn from *aishone*, relic bones that are jealously guarded and widely coveted.

Kagiri and Noniki leave their tiny village with a few aishone and all the hope they can muster, but the world is a larger, more dangerous place than they ever dreamed. Forced into a dark bargain that may cost them not only their lives but their souls, their fates intertwine with an emperor, a warrior, a graverobber, and a killer in ways none of them ever imagined, ways that could reshape the Relicant Empire forever.

This is the first book in The Relicant Chronicles, the Anime-esque epic fantasy series from international bestselling author Aaron Rosenberg.

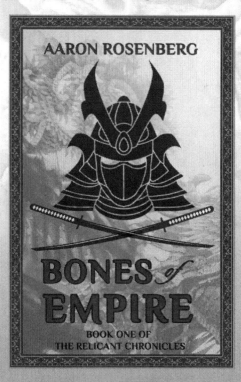

AARON ROSENBERG

BONES *of* EMPIRE

BOOK ONE OF
THE RELICANT CHRONICLES

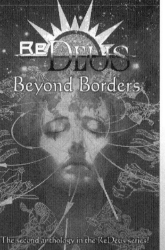
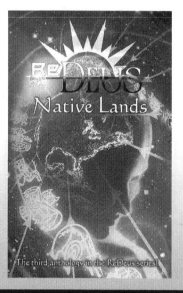